WOLF WITH BENEFITS

WOLF WITH BENEFITS

SHELLY LAURENSTON

BRAVA

KENSINGTON PUBLISHING CORP.
www.kensingtonbooks.com

BRAVA BOOKS are published by

Kensington Publishing Corp.
119 West 40th Street
New York, NY 10018

All Kensington titles, imprints, and distributed lines are available at special quantity discounts for bulk purchases for sales promotions, premiums, fund-raising, educational, or institutional use.

Special book excerpts or customized printings can also be created to fit specific needs. For details, write or phone the office of the Kensington special sales manager: Kensington Publishing Corp., 119 West 40th Street, New York, NY 10018, attn: Special Sales Department; phone: 1-800-221-2647.

ISBN-13: 978-0-7582-6522-7
ISBN-10: 0-7582-6522-0

First Trade Paperback Printing: April 2013

10 9 8 7 6 5 4 3 2

Printed in the United States of America

CHAPTER·ONE

"**A**re *you* my daddy?"

Ricky Lee Reed, originally of Smithtown, Tennessee, and only replanted to New York City a few years back, gawked at the child who'd asked him the question for a mere moment before he turned his attention to the adult female who held the child.

He'd admit it wasn't a question he expected to get, you know, *ever*. For a bunch of reasons, too, but mostly because he didn't know this woman. He wasn't one of those guys who nailed so many females he forgot their faces or names. So then . . . why was this child asking him this question? And even stranger, why was the female raising her brows and suddenly asking, "Well . . . are you?"

Wait. Wouldn't *she* know? *Shouldn't* she? Good Lord, this city. Maybe he'd never get used to living here. Ever. It was surprisingly safer than life in Smithtown, Tennessee, but it was weirder. Maybe because there were way more full-humans in Manhattan—he'd found full-humans were much stranger than shifters—and Smithtown was filled with shifters. Wolves, mostly. A few bears on the outskirts too old and big for the Pack to bother trying to make move. But all those wolves in one place with enough 'shine to take down the Russian army meant there was a lot more danger around those hills of his hometown than there ever could be on the mean streets of this city. No matter what the movies said. And yet life in Manhattan could be so strange in comparison to what he'd left behind.

He'd only come over to this bench inside the giant Sports Center, home to all of New York's shifter-run sports teams, so he could chat with the pretty female sitting there. Perhaps get her number. She was real cute, probably because of all that curly hair. Most of the females in his Pack had straight hair, but this one had blondish-brown hair with lots of black streaks that was just kind of a curly mess. Just these wild, soft curls that nearly covered her eyes and reached to her shoulders. Yeah. He liked her hair. And the fact that she was a jackal didn't mean much to him. She was still canine, like him, and he wasn't looking for his mate. Just a few dates, maybe a little fun . . .

Fun. Not fatherhood.

"No," he finally told them both. "I'm not your daddy."

The female hugged the boy on her lap and kissed his forehead. "Sorry, Denny. Maybe we'll find your daddy someday."

Now Southern politeness would dictate that Ricky Lee should just leave this whole thing alone. Not ask questions, not suggest that maybe she should keep better track of her past lovers. But he just couldn't bring himself to walk away. He was too curious.

She glanced at him. "Oh . . . are you still here?"

Before he could ask why he couldn't keep sitting on this bench, without being glared at, several more children walked up to the female. A teenager with her big brown eyes glued to her cell phone, a young boy, and a toddler female holding the boy's hand. They surrounded the She-jackal, the toddler trying to push the boy Denny aside so she could take his place on their mother's lap.

That sure was a lot of pups for such a young female.

"Who are you talking to?" the jackal demanded of the teenager. Wait. Was she old enough to have a teenager?

"No one."

"That's a lot of typing for no one."

Sighing dramatically as only teenagers managed to do, the girl asked, "Do we have to hang around here much longer?"

"I'm not leaving until I get what I want," the eldest boy said with a lot of confidence for what looked to be only a nine- or ten-year-old. "So suck it up already."

"I've got shit to do, you little brat."

"More toe shoes to buy? More positions to contort your body into until you hit thirty or so and have to resign yourself to the fact your career is over? If you want to call it a career."

The teenager almost had her hands around her brother's throat—and he knew they were all siblings, no one else could annoy a body like a sibling—when the She-jackal snapped, "Leave him alone!"

"You always protect him."

"Perhaps that's because I actually have talent bestowed upon me by the gods, which is better than mere genetics that allowed my legs to grow impossibly long."

"I hate you," the teenager hissed at her brother.

"I *live* for hatred," the boy replied. "It rejuvenates my creative fire." It was a really strange thing for a young boy to say. Really strange. But even stranger was when he glanced over at Ricky and abruptly asked, "Are you our daddy?"

And before Ricky could say in no uncertain terms, "Absolutely *not,*" the doors that led to the main training rink burst open and Ricky's hockey-playing brother, Reece Lee, flew through them.

Ricky instinctively grabbed the child in the most danger—the toddler—and moved. The She-jackal still had the boy on her lap, so she quickly stood, her arms tight around him. But she also jumped to the side, using her body to shove the older boy and his teenage sister away.

As an impromptu team, they seemed to have perfect timing as Ricky's younger brother rammed into the wooden bench they'd been sitting on, completely destroying it in the process. Ricky didn't bother to rush to Reece Lee's help, though. He knew better. A few seconds later, a seven-one, nearly four-hundred-pound hybrid barreled through those rink doors and stalked over to Reece.

The hybrid grabbed Reece by his training jersey and lifted

him up, only to slam him back down again. Reece bared his fangs and started to fight back, claws out. It wasn't a pretty fight, like one of those choreographed ones you'd see in an action movie. Instead it was more like watching a couple of pit bulls go at it in someone's yard.

"Are you just going to stand there?" the She-jackal demanded, her glare on Ricky.

"That was my plan."

"But I saw you with the smaller one earlier," she said over the snarling, growling, and roaring. "You know him."

"Barely."

Her eyes narrowed. "You're brothers, aren't you?"

"According to my momma, but I still want DNA tests to prove it."

The older boy tried to shoot past the She-jackal toward the fight, but the teenager grabbed the back of his T-shirt and held on.

"Are you insane?" the teenager demanded of her brother.

"Toni promised me I'd get to meet him!"

"I promised I'd try," the She-jackal shot back. *Huh.* The kid called her "Toni." Not "Mom" or "Mommy." Then it hit Ricky . . . these weren't her kids. At least not all of them. They were her brothers and sisters.

The teenager caught hold of her younger brother by the back of his neck, the extra flesh every canine predator child had there giving her a better collar than some strip of leather. "Toni's not about to let you get in the middle of a predator fight."

"But—"

"I keep telling you, Kyle," the She-jackal reminded him, "we're scavengers. Wait until the vultures arrive. Then you can go over and maybe get a little lunch."

When Ricky raised a brow, the She-jackal only smirked and gave a small shrug.

Deciding not to ask too many questions, Ricky focused on his brother and the hybrid—who was a damn talented hockey player—that had Reece on his back, big bear-lion hand around the wolf's throat.

Reece was putting up a good fight, though. Desperately trying to get the crazed hybrid off him. Too bad it wasn't working.

After landing a few blows to the hybrid's face, Reece glared at Ricky. "You going to do somethin'?" he squeaked out.

"Didn't you tell me yesterday to stay out of your business?" Ricky asked, grinning.

"Son of a—"

"Hey," Ricky cut in. "There are pups here. Gotta watch your mouth."

The She-jackal sighed. "Seriously?" she demanded. "I mean . . . *seriously?*"

"What?"

"He's getting the holy hell beaten out of him by a man whose hair just suddenly grew."

"That's his mighty mane. Only comes out when he's really mad."

"And you're comfortable with him basically pummeling your brother?"

Ricky thought on that, but he must have taken too long to answer because the She-jackal handed off the boy in her arms to the teenager.

"It's like I have to take care of *everything,*" she snapped at Ricky before walking around to the two fighting males and yelled over the roaring, "Excuse me, Mister . . . uh . . ." She glanced back at the oldest boy, Kyle.

"Novikov," Kyle prompted.

"Right. Mr. Novikov? *Mr. Novikov!*"

The hybrid stopped, his hand still gripping Reece's throat, his massive body still pinning the wolf to the ground. Slowly, he looked up at the jackal, mane nearly covering glowering blue eyes.

"Hi." She pressed her hand to her chest. "I'm Antonella Jean-Louis Parker. Toni for short. That's Toni with an 'i,' not a 'y.' Anyway, Ulrich Van Holtz may have mentioned that I was going to stop by today. And this is Kyle." She snapped her fingers and the boy quickly moved to her side. "Kyle really wants your autograph and although I'm sorry to interrupt your . . . wolf-pummeling, I am on a bit of a schedule." She tapped the sturdy-looking diving watch on her wrist. "So is there any way we could speed this up? Maybe you could assault the wolf later? Kyle would really appreciate it."

The boy grinned. "I would!"

The hybrid studied the jackal for several long seconds before he nodded. "Schedules, I understand." Then he looked down at Reece and roared in his face, *"Schedules! Learn the concept!"*

He released his grip on Reece and got to his mighty big feet. By the time Novikov stood, his mane had lessened considerably, something the She-jackal noticed, her eyes narrowing a bit. The hybrid faced her, his back now to Reece. That's when he mule-kicked him, sending Ricky's brother flying until he slammed into one of the many pillars around the building.

Ricky cringed. He sure bet that hurt.

"What do you want me to sign?"

"Get the shirt, Kyle." The boy took off his backpack and quickly dug out a hockey jersey and a permanent marker. Based on the jersey's colors it looked like it was from the Washington shifter hockey team. A team that the hybrid had once belonged to. That guy had belonged to a lot of teams, and to this day many of his past teammates still hated him.

The boy handed over the shirt and marker to the hybrid. As Novikov signed, he asked the boy, "So do you play hockey?"

"No, sir."

"Really? How come?"

"Because I plan to use my brilliance for something real and important, not something petty like sports."

The She-jackal cringed, her head dropping while Novikov's head snapped up.

"Sorry?"

"See, what I like about what you do," the boy explained, his hands accenting each word, his voice intense, "is the raw rage

and violence. I can use that in my work. And while you'll probably be forgotten soon after you retire, which is the way of you
athletic types whose happiest years are usually when you're in
high school"—he glanced back at his teenage sister and she re-
warded him with the one-finger salute—"*my* legacy will live on
for centuries. People will study my work, copy it. My work
will start a new art movement, a new wave of creativity born
out of blood and violence and rage. And you . . . *you*, Mr.
Novikov, will be my David."

"David?"

"Like Michelangelo's *David*? But instead my piece will be
called Jean-Louis Parker's *Novikov*, and it will be the greatest art
anyone has ever seen. And you . . . you, Mr. Novikov, will be
my muse."

The hybrid blinked and then finally asked exactly what
Ricky was thinking. "How old are you?"

"Eleven. But I don't allow my age to hold me back from my
future. Only those weak of mind do that."

Novikov sighed and handed the signed shirt back to the boy.
"I wish I could say you disgust me, but I understand you more
than you'll ever realize, kid. So go forth and kick ass."

"I will. Thank you!"

He nodded at the boy, then the jackal. "Ma'am," he said before he started back toward the rink.

But that's when the kid threw out, "And is there a chance I
can sketch you naked?"

Novikov stopped walking, his entire body jerking a bit. The
She-jackal's eyes popped open wide at the child's question, her
hand slapping across his mouth and yanking him against her
body as Novikov faced them.

"He's just kidding," she quickly said before Novikov could
ask. "He's just kidding."

The boy struggled against the jackal, his muffled words
sounding like, "No, I'm not!" But the jackal didn't release her
grip, merely smiled. "And thanks for the autograph."

Novikov nodded, grunted, and walked back to the rink, the
big doors slamming behind him.

That's when she released the boy, and using the hand not still holding the youngest brother, spun Kyle around so he faced her.

"Have you lost your mind?"

"It was just a question. He should feel privileged. The greatest artist ever known found his physique worthy of *my* precious attention. He should be bowing at my feet for such an honor."

The She-jackal stared at him for several seconds before announcing, "You're an idiot. And if you ever do that again, or I find out from someone else that you did it again, I'm going to kick your ass from here all the way back to Washington."

"Yeah, but—"

"Do you understand me?"

"As a matter of fact, I don't—"

She grabbed the boy by the back of his neck and yanked him up with one hand. He dangled a good four feet off the ground, his gaze locked with the She-jackal's. "Do you understand, Kyle?" she asked again.

"Yes, ma'am."

"Good."

She released him and shoved the signed shirt back into his hands once he landed on firm ground.

The teenager sighed. "Can we just go already?"

"We have to see Ric first. Here. Take Dennis."

The jackal handed off the youngest boy before turning to stare at Ricky. He gazed back. Smiled.

After a few moments of that, she asked, "Are you going to give her back to me?"

That's when Ricky realized he still held the little pup he'd pulled out of the way of Novikov's rage.

"Oh. Sorry about that." Ricky handed the pup over. She'd fallen asleep with her head on his shoulder, her fist shoved in her mouth. She whined a little as the transfer was made, but settled back to sleep once the jackal had her.

"Thank you," the She-jackal said, and gave him a small smile.

It was the smile that did it, more than the politeness.

"You know," Ricky began, "if you're not busy tonight—"

Pointing at Ricky with her cell phone, the teen asked, "Are *you* our daddy?"

Disgusted, Ricky stated to the jackal, "Woman, there has to be an easier way for you to get rid of a man."

"Perhaps, but I've found that there's nothing quicker. "She winked at him, then gestured behind him with her chin. "And you may want to check on your brother—he's still bleeding."

"Yeah. I think Novikov nicked an artery . . . again."

She stopped, glanced back at him. But with a little snort-laugh, she walked off without another word.

Chapter Two

Antonella "Toni" Jean-Louis Parker shoved her eleven-year-old brother inside the office by using her foot. It wasn't really a kick, though. It was more a shove.

Holding her three-year-old sister, Zia, on her hip, she followed Kyle inside while her fifteen-year-old sister Oriana pulled their five-year-old brother, Dennis, in and laughed hysterically at the same time.

"Stop condoning Kyle's inappropriate behavior," Toni ordered her sister. The pair stared at each other, then began laughing together.

"You are such a freak!" Oriana told Kyle. "I can't believe we're related."

"I don't see what the big deal was," Kyle complained, dropping into one of the office chairs. "It was just a request to sketch him naked."

"A request that should never come from an eleven-year-old *anything*. And it better not come from you again."

Kyle sighed dramatically, as he liked to do, and reminded Toni, yet again, that, "I'm an *artist*, Antonella." And what always annoyed Toni about these conversations with Kyle was his tone. Since he'd been four, he always sounded like a fifty-year-old snob explaining the difference between the rich and the poor to a struggling street vendor. A lot of people wondered how such a young boy could sound so mature and intelligently rude. They often assumed he was just mimicking his parents.

But the truth was . . . he'd developed that tone all on his own. Like his skills as a sculptor, his rude, condescending attitude seemed to be God-given. "I don't have time for these ridiculous rules that average people like you have about what you can and cannot ask."

"So much rudeness in only a couple of sentences," Toni observed.

"It's not my fault you don't understand my world."

"*I* don't understand?"

Was Kyle kidding? Antonella Jean-Louis Parker didn't understand the artistic mind? The *brilliant* mind? Toni's entire life was about understanding the brilliant mind. And not for some PhD paper she was writing or for an important article in *Scientific American*. Toni had to understand the brilliant mind because that was her life. That had been her life for more years than she was willing to count.

Because this was her family. Not just these four kids. Toni had six other siblings, ten all together. Her parents just kept breeding. Like rabbits. Or, actually, like the jackals they were. Because jackals paired for life and weren't distracted by pack issues, they bred whenever they wanted to. And Toni's parents had done just that, their latest offspring being Zia and her twin sister, both born when their mother was nearly fifty.

And although their father, Paul Parker, was, as Kyle so eloquently put it, "average," their mother, Jackie, was not. In fact, Jacqueline Jean-Louis was a world-renowned violinist. She'd performed on some of the largest stages in the world to sold-out audiences, performed in front of royalty, and had several best-selling CDs and DVDs that showed the world her skill. Yet Jackie was not only a great violinist, she'd been a prodigy. A child so talented at such a young age that she was considered brilliant.

Now to have one prodigy in a family is amazing. Most families would never, no matter how long their bloodline stretched, have a prodigy. And yet . . . somehow Toni's parents had managed to have ten prodigies out of their eleven children. Ten. In one family. True, a family of jackal shifters; but shifters were no different from full-humans when it came to how many prodigies would normally occur in one family line.

The thing about prodigies, though, was that they weren't simply brilliant. There were lots of smart, super smart, even geniuses in the world. What set prodigies apart from everyone else was their commitment. Her mother's skill with a violin would have meant nothing if she didn't spend several hours every day, since the age of three, practicing her instrument. Her sister Oriana's genetics would have meant nothing if she didn't routinely go to her ballet classes every morning and evening, six days a week, while practicing on her own, seven days a week. All real prodigies had the drive.

Lord, the drive. Toni could imagine how some people would get sick of all the family support needed to get *one* prodigy wherever they wanted to go. But Toni? Well, Toni had to deal with ten. Now, true, the twins Zia and Zoe didn't really have that drive yet. At this stage they were just naturally gifted. But little Denny, who was trying to work his way onto her lap with Zia, although only five, had already found his drive. He worked for hours before kindergarten and hours after on his paintings. Paintings that resembled actual photographs they were so painstakingly accurate. Kyle, of course, didn't call that "art." Instead he said, "Denny is still in the discovery stage where he copies everything. Although I'm confident if he gets out of that stage in the next year or two . . . he has quite the potential." For Kyle that was like calling his brother Leonardo da Vinci. Of course asking a five-year-old to quickly move through his "discovery stage" didn't seem odd to the Jean-Louis Parker kids. If you wanted to hang with them, you had to have the drive and the talent.

Tragically, Toni, the eldest, didn't have either. More than once, she'd told her mother, "I'm not really your child, am I? Just admit it." To which her mother would always respond, "You have my eyes."

"But maybe Dad isn't—"

"You have his nose, his feet, and his mother's curly hair. Just suck it up already, baby. You're a Jean-Louis Parker whether you want to be or not."

So Toni had finally resigned herself to being the "average one" among a family of prodigies. But they were also jackals, and older siblings often helped their parents raise the younger ones. It was also true, though, that most siblings Toni's age would have moved on to their own families by now. Had their own pups. But with her mother still breeding up until the twins—when finally the wonder that is flippin' menopause kicked in—and the rest of the kids being focused on their own careers—Toni just didn't feel right about going off on her own. Her family needed her. As the only one without any real skill, she was the only one who could manage all of them at one time. She had no other goal but to ensure that the rest of them reached their potential—and the age of eighteen—without going to prison.

So Toni put up with Kyle's snobbishness, Oriana's brattiness, Cherise's borderline agoraphobia, Freddy's debilitating panic attacks and issues with setting things on fire and his thievery . . . on and on it went. Her siblings all had issues, and Toni took it upon herself to keep them as reasonably human as possible. It wasn't easy. Although her siblings would never lower themselves by bumping off their competition—since they didn't consider anyone better than they were or a real threat—Toni did worry that some of them would bump someone off who got in their way. Who held them back. Once, some kid thought it would be funny to give nine-year-old Troy, the mathematician, the wrong time for an important math competition. He thought it was even funnier when a hysterically crying Troy tracked him down the next day to confront him. Sure. The crying . . . real funny. Except Troy hadn't been crying out of sadness or because he'd been hurt by the kid's actions. He'd been crying out of frustration. The emotion few in Toni's family knew how to deal with in a normal, rational way. So, those tears were no longer funny when Troy battered that kid into the ground with his backpack filled to nearly overflowing with all his hardcover math books.

Even worse for Toni, because Troy was an important prodigy, he was barely given a slap on the wrist. Not even a recommendation to go into therapy, probably because at the time, he'd been working on some important equation that his school wanted him to solve so they could brag about it in the media, and they didn't want therapy appointments getting in the way of his busy schedule. So making sure he understood beating someone out of frustration was not a good option was down to Toni. And that responsibility was something she took very seriously when it came to her siblings. Someone had to. God knew, if she didn't take it seriously, Kyle would wander around the streets asking random strangers for naked sketch time.

"I just don't see the problem, Toni. So what if I asked Novikov—"

"Shut up, Kyle."

"Yes, but—"

"Shut. It."

"This is about my art!" Kyle raged. "Don't you understand—"

Toni, not wanting to hear this particular speech again—Kyle had lots of speeches for such a young boy—reached for the back of Kyle's neck, but he scrambled over Oriana and into the seat on the other side of her.

"I'll let it go," he quickly promised. "I'll let it go."

Releasing a breath, Toni focused on the bobcat receptionist. "Could you let Mr. Van Holtz know the Jean-Louis Parkers are here?"

"Do you have an appointment?" the cat asked, not even looking away from his computer to give her eye contact.

"Yes. Remember? I was just here twenty minutes ago? Having the same conversation with you?"

The bobcat looked at her, shrugged. "And?"

Biting back an annoyed yip, Toni snapped, "As I said, we have an appointment."

"And your name?"

This was why she hated the smaller cats. Lions and tigers

could be annoying but nothing like the little ones. "Antonella Jean-Louis Parker."

"Don't you have anything shorter?"

"Just my fist," she shot back. That's when Oriana lowered her cell phone and said, "Dude, just get Ulrich before my sister rips your face off."

The bobcat sighed and picked up the phone to call the wolf they'd come to see.

Oriana re-focused on her cell phone but said to Toni, "That wolf was cute."

Toni blinked, confused. "What wolf? Ulrich?"

Rolling her eyes, Oriana replied, "No. The one you were talking to outside the skating rink. With the baseball cap."

"Oh. Him. Yeah. He was cute." But just a wolf. It wasn't like wolves were something special or unusual. Their mother was best friends with fellow former-prodigy Irene Conridge Van Holtz. A brilliant scientist and full-human, Aunt Irene was mated to Niles Van Holtz. Alpha Male of the Van Holtz Pack. And because the Jean-Louis Parkers were as close to family as Irene had, that meant that they spent a lot of time around the wolves. A *lot* of time. Not that Toni minded. Uncle Van and his Pack were fun and most of the direct bloodline Van Holtzes were amazing chefs, which meant the Jean-Louis Parkers always ate well. But bringing more wolves into her existence was not something Toni felt was necessary at this stage in her life.

"Tall," Oriana continued. "Nice shoulders."

He'd been unnaturally wide in Toni's estimation. Shoulders that wide with hips that narrow just didn't seem right.

"Nice smile."

All those teeth. Bright white teeth that he kept showing when he constantly smiled at her. Personally, she found his smile oddly threatening. As if every person he met was a potential meal.

Still, although Toni might not be susceptible to most males, she wasn't blind, either. He was a handsome wolf, but not like the Van Holtz wolves, who always reminded her of European cover models. He was too big. Too wide. Too . . . American. All those muscles and dark brown hair that just reached his massive shoulders. Amber eyes and a flat, wide nose that only barely helped to make the constant smirk on his face a little less annoying.

"Plus," Oriana went on, "he seemed to not mind your average looks and that uncontrollable mane of yours."

Slowly Toni looked at her sister. "Thanks, Oriana."

Her sister smiled without looking up from her phone. "You're welcome."

Toni seriously considered ripping that phone out of Oriana's hand since she had yet to learn the meaning of sarcasm, but Ric Van Holtz walked into the lobby before she could bother.

"Hey, guys. Sorry I couldn't really meet with you earlier. Last-minute meeting with investors."

"No problem," Toni assured him, handing Zia over to him as soon as he stretched out his arms. Ric was great with kids, no matter the breed or species, and he adored the Jean-Louis Parker pups.

"How did it go at the rink?" Ric asked, gently brushing his free hand over Zia's hair as her head rested on his shoulder.

"Fine."

"Except for that fight," Oriana muttered.

Ric's nose flared. It was a rather narrow nose, but it could flare quite dramatically when he was angry enough. "Did Novikov hurt you? Should I have him killed?"

"That seems extreme." Toni cut a warning glare at her sister, but with the brat's attention focused on her phone, there was no guarantee that she'd seen anything. "Mr. Novikov was just fine."

"He wasn't fighting with us," Kyle clarified.

"Oh." Ric quickly calmed down. "That was probably Reece Reed he was fighting then, since it's the middle of the day and Reece seems to be the only one who continues to fight that idiot."

"Novikov signed my shirt, just like you said he would." Kyle held up the shirt for Ric to see.

"Good. I'm glad he did as I told him to."

"Yeah," Oriana said, "it went great until Kyle here asked to see him naked."

Ric briefly closed his eyes. "Again, Kyle? *Again?*"

Horrified, Toni demanded, "Oh, my God, Kyle! Did you ask Ric to—"

"I will not be held back by society's mores!"

"It's not society's mores we're concerned with, Kyle," Ric kindly explained. "It's society's creeps."

"So you're saying that Bo Novikov is—"

"No," Ric said quickly and firmly. "That's *not* what I mean. And although you might be safe with Novikov or with me, that doesn't mean the rest of the world is a safe bet. You have to be careful."

Kyle motioned to Toni. "But that's what I have her for. To protect me from society's creeps."

"Really? Is that what I've been reduced to?" Toni asked. "Your bodyguard? Is that my life? Is that going to *be* my life?"

"I wouldn't worry about you having that job for long," Oriana told her.

"Why?"

"How good could you be at protecting him with those stick legs of yours?"

Toni looked down at her legs, then quickly realized she was involved in a ridiculous conversation. Again.

"You know what," Toni said, getting to her tiny stick legs. "As fascinating as this is, we have to go. We've got to make that flight."

Ric blinked. "Make your flight?"

"Yeah. Nothing worse than trying to get this group on the same flight once we've missed our original flight. We're going standard air." Toni's term for flights that catered to full-humans.

Yet when Toni looked up at Ric, she saw that he was watching her with a mix of humor and pity. "You haven't talked to your mother, have you?" he asked.

Toni immediately began rubbing her forehead. "No. Why?"

"I think there might have been a change of plan."

"No," Toni said, shaking her head. "No. No change of plan. No wacky, last-minute ideas. No." She was adamant about it. No!

Toni pulled her cell phone out of the back pocket of her jeans and took a quick look. No calls. From anyone. Her parents would have texted her, right? Called her? Something?

Unless . . .

Slowly Toni looked over at Oriana.

The younger female lowered her cell phone, gave one of her annoying smirks. "Oh. That's right," the brat said carefully. "I forgot I have a message for you from Mom."

"Really? You forgot?"

"Don't make this into a big deal," her sister warned, sounding bored. "You know how Mom is."

"Mom's not really the issue here at the moment."

"Look, it's not my job to get messages back and forth between you and our mother."

"If that's true, then I guess you won't be needing this."

Toni snatched Oriana's cell phone from her hand and threw it down the hall and into the wall. She took great satisfaction at the sound of something on the device breaking from the impact.

"*Now go fetch, bitch!*" Toni screamed at her sister.

"*You are such a ridiculous child!*" Oriana screamed back.

"*And you're a spoiled twat!*"

Ric quickly stepped between them, facing Toni. "My car can take you to your mother."

Panting, her fangs burrowing into her bottom lip as they grew from her gums, Toni nodded. "Fine."

"Great. Great." He turned and took Oriana's arm, Zia still asleep on his shoulder. Fights between her siblings never really bothered her or her twin. "Let's go get what's left of your phone and I'll call my driver."

He led Oriana down the hall, giving Toni a few seconds to calm down.

"Wow," the bobcat muttered from his desk. "Your sister's right. Your legs really are skinny."

Toni briefly thought about swiping all the cat's crap off his desk, but that wasn't something she'd do to anyone who wasn't one of her siblings. But that was the beauty of being one of the Jean-Louis Parker clan . . . sometimes you didn't have to do anything at all, because there was a sibling there to take care of it for you.

"It must be hard," Kyle mused to the bobcat. "One of the superior cats. Revered and adored throughout history as far back as the ancient Egyptians. And yet here you sit. At a desk. A common drone. Taking orders from lowly canines and bears. Do your ancestors call to you from the great beyond, hissing their disappointment to you? Do they cry out in despair at where you've ended up despite such a lofty bloodline? Or does your hatred spring from the feline misery of always being alone? Skulking along, wishing you had a mate or a pack or pride to call your own? But all you have is you . . . and your pathetic job as a drone? Does it break your feline heart to be so . . . average? So common? So . . . *human?*"

Toni cringed, which helped her *not* laugh.

And although she'd normally stop one of her brother's ego-destroying rants long before he got to the "so human" part, this time, with this particular bobcat . . . she just couldn't. Yet what she could do was get her baby brother out of here before he had to witness a bobcat male sobbing softly into his Starbucks coffee and egg salad sandwich lunch.

Because that's what was coming. Her brother might have the hands of a true artist, but his brain . . . his brain was like that of a sadistic psychiatrist who liked to see if he could force his patients to gouge out their own eyes during therapy appointments.

Lifting Denny into her arms, Toni grabbed Kyle's hand and pulled him out of the office. She'd wait for her sister and Ric down the hall.

"You going to yell at me?" Kyle asked her once they were away from the office and the bobcat's sniffling was the only thing that could be heard by their keen jackal ears.

She smiled at her brother.

Sure. They were typical black-backed jackals, which meant they fought amongst themselves whenever the mood struck them, but they were also family. And one messed with a jackal family at one's own risk.

"Nah, little bro." She winked at him. "Not this time."

Chapter Three

R icky's brother Rory Lee sat at his big office desk and
looked back and forth between Ricky and Reece. "He's
useless to me," Rory told him. "Useless! I can't use him for that
job tonight."

Ricky Lee knew as soon as he saw Reece's wounds that
he would end up having this conversation with their eldest
brother, Rory. It was something to be expected. Rory Lee
Reed was the oldest and the most uptight of the three of them
but Rory had always felt it was his role to take care of them—
even when they didn't need it.

Now, true, one could make an argument that Reece Reed
always needed someone to take care of him because he seemed
to stupidly stumble into deadly situations. But the truth was,
their youngest brother knew exactly what he was doing and enjoyed every minute of it. And Rory enjoyed acting put-upon.

And what did Ricky enjoy? Well, as it turned out, Ricky
enjoyed watching Rory get all upset while Reece willingly
walked into stupid situations to get his ass kicked. It entertained
him. Like NASCAR and good American beer.

Reece said something and Rory looked at Ricky. "What did
he say?"

"You didn't understand that?"

"With his jaw wired and his throat still recovering from that
nicked artery? No."

"I could."

"Ricky," his brother growled, "you're irritating me."

"Reece says he can do the job fine."

"How? His jaw is wired shut! Because you didn't keep him out of trouble like I told you to!"

"I'm not my brother's keep—"

"Shut up!" Rory put his elbows on his desk and dug his hands under his baseball cap and into his hair. He scratched his scalp and made lots of snarling noises.

Poor guy. He took all this so seriously. The minutiae of it, anyway. Ricky and Reece only took their cases seriously. They cared about the clients, wanted to make sure they were as safe as possible. That was their job after all. Protection specialists. That's what their business cards said. Honestly, the Reed boys couldn't have a job more perfectly fitted for their natures. When their Packmate, Bobby Ray Smith, had been discharged from the Navy, he and his best friend, Mace Llewellyn, started this protection agency. Their older Tennessee Packmates and kin were none too happy about the idea but Ricky, Rory, and Reece all felt that it was getting a bit crowded in Smithtown, Tennessee, so they'd taken Bobby Ray up on his offer to start fresh in New York. It had been a good decision for all of them.

Llewellyn Security was doing really well, their business growing every day. Though most of their clients were shifters, they happily took on full-humans. Heck, money was money. And the more money they made from the full-humans and the richer shifters, the more they could help out those shifters who didn't have the money to pay but desperately needed their help. The one thing Ricky truly loved about his kind, no matter the breed or species, was their willingness to protect each other. Sure, lions might fight wolves, wild dogs might fight hyenas, and bears might slap around everybody, but when their kind faced real danger from the outside world, from the full-humans or the full-human governments, they all worked together. It was just understood that all Pack, Pride, or Clan issues took a backseat to the survival of shifters worldwide.

Yet while the bigger shifter-run organizations like The Group or KZS handled big scale situations that might involve one or more governments, it was the smaller companies like theirs that handled individual cases. Because the less full-humans saw any evidence of the existence of shifters—the less full-humans had to die in tragic "accidents."

Mace Llewellyn walked by Rory's office. He was staring down at some paperwork and barely glanced at them, grunting out a, "Hey," before walking on. It would have been meaningless if Reece hadn't gurgled a return greeting at him.

Mace walked back several steps and slowly looked into the office until his eyes rested on Reece. "What's going on with his face?" he asked.

"Jaw's wired," Ricky told him, not one for beating around the bush.

"Why's his jaw wired?"

"Fight with Novikov."

Closing his eyes and letting out a big sigh, the lion male demanded, "How many times are we going to have to talk to you about not fighting with Novikov before a big job?"

Reece gurgled something and Ricky translated, "He didn't start it."

"I don't care!" the lion roared.

Ricky looked at Reece. "He doesn't care."

"Is something wrong with his ears?" Llewellyn asked. "Has Novikov hit him in the head so many times that he no longer understands English?"

"Just trying to be helpful."

"No. You're trying to piss me off."

Maybe a little . . .

Llewellyn pointed at Rory. "Fix this, Reed. *Fix. It.*"

Once the lion stormed off, Rory glared at his two younger brothers.

Yeah, he looked mighty pissed.

"It's no big deal," Ricky said. "You just have to find one backup. I'll still be there."

That seemed to be something Rory might be able to tolerate until Reece's eyes rolled to the back of his head and he passed out in the chair. Sweat beaded his forehead, and his entire body sporadically shook as it worked to heal itself.

The fever was actually a good thing for shifters. It allowed their bodies to heal quickly and with little additional damage. But healing shifters couldn't be left alone. They had a tendency to shift to their animal form and back to their human form several times over. Nothing harder to explain to the general public than coyotes found hanging out in a restaurant's cold storage or bears hanging out in someone's pool. So Reece couldn't go home alone and, at least in the beginning, Ricky couldn't ask one of the females of the Pack to take care of him, because the fever could make a body a little . . . amorous. Now, if their baby sister, Ronnie Lee, was around, she could do it. Fever Love, as it was sometimes called, was never directed at one's kin. But the other females in the Pack were fair game, and Reece had had enough trouble with them in his past. Which meant that Ricky would have to take his brother home . . . now.

Looking at Rory, his brother watching him with a slight sneer to his lips, Ricky argued, "I'm sure finding one more backup shouldn't be too—"

"Get out."

"But—"

"Pick up that idiot and get the fuck out of my office!"

Ricky shrugged. "All right."

Standing, Ricky grabbed Reece's limp hand and dragged him out of the chair and out of the office. He'd pick him up off the floor when they got to the elevator. Right now it was just kind of funny passing all those offices with his brother dragging along behind him.

That wasn't a good attitude, was it? No. Probably not. Fun? Absolutely!

But not a *good* attitude.

The car pulled up to the front of a five-story brownstone in the heart of an expensive downtown neighborhood in New York City.

Toni stepped out onto the street and looked up at the building. She could only imagine how expensive this place must be. It wasn't that her mother couldn't afford it. She could. *They* could. Their mother's career had been unbelievably lucrative over the years. But still . . . why? Why was her mother doing this?

"Are you giving me my cell phone back?" Oriana snapped.

The screen was cracked but it was still a workable technological instrument, which was why Toni immediately said, "No."

"I'm telling Mom."

Toni didn't know why her siblings used that as some kind of threat. It was meaningless to her.

"Whatever." She headed toward the house. "Get Zia and Denny," she ordered Oriana. She didn't look back. Didn't check to see if her sister would do as ordered. No matter what they were arguing about, the youngest of their family would always be protected and taken care of. Even while the rest of them were yelling at each other like rabid rottweilers.

Toni walked into the house, horrified to find the front door open. This was New York City. One did not leave the door open in New York City.

Yet as soon as she stepped into the hallway, Toni realized how her parents and siblings could have become distracted.

"Holy shit storm," Oriana muttered, standing beside Toni. She held Zia in her arms and Kyle held Denny's hand. The five of them stood in the hallway and gazed up at the mile-high ceilings, and down at the marble floors. The staircase was made of mahogany and seemed to go on forever.

Toni walked farther down the hall and checked out one of the adjoining hallways. That's when she realized that this brownstone had been opened up and was now connected to the brownstone next door. This place would easily fit her entire family inside it but still . . . why were they here? Why were they *staying* here?

A light breeze flowed in from the open doorway. Oriana sniffed the air. "Why do I smell dog?"

"That's just us."

"I know how my family smells." And the "bitch" was implied. "This is dog."

Thinking it was probably some stray, Toni lifted her head and sniffed. Spinning around, she walked back down the hall and out the door. She stared across the street. She watched children jump out of a big SUV, bags from a toy store in their hands. Screaming and laughing, they ran up the stairs of their own brownstone and inside.

But it was the adults following the kids inside that Toni recognized.

Snarling, she ran back into the brownstone. "Mom?" Toni called out. "Mom!"

"Upstairs! Come see, Toni! Come see!"

Toni raced up five flights of stairs and found her mother in an enormous room with a skylight. A bright open space that would be perfect for a practice room, something she was sure her mother had already noted.

"Isn't this place amazing?" her mother asked.

Toni pointed at the window facing the brownstone across the street. "Are we here because—"

"Because I think a summer in New York City is just what this family needs. Everything we could possibly want is here. The classes, the training, the—"

"First off, Mom, what classes? The kind of classes these little brats want to take have already been filled for at least six months, if not at least a full year."

Jackie chuckled. "Baby, come on. You forget what you're dealing with here."

"We still have to make calls, get recommendations from their Washington teachers—"

"I already have Jack on it."

"Your agent?"

"Uh-huh. He's already got the boys in some advanced classes at NYU. The twins in Berlitz at Rockefeller Center. Oriana will take her morning and afternoon classes with the Manhattan Ballet Company—"

"How the hell did he—"

"—Cherise will be studying under Herr Koenig."

"I heard he's an asshole."

"A horrible asshole but a talented one who only takes the best performers as his students."

Toni threw her hands up in the air. "Oh, well then . . ."

"Kyle will be taking master classes at the Steinhardt School at NYU and Denny will go to the School of Visual Arts."

"How the hell did Jack—"

"He has the kids' portfolios and recent video performances on file . . . just in case."

Toni's eyes narrowed. "Is he their agent?"

"No. He's my agent. He's just helping me out."

"Right." Toni studied her mom. "You didn't mention Delilah."

"She said she'd take care of it herself. She's eighteen now. I can't order her to go to classes."

"And we can't just have her wandering around on her own, Mom."

Her mother waved away Toni's concern. "She'll be fine."

"Mom."

"She'll be fine. And would you mind taking Freddy over to the hotel to see Irene before she goes back home?"

"Yes, of course." If her mother didn't want to discuss Delilah—and when did she ever want to discuss Delilah?—then Toni would ask her another important question. "And what about *my* job, Mom?"

Her mother blinked at Toni, her expression completely blank. "What job?"

"The one I was starting on Monday. Remember?"

"That little office job?"

"Yes, Mom. That little office job. The one I was doing part-time and had incredibly flexible hours so I could help with the kids? *That* little office job."

"I'm sure you can find something here to keep you busy."

"I'm not talking about something to keep me busy. I'm thinking long term."

"Long term . . . to what? Being an office drone? You?"

"What do you want me to do? Sit around all day?"

"Find something you're good at! Look for a real career. You have a college degree."

"In liberal arts. Not exactly beneficial in this economy."

"Oh, my God, baby. You worry about the most ridiculous things."

"And you, Mom?"

"What about me?"

"Why are you here?"

"Do you know how much I can get done being in Manhattan for a few months? This will work out great for me."

Toni walked over to the window and jabbed her thumb at the building across the street. "And those wild dogs have nothing to do with you moving here?"

"Can you think of a better neighborhood than one with fellow canines?"

"Not just canines, Mom. African wild dogs."

"We're all dogs in God's eye—"

"Mom!"

"Oh, all right!" Letting out a sigh, her mother crossed the room and leaned against the wall by the window. She glanced down. "The Kuznetsov Pack lives there."

"Mom . . . seriously? At this point it might be considered stalking."

"I'm not stalking. Just making myself available."

Toni glowered at her mother. "I can't believe how sneaky you are."

"What are you talking about?"

"You were planning this from the beginning. This was never just a little family getaway to Manhattan."

"Don't be ridiculous."

"You just wanted to make sure the Kuznetsovs were still in town." Toni glanced around the beautiful room. "This is their property, isn't it? You rented from them."

"Who else would I trust but another canine? And how dare you call me that, Antonella Jean-Louis Parker!"

"What are you talking about? I haven't called you anything."

"No. But you're *thinking* it."

Toni shrugged. "Maybe."

Ricky looked away from the TV baseball game he was watching and up at the She-wolf standing next to the couch.

"Hey, Dee-Ann."

Dee-Ann Smith. Ricky had grown up with her in Smith-town. She was closer to Rory's age and to this day they were still best friends. Ricky, however, thought of Dee-Ann as more of a sister. She'd sewn up his head when Rory had rammed it into their daddy's truck door. Sewn up his face when Reece had chucked a crowbar at him. And held his hand when, at sixteen, he was waiting to find out if his onetime girlfriend was pregnant. His girlfriend hadn't been, and Dee-Ann had been the first to hug him, then punch him in the stomach, drive him to the local pharmacy, and buy him several boxes of condoms. Something that would have started all sorts of rumors in a little wolf-run town like Smithtown if it had been any other She-wolf but Dee-Ann. She was not a female anyone wanted to start spreading rumors about. She was not a female you wanted to ever notice you.

With eyes just like her father's—cold yellow like many full-blooded wolves—she gazed down at Ricky. "Shame's not a big thing in your family, is it?"

"Don't know what you mean."

She motioned to the dog kennel in the middle of his hotel room. The Pack had taken rooms at the Kingston Arms hotel, a shifter-run establishment, when they'd first moved to Manhattan with Bobby Ray Smith. A few of the Packmates had gotten their own apartments but most stayed at the five-star hotel. Why? Because Ricky Lee's sister was mated to the lion male who owned the place. So even though their rooms usually went for several hundred to several thousand dollars a night for the general public, the Pack got their rooms for much, *much* cheaper.

"You put your own brother in a dog kennel," she said.

"He wouldn't calm down. Kept trying to rip the front door open. Look at this . . ." He lifted the arm that currently held a can of Coke and showed it to her. "Tried to take my dang arm off at the shoulder. I only got two, Dee-Ann."

"You're whining about that scratch?"

"I wouldn't call it whining . . ."

Dee-Ann stepped onto his couch, resting her butt on the seatback, her hands clasped in front of her. "Did you hear from Sissy Mae?" Sissy Mae Smith, the Alpha Female of their Pack, Bobby Ray Smith's baby sister, and Ronnie Lee's best friend.

"Nope. Why?"

"Cousin Laura Jane is coming to town. To visit."

"And?"

"Everyone knows how she broke your heart."

Startled, Ricky looked at Dee-Ann. "Yeah . . . when I was eighteen. I'm pretty sure I've recovered since then."

"I don't know. Your sister and Sissy sure are worried."

"Great. Just what I need. The pity of the idiots."

Dee-Ann chuckled. "They do seem to be making a big deal out of it."

"Because that's what they do. Make a big deal out of absolutely nothing."

"Yep."

Ricky offered his can of Coke to Dee-Ann. She took it, took a sip, and handed it back. That's when Ricky asked, "Is Laura Jane coming here tonight? Is that why you're here? To give me a heads-up?"

"No. She's not coming tonight."

"Oh. Okay."

Dee-Ann paused a moment, then added, "But your sister and Sissy Mae are coming here to talk—"

Ricky leaped off the couch and faced the She-wolf. "What do you mean they're coming here? I thought they were still out of town."

"Got in earlier today. Figured they didn't call you because

they wanted to make sure you'd stick around so they could sit down and have a real heart-to-heart about Laura Jane and how you really feel about—where are you going?"

"I don't do heart-to-hearts, Dee-Ann," Ricky told her as he grabbed his backpack from the floor and headed toward the door.

"What about your brother?"

"Babysit him until they get here. Ronnie Lee can handle him. He's almost through the worst of it."

Studying his brother, Dee-Ann's head tipped to the side. "He's trying to chew through the gate . . . with his human teeth."

"Just deal with it!"

Ricky slammed the door behind him and started toward the elevators. But the doors were opening and he could scent his sister and Sissy Mae. Panicking, Ricky charged the other way and into the nearest emergency stairwell. The heavy metal door was nearly closed when he heard his sister yell from his room, *"Reece Lee Reed! What the holy hell are you doing in a damn dog kennel?"*

As Ricky headed down the stairs, he knew he was running away. Not from an ex-girlfriend that to this day his brothers still called, "Good Lady Self-Obsessed," but from his sister and her best friend. He loved Ronnie Lee. Loved Sissy, too. But that didn't mean he wanted to sit around with them all night talking about feelings. It would be worse now, too, because the word was out that Ronnie Lee was pregnant. That meant no more liquor for his baby sister, and, knowing Ronnie, she wasn't about to let anyone drink around her when she couldn't. She hated that.

A long conversation with a *sober* Sissy and Ronnie Lee was too horrifying for words. So when Ricky Lee finally made it out onto the street from one of the hotel's side doors, he was simply relieved.

Ricky headed down the street, crossing in front of the hotel. He stopped when he saw an older She-wolf walking toward the hotel doors. She wasn't from a Pack he recognized, but his momma had raised him right. So he pulled open one of the swinging doors, smiling at her as she passed, and tipped his baseball cap.

She grinned back and nodded at him, flashing a bit of fang as the universal shifter sign of, "I know what you are!"

Once the She-wolf had made her way inside, Ricky was about to release the door when another female caught it and held it open.

"Sorry about—hey!" He smiled in surprise at the She-jackal he'd met at the rink. Uh . . . Toni! That was it.

She looked up at him. "Oh . . . hey."

"Look at that. Meeting each other again. Kind of random. Granny Reed would call that Karma. Actually what she'd call it is the devil's work, but whatever."

"Okay."

He saw that she held the hand of another little boy. He raised a brow. "You sure have been busy."

That's when she smirked and gave a little shake of the boy's hand. With big brown eyes, the boy asked, "Are *you* my daddy?"

Laughing, Ricky stepped back and allowed the pair to walk through. He started to follow, but saw one of the females from his Pack. She was on the phone and clearly looking for someone. On the tips of her toes, trying to look over everyone's head.

"Good Lord," Ricky muttered, "she's sent out scouts."

He instinctively crouched, the She-jackal taking that moment to look back. She stopped, turned, and gazed down at him. "Really?" she asked.

"One day I'll explain it to you. I'm sure you'd understand."

"Somehow I doubt it, but whatever."

The little boy shook his head. "I'm glad you're not my daddy."

"That's very wise, Freddy," the She-jackal said in agreement. "Let's be glad he's *not* your daddy."

Ricky saw that his Packmate was getting closer.

"I'd make a great daddy for any child, but I can't discuss it now."

"Because you're running away?"

"Wolves always know when to run, darlin'." And that's exactly what Ricky Lee did. Released the door, eased away from it, and took off toward his truck.

The hotel door opened and Toni smirked at the full-human who answered. She began to chastise, "That took you long en—"

"Freddy!" Giving a very rare smile, Irene Conridge Van Holtz leaned down and picked up Toni's seven-year-old brother. "How is my favorite brilliant boy?"

"My ulcer's acting up."

"You don't have an ulcer," Toni reminded him as she stepped past her mother's best friend and walked into the four-room suite Irene Conridge shared with her mate, Niles Van Holtz, Alpha of the Van Holtz Pack.

"Based on recent research, there's a seventy-three-percent chance I will," Freddy informed her.

"Only if you keep worrying about getting one."

Irene carried Freddy into the living room, closing the door with her foot.

"Where's Uncle Van?" Toni asked, using Niles's nickname.

"At Ric's restaurant showing off."

"That man does love to cook."

"Although I normally don't believe that sort of thing can be passed down, I must say the Van Holtz bloodline seems to prove me wrong."

"You're going to miss him while he's gone."

Irene sat down on one of the couches with Freddy beside her. Showing a rare moment of affection, Irene put her arm over Freddy's shoulder. Irene must be in a good mood. Because even though she'd known seven-year-old Freddy since hours after his conception, she wasn't known for her loving warmth.

To be honest, it was something that used to worry Toni. That Freddy would end up equally as uptight as Irene. Not a surprising worry. The reason the pair was so close was because they both loved science, and they were both prodigies. Irene had met their mother at a summer camp for gifted children.

That was the same summer that her mother experienced her first shift. A sometimes harrowing event that could have exposed Jackie to the world if she'd been seen by the wrong people. Although most full-humans were considered "the wrong people," Irene had turned out to be anything but. Instead, she'd been fascinated by the process of shifting and that there were others like Jackie. She'd kept her friend's secret then and now, so it was no surprise Irene had found love with another shifter.

That fact was so very important to Toni. Because although to most of the world Irene Conridge Van Holtz seemed a cold, indifferent bitch—and most of the time she was—she had another side to her. The side that loved Niles Van Holtz. The rich and talented wolf had caught her heart and managed to hold on to it for more than two decades. Uncle Van loved Irene despite her flaws, and that showed Toni there was hope for her little Freddy.

If he had friends and love, he'd be okay. She just had to make sure to keep him out of trouble now. Not easy. The more brilliant Freddy turned out to be, the more issues seemed to arise that concerned her. It didn't concern anyone else in the family. "He's only seven!" they'd say. Or "He's brilliant! Of course he's being a little weird!" Toni's concerns were often dismissed as those of an overprotective jackal sibling, but she knew better.

So when one of the bedroom doors opened and her brother's little face lit up, Toni felt good.

"Miki!" he crowed, then charged off the couch, across the room, and right into the open arms of Miki Kendrick. One-time mentee of Irene, brilliant scientist, another full-human mated to a wolf, mother to a beautiful little girl pup, and a still-off-the-grid secret hacker stalked by scary government types.

"There's my handsome boy!" Miki hugged Freddy tight, giving him a smacking kiss on his cheek that had him giggling. "Did you have fun in today's master class with us?"

"Yes. Although I realized you dumbed it down for the laymen."

"We had to. Average nuclear scientists can't always grasp what we're talking about."

"I liked when Aunt Irene made that one man cry."

Toni quickly looked at her aunt, who stared blankly back at her.

"What?" Irene asked. "He started it."

"There was mucus coming from his nose." Freddy giggled.

"I thought I told you *not* to be a bad influence on my brother," Toni reminded her aunt.

"I said I would not mock people in front of Freddy for merely being idiots. For instance, I didn't say a word about the fact that the man wore black pants, black shoes, and white sweat socks. But I refused to simply ignore his opinion on the elements of—"

"I don't care," Toni cut in. Mostly because she knew that whatever her aunt was about to say, she probably wouldn't understand. "Just don't turn Freddy into Kyle, Part two."

"How can I? Even my level of arrogance doesn't quite reach Kyle's. Although," Irene added with that serious tone, "I think Mussolini's did."

"He'd make an interesting dictator," Miki added.

And they both looked at Toni as if that information should somehow make her feel better.

Ricky knocked on the bulletproof glass of the thick security door and grinned down at the pup staring at him. "Hello, darlin'. Is Bobby Ray home?"

The pup stared at him a moment longer before turning and screeching, "Moooooooom! Wolf at the door!"

The pup's mother didn't show up at the door but the Alpha of the Kuznetsov Pack did. A wide smile on her face, Jessie Ann Ward unlocked and opened the door. "Hey, Ricky Lee."

"Hey, Jessie Ann. Your mate home?"

"Upstairs in his lair. I think he's avoiding the kids. They've been in overdrive all day now that school's out. Is everything okay?"

"Oh, yeah. Just avoiding my sister and Sissy Mae."

That made Jessie laugh. "Something I understand completely. Don't worry. If they call or stop by . . . I haven't seen you."

"Thanks, darlin'." He stepped inside and headed down the hall. "I see you've finally rented that place across the street."

"Mhmm," Jessie Ann grunted.

"Somethin' wrong?" He leaned in and whispered, "You want me to go over there and give 'em a Smith welcome?"

Jessie laughed. "Don't you dare, Ricky Lee Reed. They're paying a fortune. I mean a *fortune,* just to stay there for the summer. But I think they have motives."

"Something illegal?"

"No. Nothing that interesting."

"Then it must involve Johnny." The young wolf, Johnny DeSerio, was Jessie's adopted son. An eighteen-year-old kid with a gift for the fiddle. Could play a mean "Devil Went Down to Georgia" while Jessie Ann sang. But a strong, street-smart boy, so Ricky didn't know why Jessie Ann worried about him so.

"It does, but I don't want to discuss it." She glanced into the living room and giggling pups ducked behind the couch. "Too many big ears around here."

"Not a problem."

He kissed her cheek and headed up the stairs to the third floor, where the Pack had given Bobby Ray his own office, and there were bedrooms for visiting wolves.

The door to Bobby Ray's office wasn't closed, and Ricky walked in to find the strong, powerful Alpha Male of his Pack tickling the ribs of his baby daughter and blowing raspberries on her belly while the little darling just laughed and laughed.

"Well, hello, Daddy!" Ricky cheered from the door.

Bobby Ray froze in mid-raspberry, but Ricky Lee was dang impressed when Bobby Ray's baby girl angrily barked at him for the interruption.

"Now is that any way to talk to your godfather, brat?" Of course, she might not remember he was her godfather—the girl had six of them. Smith males believing their all-important daughters could never have *enough* protection.

Bobby Ray stood, lifting his daughter with him. "Where's her momma?"

"Downstairs."

With that, Bobby Ray tossed the child to Ricky Lee, who easily caught her. Not surprisingly, Jessie hated when they did that, but the tomboyish little girl adored it. Laughing, she clung to Ricky's neck.

"How's my favorite girl? How's my little vampire?"

"Stop calling her that."

"Hey. It wasn't my idea to name her after Dracula's first wife."

Bobby dropped into his chair. "It's the price I pay for love . . . I married a geek. And," he added, annoyed, "these dogs may run around calling her Elisabeta all day long, but to me she's just my Lissy Ann."

"I wouldn't worry." Ricky sat at the desk across from Bobby. "She's a hearty little gal. Look at these little legs. Sturdy. She'll be out huntin' and campin' with the rest of us before you know it. Won't need any fancy tents or generators with her."

Bobby shuddered a little, most likely remembering that joint Pack camping trip they'd taken with the wild dogs in Alaska. It had not gone well. No. Not well at all.

Putting his big feet up on his desk, Bobby studied Ricky a moment before stating, "So . . . guess you heard about Laura Jane."

Miki sat on the couch, but unlike Irene and Freddy, she sort of flopped on it, her bare feet landing dangerously close to Irene's thigh. How these two had become friends, Toni didn't know, because although equally brilliant and both full-humans mated to wolves, they were still quite different as women.

"So what brings you here?" Miki asked, unaware of the way Irene moved away from her extremely tiny feet. Irene was not a big fan of feet . . . or of being touched by anyone but her children and Uncle Van.

"Freddy wanted to see you before you two left tomorrow."

Irene's head tilted to the side, her brain working. She said, "I thought you guys were leaving tonight, too."

Toni kept her face blank and, after a moment, Irene sighed. "Don't tell me that woman has decided to stay here."

"That woman is your best friend and *of course* she decided to stay here. How hard can it be to move your entire family of thirteen to Manhattan at the very last minute?"

"When you have money? Not hard at all. But why?"

"Because of Johnny DeSerio."

"Is he a mobster?"

Toni sighed. "Aunt Irene, we've had this discussion. Not everyone who is Italian is a mobster—"

"I know."

"—or on a Jersey-based reality TV show."

"That I'm still not sure about."

"And he's that young violinist she met at one of her master classes last summer."

"Oh, yes. I remember. She's been going on about him for months now. Did she finally snag him?"

"Before I decide whether to be morally superior," Miki cut in, "what are we talking about your mother wanting to do with this person? Have sex with him or just—"

"*No.*" Nope. Miki was not like Irene at all. "She wants him as a student. Kind of like you and Irene. A mentor-mentee kind of thing."

"Except Irene was my thesis adviser when I was going for my PhD. Are you talking about that?"

"No. But as an artist—"

"Please. No. No 'as an artist' discussions. I've had them for two days now with your family. I'm done."

Toni had to laugh. Over the years, she'd learned to tune the "as an artist" discussions out. But those not used to it . . .

"How hard can it be to entice this boy into your mother's tutelage?" Irene demanded. "She's Jacqueline Jean-Louis, not some desperate wannabe who still dreams of having a music career."

"I love how you manage to sound arrogant for *other* people. And I don't think the problem is the kid. It's his mother. She's one of the Kuznetsov wild dog Pack and *extremely* protective of him. Word is she decked some teacher that tore into him after a competition. Her mate had to drag her off the guy. So Mom's proceeding with caution."

"Actually . . . that sounds like a solid plan."

"Yeah. I thought so."

Holding his goddaughter on his lap, Ricky asked, "Perhaps you can explain to me this obsession women have with talking things out? I mean, what is there to talk about?"

"You know how your sister is. She assumes you're still broken up over being dumped by Laura Jane."

"I was eighteen. She was nineteen. And kind of a," he covered his goddaughter's ears with his hands, "whore."

"Now, now. That's my cousin, Ricky Lee." When Ricky just stared at him, Bobby shrugged. "Who is kind of a whore."

Ricky dropped his hands. "She was seeing at least two other guys when she was going out with me. At the time, it broke my heart . . . but also at the time, when my momma didn't make blueberry pancakes on Sunday mornings like she promised, that kind of broke my heart, too."

"Not really a deep wolf, are ya, Ricky Lee?"

"Not if I can help it."

"The worst part is that now I've got to call your friend tomorrow, Aunt Irene, and tell him I can't take that job after all."

Irene frowned. "My friend?"

"Mr. Weatherford. Who hired me to work in his office this summer."

"Oh. Right." Irene dismissed that with a wave of her hand. "I told him chances were extremely high you wouldn't take the job and he should have a ready backup because he would probably find out last minute."

Toni sat up straight. "Wait. You knew Mom was going to stay here for the summer?"

"No. Not at all."

"But then why—"

"You always have to cancel your plans because of your family. Last summer it was because you went with Cooper and Cherise to Italy and then China for their concerts. The summer before that the entire family stayed in England because of Oriana's scholarship with the Royal Ballet. And the summer before *that*—"

"Okay. Okay."

"You always take these jobs and you can never actually do them—even though you so clearly want to—because of the loyalty you have to your family." She shrugged casually. "When you think about it, you've given up your whole life for your family."

"Isn't that why that idiot you were dating last year ended it?" Miki asked. "Because of your commitment to your family?"

Toni gazed at the two women but didn't respond. It wasn't until Freddy put his hand on her knee and gazed up at her with those big brown eyes that Toni suddenly burst into tears.

"Well, you can stay the night if ya like," Bobby Ray offered. "Doubt they'll come looking for you here."

"Why is that?"

"I tell Sissy that the Pack males hate staying here because the wild dogs get on their nerves."

"But the wild dogs always have pie and brownies. And tons of action movies to watch. Why *wouldn't* we stay here?"

"Because if the She-wolves think y'all hate it here, you might actually get some peace and quiet."

"Then add in the fact the dogs never keep liquor around this place . . ."

Bobby Ray grinned. "Exactly."

"She's crying, Irene," Toni heard Miki say, panic in her voice. "She's crying!"

"Well, I don't know what to do. She's never cried around me before."

"Um . . . Freddy, go into my room and get the box of tissues on the dresser."

"And nothing else!" Toni managed to sobbingly yell after her brother as he charged into Miki's room. "Just the tissues!"

Don't worry. Toni had a very good therapist working with Freddy on his stealing issues, too.

"I'm so sorry, Toni," Irene said, sitting on one side of her. "I didn't mean to upset you like this. You're not someone I purposely torment."

"It's all right," Toni said, wiping her face with her hand. "It's not your fault."

Miki sat on the other side. "You should go back to Washington. Go tomorrow. Take the job. Your family will be fine here."

"I can't leave them," Toni finally admitted to Irene and Miki—and to herself. "I can never leave them. Ever. First I'm the babysitter, then I'm going to be the spinster aunt, taking care of their brilliant kids one day. My small room filled with the knickknacks brought back by the children as they've traveled the world and lived their wonderful lives."

Irene sighed. "Were you watching the original 'Brideshead Revisited' again?"

"I'm going to be the nanny. Left alone in her room, listening to the radio . . ."

"Will Winston Churchill be giving speeches?" Miki teased. "Come on, girl. Buck the fuck up. Your family can only get you down if you let them. Look at my friend Sara. She could have let her bitch grandmother totally destroy her. But instead, she just waited until she died, threw a party slash funeral, then her whole life changed for the better."

"So you're saying I should wait until my parents die?" Toni asked flatly.

"It's a start—"

"No," Irene argued. "Waiting on death is not an option. Especially since *both* sets of your grandparents are still alive. But you do need to start weaning your family off your proverbial teat as soon as possible."

"Ew."

"They shouldn't be able to rely on you for their every need, Antonella."

"Yeah, but—"

"No, buts. This is what I want you to do." Irene put her arm around Toni's shoulders. "You are going to stay here with your family this summer. I'm going to ask Ulrich to get you a job at one of his businesses. I know he can find you something. You will take the job and you will *do* the job. While you work, you will begin the weaning process."

"They won't like it."

"I don't care. I want you to be happy, and that means you cannot and *will* not continue to be the Jean-Louis Parkers' gal Friday. Am I making myself perfectly clear?"

Toni nodded, sniffled. That's when she realized Freddy hadn't come back yet. "Freddy!"

Her brother charged out of the room with a box of tissues. She briefly thought about strip-searching him, but that seemed excessive. Instead, she yanked a tissue from the box and blew her nose.

"Now," Irene continued, "because I know how your family can be . . . and by that I mean your mother . . . I'm going to stay with all of you for at least the next month."

"Aunt Irene, that's not necessary."

"It's not a bother. Actually, I think you're doing a lot of people a favor."

"How's that?"

"Well, my sons will be in Van Holtz cooking camp somewhere in Montana for the next month. For the next two weeks, Holtz and Ulrich are going to be in Germany for that big Van Holtz family meeting and then when they get back to the States, they're going to Montana for the last two weeks of the cooking camp."

"What about Ulva?"

"Who?"

Toni smirked. "Your daughter. The one you keep saying is a

product of Satan although you also say you don't really believe in the Judeo-Christian belief system."

"Oh. Her. The demon child is going with her father to Germany. Whether she goes to cooking camp, I don't know. I don't care."

"So . . . who am I helping by keeping you here?"

"The Pack back in Washington. Apparently they find me a little terrifying and off-putting. I'm not sure why. I have no claws. No fangs. I guess, technically, I could set them on fire with that cream I accidentally made a few years back, but it's not as if I'd ever do that . . . unless, of course, I had to." She glanced off, shrugged. "But I haven't had to . . . so why worry?"

Toni and Miki locked gazes, then quickly looked away because they didn't want to explain to Irene why they were laughing. No. Explaining that wouldn't really help.

Ricky looked at his phone, saw all the missed calls from his sister, and turned it off completely. He simply didn't have the time or energy for this.

Ricky was a big fan of looking forward not back.

He adored his baby sister, he really did. But Lord, she could work an issue. Work it until it was nothing but a nub. Ricky already knew that's where this was headed. Ronnie Lee would make the whole thing an issue, and Sissy would blow it way out of proportion for no other reason than Sissy liked to blow things way out of proportion.

Still, he'd worry about all that tomorrow. Right now he was going to sit on this couch in the wild dog's big living room and watch the wild dog's extremely big TV for a few hours. The house was quiet with most of the dogs bedded down for the night, so Ricky was looking forward to a little alone time.

Of course, that alone time lasted all of fifteen seconds before he looked over and realized there was a young wolf sitting next to him. Johnny. Bobby Ray tried to pretend he'd only adopted the kid with Jessie because his mate already had plans to do just that, but Ricky knew it was because the wolf liked the kid.

True, he was in that awkward, not a pup but not a full adult either stage, which could make for some tough times, but the kid definitely had some promise. Lots of it.

And, just like Bobby Ray at that age, it seemed the boy was having some problems that at the moment Ricky Lee could easily relate to.

"Why," Johnny asked Ricky without much preamble, "do females have to make everything so damn difficult? They ask you a question, you answer, they flip out."

"Well—"

"I didn't do anything wrong," the eighteen-year-old went on. "Nothing. I answered a question. That was it. Now it's being thrown in my face." He pointed at himself. "I don't need this. I don't deserve it."

Johnny relaxed back into the couch, and moments later, the wolfdog female he'd most likely been complaining about came sauntering through the living room.

Kristan Putowski, one of the oldest Kuznetsov Pack pups, waved as she walked by. "Hey, Ricky Lee."

"Hey, Kristan." Yeah. Kristan was a cutie. And when Ricky Lee was eighteen, he would have been all over that like a bad rash. So he understood what Johnny was going through. Especially when Kristan's friendly wave to Ricky Lee turned into the middle finger just for Johnny.

"I'm not apologizing!" Johnny yelled after her.

"That ain't subtle," Ricky Lee told the boy once Kristan was out of the room.

"Subtle?"

"Yeah. Subtle. Can't go around yelling at a female shifter. They're mean, boy. All of 'em."

"I'm not scared of Kristan Putowski."

"Should be. It's them friendly cute ones that'll cut a man—and have no remorse about it." Ricky leaned in a bit and lowered his voice. "Have you two . . . ya know?"

"What? No! Never! Kristan's like a—"

"Don't say she's like a sister."

"Why not?"

"Because that's exactly what Bobby Ray used to say about Jessie Ann . . . and you saw how that relationship ended up."

"Oh."

"Besides, hoss, we both know you'd only be lying through your fangs."

The boy sighed. "I put up with her. Okay?"

"Putting up with her's good. Staying away from her's even better. At least for now. Give it a few years. You've got a girlfriend?"

"I'm too busy for a—"

"Mistake number two."

"When did I have mistake number one?"

"You need to get yourself a little girlfriend. Nothing you're planning to make permanent. Just someone to keep you out of trouble."

"I'm never in trouble."

"You will be if you keep hanging around Kristan."

"Yeah." Johnny sighed, big hands combing through his hair. "I know."

Toni dropped onto her temporary bed and blew out a breath. That's when she saw the large TV with a big red bow around it, the DVD player, and the stack of brand-new DVDs.

Her father. He knew the one thing she loved to do after a long day of dealing with her siblings was sit in front of her TV and relax.

She was nearly across the room to see what DVDs he'd picked out for her when a familiar and very welcome scent caught her attention. She charged back across the room and threw the door open.

"Cooper!" Toni threw herself into her brother's arms and hugged him tight. "When did you get back?"

"I came straight here from the airport."

Toni pulled back and looked up at her brother. "Wait. How did you know we were here?"

"I got a text from Mom when I was waiting for my layover in Geneva."

Sure. She texted Cooper in Geneva but not Toni a few city blocks away.

"I'm so glad you're home," she said. Not meaning their Washington house but back with the family. "You staying for long?"

"Well, when I got back into LaGuardia, I got a call from Aunt Irene, who told me very clearly that I was needed home because I have to share sibling duty before you snap like a twig." He smirked. "Did you really cry?"

"Oh, God." Toni dragged her brother into her room and closed the door. "I had a moment of weakness. Okay?"

"I didn't know you had any weaknesses."

"Very funny."

Coop dropped his travel bag to the floor and took off his denim jacket. "What's going on?"

"Just the usual."

"Not that usual if I've got Aunt Irene calling me. She never calls me. I don't think she ever calls anyone. Not even Mom."

"She doesn't like talking on the phone unless it's actual business."

"She doesn't like talking on the phone or she's worried the government's still listening in to her calls?"

"Both."

He nodded and dropped into a comfortable chair across from Toni's bed. "Well, big sis, I'm here to help. You. Mom. Dad. Whoever. I'll be especially efficient if you let me beat up Kyle and tell Oriana she's getting fat."

"No," Toni told him firmly. "You can beat up Kyle, of course . . . he clearly needs it. But I'm working to ensure Oriana doesn't get any eating disorders. So no comments on her being too skinny or too fat. You can, however, tell her that she seems dumb compared to the rest of the family and that her eyes are too close together."

"Oh! And her nose is pinched?"

"Absolutely."

The pair laughed and Toni felt so much better. Coop wasn't

only another sibling, he was one of her best friends. They were only three years apart, so Toni didn't have to take care of him as much as she had the others, and that maternal thing had never really kicked in. Instead, they'd spent a lot of time getting into trouble and pissing off Coop's piano teachers. Like their mother, Coop was another child prodigy. The first of the Jean-Louis Parker siblings, but not the last. Yet for whatever reason, he was also the most normal. He seemed to take after their mother the most, with very few signs of OCD, no extreme arrogance, and no penchant for setting fires.

Funny thing was, of all their siblings, Cooper had the most reason to *be* arrogant. Tall and incredibly handsome, with the body of an Olympic diver, brown eyes, and shoulder-length black hair that had hints of gray, white, and gold, Coop was an international superstar. Those who didn't even like classical music came to see him perform. His concerts were always sold-out affairs no matter what country he was in, his audience always filled not only with the wealthy but the powerful. Dignitaries, royalty, politicians—all came to see Toni's younger brother play piano. Then there were his CDs and DVDs, which had made her brother independently wealthy. And yet, at the end of the day, Coop was *still* a jackal. And that meant his family continued to be the most important thing in his life.

So when Coop was home, he helped Toni with the other siblings as much as he could. Just like their sister Cherise, who came four years after Coop. But his talent kept him on the road a lot and having him home was a wonderful treat for Toni. Because Coop got it. What was "it"? She couldn't say . . . she just knew her brother got it. And she adored him for that.

"You tired?" she asked him.

"Wide awake. Why?"

"Daddy brought me a TV and a shitload of DVDs."

Coop sat up in his seat. "You think he has *Anne of a Thousand Days* in that pile?"

Toni's eyes grew wide. "If there's a God in heaven . . ."

That was the other thing she liked about her brother. They

both had the same taste in movies and TV. A geeky taste, but still . . .

Okay. So maybe this summer wouldn't be so heinous after all.

Chapter Four

Ricky Lee had fallen asleep on the couch while watching TV, but he wasn't annoyed when a young pup woke him up by tapping on his forehead with a tiny little fist.

"Morning!" the pup said with a whole lot of doggie cheer. "The moms are making breakfast. Do you want them to include you?"

"Depends. What's for breakfast?"

The pup leaned in and whispered, "Waffles, I think. Because you're here and Aunt Jess likes you, which she says is surprising because your sister still gets on her d-word nerves. But I wasn't supposed to have heard that part."

Ricky snorted and whispered back, "Well, I'm glad you told me. I like to know everyone is happy I'm here. And I love waffles. So yeah, I'm up for breakfast."

"Okay!" the pup cheered and charged out of the room.

Chuckling, Ricky swung his legs off the couch, stood, stretched, and yawned. Then he gave himself a good, once-over shake and headed to the kitchen. The wild dog adults—male and female—were busy getting the kids fed. The wild dogs always fed their pups before they ever ate. Honestly, nothing entertained Ricky more than to watch the wild dogs and lion males dining together. Lion males did not wait for *anyone* before they ate, and in the wild, Ricky was sure that always held true. But here in Manhattan, with the wild dog Jessie Ann in charge, the lion males had learned to wait their turn or suffer her wrath. Of course, her wrath mostly involved lots of yelling, threats, and nipple twisting, but whatever she did, it was effective.

"Morning, y'all."

"Hey, Ricky!" Jessie poured him a cup of coffee and handed it to him. "Sleep well?"

"Yep. Also got to watch a *Xena: Warrior Princess* marathon on DVD. Which one of y'all is the big fan anyway?"

The adult wild dogs shrugged and said in unison, "All of us."

Of course.

"I'm going to go out on the stoop for a bit," he told Jessie Ann.

"That's fine. We'll call you when we're done feeding the kids."

Scratching his head and yawning again, Ricky made his way down the hall, out the front door, and sat on the fourth step of the stoop. It was real early for most wolves. They'd get up to go to work on time but not just to greet the day. They were mostly nocturnal. But Ricky liked early mornings, even in New York City. The sun just coming up and the people usually friendly. So sitting on that stoop, drinking that coffee, and waiting on his waffle breakfast was what he'd call a good way to start off the day.

Actually, he really couldn't think of things getting much better . . .

Toni was up, dressed, and walking down the stairs by six the next morning. Her appointment with Ulrich wasn't until around ten, but she was used to getting up early because of her siblings. Mostly, because classes started very early in the day and she needed to be around to mediate and moderate. Already, she could hear Kyle and Oriana arguing about which of them was more important and more talented, and which should be allowed to use one of the rooms on the first floor as their art studio/practice room.

Toni knew she'd not only have to find out exactly what classes the kids were taking, but she'd have to start working on a schedule as soon as possible. When dealing with so many pups at one time, schedules were critical to managing the insanity. This, of course, applied to any large family. But a family of focused, driven little nightmares needed schedules the way breathing beings needed air. It was the only way to survive without unnecessary bloodshed or jail time.

And that was what Toni did best, wasn't it? She managed the schedules of her family, negotiating agreements and timelines, while threatening important body parts when necessary.

For instance, she already had figured out how she was going to end the argument, but Cherise suddenly charged past her on the stairs. "I'll handle it," the twenty-year-old cellist promised as she ran by. "I'll handle it!"

Although she probably wouldn't handle it *well*. Cherise, the sweetest of their brood, was also the most sensitive next to Freddy. As it was, she was a borderline agoraphobic. Getting her out of the house was an unbelievable task. Funny thing was, those who booked her into concert halls all over the world thought her reluctance to travel was a negotiation tactic. It wasn't, but her agoraphobia at the very least paid well.

Still, if Cherise wanted to try managing their siblings, Toni wouldn't stop her. The way to learn was to do. Toni knew getting everyone handled today with little to no drama would not be easy, but she was ready and alert.

"Morning, sis," Coop said as he fell into step beside her.

"Hey, Coop. Did you get any sleep?"

"A little. Jet lag is kicking my butt. But you know me. I do love a nap, so I'll just sleep later."

"Great rooms, though, right?" Toni asked. "I love my bed."

Together they headed down the second-floor hallway to the last set of stairs.

"Me, too. But I have to admit," Coop continued, "I expected to find Livy asleep under my bed last night. I think I was a little disappointed when she wasn't."

Toni stopped in the middle of the hallway and focused on her brother. "Why would Livy be under your bed?"

It wasn't a question Toni asked because she was concerned that her best friend, Olivia Kowalski, was found under her brother's bed. Livy was nearly as close to Coop as she was to Toni. So Toni didn't care if Livy was asleep under Coop's bed or hers or Cherise's. It wouldn't be the first time that happened, and it wouldn't be the last. No. That wasn't why Toni was asking the question.

"Is that little bitch in Manhattan?" Toni demanded.

"You know," Coop said, turning to face her, "she'd probably be more likely to keep you up to date on her current locations if you didn't call her 'that little bitch.' "

"I only call her that when she's clearly avoiding me. I texted her last night and told her what was going on. She didn't even call me back."

"Livy hates talking on the phone. You know she's not good at it."

"Of course I know that. *I* know all of her quirks and foibles better than anyone else. But if she's in Manhattan—"

"She won't tell you that if you're just going to yell at her for not having an actual place to live while she's here."

Toni stamped her foot. Three times. "It is *not* okay to just crash at someone's house because they make the mistake of leaving the window cracked when they leave for a vacation. Who does that?"

"Livy does that. Livy's mother does that. Livy's entire family does that. *All* of Livy's kind does that. If there's one thing we can all agree on, sis, it's that *her* people are not like *our* people. So instead of ranting about it—"

"Oh, forget it! I don't want to talk about this anymore." Toni pushed past her brother and continued down the hallway. Coop, taller than Toni, quickly caught up.

"Are you pissed at me now?" he asked.

"I'm pissed at the *world* right now. I should be back in Washington, starting a boring office job while I worry about what temporarily abandoned home my best friend has recently placed her camera bag in. I should not be stuck in Manhattan hoping to beg a job off the cousin off my mother's best friend's mate."

"Come on now, you know Ulrich loves you."

"Shut up, Coop."

Her brother laughed and the sound of it made Toni smile despite the fact she didn't really want to.

"Speaking of which, did you see Mom and Dad yet?" she asked him.

"Nope. They were sleeping by the time I went to bed."

"I haven't seen Mom since before I took Freddy to Aunt Irene's hotel room yesterday . . . which makes me nervous."

"Why?"

"Don't know. Just feels like she's up to something. She wanted me out of the house for a reason last night. I mean, she'd normally take Freddy over to see Aunt Irene herself."

"You have a point." Hearing the latest argument from their siblings, Coop's head cocked to the side as they hit the top of those last stairs and started down. "Kyle and Oriana?"

"Of course. But Cherise is going to handle it."

"She is?"

"She needs to try," Toni reminded him.

"I wish her luck."

"Look, it could be worse—" Toni began as she and Coop reached the last step, but Toni's words were cut off when she saw her mother. Dressed comfortably in loose jeans, a B-52s T-shirt that was older than Toni, and her favorite battered "rehearsal" tennis shoes, Jackie headed toward the front door. Normally this was nothing for Toni to notice or remotely worry about . . . normally. But now Toni understood why her mother had avoided her and Coop last night—because her mother wasn't alone.

"Mom?"

Still walking, but not turning around, Jackie said, "I know what you're thinking, Antonella."

"You have no idea what I'm thinking or you'd probably pop me in the mouth."

"Trust me. I have a plan."

Of course she had a plan. Jackie Jean-Louis always had a

plan. She was a plotting little jackal who was always up to something as long as it benefited her career or her children. But unlike some musicians, who could be downright psychotic about their careers, Jackie was just sneaky. She never did anything to take someone else down. Jackie didn't have to because she had full confidence in her skills as a musician. Ever since she had picked up her first violin at the age of three, Jackie knew that she was unbelievably talented and no one would ever be able to bump her out of the spot she'd earned as one of the world's finest violinists. No one.

But Jackie wanted to take that next step. She wanted to be the mentor of the next "world's finest." She'd had lots of students over the years, many of whom had gone on to wonderfully successful careers. But none that were quite in her league. They'd never be quite as successful as she. Quite as well-known. She wanted that student who would turn her into The Great Master.

And that, Toni knew, explained the dog walking beside her mother. Not a shifter but an actual dog. The family hadn't had a pet since the feral cat they'd found under their home that kept hissing at them. They'd give it food and, after a few years, it wandered away. It was the perfect pet for the Jean-Louis Parkers because they only paid attention to it when they felt like it. It didn't need to be walked or taken to the vet or dealt with in any way except to toss it some food and gaze at it for a few minutes when one of the kids needed "inspiration."

But real dogs needed lots of things that no one in Toni's family was capable of providing at the moment, including her and *especially* her mother.

Yes. Her mother. Who opened the front door and told the dog, "Go take your walk, sweetie. When you're done, come back and scratch on the door. I'll let you in."

The adult dog, appearing to Toni's eyes to be a rescue her mother had picked up somewhere, saw that open door as a bid for freedom. It bolted and Toni's jackal ears immediately picked up the early-morning traffic barreling down the street.

Running purely on instinct, Toni jumped off the last step

and bolted out of the house, following that dog right into the street. Moving fast, she tackled the dog, wrapping her arms around its slim body, and made a wild leap for the opposite sidewalk.

Toni had almost made it, but the truck speeding down the street still clipped her with its fender, sending Toni flipping over the hood of a parked car to land hard on her back in front of a stoop.

When she finally got her breath back, Toni opened her eyes and saw the wolf she'd met yesterday staring down at her. He was holding a coffee mug. With an annoying amount of calm, he sipped his drink and remarked, "Darlin', at this point, I'm startin' to think you're sweet on me."

The She-jackal's eyes narrowed dangerously but when she opened her mouth, all that came out was a little "yip" sound. Ricky quickly rested his coffee cup on the wide stone handrail and rushed down the stairs to the prone female.

"Darlin', I'm sorry to waste time teasing ya. I'll call an ambulance."

She shook her head no, but when she tried to take his hand, she cringed something awful and put her hand right back down.

That's when two jackals came running over from across the street. One was an older female. Her momma, Ricky would guess. They had the same eyes. And a male, close to the She-jackal's age.

"Toni!" the older female barked. "What the hell were you thinking?"

There went those eyes dangerously narrowing again.

"Mom," the male warned, and that's when Ricky realized this was Toni's brother. He ignored the sense of relief he felt. "Not now."

"This isn't my fault," the older She-jackal argued. "It isn't."

The male tried to take the dog that Toni still held with one arm, but the animal lay flat against her, its entire body shaking.

"Poor thing." The male sighed. "It's terrified."

"Also not my fault."

The glass and metal security door behind Ricky opened, and several adult wild dogs rushed down the stairs and surrounded the jackal.

"Are you all right, hon?"

"Been better," Toni squeaked out.

"Not my fault," the She-jackal pushed.

"Grit your teeth," Ricky told Toni as he slipped his arms under her. "I'll take you back to your house."

"Oh," the older She-jackal said, suddenly looking around. "That's such a long trip . . . can't we just bring her inside here?" She smiled sweetly at the wild dogs. "You guys don't mind, do you?"

The wild dogs might not have minded, but from the way the She-jackal's two children gawked at her, Ricky felt certain they did mind. A lot.

Toni knew her mother was sneaky, but holy hell, this was some hinky shit!

Using her own daughter's brush with death to ease her way into the wild dogs' home was beneath even Jackie's usual depths. Maybe even Kyle's!

The wolf easily carried her inside the wild dogs' home and down the hallway until he reached an enormous kitchen.

Why the wolf was here at all, Toni didn't know. Maybe she didn't want to know. All Toni did know was that her life was getting weird.

The wolf placed Toni's butt on the stainless steel kitchen island so that she was sitting up. "So what hurts the worst?" he asked.

"Shoulder."

"That's what I thought. Because it's not really in its socket."

Toni sighed. "Great."

"The dog is doing well, though," one of the wild dogs pointed out.

"And that's what's important!" Jackie cheered, but when

both her children gawked at her again, she quickly added, "You're a hero! My daughter, the hero!"

A blond female wild dog pushed her way closer through the other dogs until she stood in front of Toni.

"Wolf is right," she said in a thick Russian accent, "about this shoulder. But we can fix. Hold her, wolf."

"Now wait a—" Toni protested.

The wolf scrambled up behind her, both legs around her hips, hanging well past her own long legs, and his arms around her waist, holding her tight.

"Got her!" he announced

The wild dog pulled her fist back. "I make this quick, jackal."

"Hey! I don't want you—*owwwwwwwwwwwwww! You Russian cow!*"

"See?" the Russian noted. "She's better already. Who knew jackals were so tough?"

Coop leaned in, her brother cringing in sympathy. "Are you okay?"

"No!" Toni snarled.

"Make her sling," the Russian ordered the others. She looked at Toni. "You'll be fine tomorrow. I'm impressed you don't cry like sniveling cat."

"It's not that I don't want to."

"All that matters is that you don't. I loathe weakness. Like I loathe cats." Then without another word, the wild dog walked out of the room.

"I'm weirdly freaked out," Coop muttered, "and turned on all at the same time."

Toni nodded. "I know." Glancing down, Toni said, "Why are you still holding me?" she asked the wolf.

"I'm giving you my invaluable support, and my immense charm."

"More like your immense bullshit."

"Now, now, darlin'," he teased, annoying her more. "No need to get so nasty just because you're confused by your feelings for me."

"I do not have feelings for you, other than pity for your mental illness."

The wolf laughed while Coop suddenly raised his brows at her, and Toni shook her head at her brother. Tragically, she recognized that expression. Recognized it all too well.

"Don't even—" Toni began.

"I'm Cooper," Coop announced to the wolf, grinning at him. "The younger brother. *Brother.* Not boyfriend."

Horrified, Toni snapped, "Cooper, stop it!"

"How y'all doin'? I'm Ricky Lee Reed. So glad you're her brother. I'd hate to have to fight you for her."

"No worries there," Coop volunteered. "My big sis is *very* single and not even thirty yet."

"That *is* nice to hear."

"And you already seem to know my very single sister."

"I will kill you," Toni warned. "I'm not afraid to."

"I'm glad to know she's single," the wolf said, "but she's playing hard to get while stalking me all at the same time."

"I am not stalking you."

"I feel like a little ol' gazelle calf without its momma."

Toni's eyes crossed at that pathetic visual.

"Are you interested?" her idiot brother asked. "Because as I said, she's very single, but she only deserves the best. I won't hand her off to just anybody."

"Hand me off . . . *what is wrong with you?*" Toni demanded of her sibling.

"I'm trying to help."

"I don't need help."

"I tried to chat her up," the wolf explained, "but she used y'all's other siblings to confuse me."

"Oh, the 'are you my daddy' move? Yeah. She's been using that one for years.'

"You both are aware that I'm sitting here, right? In *front* of you?"

"She had a bad breakup," Coop went on. "About a year ago. I was hoping she'd get over it sooner."

"I can help with that."

"That's what I thought. I've had a few She-lion benefactors over the years, and they all say that wolves are great for that sort of thing. The casual hook-up, I mean."

Toni looked around the kitchen. "Am I dreaming? Tell me I'm dreaming this conversation."

"We're real good for that until we find mates of our own," the wolf explained.

"See, that's what I'm thinking. Because her ex . . . not worth all this angst. Our father, who is a really great guy, still calls that man the 'pimple on the cock of humanity.' "

"Fathers love me. I've got this winning smile." And Toni didn't have to turn around to know the wolf was showing that smile to her idiot brother. "Perfect Southern manners. I never cuss. I rarely get sloppy drunk and that's only around my Pack if I do. And I treat my momma right at all times, and not just 'cause I'm afraid of her. Even though I kind of am."

"That's perfect."

"Would you two stop it!" Toni, to her horror, started laughing, hating both males for making it happen. "I'm not looking for a boyfriend."

"Not a boyfriend, darlin'. A hook-up."

"I don't need that, either from you or anyone else."

"But—"

"Shut up, Cooper!"

The males fell silent for a few moments until the wolf noted, "You do seem tense, though."

Toni's brother, tall and lanky, stepped away from his sister. "You know what?"

"Cooper," the She-jackal practically hissed. "Don't you dare."

"I should check on the kids. They're probably worried."

"About what? I'm sure they're blissfully unaware anything has happened."

"No, no. They could be very concerned. Yeah. I better check."

"I'll go with you," she said, and tried to slip out of his arms, but Ricky had a real good grip on her and no intention of letting her go. He was just too damn comfortable.

"Absolutely not! You need that sling the wild dogs are getting you."

"A sling? We can make a sling at home."

"You're right! I'll go get you one!" Then the jackal took off, leaving his sister all alone.

Yep. Ricky liked that boy.

"This is a nightmare."

"Now, now. Don't be hard on him. He only cares."

"By handing me off to a wolf he doesn't even know?"

"He probably has a good sense of things. Besides . . . my charm speaks volumes."

"Your charm makes me want to punch you in the nose."

That made Ricky chuckle. "I'm not trying to piss you off, darlin'. Just trying to get you to give me a chance."

"Why?" she had to ask. "I'm really not that interesting. I'm cute but not stunning. I'm not excessively tall. And sexually, I'm rather vanilla. So then what is it?"

Ricky decided to be honest with her. "I like your hair."

She suddenly went tense. "You don't have to be mean."

"I'm not. I like the curls. If we have sex, can I play with them?"

"I don't even know how to respond to that."

"Just say yes and I'm in."

She shook her head. "Look, I really have to go. I have an interview in a few hours."

"You need a sling and someone needs to keep an eye on you to make sure you don't get the fever."

"From a thrown-out shoulder?"

"It could happen. My brother got the fever last night. But that was from the crushed jaw and nicked artery. He's probably still passed out at the hotel."

"If your brother got the fever, why are you here?"

"I had to escape. My sister wanted to talk to me."

"Good God," she said flatly. "What was she thinking?"

Ricky heard the sarcasm but chose to ignore it. "Exactly! What *was* she thinking?"

Toni tried to move away again, but Ricky held her a little tighter.

"I'll make you a deal," he promised. "We hang out together today so I can make sure you're really all right. And if we get along . . . you go out with me."

"For sex?"

"Hopefully, but I was thinking dinner to start."

"And if we don't get along?"

"You can hit me in the nose if you're still inclined."

Toni gave a little snort. "Something tells me I will be."

"You forgot your dog outside," a black female standing in the kitchen doorway stated. Toni looked to see the thirty-pound dog she'd yanked from in front of that truck sliding to a stop by the cabinet she was on. He tried to leap onto the top of it but couldn't quite make it, so he seemed to take pleasure in grabbing Toni's foot between his two front legs and trying to chew her running shoes off.

"Oh," Toni replied. "Yeah. My dog."

The female snorted a little and held up a strip of cloth. "I have your sling."

"Thank you, uh . . ." Although she could kind of guess who this was.

"Toni," Ricky said from behind her, "this is Jessie Ann Ward-Smith."

"And you're the daughter of my son's stalker," the wild dog shot back.

"Uh-oh," Ricky softly muttered against her ear. "Watch yourself, darlin'."

Now it was true that Toni didn't need to involve herself in any of this. It was her mother's thing, not Toni's. But if Toni didn't get involved, then she'd be forced to hear about this situation all goddamn summer. It would involve scheme after wacky scheme until her mother got what she wanted. Like most geniuses at Jackie's level, she could focus on a problem and work it until her last breath. There was no getting bored for Jackie Jean-Louis. No "getting over it."

So Toni did what she had to do.

She looked the wild dog over, quickly sized her up, and went right for the superior but straightforward approach.

"Let me tell you something"—and Toni felt the wolf behind her tense at her high-handed tone—"you've got two choices. You can let your son settle happily into life as a second chair in the Ice Capades orchestra, or you can let my mother work with him for the summer and open the door to not only first chair with the New York Philharmonic but more likely a solo career. My mother," Toni went on, "is internationally *worshipped*. She doesn't waste time with artists she thinks are really nice or cute or will stroke her ego. If anything, that's what my dad is for. So what you need to know is that, yes, your son is talented. I know this not because I've heard him play but because my mother wouldn't waste time with him if he didn't have a substantial amount of talent. Substantial. There are people who'd do bodily harm to others just to have a quarter of the chance she's offering your son. And, lady, if you don't think having my mother's name on your son's résumé as his teacher, his *mentor,* is going to help him achieve unimaginable heights—then you're an idiot."

The wild dog stared at Toni and Toni stared back. When that went on for a bit, it seemed Ricky Lee began to get uncomfortable.

But as soon as Toni heard him begin, "What I think she means, Jessie Ann—", she cut him right off.

"I don't need you to clarify my statements for me, wolf, thank you very much."

"Yeah, but—"

"I don't even know you," she reminded him.

Toni refocused on Jess Ward. "Look, if you really want to find out how my mother will deal with your son on a regular basis, you might as well go upstairs and check it out, because even I can hear he stopped practicing and I highly doubt she left your house."

"Dammit." Jess Ward spun around and faced the kitchen door. She started to go through it, realized she still had the sling in her hand, and stopped long enough to toss it across the room. The white cloth hit Toni in the face and sort of hung there, blinding her.

She didn't bother taking it off.

Ricky Lee finally released his hold on the little She-jackal and slipped off the counter. He stood in front of her and pulled the sling off her face.

She had her eyes closed, and he left her that way while he fashioned the cloth into a proper sling for her.

After a minute or so, she eased one eye open and leaned around him to see if Jessie Ann had actually left the room. Once she knew they were completely alone, she leaned back, looked at him, and said something that Ricky Lee had never heard from a shifter female before. Not ever. Not once.

"I am so sorry," she whispered.

Ricky froze, thought he'd misheard her.

"Pardon?"

"I said I'm sorry." She continued to whisper, although with wild dogs and their oversized ears, they could hear anything they wanted to in their house. It made it impossible for their kids to get away with any of the crap that Smith pups managed to pull off back in Smithtown. "You know, for snapping at you."

Ricky Lee looked the female over. She *seemed* sincere. And he didn't see a weapon on her that would suggest she intended to cut his throat or anything when he turned around.

"Um . . . that's okay." He began to fit the sling on her, careful not to move her shoulder too much since he knew it still hurt her. "You do know," he felt the need to point out, "that what just happened could have easily blown up in your face."

"Yeah. It could have. But I didn't think it would. She was already waiting for me to try to relate to her on her level. You know, talk about the *Lord of the Rings* movies or how my little brother Freddy is a baby hacker. This Pack might live in the lap of luxury now, but they had some rough years on the streets when they were younger. I had to go with a straightforward approach."

"And how did you know all that about Jessie Ann's past?" he asked.

"Oh," she said while Ricky leaned in a bit and reached around her to tie the sling at the back of her neck. "There are these things called comp-poo-tors and when you ask the comp-poo-tors questions, the box gives you answers!"

Ricky stepped back and saw her wicked little smile.

"Look at you, darlin'," he teased back. "Flirtin' with me."

She laughed and Ricky knew then he'd just been charmed by a She-jackal. And the good Lord knew it had been a long time since Ricky had been charmed by anyone.

Jess Ward peeked around the open door to, she'd admit, spy on her adopted son and that jackal. In the relatively short time she'd had Johnny in her home, she'd fired two music teachers, punched another one in the face, and threatened to set another on fire. The last two her mate, Bobby Ray Smith, had handled paying off himself because he refused to visit her in prison. But some of these teachers were just rude! She got it. Okay? She understood. This was a tough business and one needed a thick skin. Blah blah blah.

Yes, she understood all that. But what these teachers didn't get was that Johnny had already had a hard life. His biological mother had died when he was thirteen. Then he was bounced around from foster home to foster home until he landed with Jess's Pack. So yeah, she was protective of him. And although she'd appreciated the honesty of the damaged-shouldered She-jackal in her kitchen who had one of the Reed boys wrapped around her like a boa constrictor, that still did not mean Jess was okay with Toni's mother. Especially when she was pretty damn sure the woman only got that dog to finagle her way into Jess's good graces.

Jess hated tricky shit like that.

So yes, she was spying. And sure, Johnny was eighteen now so she should be able to trust his judgment. But boys were stupid, something she'd learned at a very young age.

Jess could see the pair sitting on the floor of Johnny's practice room. For a fifty-something internationally known musician who'd played on the *Tonight Show,* and before the Queen of England, Jacqueline Jean-Louis sure was casual. She had on ripped jeans and a band T-shirt . . . oooh. The B-52s. Okay. So she had good musical taste outside of the classical stuff. That was nice to see. She also wore sneakers that had seen better days. She sat Indian style, her elbows resting on her knees while Johnny stared at her like Marilyn Monroe was in the room.

"When did you first start playing?" the She-jackal asked Johnny.

"My mom got me my first violin when I was five."

"Why? Did she just want you to learn an instrument?"

"No. I asked for it. I saw Itzhak Perlman play on PBS and I wanted to learn to play like that."

"How often do you practice?"

"Every day. This used to be my mom's bedroom. My adopted mom, I mean. Jess. But when she mated with Smitty, she took one of the rooms downstairs and turned this into a practice room for me so I could practice whenever I want rather than worrying about booking time in practice rooms away from the house."

"This Pack, your Pack, has been super supportive of your music, haven't they?"

A small smile curled the corners of Johnny's mouth. "Yeah. They have."

"What if they hadn't been?"

He shrugged. "I'd play anyway. I got thrown out of one of my foster homes because I practiced too much. Well . . . that and I snarled at one of the other kids when he was trying to take my Twinkie, but my God, it was *my* Twinkie."

She laughed. "Don't feel bad. I was performing with a quartet in Australia once and I ended up hitting the cello player with another player's flute because his nose was making this high-pitched whistling sound. Full-humans have no idea how those kinds of noises irritate sensitive dog ears. It's like nails on a chalkboard."

"Can I ask you something, Miss Jean-Louis?"

"If you call me Jackie, you can ask me."

"Why are you here?"

"I know you're starting Juilliard in the fall and I thought maybe I could work with you this summer. Get you ready. You'll be dealing with some serious competition at Juilliard. And those full-humans can be mean. I get that they are competitive, but telling me I have *birthing* hips? Who says that to a woman? I mean, I *do* have birthing hips but that's not the point. What I want to do with you is teach you to control your natural and correct instinct to tear out the arteries of someone who says you have birthing hips and instead, calmly blow them away with your talent. Because let me tell you—the full-humans *hate* that."

Johnny leaned back a bit, big brown eyes blinking. Jess saw him swallow before he asked, "You want to work with me?"

"Yes."

"Me?"

The She-jackal grinned. "Yes. You. Is that really so hard to believe?"

"Yes. Yes, it is."

"Johnny, you're good."

"I know I'm good. But you're . . . you're . . . you're friggin' Jacqueline Jean-Louis. *The* Jacqueline Jean-Louis. I have all your CDs. I've watched every documentary PBS has ever had on you and your CBS Christmas special three years back."

"And I've heard you play," she said, keeping it simple. Jess liked that.

Jacqueline got to her feet and Johnny scrambled up to his own. Now he towered over the jackal, like the big wolf he was growing into.

"Look," she told him, "think about it. Talk it over with your mom. I'm right across the street for the rest of the summer."

Something Jess had argued against. But her Pack wouldn't let her ignore the amount of money the Jean-Louis Parkers were willing to pay to rent the place across the street. Although, to be honest, Jess couldn't ignore it, either. It was truly a shitload of money.

"And I'm talking a casual thing," the jackal went on. "We get together, we play, we talk. We exchange ideas. I listen."

"Well . . . um . . . I'll talk to my mom."

"That should be easy enough since she's standing right outside the room, along with a good chunk of your Pack."

Jess spun around and yes, at least ten of her Pack, including Sabina, May, Danny, and Phil, were standing right behind her.

"You guys!" Jess snarled.

They all shrugged and Jess rolled her eyes, then slowly eased into her old bedroom. Johnny lifted his hands and dropped them. *"Ma."*

"Don't be mad at her." The She-jackal smiled. "She loves you. She's just watching out for you. I'm like that with my own kids—oh, my God!" she suddenly burst out, startling every canine in the room and the hallway. "My daughter! I completely forgot. And she takes it so personally when I do." She turned and rushed toward the door. "She's gonna kill me!"

While the jackal ran downstairs, Jess walked over to Johnny. "Sorry if we embarrassed you."

"What's this 'we' shit?" came from the hallway.

"Shut up, Phil!" Jess yelled back.

"She wants to work with me," Johnny whispered to Jess. He gripped her hands tight. *"Me."*

Jess still didn't know if she trusted that jackal—although because of her honesty, she did trust the jackal's daughter—but none of that mattered. Because she wasn't about to destroy her son's obvious happiness and excitement. It was something he seemed to experience so rarely that Jess knew in her heart this was an important moment for him. One of those life-changing ones.

So if Johnny was happy about this, then Jess would be happy for him.

Grinning, Jess asked, "Now can I get you that Stradivarius violin they're going to auction in Milan?"

Laughing, Johnny dropped her hands. "Ma, *no!*"

"Stop talking to me, Mom."

"I said I was sorry!" Jackie told Toni. "What made you go diving in front of a truck anyway? The dog had cleared it."

Ignoring her mother, Toni marched up the stairs of their rental home toward her bedroom. Coming down the stairs, her father stopped and stared at her. "Baby, what happened to your arm?"

"Ask your mate."

"How can you blame me for this?" her mother called up.

"Still not talking to you!"

"I see you met your mother's surprise."

Toni glanced down and realized that the dog her mother had gotten was following Toni up the stairs.

"Why is this dog following me?" she called down the stairs.

"If you don't want her, I'll just take her back to the pound," her mother replied. "Of course . . . they were about to put her down. But that shouldn't bother you."

"Oh! You are just . . . Oh!" Toni began up the stairs again. As she moved, her siblings were coming down, but one look at her face and they all glanced away and kept going. When she got to her bedroom, she stopped and turned. "Why are *you* following me?" she finally asked the wolf behind her.

"Because we agreed. I'm hanging with you today."

"My father just let you come up here to my room?"

"Yeah. I think it was my charm."

"More like Coop ran over here and told my dad about you."

He shrugged. "Whatever works. So what are we doing today?"

"I've got to get ready for an interview at ten."

"Okay."

She stepped into her room but faced him once more before he could invite himself in.

"Why don't you go downstairs and wait until I'm done."

"Okay." He stared at her a moment, and asked, "Any chance your momma is making waffles for breakfast?"

With great relish, Toni replied, "Not a chance in hell."

Then she closed the door on his disappointed face and got ready for her interview.

Chapter Five

Toni had been waiting forty-five minutes for her interview, but she didn't mind. She had a book. As long as she had something to read, Toni could self-entertain for hours. It was a gift she had.

Still, she did wonder if there really was some sort of problem going on that kept Ulrich Van Holtz and the hockey team's coach too busy to meet with her. Or were they just trying to find a way to break it to her nicely that they didn't even think she could manage the office copier? Not that she blamed them. Except for the occasional volunteer position, she'd never had a real job. Not anything she could put on a résumé.

Then again, she was probably just being paranoid and insecure. They couldn't all be away trying to figure out what to do with her, and even the snooty bobcat receptionist wasn't around.

She glanced over to her right.

The wolf, though, was still sitting there. Quietly. Staring at the wall across from them. He didn't look bored. Or annoyed. Or angry. Just . . . calm.

She hadn't said a word to him. Not because she was upset with him but because she was curious to see how long he could go without talking to her. She'd thought he would have gotten fed up by now and found a very nice way to leave. She couldn't see him storming out in a huff. That didn't seem to be his way. But politely finding an exit strategy? Yeah. That seemed more his style.

She finally had to ask, "You're not bored?"

"Not at all."

"Really?"

"I've found that if you wait long enough . . . the entertainment often comes to you. You just have to be patient."

"Okay, but it may be awhile. I don't know when—"

"That's fine. I'll just keep on sittin' here . . . lookin' pretty." He grinned at her, showing those perfect white teeth. "Enticing you with my charm."

At that point, all Toni could do was cross her eyes and go back to her book. But just as she'd settled in, the bobcat receptionist returned. He charged in through the glass door, barely glancing at her or the wolf as he passed.

Toni sat up straight, not knowing if the receptionist would be part of the hiring process, and said, "Hi. I'm here to see—"

"Yeah, yeah." He dismissed her with a shake of his head while he grabbed a messenger bag from under his desk. He had it in his fist and was just moving around the desk when the glass door was thrown open and the hockey player from the day before, Novikov, stood there. He wasn't in his training gear, but in jeans and a T-shirt, a duffel bag over his shoulder. And even though she didn't know the man very well, Toni could say with great confidence that he was definitely seething.

"What," Novikov began, spitting out the words through clenched teeth, "do you not understand about a schedule?"

Uh-oh. Toni remembered her brother Troy beginning a conversation with his onetime babysitter. Afterward, the babysitter sued for medical bills and pain and suffering, plus got a restraining order against her brother. In the end the family settled with her out of court. At the time, Troy was six and weighed about thirty pounds.

Novikov was thirty something and at least four hundred plus pounds . . . so this situation could easily end up much worse.

Trying to defend himself, the bobcat began, "I did what you ask—"

"No!" Novikov cut the cat off. "You didn't do what I asked. Because if you'd done what I'd asked, I'd be surprising my fiancée in Chicago with the wonder that is me. And later tonight, I'd be watching a bout with her and a bunch of other hot girls racing around a banked track in tight shorts and tank tops and pretending it's a sport. Instead, since last night, I've been in Iowa. Then Kentucky. Then Minnesota. None of which had my fiancée, but did have grizzlies. Lots and lots of really pissy grizzlies! Who aren't fans of polar bears *or* lion males! *And I'm both!*"

In the face of that roar, the bobcat backed up against the wall behind him, his messenger bag held against his chest. "I just got your schedule confused with Markowitz's. It was an accident."

"Wait a minute . . . you're telling me that Markowitz is in Chicago? With *my* fiancée?"

"I doubt he's *with* Blayne."

"Does Blayne know you got the schedules mixed up?"

"Well, she called—"

"Which means," the hybrid growled, "she probably felt bad for Markowitz and now she's making sure he's doing okay. You know how she doesn't like anyone to be sad. And we all know how Markowitz is a scumbag leopard who'll take advantage of any do-gooder idiot that comes along. Especially when they have legs as long as my Blayne's!" The player stalked over to the bobcat's desk and slammed really big hands onto it, making the thing nearly buckle. "But you know what's the worst part of this? What *really* sets my teeth on edge and makes me want to just twist your head around until it pops off your body? The worst part is that because of *you* I haven't had my workout to-day. I haven't had my swim. I haven't had my practice. Because of *you* I've missed almost an entire day of *my* schedule."

The bobcat blinked. "That's really more important than your girlfriend?"

Utilizing years of unplanned training, Toni dropped her book, charged across the room, and cut in front of the bobcat, her one free arm stretched out in front of her. She knew her skinny jackal arm and battered shoulder would never stop the player from getting those big hands on the idiot cat, but she felt the need to at least try because she, above everyone else, understood what was going on here.

Because Toni understood drive. The drive that one had to have in order to be the best.

So while the bobcat didn't "get" Novikov's schedule issues, Toni did. She also knew that she didn't want to spend the rest of the day in a police precinct giving a statement on a tragic shifter-on-shifter murder case.

"When's your fiancée's thing tonight?" she asked loudly in an attempt to get Novikov's attention and keep him on the other side of that very flimsy-looking desk. "Eight? Nine?"

Novikov yanked his hand back and, since it had been dangerously close to her face, she appreciated that he had enough self-control to do that.

"Eight thirty Chicago time," he snarled, blue eyes still locked on the bobcat behind her.

"Great. I know a carrier that I use for my family all the time. There're eleven of us not counting my parents, and regular planes and full-human run airports are not always the friends of jackals with pups. So I can easily get you on a direct flight to Chicago, have a car meet you at the airport to take you right to wherever she's playing her game tonight."

"It's called a bout."

Bout? Was she a boxer?

"Okay. Her bout. I can get you to her bout."

"You can do that?" he asked, looking a bit calmer.

"Just need a phone and a computer."

The player pointed at the bobcat. "You. Out."

"This is my desk."

Toni rammed her free hand against Novikov's shoulder before he could finish climbing over the bobcat's desk and strangling the feline to death. She had no illusions that she was somehow physically holding him back. Instead she was trusting in his desire not to hurt the one person who might be able to help him.

"Go take a break," she ordered the bobcat. "I won't be long."

"Whatever."

The bobcat sounded tough, but he still slinked around them and then darted out of the room before the player could get his hands on him.

"Sit," Toni firmly ordered, using the same tone she often used with Kyle.

"I'd be making everyone's life easier if I just took that cat's neck and—"

"Sit. *Now.* Over there by the wolf."

Novikov walked over to Ricky and glared down at him. Toni thought she'd have to jump between those two when the wolf only stared back. That same placid look on his face. But Novikov, instead of fighting yet another person, just grabbed the chair Toni had originally been sitting in and pulled it close to the desk.

Toni decided to ignore the fact that the chair had been bolted to the floor. Nope. It was better not to think about that little feat of strength at all.

Sitting down behind the bobcat's computer, Toni willed herself not to comment on the background picture he had on his monitor of some hot car model. So typical.

"Your full name?" she asked.

"Bo Novikov."

"Right." She gave him a small smile. "I appreciated how you handled my brother yesterday, Mr. Novikov."

"Call me Bo," he ordered. "And does he ask everyone if he can sketch them naked?"

She gave a small chuckle while typing into the Web browser. "No. Only worthy specimens."

"What happened to your arm?"

"Got hit by a truck saving a dog."

"A dog dog or . . . family?"

Toni rolled her eyes. "A dog dog."

"You risked your life to save a dog?"

"I already had this conversation with my parents—I'm not having it again!" she snapped.

"Okay, okay. No need to get snippy."

"You haven't seen me snippy," she muttered as she forced herself to ignore the pain in her wounded shoulder so she could use both hands to type.

"So why are you here today?" Novikov asked her.

She went into the site for the shifter-run airline. She had full access because the owner loved Jackie's music and because Toni worked with them so often she'd become friends with most of the staff. She didn't use them for everything—they were unbelievably expensive—but they were great for last-minute arrangements to foreign countries when the entire family was going. So many jackals in one place was pretty much asking for trouble when full-humans were around.

"Hoping to get a job for the summer," she replied without looking at him. "Looks like my family is staying here for the next few months."

"What do you do for a living?"

Toni sighed. "Babysit."

He grunted at her, and Toni glanced at him. His right leg was bouncing, his fingers were tapping the arms of his chair, and he was staring at the wall. He wasn't bored or annoyed. He was anxious. She knew the signs.

"You know what?" she said, keeping her voice light. "I bet your info is in these files. I'll dig it out, get your schedule all lined up, and you can go and skate or whatever it is you hockey players do to keep in shape. You just give me your fiancée's info on this Post-it, and I'll take it from there."

"I better not."

"It's not even noon, Mr. Novikov. You get some practice in and I'll handle everything else. Trust me. You'll get there and she'll be surprised and very happy. I'll make it happen."

He leaned back, studied her again. "Like I said, the name's Bo. And why are you protecting that bobcat?"

"I'm not protecting the idiot. I'm protecting the genius." She smiled, shrugged. "I guess that's also what I do."

"You sure?"

"You can't get on a flight this wound up. You'll startle the flight attendants . . . a lot of them are cats. You know how that'll end."

"Yeah. All right. All right." He took the pen she held out for him and jotted some info on the paper. "You don't have to get that tone. I'll be at the training rink if you need—"

"I won't need anything. Go. Now. Work out. Get your head together."

"Yeah. Thanks."

He got up, walked out, and Toni went back to work.

After a few seconds the wolf remarked, "Ya see? You wait long enough . . . the entertainment comes to *you*."

Chapter Six

Ulrich Van Holtz disconnected the call, the speaker phone shutting off, and looked over at the two females who had been sitting in his office with him for the last three hours while he was on the phone.

"They sounded . . . tense," he remarked about the bosses of the organizations they all worked for.

Cella "Bare Knuckles" Malone, his hockey team's head coach and lead contractor for the feline protection agency KZS, had her head resting on her crossed arms on his desk. It's where her head had been the last half-hour of this meeting. "I don't know what the fuck they're expecting," she complained. "They act like we've been sitting on our asses the last few months."

"Maybe 'cause your ass has been gettin' so large," Dee-Ann, Ric's mate, joked.

"My ass is perfect, canine. Don't be bitter because you got that flat ass."

"Can we have the ass discussion another time?" Ric asked, desperate to end the conversation mostly because talking about his mate's ass made him horny. That quickly reminded him that he'd be leaving the country in a few hours. He didn't want to go. He didn't like being away from Dee-Ann for so long.

Unlike some mates, Ric and Dee-Ann didn't spend unlimited time together. He had several businesses, including the Carnivores, an all-shifter hockey team that he owned and was also goalie and team captain; plus his work as one of the head chefs in the mid-Manhattan five-star and Michelin-starred Van

Holtz Steak House; and one of the team leads for his Uncle Van's shifter protection agency, The Group.

Dee-Ann, however, had one job as The Group's top agent. For some it might not seem like she had much to do with her one job. But by God, the woman did that one job to the best of her ability. She actually was home less than Ric. One time she was gone for three days and no one knew where the hell she was. Just when he was beginning to panic, he found her sitting on their couch, watching TV, icing a broken collarbone that was in mid-healing, and enjoying warm cornbread and a tall glass of buttermilk. Ric didn't ask her what she'd been up to. He'd quickly learned not to because she'd tell him. Everything. Down to the last blood-and-brain-covered detail. That was something Ric really didn't need to hear. He soon came to the realization that the only thing he needed to know about the woman he loved was that whatever she did when she wasn't with him was for the good of their kind.

Still, leaving all this on Dee's and Cella's powerful shoulders so that he could go to the Van Holtz family meeting in Germany was not something he really wanted to do.

And then after the meeting in Germany, Ric and his cousin—who, yes, he still called Uncle Van because of their age differences—would be heading out to the campgrounds in Montana for the last two weeks of the Van Holtz cooking summer camp. That meant Ric would be out of New York for at least a month.

"What have we got?" he asked, already knowing the answer.

"Nothing," both women said in unison.

"And before you ask," Cella went on, "Crush and Dez don't have anything, either." Crush, an enormous polar bear and Cella's mate, and Desiree MacDermot-Llewellyn, full-human and mate to Mace Llewellyn, were detectives in the NYPD's shifter-run division. They often worked with Dee and Cella on the more difficult cases, handling a lot of the research and managing any NYPD presence.

"Clearly we need to come up with something," Ric remarked. "I can tell the powers-that-be want Whitlan, and they're tired of waiting."

Frankie Whitlan. A gangster and conman and one-time police snitch who used the NYPD to take down anyone who got in his way or cut into his business. At one point, Whitlan had disappeared, leading everyone to think he was dead. He wasn't. Instead, he just remade himself again and returned with a business that catered to a certain type of full-human.

Very rich full-humans who enjoyed hunting shifters and stuffing them. Their trophies of lions and bears and wolves decorated their expensive hunting cabins or family homes like mooseheads.

It was something that Ric's kind simply couldn't and wouldn't ignore, but Whitlan was very smart and very good at getting lost. When they'd finally closed in on him, he'd disappeared again and had yet to come up anywhere that their three groups—NYPD for local, The Group for nationwide, and KZS for international—had people searching.

"I know we've talked to Whitlan's past associates who are still on the outside," Ric said. "But what about those inside?"

"We haven't done that yet," Dee told him.

"Then do it. Maybe if we're lucky, it'll give us something new."

"I'll—" Cella began.

Ric quickly cut her off. "No. Dee-Ann, work with Desiree and Crushek on getting together a list of names of anyone that was once a cellmate or prison buddy of Whitlan. Go back as far as you need to. Once you're ready, bring in Cella."

"Why can't I help now?"

"Because I'd like for my team to at least have a *shot* at getting into this year's championships."

"I'm working on it," Cella snarled. "But you know it's not been easy."

"You wanted to keep Novikov on," Ric reminded her, speaking of his least favorite human being. "Even after what he did to Heller."

She shrugged and made excuses. "That was an accident. Heller got in Novikov's way."

"You don't really believe that, Cella."

"Accident!"

And, as if summoned from the pits of hell Ric always accused him of originating from, Bo "The Marauder" Novikov stalked into Ric's office. No knock. No request to come in. Just throwing the door open and barreling his way into the room of his team's owner and captain, the way Ric imagined Novikov's Mongolian ancestors barreled into China.

Yet what horrified Ric was not that Novikov stood there with wet hair, a dozen roses, and a box of chocolates from the high-end chocolate store down the street under one arm, but that he held Toni under the other.

Ric would admit that until this very moment, he'd forgotten that Toni had been waiting outside for a job interview, but it had never occurred to him that he'd be putting her in danger by having her sit out in the goddamn waiting room!

"Wait!" Cella bellowed, and Ric looked away from Novikov long enough to see that Dee-Ann had been startled to her feet, her favorite bowie knife that Dee had named Big Betty out and ready to use. Which didn't really bother him unless poor Toni got in the way.

"It's just Novikov," Cella snapped. "So fucking calm down, canine."

"That boy better learn how to enter a room right," Dee muttered.

"Why are you touching my cousin?" Ric demanded.

"Another cousin?" Cella asked him. "Seriously? You Van Holtzes are worse than the Malones."

"She ain't blood." Dee-Ann dropped back into her chair.

"That makes it weirder," Cella said softly as if she were really analyzing something so damn meaningless.

Ric ignored her and snarled at Novikov. "Put her down. Now!"

But instead of putting her down, Novikov roared and kind

of shook Toni at them. To be honest, Ric couldn't understand what the She-jackal could have done to piss off Novikov this much. Although easy to rage when it came to hockey, Novikov mostly ignored the rest of the world unless they fucked with his oh-so-precious schedule. Now, if this was one of Toni's brothers or sisters, then, well . . . yeah. They probably deserved it because that was one batch of kids who could wield words the way samurai could wield swords. But this was Toni. Rational, calm Toni.

With her gaze locked on Novikov, Dee slapped the flat of the blade against her palm and warned the hybrid, "Looks like it might be time to start the killin', boy." And Dee-Ann meant that threat because she liked Toni. Amazing since Dee didn't really like many people. But she did like Toni, and Dee protected her friends.

Yet before Dee could prove how much, Toni calmly stated, "Or everyone could just take a breath and not . . . you know . . . start the killin'."

"Are you okay?" Ric asked Toni.

"I'm fine." And she sounded fine. She was even smiling. Not in a forced way, either, which he'd seen her do when she was trying to smooth over something one of her siblings had done or said. Usually Kyle or Oriana. "He's just in a rush and frustrated," she went on, "so he's having a hard time getting his feelings across without the roaring." Wait. Was she trying to explain the completely irrational actions of a completely irrational idiot?

Toni tapped her fingers against Novikov's arm. "You better go." Novikov responded by viciously growling. "Don't worry," Toni replied, as if she understood his nonsensical noises. "I'll talk to them." Novikov bared a fang and Toni's smile grew. "I promise. Now go. You don't want to miss your flight. And have fun tonight. Relax. You deserve it."

Novikov finally nodded and carefully placed her on the ground. Then he glowered at Ric and Cella and roared. Loudly. Thankfully, because their offices were underground, there were no windows to break. Novikov started to turn away, stopped long enough to look at Cella and say, "Tell Crush I'll call him tomorrow at seven p.m."

"Will do."

Ric still didn't know how the incredibly cool and good-natured Lou "Crush" Crushek and Novikov had become friends. Because Ric really liked Crushek. And he hated Novikov. So it all seemed so wrong.

The hybrid patted Toni on the shoulder and walked out. She followed him into the hallway. "Make sure you have your ID," she called after him. "You'll need it to get on your flight. And I already told your driver not to bother you with too much chatter, but even if he does speak to you when you don't want him to, tip him anyway."

With her eyes still staring down the hallway, but keeping her voice low, she said to the rest of them, "He won't tip him, but I already did just in case. I'm thinking Bo considers 'hello' and 'do you need anything, sir?' to be too much talking."

She was exactly right about that.

"I also couldn't get him a regular flight to Chicago at the time he needed, so I booked him a private one." She lowered her voice even more. "I had to charge it to the team because I didn't have his card and the company's card was in the bobcat's desk—which you may want to move. It seems kind of dangerous to have that there if there are any foxes working in your office. Now I figured charging Bo Novikov's personal flight to the team would piss you off, Ric"—and she was right!—"so I contacted the Sports Center in Chicago and let the stadium manager know that Bo was going to be in town to see his girlfriend's derby game or bout or whatever they call it. We discussed it, and he's going to set up a promo thing for hockey fans. I warned him, though, that Bo wouldn't like that, but apparently the hockey fans like the abuse, so the manager still thinks it's a good idea. This way you and the team will get some good PR. Plus, his being at that derby thing will bring attention to his girlfriend's team, which if I remember correctly, you also own." She shrugged. "So I figured it all kind of balanced out in the end. *And* this makes it a tax write-off." She continued to focus down the hallway for a few more seconds before she let out a sigh and walked into the office. She smiled at them.

"Anyway—"

"Wait," Ric cut in. "Before you go on . . . why's your arm in a sling?"

"I have one word for you, Ulrich," Toni stated flatly. "Mom."

"Oh." Ric nodded. "I see. So Novikov didn't—"

"No, no. Not at all. I was just trying to help."

Ricky Lee Reed suddenly ambled up behind Toni. Reed, like Dee-Ann, ambled rather than walked and seemed to take life as it came. Unlike his brothers, who had a little more drive. Yet Ric always felt the middle Reed brother treated Dee-Ann more as a big sister than as someone he hadn't yet nailed, which made Ricky Lee more likable to Ric than the other Reed brothers.

"What are you doing here?" Dee-Ann asked the big Southern wolf.

"Keeping an eye on Miss Antonella here."

"Good job when that Novikov is carrying her around like a load of Momma's laundry."

"I asked if she needed me to get involved and she said no. You and Ronnie Lee always go on and on about letting females make their own decision—"

"Shut up," Dee drawled. "Before I find another use for Big Betty."

"Wait." Toni looked back and forth between Dee and Ricky. "How do you two know each other?"

"Dee-Ann has always loved me from afar but she knew she could never have me."

"Betty," Dee threatened.

"We're Packmates," Ricky clarified.

"Huh," Toni said. "You're the first member of the Smith Pack I've met since Dee-Ann mated with Ric."

"She's ashamed of her poor wolf kin, so she hides us from all those rich Van Holtz friends of hers. We're not invited to

Washington for all those fancy dinners and get-togethers they have. Not even her own cousins, Bobby Ray and Sissy Mae, are invited. Off our little Dee-Ann goes, just leavin' the rest of us behind . . . sad and alone. Ain't that right, Dee-Ann?"

"What's sad is that my momma stopped me from burying you in our backyard like I tried to when I was ten. Had a hole dug for you and everything."

"Lord, you are so your father's child."

"And nothing makes me prouder. Ain't my fault your daddy's scared of him."

"My daddy ain't scared of nothin'. Especially Eggie Ray Smith."

"*Anyway,*" Ric cut in to the sibling-like bickering, "you were saying, Toni? About Novikov?"

"Actually, this is kind of interesting. Who's Eggie?"

"Antonella."

"Okay, okay. I was just curious." Toni thought a moment. "So, um, I saw on Novikov's schedule that there's a team meeting tomorrow afternoon, so the return flight for him and his girlfriend . . . or fiancée . . . or whatever . . . leaves Chicago at eight a.m., and a driver will bring him right to the Sports Center in time for the meeting. Then he can get his workout in after that."

Ric and Cella looked at each other and Ric asked Toni, "Why?"

"Well, I'm relatively certain if he doesn't get in some form of workout, he's going to be impossible to deal with. He reminds me of Dennis. He's my five-year-old brother," she told the others. "He has OCD, too, and if he doesn't get a certain amount of time painting—he's a painter—he gets completely unruly. You wouldn't think a five-year-old could do that much damage . . . but he can. And he's barely fifty pounds. Bo is *way* bigger, so I readjusted the amount of damage based on the size of the man and guessed it would be substantially worse. I figured you wouldn't want that."

"No, no," Ric clarified. "We wouldn't. But my question is why did you feel the need to help him?"

"Oh." Toni thought on that a moment. "Well . . . he looked like he needed help, and I was just sitting there." She suddenly sighed. "And to be quite honest, I really didn't want to have to testify against him if he murdered that bobcat."

"Floyd," Ric and Cella said at the same time. Floyd wasn't bad as a receptionist, but the man continued to piss off the persnickety Novikov. Then again, so did Ric—and the universe. Only Novikov's fiancée, Blayne, managed to avoid Novikov's wrath, mostly . . . as long as she was on time.

"It just seemed easier to help the man since you guys are clearly busy and I knew once he was done with . . . Floyd?" They nodded. "Yes, Floyd. I knew he'd come looking for you, and I didn't want to see you without most of your skin, Ric. We do consider you family, after all."

"Thank you."

"Look, I'm sorry if I stepped on any toes here. I'm just used to dealing with people like him, and it was nothing for me to help out. I was just sitting there."

Cella swung her legs off the desk. "He didn't make you nervous?"

"Bo? No. Not at all." She smiled. "He's very funny."

"Do you mean weird funny?" Ric asked. "Like odd and offputting?"

"No, Ric. I mean funny. As in humorous."

"He's humorous?"

Treating him like a true cousin, Toni rolled her eyes and said, "I'll let you get back to work."

"Wait," Cella pushed. "So you didn't find Bo Novikov hard to work with?"

Toni laughed. "Hard. *Him?*" She laughed some more. But when no one joined her, she cleared her throat and said, "Look, based on what I've heard from Kyle, Bo Novikov is considered the best at what he does. And there's a level of commitment and focus that comes with being the best. I understand how that is because I was raised around the best of the best. My ten sisters and brothers and my mom are *the best* at what they do. So my father and I have, over the years, learned to manage them. For their own good and ours." She thought a moment and added, "And society's."

"And what does that entail?" Ric coaxed. "Managing them?"

"Well . . . you know." When he just stared at her, she shrugged and said, "The main thing is to understand that because they are the best, their focus is incredibly myopic and that nothing you or I or anyone else says will change that. So instead of trying to change them, you work *within* the confines of that myopic vision. And while you're helping them, you're also protecting them from outside distractions that will just set them off and make your life hell for several hours to several days. I guess I'm saying that managing the best is really just a way to protect myself. Once you understand the man or the woman, the rest is really easy."

"And you understand Bo Novikov?"

"Yes," she said confidently. "Actually, he's super easy because he just lays it out there. One of my brothers doesn't let you know anything's wrong until he starts setting fires. When one of my sisters gets upset, her hair starts to fall out. So in order to prevent my brother from going to prison or my sister sobbing hysterically every time she showers, I have to guess when they're upset. Mr. Novikov is like a breath of fresh air. All that snarling and growling, it makes him incredibly easy to read." She glanced around the room. "Anything else?"

"Actually, yes," Cella said, briefly glancing at Ric. "Are you really busy right now?"

"Just waiting for my interview."

"Great. Then can you do me a huge favor?"

"Sure."

"We need to delay your interview anyway."

Clearly disappointed but trying to hide it, Toni said, "That's fine. What do you need?"

"One of our players has to get on a flight in the next couple of hours. He's sometimes easily distracted, so would you mind escorting him? Just make sure he gets on the plane. He's got everything he needs. His tickets, his luggage. Just needs to get *on* the plane to Alaska. He's going to a hockey camp for shifter pups and cubs and he's one of the guest trainers for the next week. You wouldn't mind, would you?"

"Not at all."

"Then come back here when you're done and we can have our little interview. Okay?"

Seeming surprised the interview would still take place today, Toni nodded. "Oh . . . okay."

Cella added, "You can find the player, Bert, down in the player's locker room."

"I'll take care of it."

Toni smiled at Ric and headed out.

"You going with her, Ricky Lee?" Dee asked Reed.

"Might as well."

"Good idea since your sister is still looking for you."

The wolf rolled his eyes and followed Toni down the hall. That's when Ric looked at Cella.

"What the hell are you doing?"

"Giving your not-really-a-cousin a shot at the big time."

"Or a chance to get permanent facial lacerations."

Cella shrugged. "You say tomato . . ."

Ricky Lee waited for Toni to step on the elevator before following her in. He pressed the button for the floor where the team's locker rooms were located.

"You spend a lot of time here, don't you?" she asked him.

He nodded at Toni's question. "Yep. My brother being one of the players gives me all sorts of access. Well, that and no one really asks me anything anyway."

"What do you mean?"

He shrugged. "I just mean that I go where I need to and always make sure I look like I know where I'm going. People are less likely to bother you or question you as long as you *appear* to know where you're going. It's only when you wander around with your mouth open, staring up at the big buildings or trying to sort out office numbers, that people start wondering what the hell you're doing. Thought it would only work here in the States, but it worked even when I was doing some work for the company in Japan, Italy, France."

"Really? I've been to and sometimes lived in all those places with my family over the years, and I find that surprising. I mean, you're just so . . . American."

"Lord, I hope so. Being that I was born and reared here and all." He chuckled as the elevator doors slid open. He waited for Toni to step out before he followed. "But I always looked like I knew where I was going. People may have watched me, especially in Japan. But no one ever questioned where I was going or stopped me from going there. It's always worked to my benefit."

"I'll have to try it. I'm always getting stopped."

They turned a corner and paused. Bert was just coming out of the locker room. He had a plain black duffel and a hockey bag for all his equipment.

They looked at each other.

"You know this is probably a setup, right?" Ricky asked her. "A test to see what you can handle."

"Oh, I know."

"Not sure what kind of test, though. Bert's a real nice guy . . . for a bear."

"He's probably slipped onto a no-fly list or something and they want to see how I'd get past that."

"You think you can?"

She grinned. "No problem. You sure you really want to tag along?"

"See you in action?" He returned her grin, enjoying himself immensely. "I wouldn't miss it."

CHAPTER SEVEN

Paul was relaxing on his couch with his eldest son, Cooper, watching bad mid-afternoon television and enjoying every day, average, father-son bonding.

"So how did your concert go in front of the prime minister?"

"Pretty good. You know how I like playing at the Colosseum. I'd just need Rome burning to feel like Nero." He paused. "Except with a piano. So I guess Mom's more like Nero. How about you? What have you been up to while I was away?"

"I rebuilt the motor in my Mustang. Then Freddy freaked out about something and Toni stopped him from setting fire to the house—which was good—but then he took the motor and the rest of the car apart when we were all asleep. I haven't had the heart to go back into the garage since. But I have the SUV, so I can still get around."

They continued to watch bad afternoon TV until the arguing from down the hall became so intolerable both men sighed and stood up at the same time. Together, father and son headed toward the arguing, but Paul already guessed where it was coming from. The large ballroom of the town house. It was the perfect place for a dancer to practice or a sculptor to sculpt or a painter to paint or a scientist to set up a lab. The list went on and on. And, in Paul's estimation, the room was large enough for all of his children to practice their art or music or anything else they wanted to work on. It was an enormous room!

Too bad none of his brilliant progeny wanted to share.

They'd almost reached the ballroom entrance when Cherise skulked around a corner. Poor thing. She skulked a lot. Kept to the shadows. A brilliant cellist since she was six, Cherise easily lost herself in her music. But when she wasn't playing, she was an easily frightened, constantly shivering She-jackal. It broke Paul's heart. His daughter needed to find her strength. Jackals weren't big and had no pack to call their own, but they did have each other. They had *family*. That was their strength. That's what had kept jackals going in the wild for centuries. So Paul needed to find out what would bring his daughter's natural strength out. He'd done it before with Toni by putting her in charge of Coop and Cherise when she was thirteen. He'd done it with the intention of keeping an eye on all three but letting his daughter feel what it was like to be needed, to feel important. And she'd taken that responsibility and run with it, helping him and Jackie to raise the most amazing children. Still, it was time for her to get out on her own. To live her own life. His Toni deserved that.

"What's up, Cherise?" he asked her.

"We need Toni."

"No," he said gently but firmly. "We don't need Toni. We can handle this without her."

"She should be home by now," Cherise insisted. "We need Toni."

Knowing one of Cherise's "loops" when he heard one—her "loops" being when she kept saying the same thing over and over until she passed out—Paul just walked on ahead, Coop and Cherise behind him. He stepped into the ballroom, stopping right at the entrance as a pink ballet slipper flew by and collided with Kyle's head. Tragically for Kyle, it was one of Oriana's pointe shoes, and the hard tip clocked the kid right in the eye.

"You talentless hack!" Kyle screamed, one hand over his eye. "I should rip out your Achilles tendon with my teeth!"

"Try that, you little weasel, and I'm chopping off both your hands!"

Coop glanced at Paul. "Cherise is right . . . we need Toni."

* ★ *

Toni stepped out of the limo she'd hired to transport her, Ricky, and Bert to the airport.

Newark was one of the airports she knew really well. Almost as well as LaGuardia and she had lots of connections here. She knew she could get a staff escort directly to the gate for Bert. And she might be allowed to go with him herself even though she didn't have a ticket. She wasn't sure, however, that she could get the wolf access, too. But she assumed he wouldn't mind waiting.

"Uh . . . Toni?"

Toni turned and smiled at the wolf. "Yes?"

He motioned to the limo with a jerk of his head. That's when Toni saw the claws sticking up through the roof of the vehicle. Toni rushed over and crouched down. Bert had his black bear claws dug into the roof and his powerful legs spread and braced on either side of the door.

"Bert?"

"I'm not going," he panted out desperately. "I'm not going. I'm not going. I'm not going."

Toni stood. "I think he's frightened of flying."

"What gave you that idea?"

"I don't need sarcasm right now, country boy," she snapped. Toni took a breath. "I'm going to see if I can talk him out."

"Make it fast. After a while, even people in Jersey are gonna notice bear claws through a limo roof."

Deciding not to comment on the wolf being Mr. Obvious, Toni leaned into the limo.

"Hey, Bert," she said, keeping her voice soft and soothing, like when she had to talk Cherise down from the roof of the house where she'd gone after panicking because the FedEx guy asked her to sign for a package. "Hey. It's okay. You don't have to do anything you don't want to."

"I'm not going. You can't make me go."

"No problem." She slowly, carefully leaned over, her hand stretching out to gently take his. "I just need you to retract those—*oh, my God! Not the face! Not the face!*"

* * *

Ricky didn't manage to catch Toni when she fell back out of the limo door, but he did stop her head from hitting the pavement. He took that as a win.

"Are you all right?"

"Do I still have my nose?"

"Yep. Not even a scratch."

"Then I'm fine. Help me up." He did, easily lifting her to her feet. The She-jackals sure were small. Compared to She-wolves anyway.

Toni wiped off the back of her jeans, her focus on the bear in the limo, which allowed Ricky to take a nice long look at her cute little rear.

"Stop staring at my ass, freak."

"Hey!" The limo driver stormed around the vehicle. "What the hell? What's he doing to my car?"

"Don't panic."

"Panic? Who's going to pay for this?"

"Can we worry about that later?" Toni demanded as she tossed off her sling, grabbed hold of the bear's leg, and began to pull.

"We can't worry about this later! I'm responsible for this car!" The driver crouched down and glared at the bear. "I knew I shouldn't let a bear into my car. Tacky, flea-bitten, honey-obsessed bastard!" The mountain lion driver hissed at the bear, and Bert roared back.

That's when the cops took notice of what was going on.

"We need to go," Ricky pushed.

"I said I'd get him on that plane. I'm going to—"

Ricky shoved the She-jackal into the car, hoping she'd be okay since she landed face-first on Bert's chest. He slammed the door closed and caught hold of the mountain lion by the back of his neck.

The cat hissed as Ricky walked him back to the driver's side of the car. "Get in and drive, tabby."

Ricky slammed that door shut, then walked around the front of the vehicle, waving casually at the cops coming closer. He opened the front passenger door and slipped inside. By the time he closed the door, the cat pulled into traffic and headed off.

"So where are we going?" the cat demanded. "And who's paying for my car?"

By now Toni had crawled forward until she could knock on the glass between the front seats and the back of the limo. The cat lowered the window and Toni leaned in. She gave the cat an address Ricky didn't recognize.

"He's not getting on a plane," Ricky reminded her.

"I'll figure out something."

"*And my car?*" the cat screeched, making Ricky bark at him, which made the cat hiss back and Bert roar.

"*That is enough!*" Toni bellowed, silencing all three males. "Everybody just shut the fuck up right now! And I'll pay for your goddamn limo, so shut up about it already."

"Can I get that in writing?" the cat muttered.

Toni's dark brown eyes locked on the driver. "I *will* unleash this bear on you," she warned, her voice low. "So don't test me."

Letting out a breath, she turned and dropped into the seat beneath the window.

"You're not giving up, are you?" Ricky asked her.

"No. I'm not giving up." She took a deep breath. "But I do wish I was home dealing with the devil I know . . ."

Coop didn't know how Toni dealt with this on a daily basis. The arguing. The crying. The yelling. The death threats. And those not fighting were instigating. For instance, the twins. Not even four yet, they insisted on tossing out inflammatory suggestions in any language they knew, which turned out to be a lot more languages than Coop had realized.

Cooper had always known his big sister had shielded him from a lot. As always, her concern had been keeping his focus on what he loved. His music. He clearly remembered when he was six, Toni yelling at their house cleaner because she was running the vacuum while he was practicing at the family piano. The housekeeper had never taken Toni very seriously, because all she ever did was follow their dad around and go to a regular school. When the housekeeper had ignored her, Toni had picked up the vacuum and thrown it against the wall. Then she'd screamed, "I said my brother is *practicing!*"

From that day on, Toni established her position as protector of the family. Their parents provided money, food, love, and support for their kids, but Toni handled the teachers, the schedules, the logistics, the arguments, the neurotic and oftentimes illegal behavior . . .

Cooper always knew it, but it didn't hit him until he was forced to drag Zia and Zoe off Kyle, their tiny little fists pounding his face, their sharp little puppy teeth trying to chew his nose off. Who knew such adorable little girls could be so angry? So very angry.

As the girls redirected their rage at Cooper's neck and chin, he looked to see if his father could help, but no. He couldn't. He was holding Oriana back from throttling Troy.

The yelling and arguing was so bad that finally, Jackie stormed into the room.

"What the hell is going on?" she demanded, hands on hips.

"You can't tell?" Paul asked, Oriana swinging wildly in his arms.

"Well, where's Toni?"

"She's at the job interview."

"She's not back yet?"

"Do you think this would be going on if she was here? And can you help rather than bark about our daughter?"

"But what is she doing? Having drinks with Ulrich? Enjoying a casual lunch with that other wolf she met earlier? Lounging? I mean, what exactly is my eldest daughter doing that's more important than helping her siblings?"

Toni got on the pavement, planted her feet on either side of the door, and with a yelled, "Heave!" she pulled on one of Bert's legs while the driver stood slightly above her and pulled on the other. Ricky was at the opposite door, pushing the black bear from behind.

But nothing worked. They couldn't move the bear with his claws dug into the roof.

"I'm not going!" Bert screamed. "I'm not going!"

Toni released him and fell back against the pavement.

The driver stormed away. "This is ridiculous!"

"Calm down." Toni tried to push herself up but her shoulder gave out. No problem, though. The wolf was there, grabbing her under the arms and lifting her up. "Thanks," she muttered.

"So now what?"

She sighed. "Let me see what I can do."

"Where are you going?" the driver demanded as she started to walk off.

"Just stay here with Bert. I'll be back. And yes"—she went on before the mountain lion could complain—"I'm going to pay for your goddamn limo. Just let it go already!"

"Still don't have it in writing!" he shot back after her, but Toni ignored him, walking into the Long Island airport that very few people knew anything about. It was a small, shifter-run airport with three airlines.

Two of the airlines handled exotic importing. Zebra, gazelle, cape buffalo . . . these all came in through LoupAir and Mercer Shipping. The only difference was that Mercer shipped frozen carcasses while LoupAir shipped live animals for hunting.

It was Madra Airlines that flew shifters anywhere in the world they wanted to go. Owned and operated by the enormous Madra Wild Dog Pack, Madra Airlines, a division of Madra Transportation, had been moving shifters between countries for more than a millennium. First in the boats they stole from the Vikings who raided their lands and, in turn, the wild dogs had killed and dined on, and now in, some of the most modern planes currently available.

The best thing about the Madra planes was that they were built for all shifters. From the tiny foxes who liked to steal—they were booked into seats with alarms that alerted flight attendants anytime they stood up; to the seven-foot polar bears that needed more leg and head room—they were put in remodeled planes that were originally built for military transport of trucks and Humvees; to the very demanding lion males—Madra personnel always made sure to seat them away from any cubs and had ample amounts of food on supply for their feeding needs.

That's why Toni loved Madra. Expensive it might be, but when she had to make sure the entire Jean-Louis Parker clan could get from one place to another in a timely manner and without embarrassment-inducing risks, she spent the extra cash to book them on Madra Airlines.

"Antonella?"

Toni spun around and immediately grinned. "Scotty!" She charged into the open arms of her fellow jackal. "I was so hoping you were working today."

"Is it Kyle?" he asked with a smile when Toni stepped back.

"For once . . . no. I do need your help, though." She took his hand and dragged him to the front doors of the airport and out to the limo.

"Holy shit." The jackal laughed when he saw the bear.

"He's afraid of flying," Toni told him. "Can you help?"

"With bears? You bet. Just tell me what *needs* to happen."

Ricky waited until the jackal had gone back inside the airport before he asked, "So who's that?"

"That's Scotty."

"Just telling me the man's name doesn't really help me understand."

"He runs the airport."

"Thought wild dogs run this place."

"Wild dogs *own* this company. But they hire other canines. They're a really great company if you're looking for work."

"I'm not. Do you think I am?"

"I have no idea, with you free to follow me around all day." She suddenly frowned. "You're not a criminal, are you?"

"Why would you think that?"

"Well . . . you are in the Smith Pack."

"And?"

That's when the mountain lion started to laugh. "Oh, come on! Are you really going to be insulted that she asked you that?"

"What the hell does that mean?"

"Everybody knows that the Smith Pack is either criminals or assholes. Usually both at the same time."

Annoyed and always protective of his Pack, Ricky Lee stepped closer to the cat. Instantly, the cat stood straight, fangs easing out of his gums.

"Gentlemen," Toni sighed. "Do we really have time for this?"

Ricky would make time.

"What are you gonna do, Snoopy? Without your Pack? It's just you and me."

Toni leaned in between the snarling pair. "Not really," she said, motioning toward the front doors. Ricky and the cat looked over and saw about ten males in their wolf forms standing a few feet away. Ricky didn't know any of them, but he knew wolves would always back stranger wolves against cats, because cats just really irritated them all.

That Scotty guy—was he the ex-boyfriend?—came out of the airport. He pointed at the limo. "He's in there, Craig."

The wolves trotted over to the limo.

"What are they doing to my car?"

"Tearing it apart?"

"Stop instigating," Toni told Ricky.

The wolves stood outside the limo for several seconds. Then, suddenly, one of them jumped forward, barked, and nipped at Bert's legs.

"Hey!" Bert yelled. "Cut it out!"

Another wolf jumped forward, barked, nipped.

Then they all did it, surrounding the limo and attacking Bert from both ends.

"Get off me!" he yelled from inside. "I'm not kidding! Cut it out!"

"Good Lord," Ricky muttered, his annoyance at the cat forgotten as the two stood there with Toni between them and watched. "They're baitin' that damn bear."

"That is so wrong," the cat said.

Wrong it might be, but effective. Bert suddenly exploded out of that limo, roaring, claws slashing at the wolves. He hit a few, sending them flying several feet.

"Hey, bear," Scotty said. And when Bert turned, ready to attack yet another canine, Scotty pulled the trigger on the tranquilizer gun he held. The dart slammed into Bert's neck. The black bear roared and tried to run off, but the wolves kept charging him, pushing him back, blocking him off, until he began to stumble forward . . . back . . . and then down he went like a diseased oak.

Scotty handed off the rifle to some fox standing with him and motioned to the wolves. "All right, gentlemen. Let's get the bear up and on the plane."

The wolves shifted back to human and lifted poor Bert up and carried him into the airport. One of them grabbed Bert's baggage out of the trunk and followed after them.

Scotty stood in front of Toni, his smile wide. "Told you. Easy-peasy."

"Scotty, you're the best."

"I know." He took Toni's hand and rested it on his forearm. "The best part . . . for a little extra, we'll make sure he gets back the same way. He'll wake up in New York and not even remember checking out of his hotel."

"Excellent."

"Now let's get this paperwork out of the way." He led her inside. "Would you like some champagne while we do this? You look like you need it."

The cat looked at Ricky. "He is so gonna *nail* her."

Ricky Lee took off his hat, scratched his head. "You know, cat, you are partly right."

"About what?"

Ricky rammed his head forward into the cat's, knocking the feline out completely.

Staring down at him, he said, "The Smith Pack can be a bunch of assholes."

Ricky put his hat back on and went into the airport in search of Toni.

Chapter Eight

The limo pulled up in front of the town house and Toni got out. The wolf followed. It was almost seven. She'd gone back to the office and filled Ulrich and Cella Malone in on what had happened. They didn't seem surprised, but Ric didn't seem too happy about the fact he'd bought a limo he didn't need.

After that, Toni left the office and found the wolf and the cat waiting for her. Where the driver had managed to get that nasty lump on his forehead, Toni didn't know and she didn't ask. She was just glad that he was willing to drive her home. Why Ricky went with her, she didn't know, either. If she didn't have the fever now, she wouldn't get it. Her shoulder did still hurt but nothing she couldn't manage. By tomorrow, the pain would be a faint memory.

Toni thanked the cat for his help, reminded him that he now had *in writing* Ulrich's commitment to replace his vehicle with one that didn't have a torn roof from bear claws, and said good-bye. Then she walked up the stairs to the town house, unlocked the door, and went inside.

She'd barely stepped into the hallway before Coop suddenly came at her. "Run."

"What?"

"Run," he whispered. "Make a run for it while you can!"

Ricky only had a moment to wonder what the holy hell was going on when they were there, trapping Toni against his chest, which pinned Ricky against the closed door. This was all of them, he guessed. Toni's parents, the siblings. And they were all yelling. At Toni. At each other.

"Where have you been?" her mother was demanding, one of the twins in her arms.

"Hey!" her father called out, trying to calm his brood while he held the other twin. "Why don't we let Toni have a few minutes to—"

But his attempt was drowned out by Kyle, Oriana, and another young boy as they threatened each other with all manner of things that anyone under the age of twenty-five should not be saying.

Cooper stood behind them all with another young female, both of them giving their sister what Ricky could only call a "we're so sorry" look. He knew they meant it, but unfortunately it didn't really help.

And that's when Ricky spotted her. Easing out of the library and floating silently down the hall in her all white summer dress that flowed lazily around her ankles, comfortable sandals on her feet, and a beige messenger bag hanging from her shoulder.

She looked very different from her siblings. Her hair was blonder and long, reaching down her back. She moved differently, acted differently.

He couldn't explain it, but there was something . . .

Toni went up on her toes and said loudly to the girl, "Where are you going, Delilah?"

It was the way they all fell silent that concerned Ricky. It was like they suddenly froze, suddenly aware of another's presence.

The one Toni called Delilah stopped walking, and Toni's parents and siblings all turned and looked down the hall. Slowly, Delilah faced them.

"Sorry?"

"I said where are you going?"

With a small smile that seemed permanently fixed, Delilah moved closer.

"Out for a walk," she said. Her voice was soft and . . . lilting. Not like her siblings at all. She didn't even seem canine. If he couldn't smell the jackal in her, Ricky would have assumed she was a full-human. "I won't be gone too long."

"I can come with you," Toni offered.

"No. I won't be gone too long."

"What about Cooper? Just to keep you company."

"No," Delilah said again. "I won't be gone too long."

Her voice never changed. Her attitude never changed. It was like she had one note and one note only.

"Well . . ." Toni dropped back on her heels. "Just be careful then. Okay?"

With a nod, Delilah turned away and headed off down the hallway.

The family stayed silent until they all heard a doorway somewhere deep in the house open and close.

Toni looked around at her siblings. "All right. Everyone in the living room. Calmly. Quietly. No arguing."

She started to follow after them, but Ricky caught the back of her shirt.

"Who was that?" he asked.

"My sister."

"Really?" They seemed unbelievably different to actually be related. "Was she adopted?"

Toni shook her head. "No. She's one of us. Turned eighteen a few months back." She started to walk off but stopped, glanced back at him. "I know my sister's pretty," she said, her voice very low. "But stay away from her."

"I'm not interested in her."

She nodded, then added, "Tell your brother to stay away from her."

"Because she's so young? Because she's family?"

Toni studied him for a moment before replying, "No. That's not why."

Without another word, she walked into the living room and Ricky let himself out.

As Ricky walked down the stairs, he noticed another limo sitting in front of the house. The driver opened the back door and a woman stepped out. She was full-human but covered in wolf scent. Some wolf's mate. She walked toward him, stopping at the bottom of the stairs and gazing up at him with disturbing blue eyes.

"I know you," she said. She shook her head. "No. Not you. Someone related to you. You have very similar cheek bones and eyes. That friend of Dee-Ann's."

"You know Dee-Ann?"

"I'm Irene Conridge Van Holtz."

"Ric's aunt. I've heard a lot about you. And I think you met my sister, Ronnie Lee."

She looked up at the town house. "Is there a problem?"

"Pardon?"

"You work in security, right? That's what Dee-Ann says. You and your brothers. So if you're here at my friend's house with the children I consider family, I'm wondering if you're here about a problem."

"No problem."

"Dee-Ann's cousin lives across the street with that wild dog pack, correct? That's what Holtz told me."

"Holtz?"

"My husband. I call him Holtz. Anyway, I assumed you were here to make sure there were no threats to the wild dogs."

Ricky smiled. "That was checked out before they put down their first piece of luggage."

"I see."

"Anyway, I'll let you get in and see everybody." He again started down the stairs. "Maybe you can rescue poor Toni. It's as if her kin descended on her like the hounds from hell."

"Have a nice night," she told him.

"You, too, ma'am."

Irene watched the wolf head across the street. She had to admit, she'd always thought her mate was unnaturally large, especially around the shoulders and neck. But every one of the wolves she'd met from the Smith Pack had proved to her what unnaturally large truly was. Thick necks. Enormous shoulders and chests. And bizarrely large feet—especially on the women.

Yet what Irene really liked about all wolves was how easy it was to figure out what they were thinking or feeling just by watching the expression on their faces.

And Irene knew what she'd seen when the wolf mentioned Toni.

Irene walked up the stairs and into the house, motioning for the limo driver to put her bags on the floor by the door.

While he took care of that, she headed down the marble hallway until she found the Jean-Louis Parker family in the living room. Toni stood in front of her seated family, a notepad in her hand.

"All right," she was saying, not realizing that Irene was there. "This will not be hard to manage. I'll pull together schedules for everyone, and I'm sure there is a way to manage the number of rooms we have in this place for you all to get in your work or daily practices."

"I should get the ballroom," Oriana snapped. "I need the most space."

"And the most mirrors," Troy muttered.

"Don't you have a protractor to stick in your mouth . . . pointy side first?"

"Spell protractor."

"I can spell pathetic lonely *loser!*"

"Yes," Kyle dryly cut in, "which when you hit thirty-five and your career is over you'll so definitely be."

"Enough," Toni barked. And it was, literally . . . a bark. "I alone will decide which rooms go to whom and you will suck it up when I do."

There was some angry muttering but none of the children were brave enough to challenge their sister.

Toni looked down at her notebook. "Now, let's see . . ."

That's when Irene realized something: Toni wasn't going to tell them. Anything.

So it was a very good thing that Irene was known for her cold, brutal, and heartless ability to cut through to the heart of everything. If Toni wasn't going to say anything, Irene would.

"Congratulations, Antonella," Irene said from her spot by the big entryway.

Toni's head snapped up, brown eyes locking on Irene.

"Hey, Reeny!" Paul called out. Since Jackie had dragged that poor jackal home so many years ago, he'd insisted on calling Irene "Reeny." Irene had hated it initially, but then the nickname, like Paul, had grown on her.

"Hello, Paul."

"So what are you congratulating my girl for?"

Irene feigned surprise by raising her brows. "She didn't tell you?"

With the entire family's attention focused on Irene, they didn't see Toni bare a fang in warning.

"No. She didn't tell us anything." Paul looked at his daughter. "What didn't you tell us?"

"It doesn't matter."

"Is it about your job interview? Did you get the job?"

And that's why Paul had grown on Irene. Not a lot of men had that sort of hope and eagerness in their voice when asking an adult daughter about an office job that would mostly involve using a copier.

Toni shrugged. "They made an offer, but with all that we have going on here—"

"What?" Kyle dryly asked. "You're not snapping up that job where you can be an office drone all day? What are you thinking?"

"Oh," Irene informed the family, slowly walking into the library. "They're actually giving that job to someone else. Probably a college kid since it's just for the summer. It only paid an intern stipend and was really for college credit."

"So she couldn't even get the office drone job?" Oriana snickered.

"No. But she did get the Director of Team Travel and Promotions job, which I believe starts in the six figures, comes with a company car, extensive travel, full benefits, including artery repair—apparently all those who join the team get that and

I decided not to delve further into why it's necessary—and a yearly, substantial bonus depending on her performance. I seriously doubt this will be a little office drone job for our Antonella. This is a full-time career for her. Aren't we all proud?" she asked, and began to politely applaud.

But no one joined Irene. Instead, Oriana pointed an accusing finger at her eldest sister. "You're deserting us?"

"I—"

"You're leaving us for your own . . . what did you call it, Aunt Irene? Your own *career*?"

"I thought we *were* your career," Troy said.

"Exactly!" Kyle agreed. "I have every intention of making you my personal assistant when my career takes off so that you can manage my schedule and take care of my harem of women."

Cooper smirked. "And what exactly would you do with a harem of women, Kyle?"

"*Duh.* Allow them to cook me dinner and do my laundry after they hunt me down a gazelle. Just like what Mom does. What else would you do with a harem?"

Relieved by that description from the eleven-year-old, Irene said, "You all had to know that this time would come. That your sister would be going off to her own life . . . her own family."

"Why would we know that?" Troy asked. "No one ever discussed that with us. Not once. Not ever."

"So," Cherise suddenly asked, "you thought Toni was going to stay with us forever?"

"Why wouldn't she?" Kyle asked. "We're special. We need the attention. She's just . . ."

Irene folded her arms over her chest. "Your sister is just . . . what, Kyle?"

With wide eyes, Kyle stared at Toni. "She's . . . just . . . amazing? Right. She's just amazing at taking care of us."

"So my special quality is being a babysitter?" Toni asked.

"You should feel grateful," Troy said, getting to his feet. "We *allow* you to be part of our lives. We allow you to bask in the glow of our brilliance! And you dare threaten us with leaving for some ridiculous *job*?"

Fed up, Irene looked to her best friend. "Jackie . . . do you have something to . . . to . . . by the flawed logic of Albert Einstein, Jacqueline Jean-Louis—*are you crying?*"

"I'm . . . I'm . . ." Jackie buried her face in her hands, her sobs racking her small body.

Toni, horrified, rushed forward. "Mom, please don't cry. I won't—"

Before Irene could stop Toni's next ridiculous, emotion-based words, Paul caught his eldest daughter's arm and forcibly dragged her from the room. Irene went to Jackie and helped her stand. "Come on."

Irene headed toward the door, telling the kids over her shoulder, "You all stay here until I come back."

"Or what?" Oriana sneered.

Irene stopped, turned, focused on the young girl. Focused . . . and stared.

Oriana stared back at first, but then she began to look away. Irene continued staring at her until Kyle jumped in front of his sister and screamed at Irene, *"What is wrong with you? Stop it! Just stop it!"*

Satisfied, Irene escorted her friend away, confident the children would wait like she'd told them to.

"I'm a horrible sister," Toni sobbed, her face in her hands. "And an even worse daughter!"

"You do understand you're listening to Troy, Kyle, and Oriana?"

"They're right!"

"They're selfish!"

"Apparently so am I!"

Paul sat down on the marble bench in their rental home's backyard and stared up at his beautiful daughter. "You're not doing this."

"I know," she said quickly, wiping her face with the palms of her hands. "I'm not doing this. I'm not taking the job."

"No, Toni. I meant you're not letting your siblings guilt you into giving up the chance of a lifetime."

Toni gazed at her father. "What?"

"You heard me. You're taking this goddamn job. You're taking it. You're going to do great at it. And you're going to get your own life."

"I can't desert you guys."

"Toni?"

"Yes?"

"You do know these aren't your children, right?"

Appearing disgusted, Toni snapped, "Of course I do."

"Then how can you desert them if you're not their mother? We—your mother and I—can take care of our own children."

"But—"

"We," he pushed, "can take care of our children. We had them . . . we're responsible for them." He shrugged. "It's kind of the law."

"So I'm just being pushed out? Like a lion male pushed out of a pride? You're just done with me?"

Okay, Paul recognized this. Toni's mother reacted the same way when she became over-stressed. The "nothing you say will make this better" moment.

So Paul didn't say anything. Instead he just took his daughter's hand and pulled her until she sat on his lap like she did when that internationally famous conductor's cat mauled her when she was seven. He put his arms lightly around her waist and smiled when her head dropped onto his shoulder.

"Congratulations, baby."

"Thanks, Daddy."

"So . . . that wolf seems really interested in—"

"Don't even go there right now."

Chuckling, he kissed her forehead. "Not tonight. But you know I'm not letting it go."

"I know, Daddy. I know."

★ ★ ★

"Sobbing?" she heard Irene sigh. "Really?"

"You don't understand."

"I don't understand how much you rely on Antonella? How else would I ever get our spa times together if it weren't for Toni arranging it for us?"

"It's not that."

"You don't want to have to deal with Kyle and Oriana on a daily basis? I fully understand that. Perhaps we can put them, Troy, and my demon spawn in an apartment together, and leave them there . . . forever. You'd have the rest of your kids and I'd still have my boys . . . it could work perfectly."

"Don't you see?" Jackie demanded. "I'm losing my baby girl!"

"Losing her? You mean she's growing up."

"Whatever. All I know is that my baby, my first born, is leaving me to—"

"Start her own life? Her own family?"

"Don't give me that tone, Irene Conridge. Like *I'm* being irrational."

"You are letting your emotions override your reason. That would be considered by many as irrational."

"Irene." Jackie sat down on her bed. "I don't need rational, logical Irene. I need the Irene who takes her kids to IHOP without telling her husband."

"They like the waffles."

"Wolves like waffles."

Irene sat down beside her. "I understand this won't be easy for any of you. But you have to let her go. You have to give her a chance to find out what her own life can be even if it's not going to be as groundbreaking as her siblings'."

"I never cared that she's not a prodigy. Toni is special to *me*."

"You never cared about that, but she does. She doesn't tell you, but I think part of her feels like she's . . . let you down."

"That's ridiculous."

"Of course it is. But if she can shine at this job—and from

what I heard from Ulrich, she was tailor-made for this position—she'll realize how special she is just by being Antonella. Sometimes that's all someone needs."

Jackie stared at her friend. "My God, Irene."

"What?"

"That was . . . beautiful."

"I'm not heartless, you know." She thought a moment, then added, "I can be, of course . . . but I chose not to be at that moment."

"I appreciate that." Jackie took a deep breath. "Irene . . . will you help me do this?"

"I can't believe you're asking me that."

"I know. I know." Jackie threw her hands up. "I'm pathetic. Asking you to help me manage my own children."

"No. That's not what I mean."

"It's not?"

"No. I mean if it hadn't been for you, all those years ago, always making sure the pantry was stocked with peanut butter and crackers, that the electricity bill was always paid, and that I got a good four to five hours of sleep at least every other day . . . I probably would have died a tragic but senseless death."

"Or you would have just gone to the McDonald's down the street from our old house and worked out of your office when the electricity was shut off."

"Not without you suggesting it. You kept me alive until I met a wolf shifter with a whole pack of people who ensured I didn't starve to death in a darkened room. So you don't ever have to ask me to help you manage your brilliant but extremely narcissistic children."

Jackie sighed. "They are a bit narcissistic, aren't they?"

"A bit?"

Toni sat on a nice leather couch in one of the many rooms on the first floor. The house was beautifully furnished. The wild dogs had done a great job. Although Toni still thought her mother was paying too much for this place, but there was no point in telling her that. Instead, Toni just sat on the nice leather couch and gazed witlessly across the room.

Her phone vibrated and Toni swiped it off the end table. It was a text from Ulrich.

On jet heading to Germany. Still need an answer.
In or out Jean-Louis?

Toni stared at her phone, unsure what to do. Because this was the chance of a lifetime, right? That's what her father said. But what about her family?

"Dad said they could take care of themselves. Maybe I should just believe him."

She typed the word "In," her finger about to hit SEND, when Zia ran by screaming. Not really surprising. Zia had always been a bit of a screamer. But then Zoe came charging after her . . . holding a steak knife in her hand and chanting, "Kill, kill, kill, kill!" A few seconds after that came Cherise. She hard-charged past the couch and across the living room, chanting, "I'll get her! I'll get her! Don't worry!"

Finger still waiting to hit SEND, Toni watched her siblings bolt out of the room.

"This is why you're trapped," Coop said as he dropped onto the couch beside her.

Toni glanced over. Her brother ate a sandwich and stared at her. "Why am I trapped, O wise giant-headed one?"

"Because you spend every minute trying to save us from ourselves."

"That's not what I'm trying to do here. Notice that I didn't move. I know Cherise can handle this."

Zoe ran back through the living room, still holding the steak knife. But now Zia had gotten her little hands on a big pair of scissors and was in hot pursuit. Cherise, though, was still trying to catch the youngest members of their family.

"I've got 'em," Cherise now chanted. "I've got 'em. *No one panic!*"

Coop handed Toni the other half of his sandwich. Ham and

cheese on sourdough. "I wasn't panicking," he said, setting up a large bag of chips between them. "Are you panicking?"

"Nope. She's got 'em."

"Ow!" Cherise screamed from another room. "You little viper! Give me that!"

"Okay," her brother said. "Maybe this looks bad. But we all have to learn to function on our own."

Toni heard the front door open and she looked at the archway. Delilah had returned, floating silently by, followed a few moments later by what Toni could only assume was some poor, full-human homeless person. Toni immediately looked at Coop, and he was already staring at her, his eyes wide. He was definitely panicking now.

"No!" Toni ordered. The full-human stopped and turned to her. "Go," she snapped in a harsh growl. "Go now!"

The full-human gazed at her, brow pulled down in confusion.

Delilah floated back, her hand lightly touching the full-human's arm. "It's all right," she soothed in her soft, lilting voice. "Come on. I have food for you. Something cool to drink."

"*No!*" Toni jumped to her feet. She used that same tone when unleashed aggressive dogs randomly charged her family on the streets. As canines that sort of thing happened to them more often than it did to other families.

"Out." She watched the full-human analyze the situation. He wasn't a nice man. He wasn't homeless because of mental illness or unmanageable circumstances that could happen to even the best people. Instead, he'd ended up this way because he stayed in the shadows and did things for quick money and a quick fix. But that didn't matter to Toni. She couldn't allow it to matter. Not in her parents' house.

So she did what she had to do. She bared her fangs and barked and yipped until the full-human ran off.

She faced her sister. "We had this discussion," Toni said calmly, softly. She didn't bother raising her voice with Delilah. It was ineffective and probably just made things worse.

"You were very cruel," her sister softly chastised. "He could have used a good meal."

"Again, we've had this discussion. You don't pick up strangers off the street. You don't pick up anything off the street. No squirrels, no cats, no full-humans. No postman, no Arctic foxes. Understand?"

Delilah didn't answer, she simply stared and Toni stared back.

The twins shot into the room again from another doorway. While keeping eye contact with Delilah, Toni caught hold of her sisters by the hands still gripping weapons. She yanked the knife and scissors away and handed them off to Coop—handles first, of course, because his hands were insured for nearly a million dollars. Then she grabbed both pups and held each under an arm.

"Do you understand?" she pushed her sister.

"Yes," Delilah replied. "I understand." Then she floated off down the hallway.

"I'm sorry!" Cherise yelped as she stumbled into the room. She wore shorts, and Toni could easily see blood dripping down her legs from cuts, as well as blood all over her forearms, which was probably because she hadn't used her hands to try to grab the twins—not when those hands were insured for five hundred thousand. "I'm so sorry!"

"It's all right. I got them."

No, Toni realized with an internal sigh. She couldn't go off and abandon her family no matter what her father or Aunt Irene said. Mostly because Toni was the only one with hands that could be sacrificed if necessary.

She'd have to tell Ulrich—

"Uh . . . Toni?"

Toni looked over at her brother. "What?"

He dipped his head a bit and Toni looked down to see that Zia had her phone. Her little fingers pushing on the bright screen.

"Oh . . . crud."

"Bonjour, Oncle Ric!" Zia cheered, holding the phone up for Toni to see. *"Bonjour!"*

Coop leaned in when the phone vibrated and read the new text. "And Ric replies, 'Welcome aboard, cousin!' "

"Dammit!"

Toni tried to maneuver the twins around so she could get the phone back and quickly text Ulrich a retraction, but Coop took the phone from their baby sister and began texting while walking away.

"What are you doing?" Toni demanded, following her brother with the giggling twins still in her arms.

"Telling Ric thanks for the welcome and that no matter what I text him tonight, ignore it because it'll just be my usual stupid panic."

"Cooper!"

"Ric replies that it's too late for any of that. He's already sent an e-mail to the team that you're on board. Oh, look, sis! You've already started getting e-mails. A thank-you from someone named Malone and a list of things to do from someone Russian. Novikov? Look at you with your fancy friends."

"Coop, come on!"

He stopped walking, faced her. "Let it go, sis. You're in."

Toni lifted her arms to show Cooper the twins. "And what am I supposed to do about these two? Who is going to take care of them?"

"Their mother." Toni turned and her mother stood there, smiling at her. "Just got a text from Ric congratulating me on my wonderful daughter."

Good God! How fast does Ric text? He was shooting out e-mails, sending texts . . . it was like he was a twelve-year-old girl!

Jackie took her twin daughters out of Toni's arms. "I'm going to put these two to bed." She leaned in and kissed Toni's cheek. "I'm very proud of you, baby."

"Thanks, Mom."

Jackie headed out of the room. "Come on, Cherise. I'll show you how to manage these two and protect your hands."

Cherise followed. "I was thinking falconer's gloves."

"Those are good. You also may want to look into chainmail gloves."

Standing behind Toni, Coop rested his head on her shoulder. "Chainmail gloves?"

"It worked in the Middle Ages."

CHAPTER NINE

Toni walked into the kitchen the next morning and looked over her family seated at the big wooden table, eating their breakfast.

"Anyone seen the dog?"

Kyle dropped his fork onto his plate. "You get this fancy job and now you don't even remember our *names*?"

"I don't mean *you*. I'm talking about the actual dog. I should walk him since I'm sure none of you will."

"We have a dog now?"

"You all played with her last night."

Her family gazed at her. Even her mother . . . who'd actually gotten the dog.

"Where's Dad?" Toni asked, needing to speak to someone with actual sense, but they all pointed in random directions, which didn't really help her. "Useless," she muttered. "All of you . . . brilliant but useless."

"But we are brilliant," Troy said, grinning. "And isn't that's what's important?"

"No."

Toni walked out of the kitchen and down the hall. As she neared the front door, it opened and her father walked in with the dog on what was probably the little crap leash that came with her from the pound.

"She's nice," he said, pointing at the dog. "I'll pick her up a real leash and collar this afternoon."

"Thanks for walking her and not just putting her outside."

"Of course. Besides, I think the kids should have a dog."

"They should?"

"The more interaction they have with something other than—"

"Their own ego?"

Paul chuckled and kissed his daughter's forehead. "Good luck today."

"Thanks, Daddy." She stepped back. "How do I look?"

Her father looked her over. "Like you run a banking empire."

Toni glanced down at the suit she'd borrowed from her mother. "I can shop for something new this weekend."

"You hate clothes shopping."

"I know." She sighed.

Looking up at her father, Toni hopefully asked, "Walk with me to the subway?"

"No," he said simply, surprising her. "You'll be fine on your own." Then he sort of shoved her out the door, briefly stopping to grab her backpack and shoving it into her arms. "You have a good first day, baby." He winked and closed the door in her face.

Shocked—her father loved to go walking with her—Toni turned to head down the steps and into her new life.

"Mornin'."

Toni stopped and stared. Ricky Reed sat on the stone handrail eating nuts. Almonds, it looked like.

"Morning. What are you doing here?"

"You left me hanging."

"Hanging? About what?"

"Whether you took the job or not."

"You're here at seven in the morning because you wanted to know if I took the job with the Carnivores?"

"Yep."

"You're a strange wolf."

"Some might say."

Not sure where this conversation was going, Toni said, "Look, I have to go."

"Need some company?"

"Company?"

Ricky slid off the handrail, tossed the rest of the almonds in his mouth, and gently took her arm. He moved down the rest of the stairs, and Toni was forced to walk with him.

"Nervous?" he asked.

"I guess. Hard not to be."

"You'll be fine."

Toni stopped on the street and the wolf stopped with her. "What if I'm not?"

"What if you're not what?"

"Fine. What if I'm not fine? What if instead of fine, I just suck."

"I watched you yesterday, Toni. You were made for this job."

"You're right." She nodded, desperate to believe him. "You're right. This is probably not as big of a deal as I'm making it."

"Right."

"Ulrich is like my cousin. He's family. This is probably just a cute title with some cash to make me feel better."

"Well, I didn't say—"

"I'm sure this isn't a"—she made air quotes—" '*real* job.' Right?"

He shrugged. "Okay."

Feeling better, understanding that this wasn't a real job, just something to keep her busy over the summer, Toni started off again toward the subway. When she and the wolf reached the corner, a limo cut in front of them. The driver's side door opened and the mountain lion from yesterday stepped out of the car.

Toni threw up her hands. "Mr. Van Holtz," she snapped, "already told you he'd pay for your goddamn limo!"

"I know. This is it."

Toni's mouth dropped open. "You made him buy you a Mercedes limo? Damn cats!" She swiped her arms to the side. "Get out of our way!"

"I'm here for you."

"So you can show off the new limo you *stole* from a very nice canine!"

"No," the cat snarled back. "I'm your new driver . . . bitch."

Toni smirked. "That is such utter bullshit."

"You sure are saucy today," the wolf teased.

"Quiet." She refocused on the cat. "The Carnivores are giving me a new car. Ric wouldn't waste money on a limo for me, too."

"You're still getting a new car for your personal time. The limo is so you won't have to worry about traffic and can work and take phone meetings. By the way, your new phone is in the back and I think you're supposed to be on a call right now with one of the Russian teams. Something about arranging a security detail because of what Novikov did to their coach when he was on the Minnesota team. I heard it was really ugly and the team had to sneak out of Russia."

"Isn't it called the Soviet Union now?"

"Good God," the cat sneered. "Russia hasn't been called the Soviet Union since they disbanded in the nineties."

"Well when they keep changing their name how am I supposed to keep track?" Ricky shot back. "I'm an American! Our country has only had *one* name!"

Toni rubbed her eyes. "I have to go."

"You okay?" the wolf asked her softly while simultaneously giving the cat the finger.

"I'm fine," she lied. "Today's going to be great. You'll see."

"Okay."

She forced a smile and walked to the limo. "You going to open the door for me?" she asked the cat.

"Just get in the damn car, canine."

"Bastard," she muttered before getting in the limo and answering her new phone.

Ricky walked into the Llewellyn Security offices and barely ducked a fist to the face.

"Bastard!"

Laughing, Ricky backed away from his irate baby brother. "Mornin' to you, too, hoss."

"You left me alone with them," Reece accused. "You left me alone with She-wolves who were *worried* about you. Who spent the entire time talking about you and that girl you fucked ten thousand years ago. And I, big brother, was trapped in a cage—*and unable to get away!*"

Mindy, the cheetah receptionist, giggled but quickly turned away when Reece glared at her.

"I'm sorry," Ricky said, and he really meant it. "I'm sorry. I panicked, and I ran. Just like Daddy taught us."

"Don't blame our dear, sweet daddy for this."

"He always said, when you hear the click of a gun, the growl of a momma bear, or the concern of a She-wolf . . . you run. You run like the Devil himself is on your ass. And that's what I did. And you would have done the same."

"You're still a bastard."

"I know. But I also know you understand."

Ricky patted his brother on the shoulder and headed to his office. He stepped inside, ready to get to work, when a voice from the corner of the room stopped him cold.

"Hey, big brother."

Hearing his sister's voice, Ricky headed right back to the door, but Reece was there, grinning, as he yanked the door closed. Grabbing wildly for the doorknob, Ricky desperately pulled on it, but a strong hand gripped his shoulder and dragged him over to a chair, shoving him into it.

Sissy Mae Smith, younger sister of Bobby Ray Smith, stroked his cheek. "You poor, poor thing. How hard this must be for you."

Ricky glowered at the Alpha Female of his Pack because he was aware that while his sister was honestly concerned, Sissy Mae knew better. But like many of the Smith She-wolves, she was a vicious little instigator. He'd never known anyone who loved tormenting a body more than Sissy Mae Smith . . . except maybe her momma or that lion Sissy Mae was mated to.

"You can't avoid this," Ronnie Lee said, stepping forward. Only a few weeks pregnant, she wasn't even showing, but her emotions had been a nightmare of love and concern since she'd conceived. Ricky knew this wouldn't last once the pup was born, but the thought of putting up with "concerned Ronnie" as Rory called her, was beginning to make Ricky Lee panic.

He loved his sister, couldn't wait to meet his nephew, but he wanted the baby sister who, when a few years ago he was kind of sad about breaking up with some girl he couldn't even remember now, told him, "Get the fuck over it, Ricky Lee. She's probably already fucking somebody else by now."

Lord, he wanted that Ronnie Lee back! Not this one who was stroking his head like he was a wounded dog she'd found on the side of a busy highway and needed to rush to a vet to have his leg removed.

"I know this is hard, Ricky Lee. I know how you felt about Laura Jane."

"You mean when I was eighteen? And lived by my dick?"

"It's all right. We're here for you."

Then his sister was hugging him. Ronnie Lee was *hugging* him.

Someone kill me now.

"They want *what*?"

Toni looked at the notes she'd barely managed to scribble as the interpreter for the Russian coach had rattled off the Siberian shifter team's demands for the international game. She read the demands out loud again, stopping when Cella Malone said, "That one."

Her long legs up on the table, her long black hair streaked with white and orange-red strands, Cella Malone crossed her arms over her chest and took in a deep breath before asking, "They want Novikov in a *cage*?"

"Yes. Um . . . before and after the game, and during, uh, half-time."

"And you agreed to that?"

"No."

"What did you agree to?"

Toni, getting the feeling she'd screwed up, admitted, "Nothing."

"Did you negotiate?"

"No."

"Why not?"

Toni glanced around at the table full of people and said, "Didn't know I was supposed to."

"Did you at least say no?"

"No."

"Then Yuri"—the Moscow coach—"thinks you agreed."

"But I didn't agree."

"But you didn't say you didn't agree."

"But I didn't say I agreed, either."

"Yuri won't care. As far as he's concerned, we'll be putting Novikov into a cage. Not that I blame the man. It's been a few years, but that poor bear is *still* recovering from what Novikov did to him. But Novikov isn't going into a cage. And we're not playing the Siberian team without him, because I don't like to lose. And playing against a team made up of polars, tigers, and a couple of foxes is what nightmares are made of." Cella sighed and shook her head. "I'll call Yuri myself."

"No, no." Toni shook her head and fought her desire to shift to jackal and start chewing on the furniture out of anxiety. "I can deal with it."

"Yeah," one of the department heads cut in. "You did such a great job already with Novikov in a cage and everything."

Toni glared across the table at a fellow canine, a red fox, but she bit back her automatic, Kyle-like response.

"I'm sure," Toni tried to insist to Cella, "that I can handle this. I just need you to—"

"Could you guys get out?" Cella asked everyone else.

The other department heads quickly left, leaving Toni alone with the big She-cat. She was really a stunning beauty, but Toni couldn't ignore those knuckles of hers. They were bloody and torn, like she'd just been in a fight. And everyone knew about the Malones. A tiger family of one-time Irish Travelers who had a very tough reputation among shifters. So Toni really didn't want to get on the wrong side of this woman.

"Look, kid," Cella began. "I know you're new to this, but you need to step it up. I've got a lot going on," she complained, rubbing her forehead. "And a killer headache. I mean you did a great job with Novikov and with Bert. Better than anyone else. Plus you got Ric Van Holtz's stamp of approval. All of these are good things. But don't think for a minute that your connection with Van Holtz is going to protect you. You don't get this job right . . . I'm firing your ass and Van Holtz isn't going to override my decision. So step up your game."

Toni nodded. "Yes. Of course."

"And, sweetie . . . what are you wearing?"

Toni glanced down at her mother's suit. "A business suit."

"Why? Are you selling insurance?"

"Well . . . I . . ."

"The bottom line is . . . you look uncomfortable. And uncomfortable to shifters means weakness. You don't want these guys thinking you're weak. They will stomp all over you. So grow a backbone, wear something you're actually comfortable in, and I'll handle Yuri for now. Okay?"

"Yes."

"Good." Cella swung her legs off the table, swiped up her papers, and walked out of the conference room.

Alone now, Toni dropped her head on the table. Not even lunch yet and she wanted to walk into traffic.

This had been a huge mistake. Huge. Gigantic. What had she been thinking? And even worse, she'd been getting calls and texts from her siblings all morning. It seemed that everything was currently a mess at home and now here. All because of her, as far as she was concerned.

"Hi!"

Toni's head snapped up and she looked at the woman standing in the doorway.

"I'm Kerri," the woman said, her smile bright.

Toni nodded.

"Your secretary." Oh, God. She had a secretary now? What

for? "Although I prefer admin, if that's okay. Or assistant. What-ever." The woman was so . . . perky. She couldn't possibly be a shifter.

"Yeah," she said, as if reading Toni's mind. "I'm a full-human. Married to a wonderful hyena. I love his Clan. You know, when I first met him, I totally thought he was a woman, just big-boned, but then I found out he's actually a man. He laughs at everything, like at my cousin's funeral, which was awkward, but I just adore him. So you're a . . ." She pointed a finger at her. "Jackal, right?"

Toni nodded. "That's so cool! I wish I were a shifter. Being full-human is okay. I mean I'm healthy and not unattractive. But to be able to shift into an entirely different species . . . that's so cool!"

"Uh-huh."

"Anyway, your office is finally ready."

"Office?" The bobcat had put her at a desk not far from his own, and Toni hadn't thought much about it. It was small but would do for her purposes.

"Floyd didn't tell you, right?" Kerri asked with an eye roll. "Typical. You started so quickly after being hired that we didn't have much time to set up your office. And I was making sure it was all going perfectly, so I'm very sorry I wasn't there to greet you when you got in and that you had to deal with *Floyd*." She stuck out her tongue and crossed her eyes. Seconds later, her big smile returned. "Okay! So let's go see your new office!"

Ricky had his head back and was staring up at the ceiling. There had to be a way out of this. There had to be. He was a strong, confident wolf who'd traveled the world. And yet he couldn't seem to come up with any way to get these two She-wolves out of his office.

Ronnie was still talking, practically in tears, while Sissy Mae did that annoying repeating thing.

"I know you're trying to get over this," Ronnie Lee said.

"Trying so hard," Sissy agreed.

"That you're pretending her being here doesn't bother you."

"Pretending. Such pretending."

"But we're here for you."

"We are so *here* for you."

Just when Ricky was entertaining the idea of jumping out the window, there was a short knock at the door, and without waiting for an answer, Rory pushed it open.

"Hey, Ricky, I need you to—"

A job folder in his hands, Rory stopped mid-step, his gaze bouncing back and forth between Ronnie and Sissy.

"What are y'all doin'?"

Ronnie put her hand on Ricky's shoulder. "Just talking to my brother. Is that all right with you?"

Rory lowered the folder. "Tell me you two aren't still going on about Laura Jane."

"Well, it's not like you care, Rory Lee!"

"Because I don't care! Neither does this idiot!" Rory stomped over to Ricky, grabbed his forearm, and yanked him out of the chair. "Now if you don't mind, we have actual work to do." Rory shoved the folder into his hand. "This client is having a problem with his system. Go take a look at it."

Practically running, Ricky headed out of his office. "I'm on it!"

"This conversation isn't over, Ricky Lee!" Ronnie yelled after him. "You're going to have to face this at some point!"

Inside the elevator, Ricky gave a quick wave to a still giggling Mindy while he rammed the first-floor button until the doors closed. Then he let out a breath and said, "Not if I can help it."

Toni sat at her giant mahogany desk with the state-of-the-art computer system, three HD monitors—why she'd need more than one monitor, she didn't know—and her ergonomically designed leather executive chair. She sat and she silently freaked out.

It was a gift she had, silently freaking out. Most people, especially her family, did it loudly with much crying and yelling. Using the excuse of being artists, they were always very emotional, but Toni could never afford to do that. Someone in her family had to at least *appear* calm and rational.

This was true even if she were a total and complete mess. As Toni currently was at the moment. And she had been for the last three hours, through lunch, and several phone meetings, while she sat at her fancy new desk and silently freaked out.

"Hi, boss!" Kerri said as she walked into the office. She'd quickly become familiar, something Toni normally didn't mind. But she hated that Kerri kept calling her "boss." She wasn't a boss. She'd never be a boss. At least not a good one.

"Oh, I forgot to tell you earlier. Mr. Van Holtz is out of the office for a few weeks, but he handpicked me and didn't want you to be fooled by my extremely perky nature and tendency to tell too much information about myself. He says that I'm really good at what I do and disgustingly loyal. He thinks we'll get along great—and so do I!"

She sat in the chair across from Toni. "So, now that we have a few minutes, let's discuss my role." She flipped open the top of the leather folio she had in her hand, the PC tablet fired up and ready for her notes. "What do you need from me?"

Toni sat and stared at the woman, her eyes wide.

"Ma'am?"

"I can't do this," Toni finally admitted. "I don't know what I'm doing. I don't belong here." Toni jumped to her feet. "I've gotta go."

"Go? Now? But Miss Jean-Louis—"

"I just . . . yeah."

Swinging her backpack over one shoulder, Toni walked out of her office, down the hall, and to the elevator. As the elevator headed up, she began to write her resignation letter in her head.

Of all her bad ideas, taking this job had been the worst. But that was okay. She'd be fixing that as soon as she got home. She just had to get out of here first.

★   ★   ★

Ricky really did love rich people. Why? Because they paid for everything. Things that the rest of the world thought nothing of doing themselves, the rich insisted on hiring other people to do for them. For instance . . . rebooting the monitoring system. What did rebooting entail? Pressing the restart key on the PC keyboard until the system restarted. That was it. Then everything would start up again and go back online.

The owner of this system knew that information. It was something the company always told all of their clients. Information many of them appreciated and used. But the richer the client, the less they seemed to want to help themselves. Especially the clients who were born into their wealth. They were so used to others doing for them that even the simplest task required a staff.

But Ricky didn't care about any of that because he'd just earned his company a little extra cash by rebooting a computer, double-checking that the cameras were working, and chatting up a client for an hour or so, something Ricky didn't mind doing. He enjoyed talking to people even when they had nothing in common. You just never knew what you might learn from talking to strangers.

Even better, once Ricky was done with that client, he did an evaluation for another wealthy family and was now done for the day. Realizing it was nearly four, he decided to go see how Toni was doing the first day of her job. He recognized the look of terror on her face when she'd understood that limo was for her. Most people would run, jump, and skip into the backseat, but she just looked . . . confused, then panicked.

He walked in through the huge glass doors of the Sports Center. This was the main floor where the full-humans congregated. Here they could find all sorts of kid sports for future athletes, including gymnastic classes, basketball, ice skating, hockey, whatever. There were adult facilities, too. But to get to the real heart of this place, one had to descend to the lower floors where all the professional tri-state shifter sports teams trained and had their home games. That's where the real entertainment was, but Ricky didn't quite make it down there . . .

She stood with her back against a pillar, one leg bent at the knee, the foot pressed against the concrete behind her. Long brown hair reaching her slim waist, bright green eyes ever watchful, cheekbones as sharp as her tongue. She smiled as soon as she saw him and he knew she'd been waiting for him.

He walked up to her, nodded his head. "Laura Jane."

"Hey, Ricky Lee. Your brother told me you'd be here."

"Rory or Reece?"

"Reece."

That made sense. If Reece thought he'd have a shot at nailing Laura Jane, he'd tell her anything she wanted to know. Not that Ricky blamed his baby brother. All these years and Laura Jane still looked good. Even at seventeen, there'd been something very sultry about her and it was still there, but now it had matured, been honed into something lethal.

"So what do you need, Laura Jane?"

"Well, I came to visit my kin for a couple of weeks, and your sister has not been making it easy."

"What do you want me to do about that?"

"I figure if we can show her there's no hard feelings about what happened all those years ago, she'd back off a little."

Ricky doubted it, but he was curious to see where this was going.

"And how should we show her that? That there's no hard feelings, I mean?"

Laura Jane gave one of those slow, drawn-out shrugs. The kind that used to drive him wild when he was seventeen. "Maybe we could go have dinner. Talk about old times. Show your sister there's nothin' to worry about anymore."

"You know, Laura Jane, that sounds like a real nice idea but . . ."

Ricky Lee's words of refusal faded away when Toni sprinted past him in that uncomfortable-looking suit. Charging right behind her was some full-human gal who kept calling her name.

"Uh . . . excuse me, Laura Jane. I've gotta . . ." Ricky didn't bother finishing, just went after the two women, catching up to them at the corner.

"What happened?" he asked.

"I have to go," Toni said, her arm out as she tried to hail a cab.

"But Ms. Jean-Louis," the full-human protested, "I'm sure this will work out."

"Nope. It won't. I've gotta go."

Yup. That was panic. Ricky knew the signs.

"Tell them I quit," Toni barked, her arm waving wildly at any and every cab that passed.

"Don't tell them anything," Ricky ordered the full-human, his arm going around Toni's waist and lifting her off the ground. "Just say she left for the day. Okay?"

"Yes, sir." She reached into the back pocket of her jeans and pulled out a set of keys and a piece of paper. "This is also for Ms. Jean-Louis."

Ricky nodded and, with Toni in his arms, stepped in front of an available cab. The cab screeched to a halt, and while the driver cursed at them, Ricky carried Toni to the back of the cab and pushed her inside.

He looked at the full-human. "She's gone for the day," he reminded her again. "That's all that needs to be said."

Grinning, appearing relieved, the full-human nodded. "Gone for the day. I'll take care of it."

Once in the cab, Ricky closed the door and gave the driver—who was still cursing at him—Toni's address.

When the driver finally pulled back into traffic, Ricky looked over at the She-jackal who was curled into the corner of the cab—panting.

"So, darlin'," he asked, "how did your day go?"

The wolf reached into the cab and insisted on dragging her out.

"No!" she argued, slapping at his hands. "I said take me to LaGuardia! This is not LaGuardia!"

"Come on. Once we get you inside and get you some ice cream or some hot chocolate—"

"No!"

"—you'll feel much better."

"Stop being so rational!" She grabbed the inside door handle on the opposite side and held on.

"Now, darlin'," he said, "don't make me get a pinch collar and a leash."

"I hate you! I hate my parents! I hate my brothers and sisters! And I blame you for all of this!" Toni knew she was being irrational, but she simply did *not* care.

"You're absolutely right," the wolf soothed. "And you should go inside right now and tell them all exactly how you're feelin'!"

Toni stopped trying to kick the wolf in the face and thought on that.

"Yes. I really should tell them how much they've screwed up my life!"

She scrambled out of the cab, yanking her bag repeatedly when the strap got caught on the door.

"I'm going to tell all of them exactly what I'm thinking!"

"Good." The wolf easily removed the strap from the car door. She saw him reach back into the cab and hand the driver money.

Angry at the world, Toni headed up the stairs and into her parents' rental house. But before she could say a word or take a step farther, Kyle ran into the hallway from the library.

"She's here!" he yelled. "She's back!"

And like locusts, they descended on her. Her mother. Her siblings. Her father and Cooper tried to stop them, but it was no use.

"You have to do something," Oriana ordered. "Mom can't schedule to save her or my life. I've already missed *three* classes today!"

Troy pushed Oriana out of the way. "I need you to arrange a meeting with the head of the math department at Columbia. Aunt Irene called him, but she ended up arguing with the guy."

"Because he's an idiot," Aunt Irene complained from the stairs. "At least whoever I actually spoke to that refused to let me talk to the head of the math department is an idiot. And obviously jealous."

"Jealous of what?" Troy demanded.

"That I easily raise more money for my department than he does." Irene came down the stairs, a duffel bag in her hand. "Plus, I have, according to your Uncle Van, amazing legs."

"Is that why you're walking all slow and sexy down the stairs?" Cooper teased.

"Yes." Irene pushed her way through the children and handed Toni the bag. Then she turned her around and pushed her toward the door.

"Wait," Kyle said. "Where is she going? Why is she leaving? *Stop this madness!*"

The door closed behind Toni and she could hear the arguing continue as she walked back down the steps and met up with the wolf.

"That went well," he said.

"I can't go in there," she admitted. "I can't handle them right now." She looked around. "But I have nowhere to go." She let out a sigh. "I hate my life."

"Come on," Ricky said.

"Where are we going?"

"I'm not exactly sure," he said, not making the least bit of sense. "But I swear, entertainment seems to follow you around, like a puppy after its momma. So I am along for the ride, darlin'."

Ricky showed the keys to the doorman and, without question, he sent the pair to the fifteenth floor. Once they arrived, they walked down the hallway to the last apartment. Ricky unlocked the door and together they stepped in.

"Wow." Toni sighed as she entered and looked around. "Your apartment is amazing."

"This ain't my apartment."

Toni stopped, faced him with wide eyes. "Are we doing some illegal Smith thing?"

That made Ricky chuckle. Everybody thought the Smith

Pack was always running around doing illegal shit. And, mostly, they were. But that wasn't how Ricky and his brothers were raised. Their momma didn't like "the criminal types," so she made sure that none of her boys were. Too bad she didn't really convey that attitude to her daughter, too, but Ronnie had cleaned up her act since the Pack had moved to New York and she'd mated with that big-haired lion male.

"No, darlin', we're not doing anything illegal. This isn't my apartment, but I think it's yours."

Toni blinked and her back snapped straight. "What? What are you talking about?"

"This is your apartment. You were having a meltdown in the cab when that little full-human handed me the keys and this address." He held out the sheet of paper the full-human had written the address on. Toni snatched it out of his hand and gawked at it.

"Maybe she was hitting on you," Toni said desperately. "You're cute. She was probably trying to lure you to her house so she could hook up with you."

"Awww. You think I'm cute?"

"Good God, would you focus?"

"No need to blaspheme."

"I don't even know what that means."

"You might as well accept that this beautifully furnished home is yours."

"Lies!"

Ricky pointed at the two dozen white roses on the long table underneath a mirror. "The card by these flowers has your name on it."

"What?" She snatched up the card, tore it open, and read out loud, " 'Because it's time you had a place of your own. Ric.' "

"See?"

"See?" she repeated back to him, her eyes locking on him. "*See?* Don't you understand? This is a *nightmare!*"

"You know what?" Ricky placed the duffel bag back in Toni's hand and turned her toward the bedrooms. "Why don't you go change out of that uncomfortable-looking suit?"

"Why does everyone hate this suit?"

"We don't. We hate you *in* that suit. You're clearly not comfortable."

"I know. I'm so miserable."

Ricky gave her a little push. "Go change. I'll order us some food. Chinese work for you?"

"Whatever."

Ricky dropped his head in case Toni looked back and saw him laughing.

Such a cute, confusing little thing. But, again, entertaining. Really, truly entertaining.

CHAPTER TEN

Toni eventually forced herself out of the bedroom where she'd changed clothes and into the dining room. An array of Chinese food covered the long wooden table as well as white plates; knives, forks, and spoons; and linen napkins.

"Are you expecting company?" she asked the wolf as he came in through the swinging doors with a bottle of wine and two crystal wineglasses.

"Nope. Why?"

"This seems like a lot of food."

He studied the table. "Really?"

Shaking her head and deciding not to pursue it, Toni asked, "Did you get the plates and silverware from a neighbor or something?"

"This stuff was already in the cabinets."

"You're kidding."

"This apartment is ready to go, darlin'. Stuff for the bed, towels for the bathroom, soap, toothbrushes, shampoo, even that really soft toilet paper. Anything you could want is here."

Toni pulled out one of the dining chairs, dropped into the seat, and planted her face on the table. She heard another chair being pulled out, and the wolf sat down next to her, turning the chair so he could face her.

"All right. Talk to me, darlin'. You're not insane. A little crazy, but not insane. And this . . . everything you've gotten in the last few days . . . do you know how many people would kill for all this?"

"But," she said, slowly lifting her head, "those people would be qualified."

"You are qualified."

"I'm not." She finally admitted the truth that embarrassed her. "I've never had a job."

"What do you call taking care of your family?"

"Not a job. There are loads of women and men in this world who help raise their younger siblings. There's absolutely nothing special about me."

When the wolf laughed at her, Toni's hands curled into fists and she snarled, "You know what? You can take this Chinese food and shove it up your goddamn—"

"Whoa, whoa, whoa. I'm not laughing at you. I'm laughing at how you don't think what you do is work. You know, I'm part of a Pack. And when you're in a Pack, you help take care of the younger pups. That's just how it is. Me and my brother Rory had to manage twenty pups under the age of eleven during a Reed family reunion one summer. It was only for an hour and it was the longest gosh-darn hour of my life. Especially since the Reeds fight really rough when they're pups. But you know what? Still easier dealing with those mean little bastards than you having to deal with your siblings. Do you know why?" She shook her head. "Because most pups are kind of stupid. Cute . . . but stupid. It's just about keeping them from doing any permanent injury to each other. You, however, have prodigies. Mean, determined little prodigies. Ten of them. Darlin', that's a job."

"Okay, yeah!" she exclaimed. "I'm the world's best babysitter. But *this* job . . . I was on the phone with some Russian guy who wanted Novikov in a cage and then there are all these rules about the hotel situations when the team travels. Some guys can't room together. And every time I see the coach her knuckles are bloody and I can't figure out if that's a subtle threat of some kind. And then they gave me this big office and an assistant and she's really nice even though she's mated with a hyena and I got this laundry list of stuff to do from at least six of the players and now I'm confused because I feel like I'm their assistant and Ric isn't even in town so I can't ask him anything and it seems that coach doesn't want to be asked about a goddamn thing she just keeps yelling at me because I don't know anything and apparently that's just not acceptable even though it's only my first day and—"

"Okay. Okay!" The wolf took her hands and held them. "Take a breath." He paused, then added, "Let it out. I want you breathing."

He leaned down a bit and kept staring at her until she looked him in the eye.

"I'm going to be direct with you right now. All right?"

Toni nodded at him.

"And I'm going to say what my momma said to me once . . . you need to balls up."

Blinking, Toni leaned back.

That hadn't been exactly what she'd expected . . .

"Balls up? That's your recommendation to me?"

"I'm giving you my momma's wisdom."

"Thanks. That's great. I'm going to eat now. Can you hand me those egg rolls?"

"Now wait, don't just dismiss this."

"I'm not. I'm just deciding to eat rather than locate my missing testes."

Ricky took the egg roll out of her hand.

"I was eating that," she protested.

"I took it anyway."

"Whatever." She reached for another egg roll.

"And that's your mistake," he announced.

Her mouth around the egg roll, Toni muttered, "Wha?"

"Do you know what happened when I took a pork chop from my sister?" He held up his forearm and Toni winced at the scar there. "That's from where she took a chunk out of me. Then she took her pork chop back and ate it while my mother tried to stop the bleeding. You know why?"

Toni swallowed her food. "She's psychotic?"

"Some might say. But really she's just a predator. That's what predators do."

"Okay. And?"

"And you're used to working with full-humans. Rich, fancy ones who think stealing someone's company out from under them is being predatory. And your family is used to dealing with full-humans. They know they have to act a certain way in order to do well in their chosen fields because it's full-humans giving them the money or hiring them for the jobs."

"Yeah. I guess."

"But that's not what you're dealing with at this job. Now you're dealing with predators. Ones that get on the ice and bash the shit out of each other for money."

"Couldn't you say the same thing about any pro team? Shifter or not?"

"Not really. Think about it. The team doctor has a specialty in artery repair and their team insurance includes fang-loss as a long-term disability. These are not full-human concerns, but they're ours."

"So what do I do?"

"Treat them all like you treat Kyle. He's the only one of your brothers and sisters that you don't hold back on."

"What about Oriana?"

"You're too worried she'll get an eating disorder. But Kyle is too arrogant to bother with any of that. So treat the team, including the coach, like bigger, stronger, stupider versions of Kyle."

"And what if that blows up in my face?"

"You were all ready to quit anyway. What could you lose with one more day trying it my way? Plus . . . you get to keep this place for a whole other day."

"You are way too attached to this apartment."

"Did you see the size of that TV in the living room?"

He spotted her right away. And had followed her for at least an hour. She captivated him. The way she seemed to float everywhere. The way she kept that small smile, no matter what was going on around her in this horrible city. There was just something about her that he couldn't put his finger on, but it called to him.

And he knew if it called to him, it would call to Chris.

She walked on. Easing through the busy streets, seemingly untouched by all those around her. She glided. She glowed. All men noticed her, some spoke to her, but they didn't try to stop her. They didn't try to impede her progress. And she seemed not to notice them. She stopped for a while by the street artists, studying their work. Briefly discussing what she saw, but even that didn't keep her for long.

Finally, she walked down a street he'd come to know so well since he'd moved to this horrible city and, to his shock, she walked up the stone steps to his true home and sat down in the middle, her back facing the big double doors.

He finally approached, crouching beside her. He gently took her hand and her head turned toward him, big blue eyes focusing on him.

"You search for something," he told her. "You search for truth. For joy. For happiness. You search and, finally, you've found it."

She said nothing, merely stared at him with those blue eyes, that same small smile on her lips.

"Come with me. Let me show you the truth. Let me show you the way. He's waiting for you."

She nodded. "All right."

With that commitment, he led her up the stairs. He knocked once and the doors were opened. He smiled and nodded at the acolytes who protected the doors. He could see their jealousy. They also knew that he was bringing in something extraordinary.

He led her through the temple. As they walked, she looked around, blue eyes taking it all in. But she asked no questions, did not question him or his motives. Simply let him lead her through his home, his hand holding hers.

He stopped in front of double doors deep inside the temple

and waited, giving her a brave smile. She merely stared back at him.

He didn't knock. He didn't have to. Eventually the doors opened and Chris stood there. He studied her, learned who she was just by looking at her. Chris could see into a person's soul, understand their needs and wants, and then help them find the truth about their lives.

Chris was their Savior, and soon, the world would know it.

"I'm Chris," he said, holding out his hand.

"I'm Delilah."

"I'm here to help you," Chris explained. "To guide you to the light."

Delilah dropped her hand into his, stared at Chris with those big blue eyes, and replied, "Okay."

The TV *was* nice and the perfect end to a perfectly shitty day. After downing more of that Chinese food than she'd thought she would, they ended up crashed on the couch, watching true crime shows and eating gourmet butter pecan ice cream that was already in the freezer.

"You've gotta love the defense attorneys," Ricky said after swallowing another spoonful of his ice cream. "No matter how much bull their clients are trying to pass off, they always seem to go along for the ride."

"Defense attorneys are important. You never know when you're going to need one."

"Planning to kill your third husband the way you killed your first husband so that you can get the life insurance and buy more Chanel bags, are you?"

"I'm not planning to do anything. Life is too short to spend a moment in prison. But you never know when you might be falsely accused. It happens more than people want to realize. And if it happens to me, I'd like to know that there's a defense attorney out there who's going to save my ass."

"Do you sit around worrying about being falsely accused all the time?"

"Not all the time." She shrugged at his one raised eyebrow. "I worry. That's what I do."

"And you're damn good at it."

"Yes, yes. I know. That's all I do. Sit around and worry about my family." But if she didn't worry about her family, who would? Some cutthroat agent? Some reality show producer? Toni shuddered at the thought.

"Is that why y'all broke up?"

"Excuse me?"

"Why you broke up?" Ricky asked again.

"Broke up with who . . . ?" she thought a moment. "Or is it whom?"

"Broke up with your last boyfriend?"

"Why are you asking about that?"

"Just curious."

"Well, be curious about something else."

"Breakup was that bad, huh?"

Toni rolled her eyes. "Is giving me that pity look supposed to get me to tell you everything about my last relationship?"

"That won't work? Because it's worked on others with equally large breasts as yours."

"No, that won't work." But Toni laughed in spite of herself.

"Come on," he pleaded with a smile. "Tell me somethin'. Toss this wolf a bone."

"All right, all right. He was full-human—"

"Mistake number one."

"Are you going to let me finish or comment on each new revelation?"

"Okay. Finish."

"He was—is—full-human and an eye surgeon. He was nice but very . . . particular."

"About your sexy times?"

"Again . . . *no*. But thanks for grossing me out." She shrugged. "He was just particular about how things should go. He seemed to be on a schedule."

"I figured you'd like a man with a schedule."

"Not when that schedule specifically involves me."

"Let me guess . . . he wanted marriage, right?"

"What makes you think that?"

"All full-humans want marriage. Waste of money, in my opinion."

"That's what my parents would say anytime I asked why they weren't married. Funny thing was, my ex's mother used to constantly ask when my parents were going to get married rather than living in sin. Her words. Yet my dad was home every night with his mate—"

"Hence the many pups."

"Exactly. While my ex's dad was banging his secretaries. But *my* parents are the ones living in sin? Really?"

"Full-humans do love to judge."

Toni gave a small shrug. "I don't know. Shifters can be judgmental."

Ricky waved his spoon. "No, no. It is not the same. Our kind are born with preconceived notions about each other. Cats hate dogs. Wolves hate coyotes. Nobody trusts the foxes, and everybody fears the momma grizzly. These are givens based on centuries of surviving in the wild together and putting up with each other's bullshit when eating at a Van Holtz restaurant."

He did have a point.

"So what happened?" he asked again. "*Did* he push for marriage?"

"He did. But that wasn't the main problem." Toni brought her legs up and turned her body so she could face the wolf, suddenly eager to have this conversation. She could have talked to Coop when it happened, but he'd been on tour. She could have spoken to Cherise, too, but she took it so personally when anyone hurt any of her siblings that Toni didn't want to be responsible for what she might do out of anger. There was also Livy, Toni's best friend. But if upsetting Cherise was a bad idea, then upsetting Olivia Kowalski, American-born, Chinese-Polish daughter of two take-no-shit immigrants was a mistake on a global scale.

"The main problem was that he couldn't understand the connection I have to my family."

"Of course he couldn't," the wolf said flatly. "Do you really think some full-human gal can understand leaving my bed some morning, walking out into my living room, and finding my entire Pack snoring on my floor or eatin' my yogurt while they watch the Brickyard 400?"

"Am I supposed to know what that is?"

He sighed, long and deep. "Poor, pretty Yankee. That's NASCAR, darlin'. You do know what *that* is, right?"

"Yes," she replied eagerly. "Troy and Freddy like to watch it for mathematical and scientific reasons—I think they're secretly planning to build a car. Kyle likes to watch it because he says it's fun to see what the"—and she used air quotes here—" 'average' human being does in his or her time off."

"It must be hard for ol' Kyle to be so—"

"Arrogant? Rude? Condescending?"

"I was just going to say snotty, but those words work, too."

"He's really not that awful," she admitted. "Unfortunately . . . he doesn't *know* he's not that awful."

"I have to say, though . . . I like Kyle."

"You do? Because you're one of the very few."

"I like his attitude."

"Really?"

"Oh, yeah. You know why?"

"No idea whatsoever."

"Because he is what he is. I like that in a canine."

"You're an odd man."

He scraped the last bit of melted ice cream at the bottom of his bowl. "Some might say."

"So," Ricky asked as he placed the empty bowl on the coffee table, "how did it end with your boyfriend?"

"I did something . . . reprehensible."

Ricky leaned back and waited for her to tell him what that was rather than pushing her. And she did tell him.

"I left him alone with Kyle."

"You are a cruel woman."

"I know, I know. I still feel bad about it. The man graduated from Harvard Medical School, and by the time Kyle was done with him, he had to take a sabbatical from the hospital."

Ricky started laughing at the full-human's weakness.

"It's not funny. I still don't know what Kyle said to him, but he was only in there for ten minutes. Fifteen tops. I thought he was just going to scare him off or something. Prove to him that my entire family was a bunch of spoiled brats that no normal man would want to be around. But it turned out Kyle really didn't like him. At all." She grimaced. "I think he was crying when he left. And Kyle was smiling . . . then again so was my dad, Coop, and Freddy."

"If your daddy didn't like him, that should have been a clue."

"My father has never liked any of my boyfriends."

"All full-human?"

"That's who I was around. Except for the Van Holtz Pack, but all that Pack talks about is cooking. I still make Hamburger Helper."

"I love Hamburger Helper."

She grinned. "Me, too. Any time we know Uncle Van is out of town, we invite Aunt Irene and her kids over and I make a big batch of Hamburger Helper for everybody."

"Why when he's out of town?"

She was quiet for a moment before saying, "Everything is pretty much a joke to my uncle Van except three things. His daughter, Ulva, who I decked once during a family soccer game because she made Cherise cry; the cleanliness of his kitchen; and his food. Uncle Van takes his food very, very seriously. So, yeah, we keep our Hamburger Helper nights completely top secret. And you better never tell, either."

"Your secret is safe with me. The Reeds are known for the ability to keep our mouths shut. In fact, I have a couple of cousins in Midwest prisons just for that reason."

"You know that is something I'd suggest *not* telling people."

"Funny, my momma says the same thing."

"You should listen to her."

Toni's phone rang, and she pulled it out of the backpack she had resting against the couch.

"Fancy phone," he said while she stared at it.

"It's the one I got at the job . . . and yet Kyle already has the number."

Ricky chuckled and Toni answered her phone. "Yes, Kyle? No, Kyle. No, you may not tell her she's fat. Because she's not and because it's wrong. No, you cannot push her into an eating disorder. No, you cannot convince Troy that Dad isn't really his father and he's really the slow boy Mom adopted. Can't you all just work together?" Sighing loudly, Toni closed her eyes and Ricky saw all the tension that had eased out of her over the last couple of hours come right back up. "No, you are *not* superior. You are one of us and you *will* work together. Goddammit, Kyle, I am not playing around." She looked at her watch. "Fine. I'll be home in—"

That's when Ricky snatched the phone out of her hand and while she watched, he crushed the little technological marvel in his fist. "Uh-oh . . . look at what I just did. My big, clumsy wolf hands crushed your itty-bitty fancy phone. You know what that means?"

"That you're insane?"

"No. That ol' Ric Van Holtz is gonna be real upset with me because he'll have to get you a new one. So upset he'll have to send Dee-Ann Smith to pummel me because he can't risk bruising those lily-white hands of his."

"Don't pick on Ric. He's one of my favorite not-really-cousins."

" 'Not really cousins'?"

"With a hyphen between each word. In other words, he's like family but not by blood."

"So you just make up ridiculous terms for no reason?"

"Pretty much."

Ricky shrugged. "Okay. So you wanna make out?"

"No, I do *not*."

He stared at her, waited about a minute, then asked, "What about now?"

"No!" But she was laughing and no longer tense.

"If I wait another five minutes . . . ?"

"The answer will remain the same."

"But I'm crashing here tonight—"

"When did I invite—"

"—and you can't expect me to just lie out here all alone with a beautiful woman in the very next room . . . can you?"

"Yes, I can."

"Heartless."

"So Kyle has told me." Toni relaxed back against the couch and smiled at him. "Thank you."

"You're welcome." Ricky also relaxed back, his shoulder pressed against hers. "Since I can't get you to make out with me . . . what about massaging my head?"

"What?"

"Please?"

"You mean like a . . . scalp message?"

"It's my favorite thing. And you got them strong hands. Plus"—he pulled off his Tennessee Titans baseball cap—"I've got a great head of hair. All shiny, smooth, and silky. When I'm around Mitch Shaw, I make sure to shake my hair out to make him jealous of its beauty."

She frowned a bit. "Is Mitch Shaw a lion?"

"You know him?"

"No. But a wolf mocking a man's hair can only mean he's either talking to a super model . . . or a male lion obsessed with that goddamn mane they all have."

Laughing, Ricky laid his head in Toni's lap and put his feet up on the armrest. "I have to say, darlin', I am liking you more and more."

"I'm learning to tolerate you, too."

Then, to Ricky's delight, Toni dug her fingers into his hair and gave him one of the best scalp massages he'd ever had.

"I'm just doing this," Toni muttered, "because I feel I owe you one for today. You know . . . calming me down and everything." Then, her voice stronger, she snapped, "But don't get used to it or anything. This is a one-time deal. Understood?"

"Sure."

Of course, understanding didn't mean he'd agreed to a damn thing . . .

Ronnie Lee Reed knew the girls were bored. Of course she hadn't told them not to drink. That had been Sissy. Sissy who was clearly enjoying the torment-potential of Ronnie's pregnancy.

"Isn't it great?" Sissy was saying to their fellow She-wolves. "Hanging at this great club and *not* drinking?"

They all muttered, "Yeah. Great." But they were bitter, bitter words.

"It's like we can really *talk* without worrying about liquor clouding our minds. Isn't that right, y'all?"

More muttering followed that, and Ronnie had to quickly tip her head down and focus on something else. Anything else, or she'd bust out laughing. Sissy knew it, too. This was how the pair of them had entertained themselves for years. It was wrong, Ronnie knew. But it was fun.

"Hey, y'all."

Ronnie raised her eyes and looked up at Laura Jane Smith. Funny. She hadn't liked Laura Jane when they were growing up in Tennessee together, and she disliked her even more now.

It had been such a relief when Laura Jane had headed off to stay with the Mississippi Smiths. A large Pack, full of Reed males for her to fuck with. Cousins Ronnie didn't think that much of one way or another. She had kin she was much closer to. Like, you know, her own *brothers*.

It had been the one thing Ronnie and her mother had ever agreed on. How much they disliked the relationship between Ricky Lee and Laura Jane. It wasn't that Laura Jane was, as Sissy liked to call her, "a ho."

Hell. Sissy and Ronnie were hos before they'd settled down with their mates. But they'd known their boundaries. Family wasn't off limits, but if you were just looking for a good time without any commitments, then you stayed away. That's not what Laura Jane did. She'd played Ricky Lee and several other males she'd been with around the same time. Not okay, in Ronnie Lee's book. So having the bitch coming to town to "visit with my favorite kin!" was doing nothing but irritating Ronnie's already sensitive nerves.

Rory Lee kept telling Ronnie to stay out of it. She didn't want to. Females like Laura Jane didn't understand subtlety. But she could tell that Ricky was avoiding her, and Ronnie didn't like that, either. If anyone should feel awkward, it should be Laura Jane.

But that one didn't feel much of anything. She was too busy running around, trying to look "sultry." It was the word all the boys had used about her when they were growing up.

Took a lot of effort, if you asked Ronnie Lee. Always posing and making sure your mouth is at its most pouty.

Laura Jane pulled out a chair and dropped into it. "So what are we all doing tonight?"

"Hanging out. Just experiencing life," Sissy Mae offered, her smile large. "Liquor-free."

Laura Jane managed to hold on to her perfectly sultry smile. "Really? How novel."

"So have you been enjoying your visit to our fair city?" Sissy asked her cousin.

"I have. I have. Although it's not really *your* city, is it, Sissy Mae?"

"I live here, don't I?"

"True. But you'll always be a country girl." Laura Jane's eyes narrowed the slightest bit. "Just like the rest of us."

The words were said kindly, but Ronnie wasn't fooled. Neither was Sissy Mae, which was why she was Ronnie's best friend.

Laura Jane looked over at Ronnie. "How ya doin', hon?"

"Fine."

"Got the morning sickness yet?"

"Came and went. Just like my momma."

"Good. Good. My poor sister, Sally? Lord, she went through hell during her pregnancies. Running to the bathroom to throw up nearly every damn day for nine months. Poor thing."

"Uh-huh."

Laura Jane leaned over the table a bit and said to Ronnie, "I went to see your brother today, darlin'."

Ronnie had learned long ago how not to react to just anything. It was a hard-won skill but necessary when one's best friend was Sissy Mae Smith. A She-wolf who was still banned from several countries in Asia and Europe. Of course, so was Ronnie Lee, but that was only because of Sissy Mae. It was *always* only because of Sissy Mae!

"Is that right? How is he doing anyway? Haven't seen him in a day or two. Always so busy, that Ricky Lee."

"He seems fine. Looks good." Laura Jane winked at her, and Ronnie wanted to tear the bitch's eyes out with her fangs. "Surprised about him and that She-jackal, though. It's not like him to use somebody just to get out of an uncomfortable situation. Odd-looking little girl, too. I mean, unless she *paid* to have that hair."

Unable to help themselves, Ronnie and Sissy glanced at each other and back at Laura Jane.

Then Ronnie Lee asked, "She-jackal?"

Chapter Eleven

Toni hadn't needed an alarm clock to get her up in the morning for years, because getting up late meant she'd had to deal with full-blown arguments rather than preventing them. So when the sun streaming through the big windows hit her right in the face, she instantly knew she had to get up. Although her mother made breakfast for all the kids—she loved to talk to her pups in the morning, feed them, and then send them out into the day with her favorite phrase: "You're all equally amazing. Don't let anyone tell you any different."—Toni still had to make sure that the older kids had all their supplies, knew their schedules, and most importantly, took care of basic hygiene. Oriana wasn't a problem, but Kyle and Troy often simply forgot. They became so absorbed in their work or whatever they were studying that things like brushing their teeth, bathing, or changing their socks were considered secondary.

Toni didn't consider them secondary, so she knew she had to get up. But, for some reason, Toni didn't want to get up. She was entirely too comfortable here, face down on this very warm couch that smelled really good. So good, in fact, that Toni ended up rubbing her face against that couch.

That's when the couch growled.

Toni's eyes snapped open at the same time she sat up, realizing to her horror that she'd been asleep *atop* Ricky Lee Reed's chest. Possibly for the entire night!

Amber eyes surrounded by surprisingly long eyelashes opened, and a slow, lazy smile spread across his lips when his gaze locked on her. "Mornin', darlin'."

"Why am I on your chest? Why was I *sleeping* on your chest?"

" 'Cause I'm cuddly?"

It wasn't his stupid question but his voice that made her punch him right in the chest she'd been asleep on. No man, wolf or otherwise, should have a voice that low and sexy this early in the goddamn morning!

"Ow!" he howled, his arms covering his chest. "What was that for?"

It didn't help that he was still grinning at her while he protected himself.

"You know exactly what that was for!" she snarled, then tried to scramble off him. But the wolf caught her by the hips and pulled her right into his lap, her legs straddling his waist.

Toni gasped and glowered down at the big bastard. "Are you hard?" she demanded, feeling something like a lead pipe pressing against her thigh.

That damn smile grew even wider. "Every mornin' like clockwork."

Deciding she had had enough, Toni gripped his hands and pulled them off her waist. She scooted off his lap and stood up, adjusting her clothes as she did. "You are such a—"

"Now, now. No call to get nasty just 'cause you cuddled up to me like I was a big ol' teddy bear."

"Shut up." She started to walk out, only to realize she didn't recognize where she was. "What is this place?"

"Your apartment," the wolf said, his arms slipping behind his head.

"My . . . ?" It all came back to her, and Toni shook her head. "The job. I have to quit that job."

"You're not quitting that job."

"Why not?"

"Because you keep that job and you keep this awesome apartment and that *awesome TV.*"

"What does *my* TV have to do with you?"

"I can't come over and watch it?"

"No!"

"No loyalty among you jackals. Guess the Bible got it right about y'all."

"The Bible is *biased*. Jackals are a wonderful—oh! Why am I arguing with you?" she demanded before marching off toward a doorway.

"Not a morning person?"

"Shut up!"

Silently laughing and enjoying himself thoroughly, Ricky got off the couch and followed after the angry little jackal.

She actually hadn't fallen asleep on him. Or even cuddled up to him. She'd just fallen asleep on the opposite end of the couch, her hands and feet twitching away as she ran in her dreams. And sure, Ricky could have left her over there and slept on his side of the couch, or on the other two couches in the sizable room, but it had been mighty cold in that room . . . once he'd turned the air conditioner up. So he'd pulled her into his arms and she'd happily rested on his chest like she belonged there.

Perhaps not the most honorable way to handle things, but he was a wolf, not some full-human with a lot of rules and regulations about how to run his life.

Besides, she'd felt really good in his arms and had smelled even better.

Like now. All annoyed and everything, she still smelled really good.

He tracked her down into one of the bedrooms, where she stood in front of the chest of drawers.

"What's wrong?" he asked her.

She glanced back at him. "Do you think he bought me clothes?"

"I have to say if he did . . . that would be weird."

"Yeah."

"Especially if they fit perfectly."

"Stop." She opened one of the drawers and blew out a sigh. "Empty. Good. But now I need to go home."

"What about the bag your aunt gave you yesterday?"

"I'm wearing what she gave me."

"She gave you a giant duffel bag with just one set of clothes?"

"Irene's brilliance focuses on other things."

"Other things besides logic?"

"Pretty much." She faced him. "I have to go home so I can get dressed, go back to the Sports Center, and quit my job."

"What about my TV needs?"

Her eyes crossed before she stepped around him and walked out of the bedroom.

"I'll go back with you," he suggested/insisted.

"No. I can make it back on my own."

She grabbed the duffel bag she'd left lying in the hallway and was at the front door when Ricky came up behind her.

"See ya," she said as she opened the door.

"When?"

She stopped, faced him. "What?"

"When will you see me? Tonight? Tomorrow? This weekend?"

"I'm not dating you."

"Who said anything about dating? We're shifters. Shifters don't date. That's for full-humans."

"Then what are you suggesting?"

"Sex. Preferably lots of it."

"Just sex? That's all you want?" she pushed.

"What? Do you like to talk or something?"

"No."

Ricky grinned. "So you just wanna hit it?"

"No! I mean—oh! Why am I having this conversation with you?"

"Because you're intrigued and kind of turned on. It's okay. I know you're used to full-humans and their complicated ways, but it's time for you to learn the ways of your people."

"Or I could never see you again."

"Why would you do that?"

"Because . . . it's just . . . why am I *still having this conversation with you?*" she finished on a yell.

"Well—"

"Shut up!" she spun away from him and stormed out of the apartment.

"You're dang cute when you're angry," he called after her. "Well, damn, darlin'! That gesture was just unnecessary!"

Ricky stepped back into the apartment and went looking for the boots he'd had on last night. While he searched, he laughed the entire time because, yeah . . . this was gonna be *fun*.

Kyle was waiting for his sister to come home. He knew she'd be back to check on them, and when she did, he, Oriana, and Troy had it all worked out. They were going to give her the silent treatment. Show her that they didn't need her. Not like she seemed to think they did. And then, once she understood the depth of her idiocy, they'd again allow her to manage their lives. Because working with his aunt Irene, whom they all adored, was like hell on earth.

That woman was impossible! Blunt to the point of just rude, she would cut Kyle off midsentence in order to inform him that he was wrong and remind him that he was only eleven. He knew he was eleven. He was quite aware of being eleven. He didn't need a reminder of that. Nor did he need his aunt to cut him off while he was speaking. That was intolerable!

Did Michelangelo have to go through this sort of thing? Did Rodin? Kyle doubted it. Brilliance shouldn't be forced to deal with such ridiculous things as schedules and worrying about making people cry.

And of course his dear, sweet, but clueless aunt Irene didn't understand that. She was a scientist. Yes, a brilliant scientist, but just a scientist. She was *not* an artist, so she didn't understand *anything*. She definitely didn't understand things the way Toni did, and Toni was much less terrifying than Aunt Irene, which was very important.

So when Toni got home, Kyle would let her know in no uncertain terms that he and the others would no longer tolerate any more of this ridiculous behavior from her. She had work to do, and that work was here, with her *family*. Not with strangers who did no more than follow a tiny puck around while on skates. Full-blooded bears did that sort of thing in Russia for full-humans' entertainment, so Kyle was not impressed.

Freddy ran into the kitchen, a thick and, Kyle would wager, *boring* book in his hands. He held it up for their father to see.

"Look what came for me, Daddy!"

"What's that?"

"Miki sent me a book about my favorite physicist, Henry Cavendish!"

I was right. Boring.

"I'm going to go bury it in the backyard!" Freddy cheered before charging toward the backdoor.

"You haven't read it yet," their father reminded him.

Freddy stopped, stared at the book in his hands.

Kyle's brother was *such* a canine. If anything was important to him, he buried it in the backyard, which was only really annoying when he panicked, stole something that belonged to someone else, buried it in the backyard, and then refused to tell anyone where. And for such a chatty kid, Freddy really could keep his mouth shut when he felt like it.

"Why don't you have breakfast first," their father suggested, "read the book, then decide if you want to bury it or not."

"It's from Miki," Freddy repeated as if that explained his intense desire to bury the stupid thing.

"Miki who?" Troy asked.

"Kendrick," Oriana replied. "Aunt Irene's mouthy friend."

"She's nice," Freddy said.

"You think everyone's nice."

Their father pulled a chair out at the table. "Freddy, sit. Eat. You always forget to eat."

"Oriana never forgets to eat," Kyle joked. Although he wasn't sure it was worth the trouble when Oriana's bony elbow rammed into his ribs.

"Ow! Dad!"

"Cut it out." Their father's voice was calm, but then again, he rarely yelled at them anyway. He mostly left that to Toni.

Oriana lifted her head, her bowl of oatmeal—and Kyle's vulnerable ribs—forgotten. Her nose twitched. "I think Toni's coming," she whispered to Kyle.

"What do you mean you *think*?"

"I'm still learning to separate smells. And give me that tone again, runt, and I'll bite your nose off."

"Stop it," Troy snapped. "Both of you. Now look cold and indifferent."

Kyle studied his brother. "You always look cold and indifferent."

"Then follow my lead."

They did. Kyle and Oriana sat up straight—well, Oriana had excellent posture so that part was mostly Kyle—and looked across the room, away from the back door that led into the kitchen. Yes. Toni would notice right away that she was being ignored and it would *burn*.

The back door opened and Toni stomped in.

"Hey, baby," their father said while he blatantly fed that flea-bitten mongrel their mother had brought home. What was their father doing with that dog? Didn't he have actual children of his own to care for?

The door slammed shut, and Kyle quickly saw that his big sister was angry. He immediately ran through anything he'd done in the last twenty-four hours that could cause this response, but he'd been home in his room plotting with Oriana and Troy—and avoiding Aunt Irene.

"My TV?" Toni barked. "He's interested in my TV. Unbelievable!" She started walking through the big kitchen. "Damn wolves. I hate wolves!"

"I think your uncle Van will have a problem with that," their father told her as she stormed through, that mongrel pressing itself against his leg. Most likely out of fear.

"Uncle Van can also go to hell." Toni stood by the swinging door that led into the dining room. "In fact . . . *everyone can go to hell!*" she suddenly screamed before she threw the door open and marched through it.

After a few moments of silence from a group that was never silent, Freddy asked, "Aren't you going to go talk to her, Daddy?"

"Oh, no," their father replied with that big smile he always had. What did he have to smile about? "I know that rage. I'm not about to get in front of that."

"You've seen it before?" Oriana glanced around, then asked, "From Toni?"

"No. Your mother. Of course, I'm usually the one causing it." His smile kind of grew. "But not this time. Not with Toni."

"Then who is causing it?"

"It's not one of you, so don't worry about it. But you three"—their father said to Kyle, Oriana, and Troy—"if I were you, I'd let that silent treatment plan lie for now. Just let it lie."

The three of them looked at each other, then at their father and nodded.

Because being brilliant also included knowing when not to risk life and limb by annoying their already raging big sister.

Brendon Shaw kissed the back of his sleeping mate's neck and slipped out of bed, making sure not to wake her.

Now that Ronnie Lee was pregnant, she slept a lot more and got into fistfights a lot less. Not having to wipe her blood-covered knuckles and pay off some supermodel who got a little mouthy in a bar had been a growing pleasure of his.

Naked, Brendon walked out of his bedroom, quietly closing the door behind him, and cut through the living room of the presidential suite of his hotel, the Kingston Arms. Since shifters hadn't had one of their own in the White House since 1909, he used the suite for himself and his family.

Unfortunately for Brendon, his "family" had grown beyond what he'd exactly been hoping for.

Stopping in the middle of his living room and, sighing greatly, he looked over at the kitchen bar where one of Ronnie Lee's worthless brothers stood, eating yogurt and staring at him.

"Mornin'."

"I thought I made it clear to you and your idiot brothers that you were not to just drop by."

"Now, now, big kitty. We're all family. And family is family."

"What the fuck does that even mean?"

Instead of answering, the wolf held up his bowl. "Yogurt?"

"I don't want yogurt. And I told the staff not to stock my refrigerator with that crap anymore."

Brendon had thought by not having the yogurt, he'd have fewer visits from Ronnie Lee's Pack and family.

"You did ask them," the wolf replied. "But we just talked to the wolves on staff and they made sure to set us up right. It was either that or we mock them with our howls at night."

The wolf gestured at Brendon. "Guess you're going to have to start wearing some pants to bed, hoss, once that baby comes along."

Which brother was this again? Oh. Yeah. The middle one. Ricky. He was a little less irritating than Reece Lee and definitely not as uptight as Rory, but he was still a male canine in Brendon's house.

"Eat your food and get out."

"As ya like."

Thinking about changing the locks again but knowing it would be a waste since wolves could pretty much unlock anything they wanted to, Brendon started off again. But he'd barely walked ten paces when the front door opened, and a few seconds later, another one of Ronnie Lee's wolf kin invaded his home.

"There you are," Reece Lee said when he spotted his brother. He stepped into the sunken living room, briefly stopping by Brendon to note, "Guess you'll have to start wearing pants once Ronnie's baby comes."

"It's also my baby, though you and your brothers seem to enjoy forgetting that part."

"Hope your pup—"

"Cub."

"—ain't born with a snaggle-fang like Bobby Lee's mixed-species cousin out of North Carolina. Pretty girl until she shifts, then it's a whole other thing."

"Maybe there'll be tusks like Novikov," Ricky suggested.

"I hate both of you." Brendon sneered.

"Ya can't." Reece patted Brendon's shoulder. "We're all family now. Ain't we?"

"Come and get some of this yogurt, little brother. There's even summer berries in the fridge for mixing in."

"But I like my yogurt the way I like my women," Reece said with a huge grin. "Plain and sour!"

Rolling his eyes, Brendon walked toward the laundry to get some clean clothes and consider the benefits of private schools in Switzerland before the Reed Boys had a chance to spread their Southern logic to Brendon's vulnerable child.

After fixing his own bowl of yogurt, his brother settled down beside Ricky at the bar.

"Where'd you go yesterday?" Reece asked.

"Met a girl," Ricky said around a mouthful of yogurt.

"Anyone I've already fucked?"

"Not this time. You've met her, though. She's one of the new directors for your team. Travel and promotion, I think."

Reece dropped his spoon. "That little rich jackal?"

"Yep."

"You and some rich girl? Daddy would call that a sign of the End of Days."

"Daddy just don't like rich people."

"True. Still . . . she don't seem your speed, big brother. Kind of slow lane for a Reed."

"Never needed a fast car to keep my interest." Ricky finished his food and pushed the bowl away. "Is that why you're here? To ask me about that?"

"Nah. Rory wants us at the office for a morning meeting."

"Why?"

"Big client coming in from the Sports Center. I think they want us to evaluate their fancy security systems."

Ricky nodded. "Perfect. Was planning to go over to the Sports Center anyway and spend some time with my jackal."

"Momma says jackals do the Devil's work."

"My jackal says that's just propaganda."

The pair watched Brendon Shaw walk through his living room, thankfully now wearing sweatpants.

"What about what Momma says about cats being agents of Satan himself?"

The cat stopped, glared over at them. *"Out, canines!"* he roared.

Winking at his grinning brother, Ricky replied, "I'd have to say that Momma was probably right on that one."

A brief knock on the door and Coop walked into Toni's room. "Heard you were up here raging about TVs and wolves. Kyle thinks you've had a mental breakdown from your new job that he insists on calling stupid."

Toni, fresh from the shower and having put on jeans and a T-shirt, quickly combed her wet hair off her face before grabbing socks and her running shoes. "It's nothing." She didn't want to get into it. She didn't want to talk about what had happened between her and that useless wolf.

She sat on the wooden bench by her bed to put her shoes on. "Look, Coop, I have to go into the office, but as soon as I get back—"

"Don't worry about a thing, big sis. I've got it all handled."

Toni stopped tying her laces to look up at her brother. "What do you mean?"

"Cherise and I canceled all our concerts for this summer. We're staying home to take care of the kids."

"You did what?"

"No, no. Don't get upset." Coop crouched in front of her and finished tying her shoelaces for her. "I know what you're thinking, but I needed the break. I've been going nonstop for months. And Cherise . . . let's put it this way. When I made the suggestion, she threw herself into my arms and kissed my face like I'd rescued her from a sinking boat circled by sharks."

"But Coop—"

Done with her laces, Coop placed his hands on her knees and looked deep into Toni's eyes. "You, big sis, deserve this. You *deserve* this. You've taken care of us, now it's our turn to do the same for you. Let us."

"But weren't you supposed to play for the king of—"

"If you've played for one king, trust me, you've played for them all. Our family is more important. And although Aunt Irene is trying to help, she terrifies the kids."

"I know." Toni sighed.

"And a crap-load of computer stuff arrived yesterday and she was up all night in her room putting it together with Troy and Freddy."

"Troy and Freddy were up all night?"

"Only until three, but that's when they usually go to sleep anyway." Very true. Toni tried to get them on a more normal schedule for kids their age, but their minds never stopped turning, never stopped going. When she did order them to bed early, all they did was stay up all night thinking until Freddy began to work himself into an ulcer and Toni found that Troy had written equations all over his bedroom walls. "So I don't forget!" he'd told her when she'd found him at six in the morning with a tiny stub of blue crayon in his hand and wild eyes.

"And you know how Aunt Irene is when she gets into her work," Coop continued. "So you need me and Cherise here. We can help each other and help you. For once."

Toni thought about telling her brother that she was only going into the office to quit the job she was so ill-prepared for, but she didn't have the heart. He was just so damn proud of himself. She hadn't seen him look like that since he was ten and was asked to perform for Queen Elizabeth of England in London. Although he did ask Toni later, "Is that the redheaded one?" Then he'd whispered, "Isn't she dead? Will I be playing for a zombie?" Her fault. She'd let him stay up with her so they could watch *Night of the Living Dead* while their parents were out of the house, and the babysitter was clueless.

"No," Toni had explained. "This is that Elizabeth's, like,

great-great granddaughter or something. She was born, like, a hundred years ago or whatever."

Thankfully Toni's understanding of history had improved with age.

But whichever Elizabeth that had been, Coop had had a look on his face of pure pride then, and he had the same expression now. It meant a lot to him to help his family.

So although Toni was going to quit this job because she was woefully under-qualified, she didn't have to tell her brother that. And maybe, if she was lucky, she could find a job better fit for her skills and Coop could spend the summer helping with the rest of the kids.

Hell, if it made her kid brother happy, who was she to argue?

"Thanks, Coop. I appreciate your help."

"You're welcome."

Toni stood, picked up her backpack. "We'll talk later, okay?"

"Don't worry about it. I know that new job will keep you busy."

"Yeah." Toni started to walk out but stopped. "Can I borrow your phone until later?"

"Sure, but Freddy didn't take that new one you got apart, too, did he?"

"No, no." She took the phone from her brother. "But I don't want to talk about what *did* happen to it."

Toni left the room and walked down the two flights of stairs to reach the front door. With her hand on the knob, she glanced back down the hallway and saw Oriana, Kyle, and Troy suddenly dive into the living room. Only Freddy stood his ground. He waved at her, and Toni smiled, winked, and blew him a kiss.

She walked out of the house and stopped when she came face to face with Delilah.

"Are you just getting home?" Toni asked, glancing at her watch.

"Mhmm."

Delilah tried to move around her, but Toni cut in front of her and asked, "Where have you been, Delilah?"

"Just walking."

Delilah tried to step around her again, and again Toni moved, blocking her. "Walk around where?"

Slowly her sister raised those blue eyes of hers to look at Toni. "Just around."

"You're being careful, right? Manhattan isn't Seattle."

"I know." She gently patted the oversized shoulder bag she always had with her. It kept her drawing pad, notebook, and pencils. It was her ability to draw like artists thirty years her senior that had made Delilah a prodigy. But that wasn't why Toni still kept a close watch on her eighteen-year-old sister. No. It wasn't her skills as an artist that made Delilah so unique . . . and they both knew it.

"Don't worry about me, Toni." Delilah stroked her fingers gently down the side of Toni's face, and it took all of Toni's strength not to flinch away from that touch. "I'm always careful."

"I know."

With that soft smile, Delilah moved around Toni and headed inside.

"But it's not really you I'm worried about . . . is it, little sister?" Toni said to Delilah's back.

In the doorway, Del slowly turned around, her head dipping down a bit as she focused on Toni. Her smile spread—stretched—into a leer before she closed the door in Toni's face.

Toni released the breath she always held whenever she attempted to figure out what the fuck her sister was up to.

Deciding she didn't have time for this, Toni headed down the steps but stopped when she reached the second-to-last step and saw Johnny DeSerio standing in front of the wild dogs' house and staring across the street. He was a young wolf and yet he wasn't moving. That seemed strange. Young canines were known for their high energy.

Concerned, Toni waited until traffic cleared and jogged across the street until she reached Johnny.

"Are you okay?" she asked.

"My feet stopped moving," he muttered. "I've lost the ability to walk."

"Okay. But you are standing. Standing is good. So there's been no damage to your spinal cord."

Toni moved around until she stood right beside him.

"I see you have your violin," she noted.

"Do I? Maybe I should leave it inside. I'm not very good."

"That's not what my mother says."

"Your mother is a foolish woman!" he suddenly exploded, and Toni had to move fast to stop herself from laughing. Biting the inside of her cheek definitely helped. When she finally got control, Toni placed her hand on his forearm.

"Would you like to get a cup of coffee with me?"

"I want to hide in my basement."

"I know, but I think coffee and maybe some breakfast would probably be better." She tugged his arm. "Come on. There's a coffee shop down the street."

"You really have nothing better to do than have coffee with me?" he asked.

Toni shrugged, figuring she could quit at any time. "Nope. Nothing better to do."

Chapter Twelve

They ended up in a Starbucks at the end of the street, and Toni not only got the wolf to drink a large cup of coffee, she also got him to eat several cinnamon buns and three pieces of coffee cake. Not the healthiest breakfast, but she was sure he'd work it off.

"So what is it?" she asked him when she knew Johnny was calmer. "What has you so worried?"

"Everything."

Toni smiled. "Everything, huh? So . . . the economy? Wars in other countries? Who'll win this year's Super Bowl? That everything?"

"Since I don't care about any of that . . . no."

"That's what I figured. So what is it? Really?"

"What if I'm not as good as your mother thinks?" he finally asked, taking a huge leap of faith in showing Toni his weakness, his true fear.

"You have to be," Toni stated bluntly, "because when it comes to *this,* my mother is never wrong. She's completely useless at the most basic things like math, keeping the tenses straight when she's speaking Italian, and unless she's making breakfast, she'll most likely set the house on fire if she tries to cook a meal. But when it comes to music . . . when it comes to what you do . . . my mother is never wrong."

"But"—he shoved another bit of crumb cake into his mouth—"what if she's wrong *this* time? About *me?*"

"Because you have that kind of power, right? Quite the narcissism you've got going there," she teased.

He gazed at her for a long moment before admitting, "You're right. I'm pathetic." Then he dropped his head to the table and sighed . . . dramatically.

Crossing her eyes, Toni eased her brother's cell phone out of her pocket and, keeping it under the table, quickly texted her mother. It was a skill she'd developed over the years . . . texting without looking. She'd learned it from Oriana, and it was a skill she was glad to have because of times just like these.

Starbucks on corner. It's Toni.
Need you. Another stu bout 2 b destroyed
By yer awesomeness

After a few minutes of staring at the top of Johnny's head, Toni saw her mother rushing down the street. She skidded to a halt when she reached the Starbucks doorway, took a breath, pushed her hair off her face, and calmly sauntered into the café.

Again, Toni only managed not to laugh by biting the inside of her cheek.

Jackie casually ordered a chai tea from one of the baristas before *casually* sauntering over to their table.

Her mother had become the queen of being casual after lots of self-training.

"Hey, baby," she said to Toni. "What are you doing . . . wait. Johnny? What are *you* doing here?"

The wolf's head came off the table, and he blinked wide, panicked brown eyes at Jackie.

Jackie pretended to think, her forefinger tapping her chin. "Don't we have an appointment right now?"

"I'm sorry, Ms. Jean-Louis. I . . . I . . . it's just . . ."

"Don't worry about it." Jackie waved Johnny's panicked stuttering away. "I'm terrible with appointments myself. That's what my mate helps me with. Right, Toni?"

"Sure," Toni lied, because her father would probably be late to his own funeral if Toni didn't make sure he wasn't.

Jackie went to the counter and picked up her tea, then returned and sat down next to Toni.

"So," she asked, cupping her chai tea, "what are we talking about?"

Johnny looked at Toni, his eyes begging her not to say anything.

"Movies," Toni lied. Honestly, Toni would only lie this much to help her mother.

"I love movies," Jackie stated. "What are your favorites, Johnny? Are you into sci-fi or stuff with lots of big explosions? Personally I hate chick flicks or anything that's clearly trying to make me cry. I hate that."

Knowing her mother could handle things from here, Toni picked up her backpack and slipped out of her chair.

And now, after handling this little drama, Toni knew it would be easy as hell to quit her day job.

Ricky leaned against one side of the office doorway and Rory leaned on the other while Reece stood between them, his arms crossed over his chest. Together they watched a big male lion play grab ass with his wife. Of course, it was his right. The company was partially his.

"Mace!" the full-human giggled-squealed. "Stop it!"

He had the poor little thing pinned against his desk with his big lion thighs while he man-handled—or in this case, *lion*-handled—Desiree MacDermot-Llewellyn, detective first grade for the shifter unit of the NYPD.

"Come on, Dez," the big cat pushed. "Just give me ten minutes."

"That sounds highly unimpressive for a former Navy man."

"Unlike your Marine brethren . . . Navy SEALs know how to get the job done—quick, fast, and to everyone's satisfaction. We don't just storm the beach, baby. We take the whole damn country."

Ricky looked at his brothers, and both of them crossed their eyes in disgust. Cats were bad enough, but military cats could be the worst. Combining that mane along with the ability to protect their country just made most of them completely unbearable.

"What are we doing?" a voice asked from behind Ricky and his brothers, and, he was ashamed to admit, they all reacted as any sane person would react when they suddenly had a large polar bear sidling up to them—they screamed like little girls and spun around, fangs bared, claws out, ready to fight to the death.

Eating what smelled like seal jerky, Lou "Crush" Crushek stared at them, unfazed by their panicked reaction. Unlike grizzlies, polars didn't fly off the handle at the slightest provocation. Of course, polars were also more likely to eat a person just because that beached walrus they could scent was miles away somewhere on an ice floe and, you know . . . that human was standing right *there*.

Crushek nodded at Reece. Ricky knew he was nodding at Reece because Reece was the only one of them who played hockey professionally. Reece wasn't the best the Carnivores had, but he was the one who always seemed more than willing to sacrifice himself to get between the other team and their potential goal. The wolf had had more surgery than seemed right over the last few years to repair all sorts of damage, but he truly loved hockey and his personality made him a standout with the fans.

"How ya doin', Crush?"

The bear shrugged. Crushek wasn't much for, you know, *words*. But that was okay. His mate, Coach Cella Malone, more than made up for it because that chatty kitty didn't know when to shut the heck up.

"Good," Reece said, reading that shrug as a positive response.

The bear looked over at MacDermot, who was now glaring at Ricky and his brothers. "You ready, MacDermot?"

They didn't seem a likely pair, MacDermot and Crushek, but the fellow detectives worked really well together and had closed a lot of cases for the NYPD since they'd been teamed up. A few cases that Ricky and his brothers had been involved in because of their security company.

"Yeah. I'm ready." She kissed her mate on the cheek and headed out, beautiful gray-green eyes glaring at the Reeds as she passed. The three brothers said nothing to her because they knew better. Even Reece. A full-human she might be, but Dez MacDermot-Llewellyn was always armed and always ready to shoot. In fact, she was one of the only full-humans he'd ever known who happily called Sissy Mae and Dee-Ann Smith "friends" and actually meant it.

She was almost past when she suddenly jerked toward them. All three jumped back, Reece immediately covering his face with his forearms since he felt that was the best part of him.

Sneering, she walked out the door and, chuckling, Crushek followed.

"Love you, babe," Llewellyn called after her. "See you at home."

"Love you, too," she called back.

Llewellyn walked around his desk, and when he pulled his chair out, he noticed that the three wolves were watching him. "What?" He glared at them when all three tipped their heads to the side. "Look, I'm a lion male, but I can say 'I love you' . . . and mean it. Really."

Toni sat down at the desk she was about to give up and opened up the e-mail program. She started typing, "Dear Ric," but was worried that using his nickname was too casual. So she tried "Dear Ulrich" but thought that sounded too formal.

"This isn't working," Toni muttered, her entire body drooping in her very expensive ergonomically correct desk chair. "What do I say? 'Thanks for the opportunity but I'd rather set myself on fire than fail on such a grand scale'?" No. That sounded tragically pathetic. Even for her. And she knew if she sounded pathetic that would only make Ric push for her to "keep trying!" He was a keep trying guy. A guy who thought everyone could do anything they wanted if they put their mind to it.

So she knew she had to find a way to quit and get him to not bug her about it. That would not be easy. Though he was a wonderfully nice wolf, Ulrich Van Holtz could be just as pushy as the rest of the Van Holtzes.

While she was debating the best way to handle her resignation, Kerri appeared in the doorway, a big grin on her face.

"I'm not staying," Toni said immediately, and she felt slightly devastated when that big grin faded.

"But why not?"

"Kerri—"

"I know a lot of pressure comes with this job, but—"

"It's not the pressure. Pressure I can handle. I'm just not right for this . . ." Toni's words faded off when she saw the pretty black woman standing behind Kerri but staring down the long hallway.

"Can I help you?" Toni asked.

Her eyes still focused down that hallway, the female replied, "Uh . . . yeah. I was coming in here to say thanks but . . . uh . . ."

Toni sniffed the air and almost audibly sighed. The female was a wolfdog. One of the more annoying hybrids in Toni's estimation. They were just . . . all over the place. No focus. No clarity. No sanity.

"Sweetie . . . ?" Toni pushed, frustrated because she wanted to talk to Kerri.

"Yeah. Sorry." The She-dog focused on them. "Do you guys know who that lion male is who's wearing the Los Angeles Raiders T-shirt?"

"Oh," Kerri replied, "that's the new player Coach just brought in. He's from Los Angeles." She lowered her voice. "He's very tan."

"Did Malone spend a lot of money bringing him here?"

That seemed like an odd question, so Toni asked, "Why does it matter?"

"Uh . . . because he just invited himself to work out with Bo."

"Novikov?"

Kerri looked at her, eyes widening in panic.

Toni shot out of her chair, charged around her desk, and tore off down the hall. By the time she reached the two males, Bo Novikov had the new guy in a choke hold that would kill most canines and smaller cats. Only lion males and hyenas could continue to put up a fight after two seconds of that.

The problem was, of course, that Bo wasn't about to release the cat just because he was starting to pass out. The dumb cat had gotten in Bo's way. Why did people never learn not to get in the way of those with true drive or focus? It amazed her.

What Toni assumed was the fiancée he'd been so desperate to get to now tried to pry Bo's arms off the cat while begging him to "Let go, Bo! Please!"

But Novikov wouldn't hear pleas. He wouldn't hear begging. A man like Bo Novikov would only hear one thing . . .

"You're late, Bo."

Bo turned his head to look at Toni while keeping his grip strong. "What?"

"You're late. For our meeting."

"I'm never late," he snarled. "And what meeting?"

"To go over promotion ideas for you? Remember?"

"There's nothing to remember because we didn't have a meeting."

"We did," Toni said, moving around so that she stood right in front of him with Kerri behind her. With her hand behind her back, Toni signaled to her assistant with her fingers. "I set it up first thing this morning."

"We did not have a meeting." He glowered at her. "I know when I have meetings."

"It's on your schedule."

"I know my schedule. We didn't have a meeting."

"I'm not talking your personal schedule, Bo. I don't have access to that. So I had schedules set up and sent to the entire team's phones."

Leaning around Toni, Kerri held up her tablet and said, "See? It's right here."

"I didn't get anything on my phone."

"Really? I sent you a follow-up e-mail." Christ, she was

really rolling with this lie of hers, but the lion was starting to turn blue. Seriously. Blue.

"I don't get e-mail on my phone."

"You can't get e-mail or you don't?"

"I guess I never set it up when the team got our new phones. But why should I bother? Malone calls when she wants to talk to me."

"I have a lot to do and I need to be able to get in touch with you the easiest way possible. That way I can also send you travel info and if there's a problem you can see it right away and get back to me so I can correct it."

"Planning to make a lot of mistakes, are you?"

"No. I just assume others will fuck up, so I build in padding for that so I'll have time to fix the problem myself."

That was not the answer he'd expected, but she could see he was impressed. Not that he'd admit it.

"The phone buzzing all the time bothers me during training."

"You don't need to look at it during your training. You need to look at it when you're done with your training. You also need to check out your team schedule, which should coordinate with your personal schedule. Right? This is about team business, after all." She tapped the watch on her wrist. "And you're late."

The hybrid's really big body suddenly loosened up, and he finally released his prey, the cat dropping to the floor while he coughed and slowly got his overly tan color back.

"Why don't you go wait in my office, Bo."

"Yeah. Okay. This can't take long, though. I've got—"

"Training. I know. But then, you should have been on time, huh?"

His eyes narrowed, but he headed toward her office. Then he stopped, turned, and kicked the cat so that the lion flew several feet, before walking off down the hall.

Kerri let out a breath. "Do you want me to—"

"Yeah."

"For—"

"Yeah. For today."

"Even the second string guys?"

"No. But give me their names. Maybe I'll have a meeting with all of them at once."

Kerri grinned and did a little dance, before running down the hall. Toni knew why the full-human was so happy, but none of this meant that Toni had changed her mind. She was just helping out. Especially with Ulrich out of town for a while.

Goddammit! She was just being a good person!

"Wow," Bo's fiancée said while she gawked at Toni. "You were amazing. The way you handled him. You didn't even try to separate them."

Toni frowned. "Why the hell would I try to separate two apex predators?"

The wolfdog shrugged. "I do."

Deciding that answer meant the wolfdog was either kind of stupid or kind of dangerously insane, Toni turned away from her and focused on the cat.

"I'm Blayne by the way. Bo's fiancée."

Toni nodded but basically stopped thinking about the wolfdog. "Are you okay?" she asked the cat. He was slowly pushing himself back to his feet.

"That asshole is crazy," he choked out, his throat already beginning to bruise where Novikov had gripped him.

"I'd strongly suggest you not bother Mr. Novikov. He doesn't like it."

Now standing at his full height of about six-four or -five, the lion stared down at Toni. His nostrils twitched and his eyes immediately narrowed once he'd figured out she was canine.

"Look," he began, his tone completely condescending, "sweetheart—"

"And we're done." Toni walked away from the cat, heading to her office. She simply didn't have time for stupid, and anyone who called her "sweetheart" without knowing her was just rude.

As she neared her office, Coach Malone was coming toward her. Did everyone come to work early? Toni had been planning to use what she thought would be quiet time to plan her escape. Her plan was simply not working!

"Oh, good. You're here." Malone stopped in front of her. "We need new pictures of the guys."

"Pardon?"

"You know. Promo pictures. For them to sign. You'll need to get a photographer but someone with a little talent who doesn't easily cry."

"Cry?"

"I just don't want regular ol' headshots. I hate those."

Toni took a breath. "Well, I was hoping to talk to you—"

"God, you don't need me to hold your hand through this, too, do you?"

"No, no. It's just—"

"Because I've got a bunch of shit to do and I don't have the time. So could you just make this happen? Great. Thanks! I've gotta go."

Beyond frustrated, Toni walked into her office and sat down at her desk. Bo watched her.

"Everything all right?"

"Yeah. I guess. Kerri!" she called out. The full-human appeared in seconds.

"Yes, boss?"

"Don't call me boss. And Coach Malone wants new team pictures. Is there someone you guys use regularly for this?"

"There was."

"Was?"

"After the lawsuit, we really can't use him."

"Lawsuit?" Toni focused on Bo.

"It wasn't me," he said quickly. "It was Malone. She was one of the players then, and he said he was just trying to pose her properly. She said she didn't like him putting his hand on her ass. Next thing you know that leopard had a broken cheekbone, a busted nose, and two shattered arms." Suddenly the hybrid smiled, and Toni realized he was actually quite handsome when he wasn't glowering like a sociopath. "And for once . . . it wasn't me."

"Do you want me to come up with another list of names?" Kerri asked.

Toni thought about it a moment and shook her head. "No. I think I have another completely insane option."

Bo studied her a moment. "That doesn't sound very promising."

"Yeah." Toni sighed and pulled out her cell phone. "I know."

The electronic blueprints for the Sports Center were projected up on the screen, and Rory pointed at several doors inside the Sports Center that were only known about and used by shifters. "The Center guards scented full-humans here. Here. And here."

"Did they ever get inside?" Reece asked.

"No. But the Center needs a more secure system or they may have a situation where Dee-Ann may have to get involved because some full-human saw too much."

"We could change all the locks," Ricky suggested, "but then no one could get inside but wolves and foxes."

"Nah," Reece said. "The bears will just tear the doors off the hinges. Especially if they smell food from the food court."

"Are you two done?" Rory asked.

Ricky and Reece looked at each other and back at Rory. "No," they said together.

"Look." Rory stepped in front of the screen. "This is a big job for us, so I need y'all to focus."

Reece nudged Ricky's side with his elbow. "Someone's trying to act all impressive 'cause he's up for a promotion."

"You gonna wear a suit to work now, Rory?" Ricky asked him. "And some fancy Italian loafers?"

"Can we just focus on the job?"

Ricky stood. "Reece and I will go over to the Sports Center and take a look around. See what we can fix."

"I bet Ricky Lee just wants to see his new girlfriend," Reece said.

"Girlfriend? What girlfriend?"

"She's not my girlfriend, but I am hoping she becomes my fuck buddy."

"She's a jackal."

"Shut up, Reece."

"Jackal?" Rory asked. "The Devil's canine?"

"Stop calling them that."

"Why?"

"Can't get her in my bed if my own kin are insulting her kind."

"He's got a point," Reece said, shrugging. "Unlike men, girls are weird about that sort of thing. It's like they look for any reason not to sleep with you."

Rory stared at his brother. "I think that's only you."

"It can't be. I'm so much cuter than either of you."

He saw Delilah sitting on the steps outside his church. His temple, really. Where people came from all around to meet him. To hear his wisdom. To learn about how they should manage their lives. He was there for them when no one else was. Because he loved them. He loved them all.

And yet . . . he knew that Delilah was something special. Something beyond any of the others.

Chris walked down the stairs, his bodyguards only a few feet behind. He sat down next to her. He knew that to those walking by that he looked just like any other New Yorker with his torn jeans and comfortable sandals. But they'd learn soon enough that he was far from "any other" being on the planet.

"Hello."

She turned her head to look at him, her small smile in place. She was just so innocent. So tender.

"You came back," he said.

"I did."

"Will you stay for a while?"

Her smile grew just the smallest bit. "I will."

CHAPTER THIRTEEN

She got lost trying to find Toni. That's what she got for trying to understand that phone message rather than calling to confirm everything. But she'd been sleeping when her phone went off and she was not the friendliest bitch when someone woke her before she was ready. So she'd ignored the call and listened to her messages later.

Now here she was, wandering around this goddamn Sports Center. She'd never been here before. Had no interest. She hated sports on principle. It didn't matter to her who was playing. Full-humans. Shifters. Whatever. Sports was just something that bored her into a rage.

Pulling open the doors, she walked through what turned out to be an ice rink. That probably meant hockey. She hated hockey.

She walked across the ice, stopping by some lion male and another female who were talking.

"Excuse me," she said, stepping close. "Do you guys know—"

"Hey," the lion male said, glaring down at her, "do you see I'm in a conversation?"

She nodded. "I do. And I'm sorry to interrupt. But I'm lost and I just need you to—"

The lion leaned in, sniffed her. Confused, he leaned back. "Great. Another hybrid *freak*."

Actually, she wasn't a hybrid. She was simply a shifter breed that wasn't much talked about. Her kind kept to themselves, avoided most other shifters, and didn't take kindly to being sneered at.

Just like she was being sneered at by this lion.

"Look, freak, I'm busy," the lion said, waving her away with his big, strong, overly tanned hand. "If you want help . . . go find it somewhere else. 'Kay?"

She nodded. "Sure." Walked about ten feet away. Then she carefully placed her backpack on the ice, cracked her neck, her knuckles, spun around—and charged.

Toni was heading to the Starbucks in the food court to get herself another much-needed coffee when she saw Cella Malone and Dee-Ann Smith.

"Did you find that photographer yet?" Cella asked.

"Lord, Malone," Dee-Ann snickered. "Can't you even say 'hi' first before you jump down the girl's throat?"

"I didn't jump down her throat. Did I jump down your throat?" Cella demanded.

Kind of fed up with the woman's general bitchiness, Toni admitted, "You've been jumping down my throat since I started and this is only my second day on the job."

Dee-Ann snorted, and Cella turned and slammed her fist into the She-wolf's shoulder. Toni was sure that if Cella had hit her like that, she'd have a demolished shoulder. But Dee-Ann was a She-wolf, and most She-wolves were built like NFL players anyway, so the wolf just readjusted her shoulder and said, "Don't know why you're gettin' so testy."

"Because you're irritating me."

"The wind blows and you get irritated, feline."

"Shut up." Cella pointed at Toni. "Look, I'm sorry if I've been hard on you, but I've got a lot to get done and no time to fool around with this bullshit."

"Then let me handle it."

"You?"

"Yeah. Me. If you're going to get all annoyingly psychotic, I'll just handle it my damn self."

Cella and Dee-Ann glanced at each other and back at Toni. "I think the little jackal has grown some balls since yesterday," Dee said.

"I think it's the clothes," Cella remarked. "I told you that suit was a bad idea. Besides . . . it made you look hippy."

Insulted by that—she was not hippy—Toni said, "Just e-mail me a list of things that need to get done. I'll take it from there."

"And the photographer?"

"I already have a call in with someone who should be able to do the job. If you're around later and she comes in today, maybe you can meet with—"

A pained roar exploded from the training rink, and ten seconds later, the newly hired lion burst out of the double doors. But what had Toni sighing in exasperation was the female who'd attached herself to the lion's back and dug her exceedingly long front claws right into his face, a mouthful of fangs biting into the back of his head.

"Goddammit," Toni muttered.

"Hey," Dee-Ann said. "Isn't that your—"

"Yes." Toni sighed, typically appalled.

"*She's* the photographer you called in for the team?" And that's when Dee-Ann Smith, She of the Few Words and the Scary Eyes—as the Van Holtz pups had named her—threw back her head and laughed. Why? Because she also knew the female attached to the lion male. Knew her well. Probably too well after that fistfight at the Christmas dinner they all had in the Van Holtz Washington compound.

"Who is that?" Cella asked.

"Olivia Kowalski," Toni said. "We grew up together. She's a brilliant photographer. She's worked for AP, Reuters, National Geographic—"

"But?"

"But what?"

"She's worked for Reuters, AP, National Geographic, and yet she's here to do sports shots for her friend?"

Toni shrugged. "She has issues."

Cella glanced over at the grappling female and lion. "Really?" she said with great sarcasm. "I find that so shocking."

"She's like my siblings. She's an amazing artist, but as a human being she needs a little work. But I know how to handle her."

"Handle her?"

The three females looked over just as the lion finally pried Livy off his head and threw her across the lobby. Livy hit the floor hard, rolled, and slammed into the wall. For anyone else being tossed around by an angry and terrified lion male, Toni would have been on the phone dialing nine-one-one. But this was Livy. She was . . . unique.

After Livy hit the wall, she rolled back and got to her feet. She spun, bared her fangs, and charged, ramming her entire small body into the lion and wrapping her arms and legs around him as she attacked his face with her fangs.

"Get her off me!" the lion screamed, no longer annoyingly smug and condescending, but terrified and in pain. *"Get her off me!"*

Realizing how stupid she'd been to suggest Livy for this job, Toni tried to repair the damage as best she could with Malone. "Cella, I'm—"

"She'll work," the tigress said.

Toni blinked, shocked. "What?"

"Yeah. Hire her." She glanced at her watch. "Smith, we better go if we're gonna meet up with Crush and Dez."

The pair stepped away from her, but Toni still couldn't believe . . .

"Are you sure?" she asked Cella's back.

"Yep. Something tells me that one won't be running off crying like the last photographer we had."

The "last photographer" being the guy Malone had beaten up herself, but whatever.

Kind of proud of making her first hire, Toni bellowed, *"Livy!"*

Livy pulled her sharp fangs out of the lion's skull and stared at her.

Toni motioned with her hand. "Let's go."

Livy unwrapped herself from the lion and dropped to the ground. At only five-one, she was tiny for a shifter, but her size never stopped Livy from accepting a challenge. It had made for entertaining times at school.

Livy spit the lion's blood out of her mouth and calmly walked around the still screaming cat. She went back into the training rink and came out a few seconds later with her worn backpack.

Once Livy was by her side, Toni gestured at the cat, who now had several people around him trying to help. "Was there a reason you did that?"

She shrugged. "He was rude," she said flatly. "You know I hate rude."

Toni didn't bother trying to get Livy to not attack at the slightest provocation. She'd stopped lecturing her long ago. Her friend would never change, because Livy loved who she was and, if she were to be honest, Toni loved who Livy was, too.

Most importantly, Toni's entire family adored Livy, although Livy never seemed to understand why.

"So what's going on?" Livy asked after spitting out a bit more blood.

"Got a job for you."

"Will I be whoring?"

"Not this time. I'm sorry."

"You know how I love to whore," Livy stated with that flat tone that freaked people out, because no one ever knew whether she was joking or not. It had caused some awkward times when the police were involved, but Toni could usually talk the cops out of actually arresting them.

"I know." Toni tugged the sleeve of Livy's light, black denim jacket. "Let's go get you cleaned up, and I'll tell you all about it."

"Are you sure?" the She-tiger asked. And like two well-trained monkeys, Lou Crushek and Desiree MacDermot nodded in unison.

Dee took the piece of paper from Malone, studied the mug shot of Whitlan's former cellmate. "I'll handle it."

"No," all three said in unison.

"You know," Dee told them. "If I were a sensitive gal, I might be insulted right now."

"It's nothing personal, Smith," Malone told her. "And trust me when I say that you *must* be there. But . . ." She looked at Desiree.

"You're our . . ." Desiree thought a moment, ". . . last resort kind of girl."

"What the hell does that mean?"

"You're the one we turn to when all bets are off."

"I think we should move on this as soon as we can set it up," Crushek told them. "If Whitlan finds out that we know, trust me when I say he'll find a way to get to this guy."

"Fuck," Malone suddenly hissed. "I can't."

"Why not?'"

"I've gotta go to Russia. To meet with the coach for the Siberian team."

Dee sighed. "Now?"

"Yeah. Now. Ric just told me to handle it."

"Let's not get in the way of what Cella needs to do for Ric," Crushek, the hockey fanatic, chastised. "It's team business."

"And I can't go," Desiree announced.

"Why can't you go?"

"Cap won't let me. I've had bad experiences with clinically diagnosed sociopaths."

"Bad experiences?"

Desiree scratched her neck. "I may have shot a couple. Totally in self-defense, of course."

"But the Captain would prefer answers first," Crushek kindly explained.

Not understanding the boundaries that the NYPD had to exist under, Dee re-focused her attention on Malone. "Don't you have an entire staff to help you?"

"Yeah, but . . ." Malone's gaze suddenly moved off and then she grinned. "As a matter of fact, I *do* have a staff."

★　★　★

Ricky was sitting on the stairs by one of the exit doors with Reece when Rory came up.

"Well?" their brother asked.

"Humans have been all over here," Reece said.

"Did they get in?"

"Nah," Ricky said around a yawn. "But tightening security really couldn't hurt."

"Oh, I'm sorry, little brother," Rory sneered. "Is this boring you?"

"A little." When Rory's eyes narrowed on him, Ricky quickly held up his hands. There wasn't a lot of space in this stairwell, and that made it harder to fight his brother.

Rory looked off. "What about cameras?"

"They don't have any in the stairwells, but I'd suggest we tell them to put some in here."

"And full-time monitoring," Reece added.

"Twenty-four-seven and guards trained by us. Right now the Center only has a couple of old leopards watching the place after hours."

"Yeah. That sounds good. I'll write the report."

Nodding, Ricky and Reece got to their feet. Rory's phone went off and he pulled it out of the back pocket of his jeans. He answered it and was quiet for a moment; then his eyes suddenly locked on Ricky.

"I'll ask him," Rory said.

"Ask me what?"

"It's Ronnie Lee on the phone. Laura Jane is running around telling the other She-wolves that you were so disturbed by her very presence yesterday, you ran off after some jackal. Ronnie wants to know if there were really tears in your eyes when you made a break for it."

While Reece laughed so hard he was bent over at the waist, his hands resting on his knees, Ricky took off his Tennessee Titans cap and scratched his head. Because his day had just gotten crappier.

★　★　★

Livy held up a color print of Bo Novikov trying to force a smile. "This is what nightmares are made of."

"I know," Toni agreed while she licked her spoon free of Greek yogurt. "That's why we need you."

"This isn't really my thing, Toni. I—"

"If you say you're an artist, I will hit you."

Chuckling, Livy tossed the picture back onto Toni's desk and ate more of the French fries she had purchased. After spending some time catching up, they'd gone to the Sports Center food court and had picked up their lunches. Fish and chips for Livy. Yogurt, salad, and a burger big enough to choke a rhino for Toni. She'd bypassed the fries, but now she was regretting it while she watched Livy eating hers.

"I was not going to say that. At least not to you." Livy shrugged. "But I hate sports. I hate sports guys. I hate people. I hate dealing with them. Talking to them. And portrait photography means talking to people. I also hate—"

"Yes, Livy. I know. You hate . . . pretty much everything."

"Pretty much."

"But this will be good money. *Clean* money, Liv. And God knows you can't even think about trying to do another office job."

"Why? I'm a fast typist."

"Yes. But then you throw the computer at the office manager and I'm bailing you out of jail . . . again."

"He was rude."

"You think everyone is rude. But with shifters, you'll be right and they can fight back. At the very least they'll be fast enough to duck a flying PC."

"That hard drive did ram right into his head. He was out for, like, ten minutes."

"Is that restraining order still in effect?"

"I think it expired last year. But I wasn't planning on going back to Utah anytime soon." Livy took a handful of her fries out of the newspaper they were nestled in and dropped them on the plate with Toni's burger. "Honestly, though, how much money could this really get me?"

"A lot."

"Really?"

"You should think about it. You'd be able to live some place you're paying for rather than just crashing on someone's couch . . . like the couches of people you don't know."

"It's called squatting and it has its place in society. And one paycheck isn't going to—"

"I realized that. So I talked to a few of the other teams' promotions people here and in Jersey."

"Which means what?"

"I've got you other jobs with the local shifter teams."

Livy smirked. "So you're my agent now?"

"If I have to be. Clearly your agent doesn't understand your true needs and skills."

Livy thought a moment. "Well . . . it would be nice having a place of my own eventually."

"Where are you living now?"

"Some guy left his window open on Thirty-Second Street and Fifth, so I—"

"Okay. That's enough." Toni shook her head to remove the image of her best friend climbing into some guy's temporarily vacant home so she had a place to sleep for the night. It was in Livy's nature, Toni understood that. But it was in Toni's nature to put her siblings in burrows . . . she didn't actually do that, though, now did she? "The family is in Manhattan for the summer, so you can stay with us. But come end of August, you'd better have your own, *rented* apartment, Olivia. You can't keep living this way. It's not right, especially when you don't *have* to be homeless!"

"Okay, okay. Calm down." Livy smirked. "So emotional."

"Shut up. I'm trying to help."

"I know. And thank you."

"You're welcome."

"But you do understand I have money, right?"

"Not clean money."

"It's clean . . . *ish*."

"Well, I prefer to think of you as penniless—clean or not—so that I can justify your need to live rent free."

"I don't need to live rent free. I just don't like staying in one place when there's all these available spaces I can fit into."

"I don't want to discuss this," Toni insisted. "It upsets me."

"Okay. Okay. So when do I get started?"

"Well—"

The door to her office opened—without a knock—and Ricky Reed walked in, pulled one of the chairs that sat against the wall to her desk—this one wasn't bolted down at least—and dropped into it.

"Do you ever think to yourself," he suddenly began, " 'How did I *not* know she was a delusional narcissist?' "

Livy stared at the wolf and replied, "Every day."

Ricky focused on Livy. "Hi. I'm Ricky Lee Reed."

"I'm Livy."

"Nice to meet you, ma'am."

Livy quickly looked at Toni, eyes wide, and mouthed, *Ma'am?*

"I'm not sure what you're talking about," Toni admitted. She wanted to be annoyed with him about earlier, but she was having a hard time when he looked so despondent.

"My ex-girlfriend is running around telling my Pack that I ran away from her yesterday crying."

"Did you?" Livy asked.

"No, I did not. I was just chasing her," he said, pointing at Toni. "And if anyone was crying, it was her."

"I was not crying. I was merely panicking."

The wolf suddenly looked around Toni's office. "I thought you were quittin'."

"I had to put it off."

"Why would you quit?" Livy asked. "This job seems tailor-made for you. Taking care of useless idiots."

"My siblings are not useless."

"Freddy's not useless . . . and the twins are too young to know definitely about them yet. But the rest of them . . . pretty useless."

"Shut up," Toni snapped.

"You shut up."

"You shut up more."

"That doesn't even make sense."

"Excuse me," the wolf cut in. "We were talking about *me*. Not y'all."

"He has a point," Livy kindly said, which only annoyed Toni more.

Reece Reed walked into Toni's office—again, without asking if it was okay to come in—and threw his hands up at his brother. "I was trying to talk to you, Ricky Lee."

"No. You and Rory were laughing at me, and I'm in too bad a mood now to sit around and listen to it."

"Look, I told you Laura Jane was crazy back in high school. Don't be mad at me *now* because I was . . ." Reece sniffed the air. "Because I was . . ." He sniffed the air again. Then he dropped to his knees and buried his face into the side of Livy's neck.

Livy's body tensed. She didn't like to be touched . . . ever. "Could you get your redneck nose off me?" she deadpanned.

"What *are* you?" Reece asked.

Toni briefly closed her eyes, knowing that over the years that particular question had led to all sorts of bad situations.

"Don't be rude, little brother," Ricky warned.

"Smell her," Reece ordered his brother.

"I'm not smelling anyone. It's rude."

"Seriously, though," Reece pushed. "What are you?"

"Your worst nightmare if you don't get away from me," Livy said calmly.

"Are you a hybrid?"

"No, Livy!" Toni nearly screamed when she saw her friend's hand come up and those deadly claws explode from her fingertips. "Don't you dare. He's on the hockey team and he needs his eyes."

"Then," Livy said, staring right at the much bigger wolf, "he needs to go away."

"Reece . . . move."

"Yeah, but—"

"Reece!" Toni pointed at another chair pushed against the wall. "Go sit down. *Now.*"

Grumbling, the wolf got to his feet and stomped across the room until he could drop into a chair. "I was just asking a question."

"See?" Livy, her claws thankfully retreating, said to Toni. "You're perfect for this job."

"Shut up," Toni said with a laugh.

"You shut up."

"You shut up more."

"I still don't know what you two are talking about," Ricky complained. "And we're supposed to be talking about *me.*"

"Really?" Toni asked. "Because I don't remember that being something I agreed to."

"Would it kill you to give me five minutes of your time after all that Chinese food I bought you yesterday?"

"I didn't know I owed you for the Chinese food."

Not getting the response he wanted from the jackal, he turned to her friend. And Reece was right . . . Ricky didn't know what she was. Unlike hybrids, which were sometimes a combination of scents, this female smelled like something completely different. Not bad, like some hyenas who didn't bathe regularly could smell. Just . . . different. She was pretty, though, with short, straight, pitch-black hair that had a white streak just off to the side, and dark, *dark* brown eyes. Her coloring and the shape of her eyes suggested that she was part Asian, and even though she wasn't standing, he could tell she wasn't very tall or lean but she was strong with wide shoulders for such a small female. There was a lot of power in that very compact body, which he assumed was why Reece was still staring at her. Well, that and he was still trying to figure out what she was.

"She dragged me to her new apartment last night—" Ricky began.

Toni's friend—Livy, was it?—abruptly looked at Toni. "You have your own apartment?"

"No."

"But—"

"*No.*" The jackal suddenly dug her hands into her curly hair, making it look kind of wild and even sexier. "First off, I don't think it's even my apartment."

"What does that mean?"

"And second, even if it was my apartment, as much as I love you, Livy, I'd never let you stay there."

"What kind of friend are you?"

"One that knows her boundaries." Toni took a small slip of paper from a stack on her desk and wrote on it. "Here." She slapped the paper on the desk close to her friend. "The address of where my family is staying. You *will* stay there," she ordered.

"You let her stay with your defenseless kin, but you won't let her stay at your apartment?"

"Because she's messy."

"I'm not messy."

"Oh, my God, Livy!"

"If you got a maid it wouldn't be an issue."

"I'm not getting a maid just so you can be a slob."

"Fine. I'll pay for one, you cheap heifer."

"I'm not getting a maid!"

Realizing that these two were like sisters and sensing these weird little arguments of theirs could go on *forever,* Ricky decided he had to take action. Pulling out the cash he had stuffed in his front pocket, Ricky handed over a couple of twenties to Toni's friend.

Livy stared at the money before asking, "I usually charge more for blow jobs." She said it so flatly that it took Ricky a second to realize she was being sarcastic.

"You can take that up with your momma and the Lord, but I've given you cash for you to take a cab and go away." He took the slip of paper with the family's address off the desk and put it in Livy's hand with the money. "Nothing personal, but I want Miss Toni focused directly on *me* so I can whine in peace, like a proper wolf. Can't do it with an audience. My kind considers it a sign of weakness."

Reece had eased up behind Livy and, once again on his knees, asked, "What does *your* kind consider weak?"

"Your face," Livy shot back before she got to her feet, picking up her backpack and swinging it onto her shoulder, which caused it to slap into Reece's head since he was in the process of standing to his full height. "See you later," Livy told her friend, then walked out. There was no chatter about calling each other or what are you doing later or anything about going shopping. None of what Ricky's daddy called "lady stuff." Nope. She'd said "see you later" and walked out.

Ricky had to admit . . . he liked that in a female. He especially liked that Toni didn't seem bothered by her friend's abruptness.

"So," Reece began as he started to sit in the chair Livy had just vacated.

"That ass," Ricky warned, "better not hit that seat or your face will be hitting the floor."

Reece stood back up. "You know, big brother, there are nicer ways to tell me to go."

"But none of those will you actually listen to."

Reece grunted and walked out.

Now that they were alone, Ricky looked at Toni.

"You're pouting," she noted.

"Because my entire Pack is pissing me off."

"I thought the problem was your ex-girlfriend."

"My ex-girlfriend is just a giant pain in my ass. But my Pack actually believing her . . . ? Their loyalty should be to me. Don't you think?"

Toni leaned back in her chair, her brows pulling down into a fierce frown. "What are we doing?" she suddenly asked.

"Chattin'."

"Are we friends now?"

"We're not enemies." He raised a brow. "Are we?"

"Don't threaten me with your eyebrows."

"I'm not. I'm interrogating you with my *one* raised eyebrow. If I was threatening you, I'd use both eyebrows. Like this." He leaned forward and raised both brows while widening his eyes.

When she burst out giggling, Ricky leaned back in his chair and said, "See the difference?"

No. Toni didn't see the difference, but the fact that he had the balls to actually give her a demonstration of something so ridiculous did impress her. Other than Cooper and their dad, there wasn't a lot of deliberate silliness among the Jean-Louis Parker clan. There was unintentional silliness, of course. How could there not be with Kyle and Troy around? But you'd never convince them of that.

"All right." Toni finally sighed. "Go ahead and tell me about your—"

"Oh, good. You're still here," Cella said from the doorway. Dee-Ann was beside her, leaning against the doorjamb.

"Where else would I be?" Toni looked at her watch. "It's not even two o'clock yet."

"You could have left for the day."

"I could have? Wait . . . am I only supposed to be working half-days or something?"

"I don't know." Cella waved her hand around, almost hitting Dee-Ann in the face. "Discussing your schedule is not why I'm here."

"Okay."

"You said you'd help me out, right?"

"Sure."

"Great." Cella walked into the office and tossed what appeared to be an itinerary on Toni's desk. "This really helps. Thanks."

"Wait." Toni looked down at the paperwork, then at Cella Malone. "You want me to go to . . . to . . . ?"

"Yeah."

"Why am I going to *Russia*?"

"I can't go. I have to take care of something here. And you said you'd help."

"I thought I'd help with non-coaching-related stuff. Or, I don't know . . . organize your files or something."

"This isn't necessarily a coach thing. Besides, it's about Novikov. You like Novikov."

Exasperated, "What does that have to do with *anything*?"

"Actually, this is team travel-related, which *is* your job."

"Yes, but—"

"So go over to Russia and get them to let the team in *with* Novikov but not in a cage. But remember, no Novikov, no game, and then we never get a chance at the title of best in the world."

Ricky smirked. "Did you just make that title up, Cella Malone?"

"Shut up, Reed."

Desperate, Toni asked, "But is it really that important that he goes?"

"He has to go," Ricky piped up. "The team can't win against the Russian teams without Novikov. There are mostly bears on the Russian teams."

"I don't *care*." Toni stopped, took a breath. "I just don't think it's a good idea for me, a jackal, to go to a bear-populated area to argue for the rights of Bo Novikov."

"It's better you do it than me."

"How is it better, Cella? You're the team coach *and* you're a Siberian tiger . . . so aren't the Russians your people?"

"Not really. Siberian tigers in Russia are not fans of the Malones."

"Is anyone fans of the Malones?" Dee-Ann asked.

"Shut up, hick."

"But," Toni pushed ahead, still desperate, "what am I supposed to do with Russian bears?"

"Do what you do."

"What does that even mean?"

"Look, kid," Cella said, sounding annoyingly exasperated, "you managed to control and calm down Bo 'The Marauder' Novikov without use of a stun gun or a tranquilizer dart. So if you can manage him . . . I think you can manage a couple of frickin' bears."

"Yes, but—"

"Just do it. God! Take some initiative. Woman up!"

"I just don't think I'll feel . . . safe. You know? Unsafe work situation or whatever."

"She has a point," Dee-Ann drawled. "Get her mauled by some damn Russian bears, Malone, and Ric will have your ass. She is considered family by the Van Holtzes."

"You and I have other things to handle, Smith."

"First off, don't snarl at me, hell cat. And second, just get her some dang security."

"I would send Bert . . . but he hates flying and he's still in Alaska."

"Lord, woman, don't send a player with her," Dee-Ann snapped. "Get someone actually *trained* in security." And that's when she pointed at Ricky. "He'll do it."

The wolf, who'd been staring off during most of this conversation, suddenly looked alert. "What?"

"Like you've got anything better to do."

"That's not the point, Dee-Ann. I'm just one wolf—and these are bears. Russian bears. Smith Pack and Russian bears do not mix, or do you not remember Pack lore?"

"That was like a hundred years ago. I'm sure they're over what happened by now."

Toni put her elbows on her desk and dropped her face into her hands. "This is going to be a nightmare."

"Oh, buck up, kid," Cella told her, reaching across the desk and patting Toni on the shoulder. "It'll be fine. Just don't get any of them angry or let the polars sniff you or allow yourself to be left alone with any of the Kamchatka bears who haven't eaten."

Slowly, Toni lifted her head and looked at the head coach of the New York Carnivores. "Really? That's the *best* you can do?"

"Pretty much. Good luck!" Cella walked out the door. "Come on, Smith. Let's move."

Dee-Ann looked between Toni and Ricky. After a moment,

she said, "Take good care of her, Ricky Lee. Make your momma proud."

She left and Ricky jumped up. "I'll be right back," he said before he quickly walked out of the room.

Less than a minute later, he was back, dropping into the chair he'd just vacated.

"That was fast," Toni said.

"Yeah."

"What did Dee say?"

"Before I could say a word, she said I could go with you and deal with bears or stay here and have long, meaningful talks with the females of my Pack about Laura Jane." He smirked. "Guess which one I chose?"

"Ricky?"

"Yeah?"

She leaned forward a bit and whispered, "I don't want to go to Russia."

"Come on, darlin', it won't be that bad. And unlike my younger sibling, I do know how to handle bears. Besides, with all the places you've traveled, you can't tell me you've never been to Russia before."

"Sure I have. But I've been to *Russia* Russia. You know, Moscow, Saint Petersburg, Omsk."

"Omsk?"

"Yeah. I went there with my brother. Coop's big in Russia. Which means these are all places where my mother and brother would perform before dignitaries and royals. But I've never been to bear territory in Russia. And do you know why?" Ricky shook his head. "Because my parents told me to never go to bear territory in Russia! In fact, their exact words to their offspring were 'you will die if you go to bear territory in Russia.' "

"It won't be that bad. I'll be there, and I'll have your back the entire way. Promise."

"Do you know what's really going to be the worst part of this, though?"

He gave her a one-sided smile. "Telling your family you're going to Russia?"

Toni dropped her head on the desk, not even bothering to use her hands this time.

"This is going to be a nightmare," Toni said again, this time directly *into* the desk. Not that doing so helped any.

Chapter Fourteen

Delilah Jean-Louis Parker dug through her sister's clothes. Sometimes Oriana kept cash in her dresser drawers. Since their parents pretty much paid for everything and all Oriana cared about was dancing, she rarely spent her allowance. Actually, most of the kids didn't spend their allowance and a few of them didn't realize when the money was gone. Which was a nice little boon for Delilah.

Finding a healthy wad of cash, Delilah took more than half and put the few remaining bills back in Oriana's dresser. She closed the drawer and stepped out of the room. She looked up and down the hall, saw no one around, and went into the next bedroom over.

She searched quickly and quietly, bored by anything but cash or something she could sell for cash. The best thing about her family was that they were so absorbed by what they did every day that they barely noticed anything she did.

Not finding any cash or cash-worthy items, she sat on the bed. She saw a backpack and eased the zipper open. She went through it until she found a notebook that seemed out of place. Delilah pulled it out and began flipping through the pages. Unlike the rest of her siblings, Delilah didn't consider herself one thing or another. She knew she was a good artist. For her, drawing was easy. But so was math and science. She'd been offered multiple academic scholarships before she left high school. She said "left" because she never actually graduated. Her parents thought she'd graduated. She'd *told* them she'd graduated.

Del had even managed to walk into the hall at graduation. Until, you know, that bomb threat got called in and the rest of it was canceled. Then, with the help of Troy's PC and her design skills, she'd been able to show her parents a lovely diploma.

But when you were as smart as Delilah was, who needed a real diploma or a degree? What was the point? Because even without them, she still knew she had something worthy in her hands now. Something she could really make money on.

"What the hell are you doing in here?"

At first, Delilah thought it was Toni when she heard that snarled question, but she looked up into the face of Oriana.

Putting the notebook back—why steal it when she'd know exactly where it was at all times?—Delilah stood up. "Nothing. Just being nosey."

Oriana watched her for a moment, then shook her head. "I'm telling Toni you're stealing our shit again."

The little snitch would, too.

Delilah watched her sister turn around and start to head out to find Toni. And if there was one thing Delilah was not in the mood for, it was one of "those" discussions with Toni.

So Delilah grabbed the back of Oriana's neck. Not by the extra flesh that all young canines had. This wasn't some loving correction given from one sibling to another. Instead, she just grabbed the cunt's throat and yanked her back until Del could press her mouth to her sister's ear.

"How about—" Del began.

"Get off me!"

"—you just forget what you saw, little sister?"

Oriana started twisting her body and reaching back for Del's arms. *"Get off me, Delilah!"*

One of Oriana's hands slapped Delilah's face. It hurt but Del didn't care. She'd always had a high tolerance for pain and, most times, didn't even remember the pain a day or two later. Sometimes even ten minutes later.

So it wasn't anger that had Del pressing the point of her little butterfly knife to her sister's face, right below her eye. In fact, Delilah felt nothing at all except a little bit of pleasure when her sister abruptly stopped moving.

"I'll say it again . . . forget what you saw. Or I'll make sure you stop seeing all together. Understand?"

"Yes."

Delilah held her sister a little longer. Not to make her point clear but because she was really struggling with her desire to cut her sister's eyes out of her head. But she knew if she did that . . . she'd have to deal with Toni. Delilah hated dealing with Antonella. So cutting up her younger—and prettier—sister would have to wait.

She shoved Oriana away from her, grinning when her sister hit the wall and spun around to glare at her.

Delilah dragged the blunt side of her blade across her own cheek, just so her sister understood exactly what she was risking by fucking with her. She took a step toward her, and that's when Toni's best friend stepped into her line of sight.

Quickly dropping her arm behind her back to hide her knife and closing it, Delilah smiled at Livy Kowalski.

"Hello, Olivia."

Livy moved her gaze back and forth between Delilah and Oriana. After a moment, she asked, "Everything all right, Oriana?"

Gritting her teeth, Oriana bit out, "Yes. Everything's fine."

"Good. I'm going to be crashing here for a while."

Oriana nodded. "Okay. I'll let Mom and Dad know."

"Thanks."

Oriana walked off, and Delilah went to follow her. But Livy reached across and slammed one hand against the doorjamb, blocking her way out.

The little freak leaned in, going up on her toes to get near Delilah's neck, and breathed in deep.

God, Del hated this bitch. Always had.

But at the same time, she wasn't about to engage her, either. Del shoved Livy's arm out of her way and took a step into the hallway. Livy seemed to be letting her go, but as Del passed,

Livy snatched the closed knife out of her hand. She heard the bitch expertly open it.

Delilah spun around without thinking and found her own knife pressed against her throat. The freak's head tilted to the side as she studied her.

"Threaten one of the kids again," Livy told her, "and I'll cut your throat and watch ya bleed out."

"I think Toni might have a problem with that."

"No, she won't. And we both know it."

And damn her, but Delilah knew the bitch was right.

They stopped at the hotel first to get Ricky's travel stuff. He offered to meet Toni back at the house her parents were renting, but the look of panic on her face had him quickly changing that offer to immediately promising he wouldn't leave her side.

So he opened the door first and walked in, sniffing to make sure there were no Packmates lurking around.

Toni leaned in. "Embarrassed to be seen with me by your girlfriend?"

"*Ex*-girlfriend, and no. I just don't want you to face the Smith Pack Female Interrogation."

"You made that sound like all those words were initial capped."

"They are. I'm surprised you've never heard of it. There's lots of girls in mental institutions across the United States who've faced the Smith Pack Female Interrogation."

"Okay." She pushed past him and walked into his hotel room. "This is nice."

"Yeah."

She looked up at him, her little nose wrinkling. "Isn't it kind of expensive, though? To live at the Kingston Arms rather than getting your own apartment in Brooklyn or Queens?"

"Are those actual places?"

"Very funny."

"And my sister will be bearing the hybrid freak of the hotel's owner."

"Hybrid freak?" she demanded.

"Don't worry. I'll adore the little bastard like the moon."

She rolled her eyes and walked fully into the room. Ricky followed, closing the door behind him.

"Make yourself comfortable," he told her, heading toward the bedroom. "I'll be out in a bit."

"Why did you get a suite?" she asked.

"I didn't demand it, if that's what you're thinking. Brendon Shaw gave one to me and each of my brothers in the hopes we'd stop just showing up in his apartment upstairs whenever we like."

"Did you?" she asked from the other room.

"Nope!" Ricky pulled out the trusty black duffel bag that had gone with him to all sorts of places all over the world.

"Isn't Brendon Shaw a lion?"

"Yep."

"So you fully understand that just having you show up in his house is a form of torture for a man who truly does consider himself king of . . . well . . . probably everything."

"Of course we do. That's why we do it. Plus he gets this really good Greek plain yogurt that just seems to taste better being eaten in his apartment than in ours."

Ricky packed quickly and efficiently. He'd learned to do that a long time ago. Although he hadn't traveled much out of the States when he was growing up, his father and uncles sent him and his brothers—sometimes together, most often not—to different countries to meet with other Reeds and to learn about basic defense. It was something the Reeds felt was important. Sure, most everybody called them the junkyard dogs of the Smith Pack, but the truth was they really believed in being able to defend the Pack—and definitely the Reed family— whenever necessary.

The Smiths ruled as a Pack, so to speak, because they were willing to destroy anyone who even *thought* about touching one of their own. But the Smiths were also wild fighters. Like that kid in the schoolyard no one wanted to fight because he'd pick up a shovel and smash someone's head in rather than throwing crazy punches like any normal seven-year-old. The Reeds, however, prided themselves on being smarter fighters, just like the full-blooded wolves. They'd strike at night, find the weakest points, and do their best to ensure no—or at least *less*—"collateral damage." Ricky's grandfather once compared it to unleashing the berserkers (the Smiths) from the front while the Roman soldiers (the Reeds) snuck in from behind and destroyed the enemy.

The relationship between the Smiths and the Reeds had worked for centuries, ever since they'd landed on these shores a few years before those pilgrims ever did, and Ricky respected that relationship more than he could say. He didn't see the Smiths as separate from him, but a part of his life just like his momma and daddy and siblings. And he knew the Smiths felt the same way. When Bubba Smith said things like, "Come after the Smiths and we'll come down on you like hell itself opened its doors and let out the worst of its kind . . ." he wasn't just talking about protecting blood relatives. He was talking about *anyone* considered one of the Smith Pack. That was the Smith philosophy.

So when the Reeds raised their pups, they raised them to "protect their own," which meant protecting blood kin and Pack kin. It meant protecting their siblings and their cousins as well as old Missus Sandy Mae up the street who often ended up on the wrong side of full-humans in a nearby town because she was kind of crazy.

And protection was something the Reeds did not take lightly.

That's why working for Llewellyn Security was such a great job for Ricky. Not only did it allow him to protect the New York Smiths, a job he'd been born into, but also protect others for money, a job that helped him have a very healthy retirement fund as well as go on little excursions like this one.

Of course, it didn't hurt that he was getting to go with sexy little Toni Jean-Louis Parker. Nope. That didn't hurt at all.

"Speaking of protection . . ." Ricky studied the unopened

box of condoms in his medicine cabinet. After a moment, he shrugged and grabbed one box . . . then the second. "Couldn't hurt," he murmured after tossing the boxes into his duffel bag.

Ricky lifted his head, sniffed the air. *Rory.*

By the time he made it back into the small living room, his brother was walking through the door. His expression told Ricky he was not happy.

"You're going to *Siberia*?"

"No. We're going to Russia. Probably some place close to Moscow. Right, Toni?"

She reached into her backpack and pulled out the itinerary she'd been given by Cella Malone.

"We're going to Lake Baikal. Wait." She blinked, lowered the paper. "That *is* Siberia."

Ricky's eyes crossed. *Good Lord.*

"We're going into Siberia?" Ricky demanded.

"That's probably where the team is from. Most of the Russian teams likely train there off season." It made sense. She doubted any nosey full-humans were going to bother the shifter-only teams while they were training for games in Siberia. And Lake Baikal had freshwater seals, which the polars probably loved.

She looked at the wolf and immediately felt bad for him. He hadn't signed on for this. Moscow, or a place *close* to Moscow, was one thing, but asking him to travel to Siberia was definitely asking too much of the man.

"Look, Ricky, you don't have to—"

"I've already contacted Vic," Ricky's brother said, and walked around the couch Toni was sitting on and laid a case he had on the coffee table. He opened the case. "He'll be meeting you at the airport and he'll get you to Lake Baikal."

Toni, confused by all this, held up her own papers. "I have an itinerary."

"I know, darlin'," Rory said while at the same time removing the paper from her hand and putting it back into her bag.

"It'll help you once you get there, but I want to make sure y'all get there safe and then *stay* safe once you arrive. Vic will make sure of that."

"Who's Vic?"

"Dee recommended him awhile back. He helps our company when we need contacts in Eastern European countries."

"He was born and raised in Chicago, but his area of expertise is Eastern Europe," Ricky explained.

"You look worried," Toni told Rory. "I feel like I should be freaking out. Should I be freaking out?" she asked Ricky.

"No. Everything's going to be fine. This is just a precaution."

"How come Cella Malone didn't have to take these kinds of precautions?"

"You said it yourself, darlin'. She's a Siberian tiger *and* a Malone. No one's messin' with her."

"But it's probably best she's not going," Rory admitted. "Her reputation ain't much better than Novikov's with the Russian teams, and she probably would have asked Dee-Ann to go with her . . ."

The brothers stared at each other, then started laughing.

"Lord," Ricky finally said, "that would have been very bad."

"What does that mean?"

"It's just better that *you* are going," Rory insisted. "Now, you have your passport, right?"

"As much as my family travels? My mother's agent actually has a schedule when we all have to get our passports renewed."

"Excellent." Rory waved off his brother. "I know you've got what you need. I've already touched base with Llewellyn and he's arranged with that company y'all are flying with. Madra Air?"

"Yeah."

"He says just bring your nine, but nothing else."

Toni sat up straight. "You're bringing a gun on a plane?"

"Don't worry about that."

"I'd rather not end up on Madra's Do Not Fly List if you don't mind."

"Don't worry about that." He looked at his brother again. "So Dee-Ann has already contacted Vic for us. And he's still in Russia?"

"For now, yeah, he's been helping with tracking Whitlan."

"Wait," Toni cut in. "Who the hell's Whitlan?"

"Vic will get you whatever you need once you get to Russia," Rory went on, ignoring her.

"Better be more than a nine," Toni muttered, and she realized that both brothers were staring at her. "These are bears and Siberian tigers. A nine isn't going to do anything but irritate them."

"How do you know that?" Rory asked.

"When you're a small canine in a world filled with big cats, wolves, and bears, you find other ways to fight. Trust me, if full-blood jackals had thumbs, they'd know how to take down lions with a .416 Remington, too."

Ricky grinned. "Too?"

"Could you two flirt later?"

Toni growled at Rory. "I wasn't flirt—"

"Y'all need to remember that these Russian bears are not to be trifled with," Rory went on. "So if it looks like things are getting out of hand"—he looked directly at his brother—"let Toni do the talking."

Toni blinked. "*Me?* Why me?"

"If you can calm down Novikov, then Lord, woman, you can calm down damn near anybody."

"Thank you?"

Rory walked around the couch until he was right in front of Ricky. "Listen to me, little brother. Things explode out there, you let Vic do what he does best and you get yourself and our little Toni here out. Don't try to be anyone's dang hero."

"That's Reece's weakness, Rory. Ain't never been mine."

"Keep it that way."

The brothers stared at each other a few seconds longer, then they hugged.

And that's when Toni finally yelled out, "Is anyone else concerned that we're doing all this just to negotiate a contract for a goddamn sports team?" She threw her hands up in the air. *"Anyone?"*

The brothers pulled away and Ricky admonished, "You shouldn't blaspheme."

Toni's eyes crossed. "Shut up."

They walked right into the middle of a melee. It wasn't pretty, either. Fists and legs flying, screams and snarls and yips filling the air.

But Ricky had to admit he was impressed. Because while the two oldest were trying to figure out what to do, Toni walked right into that pit of swinging arms and legs and began yanking pups apart and tossing them around the room until she got to Oriana, who was too old to toss anywhere.

"That is enough!" Toni bellowed over the continuing screams and threats while she held her fifteen-year-old sister in a nice little choke hold. *"I mean it!"*

That seemed to calm them all down, and she pushed her sister away before facing Cooper and Cherise. "Where's Mom and Dad?"

"They went out with Aunt Irene."

"When?"

Coop looked off, clearly embarrassed, and admitted, "Fifteen min—"

"Fifteen? You couldn't keep them under control for *fifteen* minutes?"

"It's not his fault," Cherise chimed in from behind Coop. "He was practicing and I told him I'd take care of the kids, but things spiraled so quickly . . ."

Toni folded her arms over her chest and gazed down at her feet.

"Hey," Coop said, putting his hand on Toni's shoulder. "It's not a big deal. We'll figure this out. We'll make it work. Just give us a little more—"

"Time?" Toni asked, looking up at her brother. "We don't have time. I'm going to Russia tonight. For work."

"You're deserting us?" Kyle scrambled to his feet and gawked at his sister. "You're deserting us for that ridiculous *job*?"

In that second, Ricky saw Toni begin to waffle. She didn't want to desert her family.

She began to speak, probably to change her mind, but Cherise came around Cooper and stood by Toni's side. "Yes, she is going. Toni's going to Russia. Without us." Cherise smiled and it was a very pretty smile. She should do it more often so she didn't always look so terrified. "And we're going to be very proud of her when she goes."

"But Kyle the idiot is right." Oriana glared at her brother. "As much as I loathe to admit it." She focused on the rest of them. "She can't just go off and leave us! Nothing has been organized. Mom and Dad don't know what they're doing. Coop is busy preparing for his next concert, and his agent is constantly calling here about another record deal with the London Philharmonic, and Cherise is just goddamn hopeless."

Cherise frowned. "Hey."

"And you think you can just *leave*?" Oriana demanded of her eldest sister.

Toni looked over the faces of her siblings before replying, "Well—" she began, but that's when Ricky grabbed her around the waist and walked out of the room.

"Excuse us, y'all."

"Hey, country western fellow!" Kyle barked. "Where are you going with our sister?"

Ricky took Toni out into the hall and to the stairs. "Go upstairs. Pack."

"But—"

"No, 'but,' woman. Just do it."

Freddy walked around Ricky and took his sister's hand. "Come on, Toni. I'll help you pack."

The little boy started up the stairs, glancing back at Ricky and winking at him.

At least one of her siblings thought about someone other than himself. It was a nice change.

Ricky returned to the large living room and faced the children. "Now, y'all," he began, "I know it's hard to let your sister go when you need her so badly. But you really have to let her do this. You have to grow up a little and show your sister what big boys and girls you are." He gave them his best smile. "Right?"

After all the pups stared back at him, it was Kyle who dramatically threw his arms up in the air, rolled his eyes, and fell back on the couch behind him while Troy muttered, "And the common man speaks."

"You should bring something pretty," Freddy told Toni while he watched her pack, his little body on top of her dressing table.

"Why?"

"Because." He gave her an adorable closed-mouth smile and looked up at the ceiling.

"Frederick Jean-Louis Parker . . . what are you getting at?"

"I may be a kid, Toni, but I'm not a *child*." Yes, he was. "That wolf likes you. And you like him. But you have to look pretty. To keep his interest. So you two can be boyfriend and girlfriend and he can give you things that you can sell for profit."

Chuckling to herself, Toni folded another pair of jeans. "Where do you get this stuff from, Freddy?" She knew it wasn't from their mother or Aunt Irene. And it definitely wasn't from their dad, who to this day referred to himself as a male feminist, "because I have too many girls of my own now not to be."

"Delilah."

Toni froze in midpack at Freddy's answer, her folded jeans held over her case. "You've been spending time with Delilah?"

"A little. She's nice and fun."

Toni forced herself to continue packing and to keep her voice casual. She knew if she overreacted, Freddy would panic. Freddy and panic were two words that were very bad together. Very bad.

"She's fun? Really? What have you two been doing?"

"Making money for the orphans. First at home, but she said we'd start here now. A lot more orphans in New York."

Unable to keep packing, Toni turned and gazed at her baby brother. "Making money for orphans?"

"Uh-huh."

"How have you been doing that?"

Freddy looked at the open bedroom door. "I'm not supposed to tell," he whispered.

"You can tell me. You know that."

Freddy's trusting smile broke her heart. "I know I can." He motioned her close. When she stood right by him, his little knees pressed against her hips, he said, "Sometimes we just sit in the park and I look sad and Delilah asks people for money. Sometimes they don't want to give it to her or they want her to go somewhere with them to give her money, but she doesn't want to do that. So she makes up stories to tell them. I know that you and Daddy say we shouldn't lie, but to help orphans, I think it's okay. Don't you?"

Instead of replying to that, Toni asked, "What do you two do other times?"

"Delilah gives me this little TV to watch and a headphone that I can talk into while she plays cards with some people. Then I . . . I . . . I . . ." His little face screwed up as he tried to think of the right words.

"Count cards?"

"That's it!" He grinned. "It's easy for me."

"No one notices what she's doing?"

"No. But I think that's because they're mostly men and they stare right at her, but they don't see the thing she wears in her ear. They stare at her a lot. Probably because she's so pretty." Freddy frowned. "What's wrong?"

"Nothing," Toni lied. "But you're starting classes on Monday. You won't have time for all this once that happens. Okay?"

"Okay."

"Hey." She placed her hands on either side of his hips and leaned in. "Will you do me a big favor?"

"Sure!"

"I'll need travel supplies. The *good* stuff."

"You want me to hit Mom's stash of those fancy chocolates?"

"You read my mind."

She quickly gripped her brother's nose with her lips and twisted around while he giggled and pushed at her. Then she wrapped her arms around his waist, kissed his neck, and lifted him off the dresser. She spun him around once before putting him on the floor.

"And when I'm gone—"

"I know. Don't let Kyle make me feel like a loser because I'm not an artist. And don't let Troy make me feel like a loser because he's older and thinks he's smarter than me."

"And?"

"Don't steal. Don't set the house on fire."

"Good man. Now get what you can and bag it for me."

"Okay!" He charged out the door, and when Toni heard his little feet hit the stairs, she started for the doorway. That's when she was grabbed from behind and dragged back toward her bed.

She wasn't really startled by that grab, because she'd known that Livy had been asleep under her bed the entire time. Livy wasn't the normal guest that people had over. She really liked that feeling of sneaking around someone's home even when she'd been invited, and no one in the entire Jean-Louis Parker family gave a shit.

"Don't even think about it, Antonella," Livy said in her ear as she wrestled Toni back.

"I'm going to twist that bitch's neck until it snaps," Toni snarled, desperately fighting the strong little arms wrapped around her. "I'm going to put her down like the sick pup she is!"

Toni was thrown on the bed, and Livy climbed up on her chest, pinning her down.

"You're not being rational," Livy said calmly.

"Fuck rational! She dies tonight!"

"Uh . . ." Ricky said from the doorway. "Is everything all right?"

Livy motioned Ricky in with a tilt of her head and said, "Get in here and close the door."

Ricky's grin was *huge*. "Well, all right then."

"This isn't about you, hillbilly." Livy looked down at Toni. "You need to calm down. You can't go around killing your relatives. Even when they deserve it. As you know, I've tried and it just didn't work out well for me. Those ankle bracelets they use to monitor your movements are really *not* comfortable."

"That horrible bitch is using my baby brother to scam people."

"Who?" Ricky asked.

Livy smirked. "Delilah."

"The blonde?"

"Yeah," Livy replied. "And what really bothers you," Livy said to Toni, "isn't that it's just one of your siblings, but that it's Freddy."

"Because Freddy's the only one she could scam into doing this. Kyle and Oriana won't go near her. Zia and Zoe cry whenever she's around. Troy could do it and probably would, but he's such a ballbuster, he'd want hard cash from counting cards. And he'd never believe that orphans story."

Hands in the front pockets of his jeans, Ricky asked, "Isn't Troy, like . . . nine?"

"Your point?" Livy asked.

"And not to be indelicate, but . . . aren't y'all kind of rich?"

"Kind of rich?" Toni pushed Livy off her and dragged herself up until she was sitting. "My mother could buy the property we're currently sitting in outright . . . and in cash. But my sister likes to scam people for money. Do you know why?"

"Just another bored rich girl?"

"I wish. The twins are bored little rich girls. I can handle bored little rich girls."

"But sociopaths . . ." Livy muttered.

"Now come on," Ricky said. "I took psychology in college—"

"You went to college?" Livy asked, which got her a punch in the ribs from Toni. "Ow! It was just a goddamn question."

"—and y'all shouldn't be bantering around words like sociopath when you're talking about a family member."

"Believe what you want." Toni swung her legs over the edge of the bed so that she and Livy were sitting right next to each other. Toni thought a minute and decided what she had to do.

"I've made my decision. I obviously can't go on this trip. I can't go."

That's when Livy slammed Toni to the floor and pinned her there—because the woman simply didn't know the meaning of the word subtle.

Ricky grabbed the small but surprisingly strong and vicious female off of Toni.

"Tell her," Livy ordered him once he'd gotten her off Toni. "Tell her that she *is* going."

"How can I go now?" Toni shot back. "At first I thought I just needed to deal with the schedule issue, which is challenge enough. But now . . . after what I've found out about Delilah?"

"Excuses!" Livy accused, pointing a damning finger at Toni. "You're using bullshit excuses to get out of this. Because you're scared."

"They're bears! Of course I'm scared!"

"Not of the bears, you idiot." Livy swung her arms until Ricky was forced to drop her. Then she re-adjusted her T-shirt and denim mini-skirt. "You're scared of change. You're scared of taking this chance and going out on your own."

"They need me."

"Because you've made them helpless. Which, I'd like to remind you, is not your job. Your job as the eldest jackal sibling is to prepare them for life on their own."

"But what about Delilah?" Toni demanded. "She's a problem all on her own."

"Isn't that something your parents should be concerned with?" Ricky asked.

"My parents are in denial. I'm not."

"*I'll* watch out for Freddy," Livy said.

"I can't ask you to—"

"I'll watch out for Freddy, so just suck-it-the-fuck-up already."

"Don't curse at me, whore!"

"Birthing cow!"

"All right!" Ricky cut in before he was hurt trying to stop these two females from getting into a claw match. "That's it!" He focused on Toni. "The bottom line is, if you don't take this trip, I can assure you that Cella Malone is going to fire your ass, no matter whose cousin you are."

"I don't care," Toni said, her voice firm. "Let her fire me. I'm not leaving. At least not until we get things . . . organized."

"Organized?"

"Right. Once I get their schedules organized, everything will be fine. That'll just take me a couple of days. Cella won't mind that, I'm sure."

Toni walked out, leaving Ricky and Livy standing there, gazing at the open door.

"Will that Cella Malone chick mind that?" Livy asked him.

"She sure will."

"Then we have to take away her excuses."

Ricky shrugged. "I may have an idea." He pulled out his phone. "But my baby brother won't like it."

"Your baby brother? Was that the other wolf who was in the office with us?"

"Yep."

"Then I don't give a shit he won't like it."

Ricky laughed and began making calls.

Chapter Fifteen

Paul stepped out of the cab and held his hand out so that Jackie could grab it. He helped her out and then held his hand out for Irene. She, as always, completely ignored it, and got out on her own. He didn't take that personally, though. He never had. It was one of the main reasons they'd gotten along so well. Paul never took anything Irene did personally. She was so brutally direct and unwaveringly honest, it didn't make sense to get all worked up when she said things like, "I'd prefer you not touch me" or "Are you staring at me because you have a question or because you're planning to kill me at your earliest convenience?"

Paul, the first and only born of his hippie mom, loved that directness. He loved that he knew his beautiful mate would always be safe around Irene Conridge because she never bothered to lie. And, when they started having pups, that his kids would be safe around her. He hadn't been crazy about the wolves that became part of their lives when Irene had hooked up with Niles Van Holtz, but it made sense. Irene simply didn't fit in with full-humans even though she was one. She needed a predator for a mate . . . even if that predator was an obsessive-compulsive wolf.

And, over time, Paul and Van had become buddies. Sort of. And Van treated all the Jean-Louis Parker kids as family and Pack, which meant a lot. So it had all worked out.

Like now. Having Irene around while they were staying in

New York was great because it kept Jackie happy. The pair of them could sit around gabbing or making fun of the kids or obsessing over the future of the kids' educations. And while they did that, Paul could do what he really loved to do . . . watch TV, read a book, and fix up old cars.

It was turning out to be a really nice summer with Irene around.

The trio reached the stone steps outside of their rental house and began to climb. Paul glanced over his shoulder and saw a limo parked a bit down the street. He didn't know why it was there or why he noticed it.

Jackie pulled out her keys and had them in the lock when the door opened and that country wolf was standing there. Man, this kid was really making a hard run at Paul's baby girl. Something that would normally set Paul's hair on fire, but after that last idiot had made her miserable, the wolf seemed like a good way to transition *away* from that past relationship and into more promising ones.

"Richard Reed?" Irene said, because she wasn't about to call anyone Ricky Lee. "Why are you here?"

"Miss Irene. Miss Jackie. Mr. Paul."

"Please don't call me that," Paul practically begged as they all moved into the hallway and Paul closed the door. He felt old enough without adding "mister" before his first name like he should be wearing an ascot.

"I need y'all to do me a favor and just go along with what's about to happen."

Paul blinked. "Why? What's about to happen?"

There was a knock on the door Paul had just closed and he pulled it open again. "Good Lord," he muttered, staring up at the behemoth standing in his doorway. He looked at Ricky. "Toni's bringing stray hockey players home with her now?"

"Actually I asked Mr. Novikov here. To help out."

"Help out with what?" Irene asked, her gaze locked on the man lumbering into their home. "Are you planning to kill all the children so they'll no longer be a bother?"

"Irene," Jackie chastised. "Not the right response."

"Because it's morally wrong or because you're afraid he'll get mad and kill us, too?"

"Both!" Jackie snapped.

"Hi!" A pretty black woman popped out from behind Novikov. She had a bright, wide smile and adorable dimples, but Paul didn't understand why she was here or why Novikov was here. What the hell was going on?

"I'm Blayne. Bo's fiancée. I'm here to help, too."

"Except I didn't ask her here to help," Novikov replied, his cold blue eyes looking around the hallway like he was trying to figure out how to destroy the walls to get to the weak pups within. "But she's worried I'll make your kids cry."

"No, no," his fiancée quickly cut in, trying to laugh it off. "He's very good with children. He has to be." The wolfdog gripped his thick arm with very strong-looking hands. "You *have* to be."

"If you're once again talking about our future offspring, I already told you that as long as they understand schedules and time management and focus . . . we'll be fine." He locked those cold, dead eyes on Ricky Reed. "Where are they?"

"I'll show you."

"You will?" Paul asked, trying to ignore the fact his voice broke.

"Just go along with this," the wolf said again before heading down the hallway.

Paul looked at Jackie and Irene. Both females shrugged and, not knowing what else to do, followed after the wolf and the two unstable-looking hybrids.

Their children were in the living room arguing. Paul had left them that way more than an hour ago, and it didn't seem as if much had changed except that Toni had joined the fray.

She was standing next to a dry-erase board that had a very large claw mark ripped through it.

"This," Toni said, pointing at the dry-erase board, "was not helpful, Oriana."

Paul's fifteen-year-old baby girl had started shifting her entire body at fourteen and was now learning to control that power, which meant that she liked to whip her claws out at the slightest provocation.

"You always side with Kyle and Troy," Oriana accused. "I'm sick of it."

"I do not always side with them."

"No," Kyle corrected, "she always sides with Cooper and Cherise."

"Why are you even here, Cooper?" Troy demanded.

Raising his hands and dropping them, Cooper asked, "What are you attacking me for? I've been trying to help you little bastards."

"Well, good job, big head."

Cooper's eyes narrowed and he took several steps toward Troy, but Toni caught his arm and held him back. It was a rare thing to see Cooper's temper, but Kyle and Troy always managed to get that anger out of him.

Ricky Reed stepped forward and said, "Toni, I brought you and your kin some help."

Toni looked over and her eyes widened at the sight of Bo Novikov. Then Kyle perked up and said, "Mr. Novikov! Are you here to pose for me?"

"No!" Novikov and Toni said simultaneously.

Toni focused on the large hybrid. "What *are* you doing here?"

"Reed's idiot brother called me—"

"I do have a name, hoss."

"—and said you needed help with schedules and organization."

"But don't you have practice?"

"Malone canceled it for tonight, which meant my other option was another thrilling dinner with a bunch of never-shutting-up wild dogs."

"They love you!" Blayne said with a huge grin.

Novikov glanced at his fiancée and back at Toni. "See what I mean?"

"Hi, Toni!" the wolfdog cheered.

"Oh." Toni frowned. "Hi, um . . ."

The wolfdog's smile slowly faded. "Blayne. Blayne Thorpe."

"Uh-huh."

"We just met this morning?"

"Uh-huh."

She tried again. "Bo's fiancée?"

"Oh. Right. Bane."

"Blayne."

"Right." Toni turned back to Novikov. "So you're here to help?"

"What makes you think *you* can help us?" Troy asked, sounding particularly snobby. "I mean you're just a sports guy, right? You're like Oriana . . . only with skates."

"Physique wise, though," Kyle pointed out, "he is perfection." When everyone stared at him, Kyle added, "Perfect for a sculptor like me."

"Okay."

Novikov walked over and stood next to Toni so that he towered in front of the kids. He was like a giant wall.

"What I am, small child I can easily crush with one hand, is the best hockey player in the States. Not one of the best. I'm *the* best. And I ensure I stay the best with focus, determination, and a willingness to destroy anyone who tries to get my puck. What ensures that I stay on point with all that I have to do in a day is maintaining my schedule and organizing my life. That's my fiancée, Blayne." He pointed over at Blayne, but she was still staring at Toni. "She's all over the place. Schedules mean nothing to her. She writes lists but she doesn't follow them. That's probably why she's a plumber."

That's when he had Blayne's full attention. "I like being a plumber."

"But you're not the best plumber."

"I'm one of the best plumbers in the Manhattan area."

He looked back at Paul's children. "*One* of the best," he repeated. "See what I mean?"

"But you can help us, right?" Kyle asked.

"I *will* help you. It's the least I can do for your sister."

"For Toni?" Troy briefly studied his sister. "What do you owe her?"

"I'm the best in the States. And she's going to help me get to Russia to prove that I'm the best *in the world.*" He looked at Toni and, for the first time since walking into their home, the hybrid smiled. It didn't make him look any more approachable or nicer but it still helped . . . a little. "Right, Toni?"

Toni swallowed and, with a sigh, nodded her head. "Yeah. That's right."

"Then you better get going."

"Are you sure you want to do this?" Toni asked. "They're really horrible children."

"Where's the loyalty?" Kyle demanded.

"They're not horrible," Novikov corrected. "They're just determined. I understand determined. I can handle determined. What I can't handle is telling me my wedding will start *around* three o'clock."

"Are you still bringing that up?" Blayne snarled.

"Yes!"

"You'll need a new dry-erase board," Toni pointed out.

"I don't like dry-erase boards." He looked at the kids. "Can anyone tell me why?"

Kyle raised his hand and when Novikov pointed at him, he answered, "Because they can be erased?"

"Exactly. There's no permanence. But I saw an office supply store a few blocks away. Let's go get those giant Post-it notes that we can stick to the walls. Actually, let's get an array of sizes of Post-its. In different colors. And multicolor permanent markers. Permanent. Not erasable. That way we can color-code things permanently. I like color-coding." He pointed at the twins, Freddy, and Dennis. "These very small ones will stay here. I won't be responsible for their safety. But I'll take these three with me." He pointed at Oriana, Kyle, and Troy. "I can tell they'll be the most trouble during this process." Yet that didn't seem to bother him.

"Can I come?" Blayne asked.

"No. You'll wander the aisles and want to buy things that aren't needed for this process. But I will pick you up a couple of those giant Butterfingers that they sell at the cash register."

Blayne grinned. "Okay!"

"You three," Novikov ordered. "Let's go."

And for the first time Paul could think of, his three middle children got to their feet and followed after someone *without question*. It boggled his mind.

"Where are you going?" Jackie asked Toni.

"Russia. To negotiate with bears."

"Don't worry, though," Ricky Reed told them, putting his arm around Toni's shoulders. "I'm going with her to protect her."

"Because Russian bears love wolves so much?"

The wolf grinned. "Mr. Parker, is that what you Yankees call sarcasm?"

Livy Kowalski walked into the living room. "Your bag is packed and ready to go," she told Toni. "Your limo is waiting outside."

"Yeah, but—"

"No buts, canine. Just go. You need to do this."

"She's right," Paul said, moving to stand in front of his daughter and taking her hands in his. "Is this part of your job, baby?"

"It is."

"Then you have to go."

"Or I could quit."

"Let me ask you this . . . do you want to quit? And before you answer, I'm not asking if you think you should quit or if you think your siblings want you to quit. I'm asking you if you *want* to quit?"

Toni was silent for a long moment before she replied, "I don't think so. At least not yet."

"Then go get your plane and do your job."

"And you guys?"

"We'll be fine. I promise." He leaned down and kissed her cheek. "I love you, baby."

"I love you, too, Dad."

"And be careful."

"Yes, sir."

Toni headed out, stopping to hug her mother and Irene. She motioned for Cooper to follow her.

Ricky Reed nodded at Paul. "I'll protect her with my life, sir."

"You better," Paul told him plainly. "Because I will kill you if anything happens to my daughter. And I mean anything."

"I understand, sir." And Paul believed him, which was surprising because Paul rarely believed wolves unless it was Niles Van Holtz.

Jackie faced Paul once the kids were down the hall and at the door, saying their good-byes to Toni. "We're letting our daughter go off to negotiate with *bears*?"

"No. We're letting our daughter go off and be an adult. It's time, Jack. You know that."

"I know. I know."

He wrapped his arms around his mate and hugged her tight. "Of all our kids, she's the one I know can handle herself in any situation. So don't worry."

"Okay."

They held each other for a bit until Jackie asked, "Where's that dog you insist on keeping around?"

"I like that dog. She's the only one in the family who doesn't talk back."

"Excuse me." Blayne, who Paul hadn't realized was still in the room, smiled and gave a little wave. "Your dog is under the couch."

Still holding on to each other, Paul and Jackie leaned over a little so they could look under the couch.

"Huh," Jackie said. "She sure is."

"That's kind of Bo's fault," Blayne explained. "He scares regular dogs. He doesn't mean to, of course, but there's no helping it."

Paul shook his head. "That's fine. It's not a—"

"I'm really excited he'll be spending some time with your

kids," Blayne went on, cutting Paul off but somehow not being rude about it. She just seemed to have all this energy that simply could not be contained. "I plan to have a whole busload of kids myself, and he needs to learn how to deal with children without making them cry or hide or scream hysterically."

Jackie tensed in Paul's arms, so he held his mate a little tighter, keeping her in place.

"He's such a great guy, but no one ever sees it because, ya know, the glower and all *is* off putting, but that's just his focus. But now that I've met your kids, I see you guys totally understand that. What's it like having so many prodigies in one family?"

"Well—" Paul began.

"Although I don't know if they'll all be like Bo. I'm honestly terrified they'll all be like me. I'm not sure how he'll handle that. But this is a good start, don't cha think? Let him deal with kids just like himself and then I can ease him into more . . . challenging children. Yeah. That's a good plan."

"O—"

"Anyway, it's really nice of you guys to let us stay here. We'll just sleep on the couch. Don't worry"—she grinned and winked—"no hanky-panky while we're here."

Paul held Jackie even tighter. "You're staying here?"

"Oh, yeah. I thought maybe a day for this thing but after meeting your kids and realizing how much like Bo they are . . . you're looking at a minimum of a two-day but more likely a three-day ordeal to get them all to agree. But according to Ricky Lee, most classes and whatever don't really start until next Monday, so that's enough time. I wouldn't worry." She stepped closer. "I just have to say you two are *such* a cute couple and I think we're going to be such great friends!"

Paul's grip on his mate at this point was so tight, he was surprised he hadn't broken any of her ribs. But he had to take the risk because Jack hated people who, in her words, "chatter on." And holy hell could this wolfdog chatter! And too much chatter meant that every once in a while, Jackie started swinging, and Paul really didn't want to have to listen to the whining that would inevitably arrive come practice time once Jack's knuckles started to swell. It was really hard to play violin when one's knuckles swelled.

"While we're waiting for Bo to come back with the kids," Blayne went on, "would you like to go get some coffee or—"

Irene suddenly took hold of Blayne's forearm, gripping her tight. Like Paul, Irene knew how to read Jack like a book. It helped them work together to keep her calm. "Come with me," Irene ordered.

"Where to?" Blayne innocently asked.

"Any place where we can intelligently discuss why your fiancé is so freakishly large and inhuman looking. Was he subject to radiation while in his mother's womb?"

Jackie snorted a laugh and quickly buried her face against Paul's neck while Paul bit the inside of his cheek hard so he didn't laugh.

Blayne stopped walking right outside the living room and frowned at Irene. "Wait . . . what?"

CHAPTER SIXTEEN

Nothing like a nearly fourteen-hour flight to make a girl miserable.

Even though flying on Madra Airlines meant that Toni and the wolf could stretch their legs out since the plane was designed with Russian and Alaskan bears in mind. They also got to choose between entrees like cow, gazelle, buffalo, zebra; and for the polars, whale and seal blubber.

Other than that, it was still the same, excruciatingly long flight it always was whether a shifter-run flight or full-human.

Dropping her bag to the ground, Toni took a long, much-needed stretch, then did an allover shake.

Once done with that, Toni pulled out the itinerary from the back pocket of her jeans.

"Okay. Now we need to get to . . ." Toni's words faded out when she sensed someone standing in front of her. Slowly, she raised her gaze up and up and up some more to the male standing in front of her.

"Hi ya," he said, and smiled at her.

"Hello."

"I'm Vic Barinov."

"Hey, Vic," Ricky said, holding out his hand and shaking.

"Ricky Lee. Long time." He motioned with his head. "Let's go. I've got a car waiting for us. It'll take us to a private airstrip."

Toni looked down at the itinerary. "But we're taking the Trans Siberian Ex—"

"That's changed," Barinov told them. "You don't want to be caught on a train if there's a problem."

Toni, completely confused, shook her head. "I don't . . . I mean . . ." She looked at the two males watching her. "What I'm trying to say is . . . you both know I'm only going to negotiate a deal between our *hockey* team and the Russians', right? It's not like I'm Double O-Seven, trying to set up an arms deal."

A low rumble rolled out of Barinov while Ricky just grinned at her.

"Ain't she cute?" the wolf asked.

"Very. Let's go."

Great. Another male ignoring her.

"Who is that guy?" she asked Ricky.

"That's Vic Barinov."

"I know his name, Ricky Lee. Who, and for that matter, *what* is he? Because he's not just some security guy."

"He's a former Marine or Navy SEAL. Something like that. Born and raised in the States, but his parents were born and raised here in Russia. His daddy's Kamchatka grizzly and his momma's Siberian tiger."

"*He's* our protection."

"Trust me, darlin'"—Ricky laughed, putting his arm around her shoulders—"that boy ain't gonna cause any problems if it means he'll have to deal with Dee-Ann Smith for even two seconds."

Toni thought about that as they headed toward the exit, pushing past tourists and locals rushing to their flights. And Toni realized . . . Ricky was absolutely right. No one wanted to deal with Dee-Ann if they didn't have to.

Devon "Junior" Barton had been on Iowa's Death Row for more than ten years. He'd started out with life, but after killing a couple of fellow inmates, he earned a cell on death row. Not that he cared. Junior didn't care about much. He hadn't cared about the addicts he'd sold drugs to. He hadn't cared about the dealers he'd hired that, when they'd cheated him, he'd beaten to death with pipes. He definitely hadn't cared when he'd strangled the life out of his third wife or that his daughter had been watching when he'd done it.

Junior Barton didn't care about much. What was the point? He did get bored a lot, but there were always those who wanted to save him. The religious ones who wanted to save his soul—they were always fun to torment. And the ones who just wanted to save his life because they thought the death penalty was wrong. And, when he was really bored, he could write his daughter and with just a few well-placed words, turn her life into a flashback nightmare that sent her screaming to her therapist.

It really didn't matter to him; it was all just a game.

So when that really big C.O. suddenly appeared at his cell and told him he had visitors at one in the morning . . . Junior didn't really care. He'd assumed it was time for a beating from the guards, but this particular guard—a big black guy named Gowan—didn't spend much time around the others. He didn't speak much in general and most of the other inmates gave him a wide berth. The crazy ones never threw shit at him when they flipped out, and the dangerous ones never tried to cut him or gouge out an eye. There were other big, black guards at this prison, but this particular one . . . he was different.

So when Gowan kept walking until they reached the same room where Junior had met that priest he knew he could easily make fall in love with him, he began to wonder what was going on. And he wondered if it would be something fun.

"Sit," Gowan ordered. He was an abrupt kind of guy but never rude. He didn't get enjoyment out of torturing inmates like some of the other guards. He just did his job.

Junior sat down at the long table and waited for Gowan to shackle him to one of the metal legs, but he didn't. That was the strangest thing of all because everyone knew that if Junior had the slightest chance, he'd cut a bitch. Cut a face right off . . . and had. A doctor that was helping him after a fight.

She'd been kind of pretty, too, but not anymore. Not once he was done with her.

Gowan stepped back by the door and stood there, waiting.

That's when Junior realized that no other C.O. had ever taken him anywhere without a partner. Usually more than one.

What was going on?

Curious, but Junior didn't say anything. He didn't ask Gowan what was going on. Mostly because he didn't care.

Finally, after about fifteen minutes or so, the door opened and three people walked in. One was another really big guy. He looked like a biker Junior once knew. Maybe. Another was a female. Really pretty. Long black hair with some red and white streaks in it; tall; big tits that sat high on her chest. He bet she had a tight pussy, too. Man, would he love to find out. The third person was a woman, too. She had short hair, but wasn't really pretty, and had lots of scars, but it was her weird eyes that he noticed first. Her eyes reminded him of a pit bull he once used for protection. That dog had the same colored eyes.

The three strangers walked into the room, and the hot one sat in the chair opposite Junior. The biker stood behind her with his back against the wall, and the one with the dog eyes sat kitty-corner from the hot one.

"Mr. Barton?"

Junior didn't answer, just stared, waiting to see where this was going.

"I won't bother with introductions," she went on, a smile on that pretty face. That pretty face just begging to be destroyed. "Instead I'll get right to it. We're here for information. About one of your old cell mates." She studied Junior a moment, then said, "Frankie Whitlan."

So that's what they wanted. They wanted good ol' Frankie. Junior didn't have friends, but neither did Frankie. But they both understood the world they lived in and how the barter system worked.

"I haven't seen Frankie Whitlan in a lot of years. Not much I can tell you about him."

"We're not looking for anything recent. Just some details that perhaps no one else would know but the man who once shared a cell with him."

"And what do I get out of giving you information?"

"What would you like . . . within reason, of course?"

"You could start by getting on your knees and sucking my cock. Then we can take it from there."

The biker's entire body tensed and he growled. A low, rolling growl that made Junior laugh. Guys always thought they sounded scary when they growled.

The hottie smiled. "That's not going to happen, sweetie. Sorry."

"Then I don't know what you're hoping to get."

"You're really not going to help us, are you? I can see that in your cold, dead little eyes."

Junior didn't answer because there was no point. The hottie seemed to understand him perfectly.

She looked over her shoulder at the biker, and Junior prepared himself to get slapped around by the guy.

The biker pushed away from the wall and walked toward Junior . . . then past him and to the door. The hottie got up and followed him, leaving Junior alone with the plain girl.

That one waited until the door closed behind her two friends and the guard, then she brought one long leg up and dropped it onto the metal table.

"That's a mighty big foot you've got there, princess," Junior remarked.

The plain one didn't say anything, just brought up the other leg, crossing them at the ankle, and folding her arms over her nonexistent chest.

Junior stared at her and waited. She stared back.

And she kept staring . . . and staring . . . and staring . . .

Cella sat on Crush's lap and rested her head on his big shoulder. "Mom invited us for dinner this weekend."

"Okay."

"Are you coming for me? Or are you coming because you

get to hang with my dad and hear more stories about the good old days of shifter hockey?"

"Why does it have to be one or the other with you?"

Cella laughed and snuggled in closer.

"How long should we leave them in there?" Pete Gowan asked. He was beginning to look a little nervous.

"Give them a few more minutes."

"Yeah, but . . ." The leopard male shifted from one foot to another. "I'll have to explain if anything happens to him."

"Would I leave you hanging, Gowan?" Cella asked her fellow feline.

"Yes."

Crush laughed. "At least he's not delusional."

"Quiet, you."

After another fifteen minutes, there was a knock on the door. Gowan quickly opened it and then, just as quickly, all three of them choked from the smell and turned their heads.

Once Smith was out of the room, Gowan slammed the door shut. "Before I go back in there," he snarled, "what did you do, canine?"

Smith shrugged. "Nothin'."

"Then why," Cella demanded, "did he shit himself?"

Another shrug. "I don't know. He suddenly pissed himself and then took a shit."

"No way, Smith." Gowan shook his head. "The man has been clinically diagnosed by three separate psychiatrists, including the one working for his defense team, as a sociopath. So you must have done something to him because"—Gowan opened the door, looked in again, and closed it—"he's in there sobbing. Sociopaths don't sob, Smith. They don't know how to sob unless it's to get what they want."

"Maybe he's faking it," Cella suggested. "Sociopaths can fake anything."

"No," Smith said. "He's not faking it."

Try to help a canine and this is what I get . . .

"Then what did you do?" Gowan pushed.

"Nothing," Smith insisted. "Just stared at him."

"You didn't hit him?" Gowan asked. "Cut him with that knife of yours? Shoot him in the knee cap?"

"No."

"Any reason I need to rush him to the infirmary?"

"No."

"Did you at least find out anything?" Crush asked.

"Yep."

When the wolf said nothing else, Cella began rubbing her eyes so that she didn't get into a fistfight with Smith.

"How about you tell us what he said," Crush prompted, because the bear had way more patience than any cat.

"Whitlan's got a kid. A daughter."

Cella sat up in Crush's lap. "A daughter? Are you sure?"

"He wasn't lying to me," Dee said about Barton.

"Where is she? Did you get a name?"

"He didn't have the kid's name, but he had her mother's."

Crush stood, carefully placing Cella on her feet. "Good work, Dee."

"Thank you kindly." She looked up at Gowan. "Sorry about the mess, hoss."

"Yeah. Sure." He pushed open the door and entered the room. Smith looked in at the convict and said, "Bye now, darlin'. Thanks for all your help!"

Cella cringed when she heard a sound familiar to any Malone who'd attended a St. Patrick Day's parade.

"Jesus, Smith!" Gowan exploded from the room. "You made him throw up! *God! He's throwing up all over the goddamn place!"*

Smith shrugged and came over to Cella and Crush. Another shifter, a black bear, waited to lead them out, the security cameras conveniently and temporarily turned off.

"What did you really do to him?" Cella had to ask her.

"Nothin'."

"Smith," she said, stopping by the bear. "The man shit, pissed, and vomited after spending less than thirty minutes with you. There has to be a reason."

"Got me. All I did was stare at him until he told me something I could use."

The bear looked Smith over. "Did you stare at him with those eyes of yours?"

"I have my daddy's eyes."

"Annnnd, we now have our answer," Cella announced before they made their way out of the maximum security prison and headed home.

CHAPTER SEVENTEEN

As soon as Toni stepped off the small plane in Siberia, she remembered to turn her cell phone back on and it immediately began to go off with texts.

Toni had turned off her phone before she got on the plane in Long Island. She always turned it off when she got onto flights. She didn't use it for entertainment like most of the universe. It was strictly for communication. Usually, this wasn't an issue. But that's because she traveled with most, if not all, of her family at the same time. However, right now, her family was back in New York and eight hours behind her current time zone, which meant that by now . . . they were just starting to get the full Novikov organizational treatment.

And after reading the first couple of texts, she knew that they were not enjoying it.

Toni stood in the middle of the tiny airport and quickly responded to Oriana, then Cooper, then Kyle. She was about to respond to Troy when a hand pressed against her back. Without thinking, she spun and swung her right fist.

Shocked but instinctively blocking that wildly swinging fist, Ricky quickly stepped back, his eyes wide.

"Oh," she said, pulling her hand back and scratching her neck. "Sorry." She turned away from him and began typing again on her phone.

"Are you all right, Toni?"

"Yeah. I'm fine. Just . . ." She got a reply from Oriana and ended up shaking her phone in her now-sore fist and gritting her teeth. *"Ridiculous, demon children!"*

"Ooookay." Ricky stepped closer to her but didn't touch her this time. "We have to go."

"Go?" she snapped. "Go where?"

"We're taking a helicopter to Lake—"

"Christ! Now we have to get on a helicopter?"

"Well, to get to this particular location—"

Fed up, "Oh, whatever!"

She stormed off, just expecting Ricky to follow.

Ricky watched the She-jackal march off as Barinov eased up behind him.

"What the hell—" the hybrid asked.

"I have no idea. I've never seen her like this before."

"Well, she needs to calm down, Reed. If she goes at the bears like that . . ."

"I know. I know." He shrugged and started to follow. "Maybe she's just tired. We were on a fourteen-hour flight, then that six-hour flight on a smaller plane."

"Should we get a hotel tonight and wait before we meet with the bears?"

"They're expecting us tonight, I think. Plus, I'm afraid what she'll do if we try to stretch this out the tiniest bit."

The males arrived at the row of glass doors where people came and went. Toni stood on the other side—screaming.

"Are you two coming or what?"

Ricky glanced at Barinov. "Maybe a good night's sleep is what she needs."

"Or some puppy Prozac."

"Stop."

The helicopter flew them to a small full-human city just an hour or two outside a little-known and never discussed shifter-only territory.

"I have a car waiting," Barinov told them. He carried a small bag in his hand and led the way to a Range Rover that looked as if it could handle all sorts of terrain.

Ricky held the door open for Toni and she got inside, leaning back into the comfortable seats and resting her bag next to her.

"How are you holding up?" the wolf asked her.

Toni texted Kyle back, informing him that it was definitely illegal to put anything in anyone's food that "might make them, ya know . . . kinda sick."

Making someone "kinda sick" was not okay!

She reminded Kyle, once again, that if he ever went to jail for *anything*, no one in the family would pay to have him bonded out. No one.

Hitting SEND, she finally looked up at the wolf and asked, "What?"

"I said how are you holding up?"

"How do I look like I'm holding up?" she snapped, because it was such a fucking stupid question. "I'm exhausted. I'm stressed out. And I just want to get this stupid trip over with."

"All right then." He gestured out the front window. "Vic here tells me we're almost at the hotel."

"Hotel? Why are we going to the hotel first? I thought we were going straight to meet with the bears."

"Nah. Not tonight. It's way too late. A good night's sleep and—"

"You're not listening to me," she told the wolf. "I want to see the bears. I want to see the bears *tonight!*"

Ricky stared into the backseat at the She-jackal he was beginning to believe was losing her dang mind. And whether she was or she wasn't, for safety reasons, there was no way he could let Toni meet up with those bears tonight. It would have to be tomorrow after she had a shower, some sleep, and maybe some valium if he could get his hands on any.

"That's not in your or the team's best interest, Antonella."

Toni dropped her phone in her lap so she could ball her

hands into fists. "I want to see the bears now. Now! Do you hear me? Now!"

"Not going to happen, so you might as well just suck it up."

"I hate you!"

"Well, I'm not liking you much right now either, darlin', so that only seems fair."

Frustrated, Toni tried to roll down her window by pushing on the button. Ricky didn't know what was going on, but the window didn't go down. That's when she started punching the window with her fists.

"Hey," Barinov said low. "Reed."

"What?"

"You know what's going on here, don't you?"

"No," Ricky quickly shot back. "That is *not* what's going on here."

"Are you kidding? What else could it be?"

Ricky shook his head. "It's something else. Exhaustion or sudden onset of mental illness. That's it."

"You're serious?"

"I'm very serious. I'm telling you, it's not . . . *that.*"

Ricky glanced into the backseat to see Toni pawing at the window with her hands because she still couldn't get it to open.

"I'm trapped," she snarled at the air. *"Trapped!"*

"Nope," Barinov muttered. "It couldn't possibly be *that.*"

They reached a large hotel that straddled the border between full-human and shifter territory.

Toni stepped out of the vehicle and looked up at the building. "Here?" she asked. "We come halfway 'round the world and you bring us to a chain hotel? We might as well have met them on the Jersey Turnpike."

Ricky looked at Barinov. "Could you get us checked in?"

"Sure."

Once the hybrid had gone inside the hotel, Ricky faced her. "Look, darlin', I'm tryin' desperately not to get real cranky with you. But you are pushing my last redneck nerve."

"What does that even mean?"

"It means we're in a foreign country and in a hostile part of said foreign country, at least where our kind is concerned. My whole goal is to get you home safe and sound. Your father made it clear that he would accept nothing less. And getting you home safely means that you don't piss off bears. And the way you're acting right now . . . you're gonna piss them off."

"Fine."

Ricky frowned. "Fine?"

"Fine."

Maybe she was being a little . . . terse. Toni was willing to admit that. She probably just needed some sleep. It had been an excruciatingly long trip and dealing with the texts from her siblings hadn't helped.

Ricky nodded. "Then let's go."

They entered the hotel and Toni was pleasantly surprised to find that the interior had a wonderful look and feel to it. Like a hip, sixties apartment, but nothing felt dated or old. It actually felt quite modern and European. She loved it.

Not that she'd admit that now to Ricky.

By the time they reached the front desk, Barinov had already gotten their rooms. His Russian was fluent and his accent almost as good as the twins'—although their accent was flawless after watching some Russian language movie on cable one afternoon. More than one person had asked Toni and her mother what Russian adoption agency they'd used.

Barinov handed Toni her electronic key and, without a word, headed toward the elevators. They went to the ninth floor and walked down the hall.

"This is your room," he said, briefly stopping in front of it. "I'll be in the room to your left. Reed in the room to your right. If you need either one of us—"

"Oh, please." Toni used her keycard and went inside. She closed the door in the faces of the two males, not even in the mood to say good night. She stepped farther inside and took a good look around. She was as impressed with her room as she was with the hotel's lobby. This would be a nice place to stay for the next few days.

Placing her bag on the dresser, Toni sat down on the bed. Her cell phone vibrated and she sighed. She'd gotten three texts at the same time. Oriana informing Toni that she could not "exist under this regime!" Kyle begging her to re-think her stance on his sketching a naked Novikov. And Bo Novikov imploring her to get her little brother to stop asking him about sketching him naked. "It's beginning to make me uncomfortable."

Unable to answer any of those texts, Toni tossed her phone on the bed and fell back against the mattress. She could do this. She *would* do this. All she needed was a little room service and a good night's sleep.

Vic focused on Ricky.

"What?" Ricky asked him, annoyed although the hybrid hadn't actually done anything yet.

"Are you going to admit the problem now?"

"She's just tired," he said again. "By tomorrow, she'll be—"

"Even worse." Vic briefly pursed his lips. "I always thought you weren't as stubborn as your brothers. Guess I was wrong."

"No call to get nasty."

Shaking his head, Vic headed toward his own room. "See you in the morning."

"Yeah." Ricky waited until the door to Vic's room closed, then stood in front of Toni's door for several more minutes. He stared at it, debating with himself if he should stand out here all night or not.

When he didn't hear anything hysterical coming from inside, he decided to go to his own bed. Room service would be shutting down soon and he really needed something to eat. A steak and fries would really hit the spot.

"All she needs is sleep," he softly reminded himself. "A good night's sleep and she'll be just fine."

CHAPTER EIGHTEEN

The unfamiliar ring of his in-room phone woke Ricky up the next morning. He'd managed to get a few hours' sleep the previous night, but it hadn't been easy. His body was still on New York time, but he had a job to do. So Ricky picked up the still-ringing phone off the receiver.

"Yep?"

"Ready to face the day?"

Ricky growled. "You are too damn cheery."

Vic laughed. "See you in thirty?"

"Yeah. That'll work."

"We'll go get breakfast down in the restaurant."

Ricky grunted, sounding a little like his daddy at that moment, and hung up the phone. He took a shower and put on black jeans, black T-shirt, black boots, and secured a holstered .45 semi-auto to the back of his jeans that Vic had given him when he'd arrived in Russia. He pulled a denim jacket on to hide the weapon and left his room to go over to Toni's. He knocked but there was no answer. He knocked again.

By now, Vic was standing next to him.

"Nothing?" he asked.

"Nope." Ricky looked down one end of the hall, then the other. When he didn't see anyone around, he leaned in, pressed his nose against the doorjamb, and sniffed.

Ricky stepped back. "She's in there."

Vic reached into the back pocket of his jeans and pulled out a keycard.

"Had an extra for her room made?"

"Yep."

Vic was just reaching for the door when it opened from the inside. The two males instinctively reared back, but Toni only smiled.

"Sorry I took so long to get to the door. I just got out of the shower a few minutes ago."

Dressed in blue jeans, sexy, knee-high brown boots with three-inch heels, and a plain white T-shirt, Toni motioned both men in. "I'm almost done," she said.

"Okay." Ricky closed the door. "Vic suggested we get breakfast downstairs in the dining room."

"Sounds good," she said from inside the bathroom, the door open. "The room service was good, too."

She stepped back into the room with a towel. Her hair was dripping wet, thick curls reaching past her shoulders, bangs in front of her eyes. "Did you both sleep well?"

"Yep," Ricky replied.

She smiled—appearing much more relaxed than she had been last night—bent at the waist, and flipped her hair over. While Toni proceeded to carefully squeeze the water out of her hair with the towel, Vic bumped Ricky's shoulder with his own. When Ricky glanced over, Vic motioned to the bedroom door with a jerk of his head.

Ricky looked behind him, his eyes immediately widening at what he saw. And what he saw was paw marks on the back of the door. As if a wild animal had been locked in a room and unable to get out.

Disgusted, Ricky returned his attention to Toni. She stood straight, shook her hair. The curls were shorter now, getting curlier as her hair became drier.

"Okay. I'm ready." She threw the towel back into the bathroom and grabbed a small backpack and thick file folder from her bed. She walked to the door, pulling it open with her free hand.

"What happened to the back of the door?" Ricky asked her.

"Huh?" Toni asked, eyes wide as if she didn't know what he

was talking about. She continued to keep moving, saying nothing more.

"Going to say it now?" Vic asked him.

"No. I'm not." He pointed at the hybrid. "I know it'll be impossible for a bear-tiger freak of nature to understand, but although every dog may be a canine, not every canine is a dog."

"Did you get that from your college Logic one-oh-one class?"

"Maybe."

"Come on, guys," Toni called from the hallway. "Let's go. I've got a lot of work to get done today."

"Just leave it," Ricky warned the hybrid. "She's fine."

"If you say so."

"Watch that tone, son."

Vic chuckled and walked out of the room; Ricky followed. Still disgusted.

She saw the girl, Delilah Jean-Louis Parker, sitting on the steps in front of that church. She couldn't be more than eighteen or nineteen, but Miss Parker was strikingly beautiful.

It was extremely late when she sat down beside the girl. Glancing over her shoulder, she realized that Parker wasn't alone. At least three men, probably members of the church—or cult, depending on whom you talked to—were standing in the shadows, there to protect Parker.

That was all right. She had her own backup.

"Hi," she finally said to the girl. She knew she had a "warm way about her" as it said in her evaluations. It was something she used to her benefit.

"Hello." Parker looked at her. She had a soft smile and dead eyes.

"I got your message through our mutual friend and we are definitely interested."

"Okay."

"We're willing to pay you—"

"I want a million. In this account in the Cayman Islands." She handed over a piece of paper with numbers on it. "Get me that and I'll give you what I have."

"A million? That seems . . . substantial. For something we're not even sure will work."

"A million or you get nothing."

"Look, Miss Jean-Louis Parker—"

"Gasp," Parker said flatly. "How do you know my name? Oh, no. If you know my name . . . you know where I live. What will I do now? The horror. The horror." Parker leaned in a bit. "Is that what you wanted to hear? Was that the reaction you needed?"

A girl this one might be, but smart. And cold. Ice fucking cold.

"I'll talk to my superiors, Miss Parker."

Parker gave a little shrug, her small, misleading smile still in place. "Okay."

Tucking the piece of paper into her jeans pocket, she stood and walked down the steps and out onto the street. She walked a block until her team picked her up. She got into the Town Car and closed the door.

"Well?"

"Snotty little slit."

"We know where she lives."

"Strong-arming this girl isn't going to work. Not with this one."

"Then what do you want to do?"

"We'll see if we can find it on our own."

"And if we can't?"

She thought back on her superior's excitement when she'd shown him the information one of her contacts had sent her. "Then we give the bitch what she wants."

Although Toni had been to Russia before—several times, in fact—she'd never been this far outside a major city. She'd never been to Siberia.

And Siberia was, in a word, astounding.

So lush and green. Not at all what Toni expected.

"Beautiful, isn't it?" Barinov asked as he glanced at her in the rearview.

"It is. I guess I expected—"

"A snow-covered wilderness?"

"It's Siberia."

"There's summertime here, too. It's actually kind of extra hot for this time of year. Nearly sixty-five Fahrenheit when I checked this morning." Considering Toni had just left what she considered the oppressive heat of the East Coast, she had to chuckle a little.

The drive took a good thirty minutes until they reached the location where they'd be meeting with the bears. A ridiculously large . . . well . . . palace. Yeah. It was a palace. Not a mansion. Not a castle. A palace.

"Good Lord," Ricky muttered.

Barinov chuckled. "This is the house—"

"House?" Toni asked, incredulous.

"—that belongs to whoever is currently running this town. And for the last century and a half, that's been the Zubachevs."

"Why do I know that name?" Ricky asked, yawning and taking off his cap to scratch his head.

"Lots of Zubachevs in the States, a bunch of them in Maine. Like my mother's family, they're from Kamchatka."

"Lovely." Ricky put his hat back on his head. "Just lovely."

"What's wrong?" Toni asked.

Barinov shrugged. "Kamchatka bears kind of hate—"

"Canines," Ricky filled in. "They hate us a lot. Wolf. Jackal. Wild dog. Foxes. Doesn't matter the breed or where you fall in the genetic line, if you've even got a bit of canine blood in you, they hate you."

Barinov pulled to a stop in front of the palace. "It's called the one-eighth rule."

"The one-eighth rule?"

"If there's more than one-eighth canine blood in a shifter, Kamchatka bears consider them canines."

"And let's face it," Ricky said, grinning at her, "we all know there's a little canine in everybody."

She rolled her eyes but couldn't help smiling. Such a goofball, this guy.

"Any special instructions before we get out of this car?" Ricky asked Barinov.

"Yeah. No sudden movements. Even if there aren't any grizzlies within a mile of you, no sudden movements. None of them will like you, just accept that now. And all of them hate Novikov."

"That boy sure has made a name for himself."

"It's not his fault," Toni felt the need to remind them, since she was sure that one day she'd be having the same conversation about any or all of her siblings. "When you're the best at what you do, it's hard to remember there are other human beings standing right next to you."

Ricky turned, rested his arm on the back of his seat. "How long have you been practicing that speech?"

"Since Kyle was six. Only this time I didn't add, 'it's hard to remember there are other human beings standing right next to you, Senator' or 'your honor' or 'Mr. Prosecutor.' "

"The thing you need to keep in mind, Miss Parker—"

"Just call me Toni."

"That's Toni with an 'i,' " Ricky felt the need to explain. "Not a 'y.' "

"Right. Well, what you need to keep in mind, Toni, is that no matter what the bears here say, all they care about is keeping their territory safe, playing hockey, and making money off hockey. Keep that in mind, and you should be just fine."

The front doors to the palace opened and very large males began to walk through those double doors. Toni had assumed the double doors were there just to look fancy; now she realized they needed to be there to allow males that wide to enter and exit the building.

Toni nodded and reached for the door handle. By the time she was stepping out of the car, Ricky was there, his hand pressed into the small of her back.

"No matter what," he told her, "just remember I'm here. Vic is here. You're not on your own, darlin'."

"I know that," she said honestly. "Because otherwise I would have made a wild run for the woods by now. Jackals are brave when our pups are around, but we're not stupid."

Toni headed up the stairs with Barinov leading the way. He spoke in Russian to the bear standing at the top of the stairs, a grizzly who was surrounded by a bunch of other bears that ranged from grizzly to black to polar to speckled.

"Ivan Zubachev," Vic finally said in English, "this is Antonella—"

Zubachev cut Vic off with an angry snarl. "That American bitch, Malone," he grumbled in an impossibly low voice, "sent this *dog* to talk to Yuri Asanov. Greatest hockey coach to ever live?"

Toni fought the urge to roll her eyes. She had to agree with Kyle. She simply did not understand the love of sports.

Instead of pointing that out, she said, "Miss Malone apologizes for being unable to attend, but she had a prior—"

"I don't want to hear! Your mere presence insults this team. Insults Yuri Asanov. Go, pet doggy. No one wants to talk to you."

"Wait a minute." Toni couldn't believe what she was hearing. "I do understand you're upset about this, Mr. Zubachev. But I am authorized to negotiate with Mr. Asanov and the team."

The bear glowered down at her. He had to be at least eight feet tall while human. She didn't even want to imagine how big his bear form was.

His lip curling, he growled, "I hear dog barking . . . but it means nothing to me." He gestured with his hand. "Go, little dog. Go play in next town with other dogs. There's no place for you here."

With one last glower, Zubachev turned on his heel and stalked off. The rest of the bears followed him.

Rage ripped through Toni's system. She heard roaring in her ears. And as she saw those double doors begin to close, the proverbial leash she'd always used to keep herself calm in any situation snapped.

* * *

Ricky stared at the empty spot where Toni had been standing. Usually he reacted quickly in dangerous situations, but he had to admit he just never expected anyone to suddenly bolt *after* bears. Away from bears, yes. But after?

"Fuck," Vic snarled. The hybrid charged up the stairs after her, but by the time he got to the doors, they were shut in his face and locked.

"Can we kick in the door?" Ricky asked as he ran up behind Vic.

"This palace was built by bears just before the Russian civil war hit Siberia in 1918. And none of the things that happened in the rest of Siberia happened here, because no one could get past the bears who guard this territory or their incredibly strong wooden doors."

"We can't just leave her in there."

"I don't think we have a choice." Vic shrugged. "But her mangled body should be tossed out here anytime now."

Ricky gawked at the man. "Not. Helping."

Toni was aware that hands were grabbing for her as she moved around unbelievably large men to reach her goal. But she was fast and she was scrappy, so she ignored those hands until she'd gotten to the front of the group and jumped in front of Ivan Zubachev.

She stopped and held out her arm, palm out. "Hold it just a second, Poppa Bear."

Zubachev did stop walking, but his expression suggested he wouldn't wait for long.

"You'd do well to move from my way, little, tiny dog."

"I thought I was here to talk business."

"That cat bitch was supposed to come. And yet she is not here, but you are. I don't talk to dog."

He started to move forward so Toni took several steps back, her arm still held out. "You don't want to talk to dogs? Do you think I want to talk to you? Do you think I'm comfortable around human beings *this* large? I'm not. But I have a job to do, so I sucked it up and I came here. And now you won't even talk to me. How is that acceptable?"

"I don't talk to dog," he repeated, and Toni knew he was serious. He was not going to talk to her simply because she was canine.

Bigots!

So if the bear was going to be as difficult as all stubborn bears could be, then Toni was going to be as difficult as all dogs could be.

"Leave by door," the bear said, walking around her with the others following. She watched them all lumber by and, once they were a healthy distance away, Toni yipped. Several times.

The bears stopped. Zubachev covered his ears, spun to face her.

"What is that noise?" he bellowed.

"That's how jackals talk. I'm a jackal, not a dog. Dogs bark. Jackals yip."

"Well, stop it!"

Toni shook her head. "No."

She yipped again.

Zubachev dropped his hands to his sides and took an angry stepped forward. "Stop it," he ordered. "Or we make you stop."

"You'd have to catch me first, and I can assure you . . . jackals are way faster than bears. Because we have to be. And this place you have"—she raised her arms and spun in a circle—"has wonderful acoustics. I can hide all over the place and just make this noise all . . . day . . . *long.*"

Then she began yipping and yipping and yipping.

Ricky and Vic pulled away from the door.

"Good God, what is that noise?" the hybrid demanded.

"That's the soothing sounds of your local jackal."

"Are they cries for help?"

"Nope." Ricky shook his head. "Just her saying 'hi.' "

Vic's eyes narrowed. "It makes me want to kill."

And that's what was worrying Ricky. Especially when he

heard the distinctive angry roar of bears coming from inside the building.

"She's going to get herself killed," Vic warned.

Ricky stepped back and studied the front of the building. "Come on. We've gotta find a way in."

"Make her stop!" a polar screamed at Zubachev in Russian. She knew what he was saying only because he used phrases that one of Coop's piano teachers, a great player from Moscow, had used. Usually just before the man whacked her brother's hand with the riding crop he kept on him at all times. Toni had let that go the first time it happened, but the second time he'd done it, she'd decked the prick and that had been the end of her brother's relationship with that particular piano teacher.

Zubachev tried to grab Toni, but she was, as she'd said, too fast for him. Plus, unlike many canines, she'd taught herself to climb when she was eight because a rich cub from the Pride near their home had told her dogs couldn't climb. Toni had felt it was her duty to prove all cats wrong.

So she now stood comfortably on top of one of the big statues lining the marble hallway.

"You know how to stop me, Ivan."

The grizzly glowered up at her.

"You know how to stop me," she repeated. When he still didn't reply, she began to howl for her siblings. It was a sound that her family always found soothing. It meant that someone was there to watch out for you, to care for you. Others, though—like bears, lions, hyenas, cheetahs, leopards, et al.— found the sound so painfully annoying that they couldn't get away from jackals fast enough.

"*Fine!*" Zubachev roared, and she could tell saying that clearly pained him. Which, Toni would privately admit, she kind of enjoyed.

She stopped howling, and Zubachev said, "I will talk to Yuri about meeting with you about bastard freak."

"That's all I ask."

"But you will not make that noise again."

"Okay."

"Because it annoys."

"I know. It is annoying." Then again, so were bears being bigots.

Ivan pointed at a black bear. Toni felt kind of bad for that bear. Height-wise he was considerably smaller than the grizzlies and polars. But width-wise . . . he was built like a mountain. "Help the canine down."

"I can do it." And she did, moving expertly down the statue until she was on the ground.

She stared up at the bear. "So what's next?"

"This way, little dog."

"Or you could just call me Toni."

"Could. Won't."

Deciding not to argue the point, she followed the group down the giant hall. It reminded her of Versailles in France with its stately marble floors and floor-to-ceiling mirrors lining the entire hallway. Everything was ornate but a little too much for her taste. But as they began walking, Ricky and Barinov came charging out of one of the large rooms, their weapons drawn.

The room the two males emerged from was on the other side of the house, so they must have run around the very wide palace to get to it so quickly.

"Are you all right?" Ricky asked her. For once she didn't see a smirk on his face but true concern.

"I'm fine." But just as she said that, her phone vibrated. Another text. Sighing, Toni dug her phone out of the back of her jeans. It was from her mother.

Question . . . did you tell Novikov he could change the flooring?
In our RENTAL house?

Toni didn't even know what the hell that meant. And why was her mother asking that question so late at night? Late for New York time anyway because it wasn't even four in the morning there. And what the hell was going on back there? Why were they all being so ridiculous?

"Toni?"

She looked up at Ricky. "What?"

"Your neck is getting all red."

Toni rubbed her hand across her throat. "Oh. That. Yeah. That happens sometimes."

"Can I help?"

"No one can help." She shoved her phone back into her jeans. "Let's just get this done."

Maybe, just maybe, if she could get through this negotiation quickly, she could catch a flight later tonight and get home before her entire family imploded.

Yes. Excellent plan.

Toni faced Zubachev. "Let's get this going, Mr. Zubachev."

He nodded and again headed off down the hall. They all followed until he reached a room. He stepped inside and waited for Toni, Ricky, and Barinov to follow. Once they were in the room, he said, "Wait here."

Zubachev walked out, closing the door behind him. The three of them stared at each other until, with a shrug, they all took seats on the available chairs and couch. And they sat in that room for nearly three hours before Zubachev returned.

He looked at Toni. "Come back tomorrow. Nine in morning."

Then he walked out.

Shocked, Toni stared at where the bear had been, but Barinov stood up and asked them, "Hungry? Because I'm starving."

"Wait. Is that it?"

"Until tomorrow."

"I don't understand. Why am I not meeting Asanov today?"

"Could be lots of reasons." Barinov thought a moment. "But chances are they're just making you wait."

He headed toward the door, and Toni scrambled out of the chair. "But they'll see me tomorrow, right?"

Barinov faced her. Shrugged. "Probably. Maybe. It's possible."

Ricky gazed down at her. "Darlin', your neck's gettin' red again."

★　★　★

In the early morning, the sun barely up, Bo Novikov stood in the backyard of the jackal family's rental home.

It was a really nice place. Good for kids. Well, good for most kids. Not these kids. These kids were demons from the pits of hell.

Bo liked them.

Especially Kyle. That kid had a great future as an amazing artist . . . or he would one day be poisoned by a mate. Either one was possible.

Still, Bo had not done what he'd set out to do. Not yet. He hadn't gotten the schedule for these kids set up. He had to admit, he'd thought it would be easy. Blayne had tried to warn him. She said it would be like working with ten little Bos. As always . . . she'd been right. Well, actually nine little Bos. One of the pups, the eighteen-year-old that everyone got quiet around whenever she breezed through the room, didn't need a schedule. She said she had classes but doing what or with whom, Bo had no idea and he didn't really care.

But the others . . . the others *all* had classes. Even the three-year-olds. The twins would be going to Berlitz next week to learn *more* languages. They'd already cursed at Bo in German, Russian, and Cantonese. Three languages he knew a bit because he'd been cursed at in those languages by players he'd gone up against over the years. In fact, Bo could curse in almost all languages for that simple reason.

Yet negotiating the busy schedules of nine pups with one extremely busy parent and one not-so-busy parent was a lot harder than he'd thought it would be, exactly because those nine kids had Bo's drive. They didn't want to give an inch. They didn't care that if they went to a later-in-the-day advanced class in whatever their specialty was, their siblings could easily go to their earlier-in-the-day advanced class. They didn't care that if they gave a little, the entire family would be better off. All they cared about was having time to do what they loved and what they were good at.

Yeah. Bo admired that, but it sure did make things harder. Too bad for the brats that Bo had made a commitment, and once he made a commitment, that was all that mattered to *him*. So he wasn't giving up, no matter when Toni came back. Although Toni's mother, Jackie, had heard from her daughter and it looked as if her trip would take a little longer than Toni had planned. Maybe Bo should have warned her that negotiating with Russians was one of the harder—and more entertaining—things one could do in life. Bear or full-human, Russians were tough negotiators.

Bo heard rustling from nearby bushes. He turned in time to see one of the Parker kids crawl out. Hands, face, and the knees of his jeans covered in dirt, the little boy stood up but froze when he saw Bo standing there.

"What were you doing?" Bo asked the boy.

"Um . . . digging?"

"Are you asking me or telling me?"

The boy stepped closer. "It depends if you'll tell on me."

"Where you burying a body?"

Eyes wide, the boy shook his head. "No, sir."

"Then there's nothing to tell."

A huge smile now on his face, the boy said, "I'm Freddy."

"The seven-year-old."

"Right."

"Did you bury something important, Freddy?"

"Important to me."

"That's all that matters."

"I only bury things that are important to me."

"Why?"

"I believe it has a lot to do with my canine ancestry."

"Like when a dog buries a bone?"

"Exactly! Toni doesn't like that example but it seems the most accurate scientifically."

Jeez. Bo kept forgetting exactly how smart these kids were because it never occurred to him to analyze the fact that he liked walrus blubber jerky or that he had to constantly fight his desire to sleep all day until Blayne brought him dinner.

The boy studied him for a moment, then asked, "Don't you mind being here?"

"No."

"Is that because you're a lot like Kyle?"

That made Bo smirk. "No."

Freddy walked over to Bo until he stood only a few inches away and gazed up at him. Then he waited. At least that's what it felt like. As if the kid were waiting for something. Bo didn't know what but it felt weird just standing there, so he said, "You're up kind of early."

"Not for me."

After that statement, the kid said nothing else but continued to stare. Finally, Bo couldn't take it anymore.

"Is there something you want to ask me, Freddy?"

"Can I stand on your shoulders?"

"What?"

"Can I stand on your shoulders? Just for a minute or so."

"Why?"

"I want to know what it's like to be tall."

Bo was about to explain that the chances of a jackal being as tall as him—a lion-polar bear hybrid—were impossible but decided against it. In fact, he could actually hear Blayne in his head telling him *not* to tell Freddy that. So, Bo instead crouched down and held his arm out. The boy grabbed it with both hands and Bo lifted him, placing his small feet on his shoulders. When he had the boy secure, Bo's hands wrapped tightly around Freddy's ankles, Bo stood tall.

"Woooooooow," Freddy sighed out. "I can see the entire *world* from here."

That made Bo grin a bit.

"I bet you love being this tall, Mr. Novikov."

"I don't mind. It makes it easier to find Blayne in a crowd. She tends to bop around when she walks. Like she's on springs or something. So I just look for the top of her head to suddenly appear and I can usually track her down in a timely manner."

"I like Blayne. She smiles a lot."

"She does."

"And she's good at keeping me calm."

"That's very important for you, isn't it, Freddy?"

"It is. Otherwise I do things I'm not supposed to. Toni's excellent at keeping me calm but Blayne's good at it too."

Of course, Blayne's calming abilities probably came from the years of anger management classes she'd been forced to go to—usually by court order.

Bo didn't know how long the pair stood there, but it was a nice, easy way to start the day.

"Bo?"

Hearing his fiancée's voice, Bo glanced over at Blayne. "Hey. What's up?"

"Everything all right?"

"Just staring at the world," he replied.

Grinning, Blayne walked over, clapped her hands together, and held her arms out to Freddy. "Your mom is looking for you, Fredster."

"Okay."

The boy leaped from Bo's shoulders and into Blayne's arms. Thankfully, Blayne was on a derby team, so she managed to easily catch Freddy and not fall on her ass even though he was leaping from such a great height.

She placed Freddy on the ground, and he charged toward the back door. "Thank you, Mr. Novikov!"

"You're welcome."

Blayne smiled up at Bo.

"What?"

"I'm just so—"

"Is there a reason you came out here," he cut in before she could tell him once again how proud she was he had managed to not kill any of the Parker children, "or was it just to make sure I hadn't stomped on the small ones?"

"I've said it before and I'll say it again. You don't always watch where you walk. But that's not why I'm out here."

Bo sighed. "Then why?"

Taking Bo's hand, Blayne led her mate and future husband back into the Jean-Louis Parker house and to the ballroom on the first floor. Right where Kyle had had workers set up a giant block of white marble. And standing right by that were an arguing Kyle, Troy, and Oriana. Those three argued all the time. Really. All. The. Time.

"You are such a little shit, Kyle!" Oriana yelled at her brother.

"I need the space!" Kyle barked back.

"So do I!"

"What about me?" Troy demanded.

"You do equations," Oriana reminded her brother. "What could you *possibly* need all this space for?"

"Wall space. So I can put up my equations," he said, his hand gesturing down the long hall, "and see them in one long stream."

"You're an idiot," Oriana sighed. "Just a big-headed idiot."

"And you're an uptight little—"

"That's it," Bo cut in, impressing Blayne with his no-nonsense approach to children cursing at each other. "Enough of this."

"You might as well forget it, Novikov," Kyle said, rocking back on sneakers that lit up when he walked, reminding Blayne that this confident little kid was only eleven. "The workmen have already gone. So the marble stays put."

Bo snorted. "Really?"

Walking over to the enormous piece of beautiful marble that Blayne assumed Kyle was planning to whittle down into a statue, Bo gazed at it a moment. He moved around it. Then he grasped the marble from behind and, with a grunt, dragged it across the floor like he was moving a filled refrigerator.

Blayne covered her mouth with her hands when she saw that Bo was leaving deep gouges in the hardwood floor.

Once across the room, Bo released the marble and came back over to the kids. They were gawking at him, fear mixed with envy mixed with admiration.

"Do not bring any more giant pieces of marble in here, Kyle. Understand?"

"Do you know how much that weighed?" Kyle asked, still gazing.

"In fact," he told all three, "no more trying to claim this

room for yourselves. I'm taking it over for now. I need more space than the library."

"It took ten full-humans to move that," Troy added. "Ten."

"Full-humans are naturally weak. You shouldn't hold that against them."

"We're not," Oriana muttered. "You're just freaking us out."

"Then you better not piss me off." Bo looked at each child before asking, "Understand?"

All three nodded.

"Good. Now, I'm hungry. Let's feed." He walked out, winking at Blayne as he passed by.

The two boys followed after him, Kyle noting that Bo was "Magnificent."

Oriana stopped by Blayne. "I know," she said about her brother. "I know."

"Well . . . Bo *is* magnificent." She'd just never expected an eleven-year-old boy to be comfortable enough to say that out loud.

CHAPTER NINETEEN

By the third day, Toni truly thought her head might explode. For three days she'd been forced to sit in this room. For three days, she'd been forced to wait for hours until someone came in to tell her to "try again tomorrow." And for three days she'd been forced to keep her temper under control.

Although Toni hadn't realized she had a temper quite like this. The more they made her wait, the worse it was getting. What made it even worse were the two males she was stuck with.

She looked across the room. First at Vic Barinov. He was reading a book on the Teutonic knights and their battles.

Really? *Really?* Was reading about Teutonic knights seriously that important? When her entire life was falling apart around her?

Knowing she was moments away from biting the man's nose off, Toni turned her gaze to the wolf. Unlike the hybrid, he wasn't reading anything. He was just sitting there, placidly staring at the wall. How did he do that? How did *anyone* do that who was not already in some sort of catatonic state?

This whole situation was insane! And making her absolutely crazy. Even worse were the regular texts from her family. Text after text after text with just enough information to have Toni seriously worried for their collective safety.

And did any of that concern the bears? Well, she had no idea because she hadn't spoken to any of them. Instead, a bear led her into "The Room" as she now called it, left her there for hours, and then another bear led her out.

Well you know what? Today was going to be different. Today she was going to stand up and say, "I've had enough!"

But before she could, the door opened and some bear looked at her and said, "You can go now."

With a yip that made the black bear stumble away from the doorway, Toni got to her feet, grabbed her backpack, and stormed out of the room. She didn't look back to see if the two males with her were following, because she no longer cared. She no longer cared about them. Or this job. Or these bears. Or anything else in the universe. She was fed up with everyone and everything.

Toni reached the car first and tapped her foot while the two males ambled up. Barinov remotely unlocked the doors and Toni got inside. She tossed her bag to the floor, pulled her legs up on the seat, and wrapped her arms around her calves. She worked to control her breathing because she knew a panic attack was coming on. Yes. Like Freddy and Cherise, Toni did get panic attacks, but she'd worked hard over the years to control the problem since she couldn't afford to have panic attacks while her siblings were.

And just a few days around bigoted bears seemed to have ruined all the good work her therapist had done. This was unacceptable!

"How ya doin', darlin'?" the wolf asked her from the front passenger seat.

Toni dug her fingernails into her hands and lied, "Fine."

Ricky turned on the TV in his room, then quickly turned it off again. He didn't know Russian, wasn't about to start learning it now, and there was just something upsetting about watching a John Wayne movie dubbed into any other language but good ol' American. Or, as his sister liked to correct him, "You mean English, dumb ass?"

So Ricky grabbed his laptop and fired up one of the movies

he had on his hard drive. He was just getting into the original *Ocean's Eleven* when Vic knocked on his door.

"We both know you have a key," Ricky called out.

A few seconds later, the hybrid was in his room. "Of course I have a key, but that doesn't mean it's right for me to just walk in without asking. I'm not a housecat, ya know."

"You're actually talking about lions, aren't you?" Ricky took his Titans cap off and dropped it on the side table. "All right, how long is this going to go on?"

"Not sure."

"Because I'm gonna be honest with ya, Vic. I'm not sure how much longer she's going to—"

Ricky abruptly stopped, his gaze moving to Vic's. They moved together, both of them heading for the doors that separated Ricky's room from Toni's. Vic opened the first door and Ricky kicked in the second, assuming it would be locked. They went through and immediately stopped.

"Holy shit, Rick."

"I know."

It was like a tornado had come through the room. Everything in it had been ripped apart. The comforter, the sheets, the blankets, the pillows, the bed, the dresser, the desk, the TV, the stand the TV had been on. All of it. And it all hadn't been smashed, or tossed aside in a pouty little girl rage. No. This was dog damage. Claws and a canine body had done all this.

And now . . . that canine was ripping at the bedroom door, trying to scratch and bite her way out. It was as if Toni had forgotten she had thumbs.

"Now can I say *it*?" Vic asked.

Ricky sighed. "Yeah. Go ahead."

The hybrid leaned closer. "Separation anxiety, dude."

Ricky, as a fellow canine—but like Toni, not a dog—was ashamed to say it, but yes. This was clearly separation anxiety. She was having separation anxiety because she was away from her family. And the longer the bears made her wait, the worse it was getting.

"So what are we going to do?" Barinov asked.

"The only thing we can."

Toni knew she was losing it, but she couldn't help it. But what surprised her was that Ricky let her continue losing it without actually doing much more than keeping her away from the front door.

When she went for the bed again, digging her way down until she hit springs and wood—he didn't stop her. Even when she started chewing up the wood and springs and spitting them across the room—he didn't stop her.

When she began to attack the glass doors that led to the balcony, he didn't stop her then, either.

But when it got dark later, sometime after eight that evening, the wolf suddenly picked up her jackal body, pushed her into his empty duffel bag, and left the hotel. Maybe they were going home! Maybe the bears had said they refused to meet with some lowly canine. Maybe . . . maybe . . .

Still in that bag, Toni was unceremoniously dropped into the backseat of the car and they began moving. After about forty-five minutes, the car pulled to a stop, the bag with Toni still in it was dragged out of the backseat, unzipped, and turned over.

Toni landed on her back. She gazed up at the wolf.

"According to Vic, we're now in canine and cat territory. This is your opportunity to run. Run your little heart out. Get it out of your system. Because maybe once you do that, you'll be able to think straight and get this goddamn job done." He threw up his hands. "Look what you've done to me. Now I'm blaspheming as bad as you!"

Toni turned over and stared into the dark but lush Siberian landscape near Lake Baikal. God, she did want to run. She wanted to run until everything in her hurt.

She started to get to her four feet when a large, bushy tail flicked her snout. Once, twice. Ricky had shifted into his wolf form, and he had his ass in her face. Rude!

Toni jumped to her feet, onto the wolf's back, and over him.

She tossed her tail into his face before she took off running. She glanced back, saw the wolf right behind her.

Laughing, Toni picked up speed and ran her heart out.

Reece was ordered to the main floor of the shifter area so that he could be photographed. He didn't mind being photographed. Unlike his brothers, he was real photogenic. Still, having to sit here, waiting to be primped and probably oiled up like some porn star did make him a bit uncomfortable. And when Reece was a bit uncomfortable, he started to look for things to do. Things he probably shouldn't do but couldn't keep himself from doing because he bored so easy.

It wasn't his fault, he'd just been born that way. According to his momma, he was like that as a baby, too. "Couldn't leave you alone for five minutes, Reece Lee Reed," his momma still said to this day. "Because once I turned my back, you'd find something to get your dumb ass into."

Yet what many didn't understand was that Reece didn't always have to look for trouble. Sometimes trouble found him. Sometimes trouble slinked its way right up next to him and sat down on the bench beside him.

Like now.

"Well, hi, Reece Lee."

Eating his cheesesteak sandwich, Reece said, "Hey, Laura Jane."

"Heard your big brother left town." She pressed her hand against her chest, her tight, white V-neck T-shirt showing off her cleavage. "I hope that's not because of little ol' me."

"Huh . . . Rory left town?"

Laura Jane's left eye twitched the slightest bit.

Reece knew that Laura Jane had always thought he was stupid. And sometimes he could be. But mostly he just liked to irritate people by being dense. It was one of the main reasons Bo Novikov insisted on beating him up at every opportunity. Honestly, Reece should leave the short-tempered hybrid alone, but he couldn't help himself. The man was just so uptight!

"Not Rory," Laura Jane said, still managing to keep her voice sweet and sultry. "I'm talking about Ricky Lee."

"Oh. Yeah. He's in Russia." He took a big bite of his sandwich, chewed a bit, then added, "I'm sure it had nothing to do with you, though."

Laura Jane cleared her throat and wiped away the bit of cheesesteak that had hit her cheek. Lord, he was rude. Rude!

The She-wolf tried again, moving closer to him on the bench, making sure to lean in so he could see down her top. Nope. No bra there. Although one was sorely needed.

"You know, Reece Lee, I've been hearing such good things about you on the hockey team."

"Really? Because most say I'm just a big ol' battering ram. 'No technique,' I hear a lot. No style. All abuse."

"That's kind of sexy."

"Really? My momma says it's sad that she'll end up taking care of me when I become brain damaged."

Reece could see Laura Jane's patience beginning to wane, but she was on a mission, so she'd hold it back if she could. He wondered what she was up to. Was she really so desperate that she thought getting between the Reed Boys was a good idea? Or, more important, even possible?

The title "Reed Boys" was not given out lightly to just any Reed males. Siblings had to earn it and then keep it, and they kept it with loyalty. Reece might torment his brother on a daily, sometimes even an hourly, basis, but that didn't mean he'd ever screw a woman Ricky was interested in.

What Laura Jane didn't realize was that Reece could fuck her on this bench, in front of God and everybody, and he was positive Ricky Lee wouldn't give a damn. He wouldn't have given a damn two weeks ago, but he especially wouldn't give a damn now. Not with that little She-jackal in his sights. He knew what had Ricky fascinated, too. It was probably that hair. All wild and curly, it always looked like Toni had just rolled out of bed after a great night of sex. There were few men who could resist that sort of thing.

Still, Reece did want to know what Laura Jane was planning. As it was, she'd effectively wound up his sister. So much so that Ronnie Lee had actually called back to Tennessee to complain. Ronnie Lee did not call back to Tennessee for much. Even when she got pregnant, it was Reece who told their daddy, who told their momma, who called Ronnie Lee to yell at her about not calling home herself. See? That's how families were supposed to work. In a nice, complete circle of annoyance.

"You know, Reece," Laura Jane softly suggested, her boob now brushing his arm. "Why don't you and I go somewhere and talk. I'm worried about Ricky Lee. I swear I didn't come here to cause him any problems."

To be honest, Reece would rather throw himself off a mountain, but to find out what this self-centered little twat was up to—

"Hey," a low voice snapped at him. "Hillbilly. Are you coming or not? I've been waiting for you."

Reece looked up at the tiny female who smelled like nothing he could remember scenting before. She wasn't a hybrid, but she wasn't any breed or species he'd been around. And she wouldn't tell him what she was. So what was she? It was driving him nuts!

"You have?"

"I'm taking your picture. Remember?"

"You're the photographer, huh?" Reece shrugged. "Okay, uh . . ."

"Livy." She motioned with her head. "Come on."

Reece began to stand, but Laura Jane gripped his arm with surprisingly strong hands. "Excuse you," the one-time debutante practically barked at Livy. "But we were talking."

"And we have an appointment, so fuck off."

Laura Jane slowly stood. "Are you really coming at *me*?"

"Lady, I'm trying to be nice to you. But I wouldn't push your luck with me."

"You? Tiny little hybrid freak? What are you going to do?"

"Morally reprehensible things that most good people would be appalled by."

The She-wolf gawked at Livy, unused to not only the flat tone but the weirdly phrased threat.

Laura Jane looked at Reece, but all he could do was shrug. What did she expect from him?

Disgusted by his lack of reaction, Laura Jane glowered down at Livy. "Get out of my sight, freak," she ordered.

Reece didn't know Livy well, but something told him it wasn't the words that had upset her, but the shove Laura Jane added to those words, her hands harshly pushing at the smaller woman's shoulders. Because that's when the butterfly knife was expertly flicked open and sliced across Laura Jane's arm.

Shocked—shifters fought shifters only with fangs and claws; never weapons—Laura Jane stumbled back from Livy. The pint-size female slashed the blade again, this time cutting across Laura Jane's chest. Reece saw blood from both wounds.

The blade was flicked closed and slipped into the back pocket of Livy's jeans, and then she pulled back one hand, claws out, and slapped Laura Jane across the face and neck. Livy kicked the She-wolf to the ground and landed on top of her, her hands slapping Laura Jane over and over again until the She-wolf was out cold and covered in her own blood.

Livy got up, cracked her neck, and walked over to Reece. He stared at her, wondering whether she was about to slap him around. But she grabbed the other half of his cheesesteak and began eating.

"So are we going to do this or what?" she calmly asked.

"Yeah," he said quickly, trying to ignore the blood-covered claws that were still out and wrapped around that bread and meat. "Yeah. Sure."

Reece got to his feet, but he looked over his shoulder to see Ronnie Lee, Sissy Mae, and the New York Smith She-wolves standing there watching them. Lord, this wasn't good. Laura Jane *was* a Smith, after all. And Smith loyalty meant everything, even when a Smith didn't necessarily deserve that loyalty.

Yet if Livy was worried . . . she didn't show it. In fact, she showed no fear at all. Eating his delicious sandwich and staring back at the She-wolves, she waited.

When Livy ate the last bit of the sandwich, she swallowed, burped.

"You ready?" Livy finally asked him.

"Yeah. I'm ready."

"Good. I've got a list of other meatheads to do, too."

She walked off and Reece looked back at his sister, wondering what she'd do.

Sissy Mae walked over to her cousin, looked down at her, stared for a moment, turned on her heel, and walked off. Without a word, the other She-wolves followed, including Ronnie Lee.

That's when Reece knew they'd been watching what Laura Jane was up to even before Livy had arrived—and they hadn't liked it. Slapping her around themselves wouldn't have been too cool, but letting someone smaller and meaner do it . . . the males of the Pack wouldn't get in the middle of that. So, as far as the New York Pack was concerned, it was over.

Reece blew out a breath, stepped over Laura Jane's still unconscious body, and walked into the room Livy was using to shoot the photographs.

She was adjusting lights when he came in—her claws now gone, her hands clean—and she motioned to a metal stool.

"We'll take a few safety shots first before I try some different stuff."

"Okay." Reece sat down, watched the female move around the room. Finally, he just had to ask her.

"What the hell are you?"

She glanced at him. "None of your damn business," she told him mildly. "Now take your shirt off and look pretty."

Chapter Twenty

They ran for over three hours. Three hours of nonstop movement through lush, gorgeous wilderness.

Ricky wondered what the land looked like when it was covered in the snow and ice Siberia was famous for. But this would do for now.

They finally came to rest by the Range Rover, both collapsing next to the tires, both panting with tongues hanging out. They stayed that way for a while until Ricky realized that other canines were roaming in the dense forests. Not wanting to get into a territorial spat with Russian wolves and foxes, he got up, put on his jeans, and tossed the rest of his clothes in the car. He held the door open and Toni leaped into the backseat. She rested on her side while Ricky got in the driver's seat and headed back the way he'd come. When they returned to the hotel, he went in through the front doors, topless and shoeless. The front desk staff watched him but no one said anything. Maybe they thought the American had drunk too much of the local vodka.

He cut through the hotel until he reached the back. Completely unfazed by the locked doors there, Ricky got them open and let Toni in. Still in her jackal form, she trotted up the stairs until they returned to the ninth floor. She went to her door, but Ricky shook his head. "You can't stay in there, darlin'. That poor room has been through hell and back." He jerked his head at his own door while he pushed the keycard into the lock. "Come on. You can crash in here tonight."

Toni followed after him and once inside, she charged across the room and dove headfirst into the couch. She rolled around there for a good minute, wiggling her back against the cushions. Ricky went into his bathroom, grabbed a towel, and took it out to the now-happy canine.

He tossed it at her so that it covered her completely. A few seconds later, she'd shifted back to human and now he had a damn sexy woman wearing only a towel in his room.

This was one of those moments his daddy would say, "Proof that life is good, son. Life is very good."

Toni put one hand behind her head and gazed up at the ceiling.

Okay. She'd admit it. She was having a bad case of separation anxiety. Only wolfdogs admitted to having this issue, but all canines suffered from it now and again.

But after tearing apart her hotel room and then that wonderfully luxurious run through the woods, she was feeling damn good. Not only that, she had to admit she was feeling a little . . . well . . . worked up.

Usually, she spent so much time worrying about her siblings that Toni didn't focus too much on that side of herself. She simply didn't have the time or the inclination. Yet lying here on this couch, wearing only a towel, with a very cute, bare-chested wolf standing over her, she was having all sorts of thoughts she didn't normally entertain.

And, they were thousands of miles away from her family. Just the two of them in this room . . . alone.

"Darlin'," the wolf practically growled, "you keep looking at me like that and we're gonna have a problem."

"Looking at you like what?"

"Like you could eat me alive."

She shrugged, her gaze moving across the room. "Maybe I could."

"Uh-uh," Ricky said, stepping closer to the couch. "If you're gonna hit on me, Antonella, you need to look at me."

Toni did and they ended up staring at each other for a long moment.

Finally, Toni admitted, "I have no idea what to say next."

"Why do you have to say anything?"

"Don't I need to?" she asked honestly. "To entice you into bed?" She'd always had to work harder than the pretty full-human girls at school and in college. Toni always had to engage men first with her intellect and then let them find their way into becoming sexually interested in her.

But Ricky Lee only laughed. "Darlin', you really have been hanging around too many full-humans."

He slowly dropped to his knees beside the couch. "Do you know what I need to entice me to bed?"

"What?"

"You looking at me the way you're looking at me and . . ." Ricky carefully pulled the towel off her body. "This."

Toni knew she had scars. It was hard to grow up a predator and not have scars, but she also knew it was something fellow predators didn't give a shit about. Ricky would never suggest medicinal pads she could place on her scars to make them fade or kindly suggest a good plastic surgeon who could help her out. Her scars didn't matter to him, and that had her toes curling.

Ricky studied her body for a long moment, his gaze moving from head to toe and back again. When his eyes focused on hers, he said nothing because there was nothing to say.

Raising herself on her elbows, Toni leaned in until their faces were only inches apart. "I think," she teased, "I'm still a little anxious. Being away from my family and all."

"Really?" Ricky said, his grin wide. "You know, darlin', I think I can help ya with that."

"I really hope so, because I am desperate."

"Oh, yeah?" He leaned in closer, but still didn't touch her. "Then you better prove it before I get scared off and make a run for it."

So Toni did. She proved exactly how desperate she was.

★ ★ ★

Ricky wouldn't lie. He'd kissed a lot of women over the years. Many of them predators. Quite a few who were full-human. But there was something about this passionate, but shy kiss that made his knees weak and his heart race. Something he didn't remember ever happening before. At least not like this.

Toni's arms slipped around his neck and she pressed her mouth against his. Her lips parted and he felt her breath seconds before her tongue eased into his mouth.

Ricky melted into that kiss. He couldn't help himself. It was such a sweet kiss. And somehow, supremely honest.

While still holding on to him, Toni got to her knees on the couch, her breasts brushing against him as she moved. Her hands slipped into his hair and her fingers flexed, massaging his scalp.

Growling low, Ricky stood and grinned down at Toni. "Now that was just mean."

Toni's smile was purely devious. "Not mean . . . just calculated."

"I like calculated." He wrapped his arms around her waist and pulled Toni up until they were eye level. He kissed her. Hard, pushing her, needing to know that this was what she really wanted.

She eagerly returned his kiss without hesitation, her grip tightening around his neck.

That was all Ricky needed.

He lifted her off the couch and took her to the bed. They fell onto it, Ricky's body pushing her into the mattress.

Ricky Lee Reed was a big wolf with wide shoulders and muscular thighs. When she'd first met him, Toni had found them a tad off-putting. She kept thinking it was too much body for a woman to handle. Now, however, she knew she'd been wrong. Nothing felt better than having this wolf's narrow hips between her thighs, his strong chest pressing against her breasts.

Toni felt safe and turned on all at the same time.

Ricky dragged his fingers up her thighs, her hips, the sides of her breasts. Toni arched into those hands, her head thrown back. Who knew such big hands would feel so good?

Resting his hands on her hips, he leaned into her, taking her mouth with his. Claiming it as his own.

Toni reached between them with her right hand, lowered it until she could cup his cock through his jeans. Ricky groaned and buried his face against her neck. She tipped her head to the side, giving him better access as she found his zipper, undid it. She slipped her hand inside. He hadn't bothered to put his boxer briefs back on when he'd dressed by the car. She didn't mind. It just made it easier to run the tips of her fingers around his cock.

Fangs grazed Toni's neck before Ricky was kissing her again.

After several minutes, he leaned back a bit, gazing down into her face. His eyes had shifted to a vibrant blue, meaning the Reeds had some Arctic wolf in them.

"I can't wait anymore," he told her plainly. There was no smirk. No easy patter. Just a desperation in those Arctic wolf eyes.

"Me, either," she admitted.

"Thank God." He got up and reached for his jeans.

"Wait," she said, and she almost laughed when he stared at her in abject horror. "Tell me you have condoms."

"Condoms?" He acted like he didn't even know the word. Then he blinked, nodded. "Right. Condoms." With his cock hanging out of his unzipped jeans, he tore across the room and began tossing clothes out of his luggage. He finally held up a box of condoms, facing her with a huge, triumphant smile.

When Toni frowned, Ricky quickly added, "I was hopeful is all. Just hopeful. A man can be hopeful."

Knowing that he'd brought those condoms for her didn't upset Toni nearly as much as she'd thought it would. So when he just stood there, cock hanging out of his jeans, his blue eyes silently begging her, Toni could only ask, "Are you just going to stand there or get over here and do me?"

When Ricky dived for the bed, Toni could only squeal and speed out of the way.

★ ★ ★

Ricky managed to catch hold of Toni before she rolled off the bed.

"Sorry," he said when he pulled her back to safety. "I didn't mean to . . ."

He stopped talking when he realized she was laughing, her smile wide.

"Someone is a horny little monkey," she teased.

"Just for you, darlin'." He laughed. "Can't control myself."

She shook her head. "I don't want you to." She reached up, pressed her hand to his face, stroked his cheek. "I don't want you to control yourself."

So he didn't. Instead he kicked off his jeans and put on a condom. Then he got on his knees, leaned back on his heels, and reached for Toni. He didn't have to reach far. She got up and put herself in his arms, trusting him in a way most predators would not. Wrapping his hands around her waist, he brought her up and then down, right on his cock. She gave a startled yip, then wrapped her arms around his neck, her legs around his waist.

"Kiss me again," she told him. "I really like it when you kiss me."

Ricky had no idea why he enjoyed hearing those words so much. It wasn't simply that he liked kissing her, too. Maybe it was more because her words were direct and simple and that's what he liked so much about Toni. No matter what was going on around her or, in this particular case, inside her, she was always direct. Although he had to admit, there was very little about her that was simple. Except now. When it was just the two of them.

He kissed her, kept kissing her, while he started to fuck her. Slowly, carefully. Not wanting to scare her off or hurt her. It wasn't easy, though. She was so tight. It was obvious she hadn't fooled around much since she'd broken it off with her last boyfriend.

Ricky kissed her harder, realizing he didn't want to think about her last boyfriend. And he definitely didn't want her to think about her last boyfriend.

No. All Ricky wanted at the moment was for her to think about him and his cock and his hands on her. He'd make sure that was all she thought about.

Holy shit. So *this* was what she'd been missing with her safe, full-human boyfriends? No wonder Coop kept trying to push her toward other shifters. She thought he was just being a bigot. But no. Not really.

Ricky's grip tightened around her waist as he stroked into her, his cock pushing in and out of her again and again.

Toni dropped her forehead against Ricky's shoulder, her fingers digging harder into his hair. She knew he liked that, and it was all she could really manage when she wasn't kissing him back.

She began to squirm. Her entire body feeling hot, her nipples getting so hard they hurt. She shuddered, unused to feeling this intense.

Toni wouldn't realize it until later, but it was during this part that she stopped thinking about anything. Anything but what was going on between her and Ricky. She didn't worry. She didn't analyze. She didn't plan. She just let him rock his body against hers until she began to tremble. Until she began to pant and groan into the man's thick neck. She got so lost in what she was doing that when she came, her entire body gripping Ricky tight, she didn't know she'd lowered her hands to his back, unleashed her claws, and dug them into his spine until he climaxed, shuddered, and said, "Ow," into the silence.

Realizing she was buried in the man up to her cuticles, Toni automatically ripped her claws out.

Ricky yelped, his body jerking from the pain. Cringing, Toni leaned back. "Oh, God. Ricky. I'm so sorry."

"It's all right." He kissed her neck, apparently ignoring the sweat there, and added, "I had an uncle who always said if a She-predator don't rip up some part of your body during sex, you ain't doin' your job right."

Disgusted *and* amused, Toni shook her head and begged, "Please tell me that discussion didn't take place until you were at least eighteen."

"More like sixteen. But don't worry. My momma didn't let him in the house after that until Reece was eighteen. And she still don't speak to the man whenever he comes for Thanksgiving dinner."

Ricky, still buried inside her, kissed her collarbone, her throat, her chin. "So, darlin' . . . feelin' any better?"

Smiling, Toni wrapped her arms around Ricky's neck and admitted, "Better . . . but still a little tense."

"Well, we can't have that." Ricky stretched her out on the bed, grinned down at her. "Not if you're going to deal with those nasty ol' bears and all."

Toni grinned back. "That's my feeling *exactly*."

Ronnie Lee was eating popcorn and relaxing on her couch next to Shaw.

She had to admit, the lion took mighty good care of her. He always had, but he seemed to be thoroughly enjoying her pregnancy. And was more than happy to sit on their couch, watching the "lady network" as he liked to call it. They both had a thing for those really bad movies where some woman finds out her millionaire husband has been sleeping with her best friend and babysitter before discovering that the gardener is a serial killer and she's really in love with the humble but no-nonsense detective who saves her at the last minute.

They also enjoyed the movies based on true stories. Their all-time favorite was still the one about Betty Broderick. It didn't matter how many times they'd seen it, they never missed a chance to watch it again. And it was on tonight.

So they felt much annoyance when Reece Lee came busting into their home at all hours—actually ten p.m.—and went through the boxes she had stored in her closet. Her momma had sent them to her from her room after one of their fights. The note that accompanied those boxes had said it all: "Here's your stuff."

Shaw let out a big sigh, his whole body going rigid when he saw her idiot brother opening closet doors and pulling out all those boxes she'd unceremoniously shoved away.

"Reece Lee Reed, what the holy hell are you doing?" Ronnie demanded.

"Don't mind me. Just looking for something." He began pulling the top off the boxes and digging through them like a rabid chipmunk.

"*Reece.*"

"The more you bother me, the longer this will take."

"Maybe if you told me what you were looking for . . ."

"I doubt you remember it, but you always had one."

Ronnie and Shaw looked at each other, then shook their heads. Of her three brothers, Reece was definitely the most . . . difficult.

Ronnie offered Shaw more popcorn, and when he began to eat again, she felt better. She really only worried when the man stopped eating. Then hell was about to break loose.

After thirty minutes or so of her brother digging away, Ronnie asked, "Any word from Ricky?"

"He's still in Russia. Not sure when he'll be back. Apparently the bears aren't playing nice."

"They never will," Shaw mumbled around a mouthful of popcorn.

"Why do you say that?" Ronnie asked.

"Russian bears are notoriously difficult to negotiate with. I still don't have a hotel in that country because Russian bears are so damn difficult."

"Well, I hope my brother's being safe."

Reece shrugged, now going through a box of old children's books. "He always is. You'd only have to worry if it was me going over there."

At least Reece was self-aware of his limitations.

"Hey," Ronnie asked, "who the hell was that girl you were talking to today?"

"You'll have to be much more specific than that."

"The one who cut the tar out of that bitch Laura Jane."

"Someone cut up Laura Jane?" Shaw asked, grinning.

"I couldn't do it, of course," Ronnie reminded him. "I am part of the same Pack and she hasn't done anything to me. But this girl went after her with a blade and her claws. It may take her, like, two whole *days* before her wounds heal."

"That's why I'm here," Reece said. "I can't figure out what she is."

Ronnie blinked. "What she is?"

"Yeah. She won't tell me. It's driving me nuts!"

"Oh, Lord, Reece. You're not interested in this one, are you?"

"Nah. She's way too terrifying. I've seen Laura Jane in a fight and that small female didn't even give that She-wolf a chance to be her dishonorable fighting self. She beat Laura Jane to being dishonorable. I can't date anyone like that. But I do enjoy that in a friend. She'll make a good friend."

"You're such an odd boy."

"Here it is!" Reece exclaimed, holding up a very old book.

"What is that?"

"Don't you remember? This is *The Infamous Book of Smells.*"

Shaw's head snapped around. "The what?"

Surprised, the siblings looked at the lion.

"You never had *The Infamous Book of Smells?*" Reece asked.

"Was I supposed to?"

"How were you able to tell the difference between grizzlies and black bears?" Ronnie wanted to know. "Or mountain lions, cheetahs, and leopards?"

"I learned as I went. Isn't that how you guys did it?"

"Eventually, but every Pack pup starts out with—"

"The Infamous Book of Smells?"

"Exactly."

"Which is what exactly?"

Reece brought the book over to the table. "It's scratch and sniff for kids. With the scent of different breeds and species. I learned so much before I even cut my first fangs."

"Yeah, but that's an old copy," Ronnie reminded him.

"You think the scents have faded?"

"No. But it's not the most updated."

"I know. That's what I want."

Sitting on the chair closest to Shaw, Reece began on the first page and went through each. Scratching and sniffing. Scratching and sniffing.

Fascinated, Ronnie watched her brother until he suddenly stopped at a page. Scratched. Sniffed. Scratched. Sniffed. Studied the page. Scratched. Sniffed.

"This is it. This is the one." He looked at the page again, his brow pulling down.

"What is she, Reece?"

He looked up at her, still frowning.

"Show me," she pushed, now completely curious. She had to know!

With a shrug, Reece turned the book around and held it up the way their pre-school teacher used to when she would read a page, then show the class the accompanying picture.

Ronnie's mouth dropped open before she demanded, "Good Lord, Reece Lee Reed! *This* is the woman you want to be friends with?"

"Now more than ever!"

Shaw threw up his hands and Ronnie just sighed. Her brother . . . some days . . . honestly, some *days*.

CHAPTER TWENTY-ONE

Toni had just rolled onto her back, her entire body taking a long, luxurious stretch when there was a knock at Ricky's door and it opened. Without warning.

She yelped and pulled herself into a ball. Ricky immediately stretched his body over hers, blocking her from Vic Barinov's sight.

"Oh. Sorry. Was I interrupting?"

"Yes!" Ricky yelped. "You were."

"Sorry. But you guys do have to get ready if we're going to get to your meeting with the—"

"Meeting?" Toni scoffed.

Now, after a night of free-running through the beautiful Siberian wilderness and getting wonderfully tossed around the bedroom by Ricky Lee Reed, Toni's sense of panic was no longer clouding her mind. Instead, she just felt annoyance at the bears wasting her damn time.

"They're not going to meet with me. They have no intention of negotiating with me. We might as well just head the hell home rather than waste another damn day on this bullshit."

Barinov shrugged. "Of course. I'll get the car ready and let the hotel know we're checking out."

Ricky grabbed the sheet and pulled it up so it covered Toni all the way to her neck. Then he sat up, his body still blocking her, and said, "Wait."

His hand on the doorknob, Barinov looked back at them.

"Do you know what's going on with these bears?" he asked.

Toni didn't know why Ricky was asking Barinov about anything. Other than ensure they arrived on time and that Toni was safe, he didn't seem too involved in any of this drama.

"You know"—Barinov began—"I really shouldn't get involved."

See?

Ricky reached down and grabbed his jeans from the floor. He pulled out his cell phone and speed-dialed a number. He put on the speaker and for a few seconds they sat around silently listening to the phone ring.

"Yep?" a voice answered from the other end, and Barinov immediately rolled his eyes, momentarily reminding her of Kyle after he'd been caught tormenting Oriana about her non-existent weight problem.

"Hey, Dee," Ricky said into the phone. "How ya doin'?"

"Fine." There was a pause, then Dee asked, "You back in New York?"

"Nope. These Russian bears are being real difficult."

"Mhmm. Never liked them Russian bears."

"We haven't mentioned you," Ricky told her. "I don't think they would have fond memories of you or your daddy."

"Heh."

"Anyway," Ricky went on, "I'm not sure what to do. Any suggestions?"

"Isn't Barinov there?"

Ricky looked up at the hybrid. "Yeah. He's standing right here. But he said he shouldn't get involved."

There was a long sigh from the other end of that phone. "Take me off speaker," Dee ordered, "and hand Barinov the damn phone."

Ricky did just that and after baring a rather long fang, Barinov put the phone to his ear. "Hey, Dee—Well . . . yeah, I . . . no need to get nasty, Smith. Yeah. Fine. Whatever." Barinov disconnected the call and tossed the phone back to Ricky.

"You're a prick," the hybrid snarled.

"I'm a Reed. We were never taught to play nice with others."

Barinov stepped away from the door and looked over

Ricky's shoulder to focus on Toni. "You were negotiating with the bears as soon as you stepped out of the car the first day," he abruptly told her.

Startled by that response, Toni sat a little taller, holding the sheet to her chest. "Wait a minute . . . what?"

"You didn't know?"

"Did I look like I knew?"

"It was hard to tell with the whole separation anxiety thing." Then Barinov focused on Ricky and smirked.

"Oh, my God," Ricky muttered, placing his phone on the end table. "He's never going to let that go."

"Let me ask you"—Barinov stepped closer to the bed—"did you research negotiation techniques before you came here, Toni?"

"Of course."

"Did you research negotiating with Russians?"

"No. But I've negotiated with Russians before."

"About your family?"

"Yes."

"The powerful music family that everyone kind of loves?"

"As long as you don't know 'em personally," Ricky tossed in.

Toni shoved Ricky's shoulder and answered Barinov at the same time, "Yes."

"Then that is completely different from negotiating a business deal about hockey."

"Why is that different?"

"Your family is a bunch of American artists that the Russians—who love music like they love air—are going to treat differently during negotiations. Especially if they're dealing with a family member. But hockey is a much-beloved sport *and* a very important Russian *business*. Especially to the Siberian bears."

"So the delay . . . that's all a—"

"Negotiation tactic." Barinov shrugged. "I really thought you knew."

"No. That's what was making me crazy. I didn't understand why they weren't meeting with me. When I've helped negotiate deals for my brother and sister, I was *always* treated wonderfully. I guess I expected the same thing this time."

"You could have said something, Vic," Ricky told him.

"People don't hire me for my opinion, Reed. You know that."

"I'm not people," Toni said. "I'm desperate. I *need* your opinion. I have to get home before my entire family is decimated by their insanity. And I have to point out . . . that's a real short trip for them."

"You gonna help us, hoss?" Ricky asked.

"I'm not used to getting involved."

Toni moved close behind Ricky, laid her chin on his shoulder, smiled sweetly. "Please?" she begged. "For me?"

"You don't even like me," Barinov accused.

"I could learn to like you . . . if you help me."

He chuckled. "Yeah. All right."

Toni gave a happy yip, but Barinov barked back and said, "Do not make that noise around me. It makes me want to go outside and tear the bark off trees."

"So what's the first thing we should do?" Ricky asked.

"First . . . we cancel today."

"Cancel?"

"If they want to play hardball . . . so will you. Besides, we have to meet someone."

"Someone who can also help?" Toni asked, trying not to sound too hopeful.

"Yep. Someone who can also help."

She yipped again and now both males barked, "Toni!"

"Sorry. Sorry. Habit."

It was late when Livy worked her way through an open window in the kitchen.

Yes. She had keys. Toni always gave her keys to whatever home or hotel suite she and her family were staying at when Livy was around. And if Toni didn't give the keys to her, because they were having one of their ridiculous arguments, then Toni's parents gave Livy the keys. Paul and Jackie loved Livy. She didn't know why, though. Most shifters, without even knowing what Livy was, didn't like her, but especially jackals. In the wild, full-blood jackals and her kind went at it like dogs and cats.

Then again, nothing stopped their kind from fighting anyone off. That's what they did. That's what Livy's ancestors, mostly witches and healers, liked about the animal. How vicious and fearless it was. So while a lot of others were learning to shift into giant, apex predators, her people were becoming small and deadly.

When Livy was a little girl, she didn't understand how come she wouldn't be shifting into a cool animal like the other shifter kids her parents knew. But now that she was an adult . . . she loved what she was. Adored it. Just like she adored her best friend.

Toni was an unusual girl. She didn't think she was. She saw herself as average. And, compared to the rest of the Jean-Louis Parker brood, it wasn't surprising she felt that way. Yet Toni was definitely unique. Naturally maternal. Naturally kind. And constantly on Livy's ass.

That's when Livy realized that she'd been accepted as family by Toni when the woman—a girl at the time—began to manage Livy's career. Or, at the very least, manage Livy's agent, while attempting to get her to live a certain way. It drove Toni nuts that Livy could and often did live anywhere she had to. She had no problem taking over someone's house for a couple of days when she saw them leave with some luggage. She made sure not to destroy anything and to replace anything she may have used. True, Livy could afford her own place and she had one in Washington, but she really liked living in other people's space. It was always so fascinating. You never knew what you'd learn from complete strangers.

Livy opened the refrigerator and reached for a bottle of orange juice.

"Hi!"

Livy spun and hissed, baring her mouthful of fangs.

The wolfdog jumped back, her hands raised to protect her face. "Sorry! Sorry! I didn't mean to startle you!"

Actually . . . she hadn't startled Livy. But the wolfdog was just so damn perky. It was irritating. Really, really irritating.

"Still here?" Livy asked, being bitchy.

The wolfdog glanced down at herself. "I think so . . . right?"

Letting out a sigh, Livy turned back to the refrigerator and took out the orange juice. She opened the bottle and was about to start drinking from it when the wolfdog held out a glass for her.

"What's that?" Livy asked.

"Something for you to pour your juice into. So that you don't have to drink right out of the bottle."

Gazing at the wolfdog, Livy put the bottle to her lips and drank. For a real long time.

The wolfdog's eyes narrowed and a little spot on her cheek twitched.

When Livy was done, she smacked her lips—loudly.

"That was good." Livy sighed. Then she held the bottle out to the wolfdog. "Want some?"

"No, thank you."

"You sure?" Livy pushed, shoving the offending bottle with her saliva all over the rim closer. "It's really good. No pulp!"

"No. Really. I'm fine."

Shrugging, Livy screwed the top back on and put the juice back in the refrigerator.

"You're just going to leave it in there?"

Livy closed the refrigerator door. "Yes! It wouldn't be right not to share, now would it?"

"But . . ."

Livy stepped close. "But . . . what?"

When the wolfdog didn't say anything, Livy started off toward the swinging door.

"But you slobbered all over it!" the wolfdog yelled before Livy could make it through that door.

Slowly, Livy faced the canine. "You know what, Blayne?" Livy said mildly. "You're absolutely right. I did." She leaned forward and lowered her voice. "And it felt *good.*"

The wolfdog gasped, her mouth dropping open, but before she could say anything else, Livy walked out.

Halfway down the hall, she passed Coop. "Hey," Livy said, grabbing his arm. "Do me a favor."

"Sure."

"If you're going to the kitchen, make sure to drink out of the orange juice bottle that's right in the front. The one with no pulp."

"You're the only one who drinks the one with no pulp. The rest of us like pulp."

"I know. Just trust me on this."

Coop shook his head. "You're messing with Blayne again, aren't you?"

"Well, your sister's not here to do it, so I'm covering." She squeezed his forearm. "That's what friends do for each other, Coop."

"Torment the innocent?"

"Yes. Exactly."

They drove back to the territory that Ricky had taken Toni to the night before where they'd run for hours. Honestly, the land was even more beautiful in the day. So lush. And Ricky actually would love to come back in the dead of winter. To see all this covered in ice and snow. It must be amazing. Especially Lake Baikal itself.

Vic took them past the wooded area they'd run through and down a road until they reached a village. He pulled up in front of a small house with a pack of children running around.

"Where are we?"

"This is the home of Genka Kuznetsov."

"Wait." Ricky scratched his head. "Kuznetsov?"

"What's wrong?"

Toni leaned forward. "Are they related to the Kuznetsov Pack in New York?"

"Do not mention the New York Kuznetsov Pack or your association with them," Vic warned.

"Why not?"

"Sabina Kuznetsov is the daughter of Anton Kuznetsov. Her Pack of orphaned wild dogs took Sabina's last name because they thought it sounded cooler than Jessica Ward's last name, which in New York is true. Unfortunately, the reason Sabina ended up in New York was that her father was pushed out of the Pack by Genka who, to this day, loathes her brother with the fire of a thousand suns."

"That's a lot of heat," Ricky noted.

"Exactly."

"Then maybe we shouldn't be here."

"You need information. And that's what the Kuznetsovs trade in. Information."

"Okay."

Vic looked between them. "You two ready?"

"Yep."

They got out of the car, and adult wild dogs seemed to appear from everywhere. Surrounding the house and especially the kids, protecting them.

An older She-dog walked out of the house and stood on her small stoop. She had hair that was filled with a riot of colors like gold, brown, red, and white, but mostly blond. Lots of blond. "Why are you here, Victor Barinov?"

"I've brought friends for you, Genka. They need your help."

The wild dog lifted her head, sniffed the air. "At least this time they're canines. Unlike you."

"I'm not canine, nor am I empty handed." He lifted both his arms. In one hand he held two bottles of very expensive vodka. In the other, he had a basket filled with good French and Italian cheeses and water crackers from England.

That's when the wild dogs no longer looked suspicious but instead raised their own arms in greeting, calling out Vic's name. Genka opened her front door. "Come friends, come. Let's sit inside and enjoy this wonderful bounty our friend Barinov brings us!"

So, that's what they did.

★ ★ ★

Toni had to admit, she was fascinated. And extremely annoyed. Not at the wild dogs. Once they got some gifts, they were in great spirits. But the bears were playing games. Games that annoyed her.

"I like Novikov," Genka said plainly, her English heavily accented but easily understood. "He is strong like polar but mean like lion. He is hybrid like you, Victor Barinov, but with talent."

Barinov snorted. "Thanks, Genka."

"Welcome." She lit a cigarette, took a long drag, then pointed the cigarette at Toni. "You know, problem is not that Novikov kicked Yuri Asanov's ass."

"And Novikov truly kicked Yuri Asanov's ass," Genka's older sister commented as she walked into the room and dropped onto the couch across the small living room.

"The problem is that he made the entire team look bad. They look weak. Now they want to make him look weak."

"I can't help them do that," Toni said, shaking her head.

"Of course not. You are canine like me. We are loyal. Not like cats." Genka looked pointedly at Barinov.

The hybrid threw up his hands. "Are you just going to abuse me while I'm here, Genka Kuznetsov?"

"Yes," both Genka and her sister said together.

Genka again focused on Toni, took another drag from her cigarette. Toni hated the cigarette smell, but she wasn't about to say that. God knew, she'd put up with worse over the years for her family; she could do the same for the team paying her so much money.

"See, they don't tell you truth, little American," Genka said, reaching for the bottle of vodka on the table and pouring herself another shot. "First off, those bears can all speak English as well as me, no matter how stupid they may act around you. In Russia, we all learn English at some point in school. Also, you think you are waiting to meet with man in charge. But Yuri Asanov is not in charge."

"He's not?" Toni asked, surprised. "But he's the team coach."

"He is coach. And he is important. But he is not who you should be negotiating with. In shifter sports in Russia it is who pays the bills who controls the team."

"And who pays the bills?"

Genka blew out a long plume of smoke, her dark brown eyes on Toni before she finally said, "Ivan Zubachev."

"What? But we talked to him. He met us on the first day."

"Right. And you didn't know him. You didn't greet him as the one in charge. So now he plays games. He's very wealthy, so he has little else to do but fuck with the Americans."

"The Zubachevs have run this territory and this team," Barinov explained, "since Vadim Zubachev told Stalin to suck his dick."

Toni thought a moment and finally asked. "Wait, I'm sorry, but . . . does the Russian full-human government know you exist here?"

"They've known for centuries at least," Genka said.

"And they've never said anything? They've never come after you?"

"They tried." She held up her forefinger. "Once. Sent an entire army to wipe us out for being different. For being who we are. The men never came back." She smirked. "But we ate well that winter. Like kings."

Ricky nodded. "All right then."

"So it's Zubachev I need to negotiate with?" Toni asked.

"It is. Like most bear, he is difficult. Stubborn. Like most Russians . . . he is difficult. Stubborn. He won't make it easy on you."

"So what can *I* do to make it easier on me?"

"Gifts always help. But, my little darling, your problem is, Ivan Zubachev and his entire family are rich. Like they-can-own-your-Manhattan rich. There is little you can offer him that he does not have or cannot buy, so you'll have to come up with something unique. That *only you* can give."

"Great." Toni sighed.

"What does he like?" Ricky asked.

Genka shrugged. "Hockey. Women. Although," she said, looking at Toni, "you're not his type. Too small, like bird."

"Hey."

"Hair too messy."

"I like your hair," Ricky reminded her.

"Not helping me."

Ricky loved watching Toni's face when she was forced to down a shot of vodka. It was considered rude in Russia not to drink during a toast. So she'd winced and cringed her way through it, but managed well enough. The woman was definitely determined. He liked that about her.

After a hearty lunch and a good-bye filled with hugs and a promise to the wild dogs that they'd get a private audience with Bo Novikov himself—"We have cousins in Mongolia who want to meet him, too. We bring them," Genka had promised—they'd headed back to their vehicle.

Ricky had just pulled the back passenger door open to let Toni in when Barinov's phone went off. He smirked at the caller ID and answered.

"Barinov." After a moment, he walked around the car until he reached Toni. He handed her the phone. "It's Ivan Zubachev, *ma'am*."

Taking the phone, Toni answered. "Yes? Oh. Hello, Mr. Zubachev. Did I? I missed today's appointment? Oh. I am so sorry. I don't know what happened. So much going on, I guess. But don't worry, I'll be there tomorrow. Ready to negotiate away!"

Ricky and Vic chuckled at her tone.

"Yes. Of course. Tomorrow then."

She disconnected the call. "He is *pissed*."

"Russians hate lateness," Vic explained. "And not showing up at all . . . considered very rude."

"Then he shouldn't play games with me. I deal with that every day with my family, but I love them so I put up with it."

"Then tomorrow we're on." Vic grinned down at her. "You ready for that?"

"I can't wait." She got into the car and Ricky closed the door and faced Vic.

"Here." Vic handed Ricky the keys to the car.

"Where are you going?"

"I'll walk back. Work off the vodka." He pointed to a road that shot off from the main one they'd traveled. "Go that direction and it'll take you to Lake Baikal. The shifter-only portion. It's open to all breeds and species."

"You don't want to come?"

"Seen it." Eyes like a cat's glanced at Toni and back at Ricky. "You guys have a nice time. I'll see you back at the hotel."

Ricky snorted. "Seriously?"

"I know how you canines are, Reed. You say it's nothing, but it's everything. Just suck it up already."

Laughing, the big hybrid walked off, and Ricky didn't bother to argue with him. Instead, he opened Toni's door.

"Out," he told her. She immediately stepped out.

"What's wrong?"

"Nothing." He closed the back door and opened the front passenger side. "Since we've got the rest of the day, we're going to sightsee."

Blinking, appearing surprised, Toni said, "Really?"

"Don't you want to?"

"Yeah." She thought a moment, and a bright smile bloomed across her face. "Yeah. I'd really like that."

"Then get in, darlin'. Because I have no idea where we are going."

"It's called a GPS, Reed. It's already built into the car."

"Get in, smart ass."

Giggling, she did as he said, for once not bothering to argue. For once.

Seven in the morning and Coop walked downstairs to get in some practice before the rush began. The grand piano he'd or-

dered had been placed in the main ballroom. The one everyone was fighting over. But when he walked in, the piano was
gone and Kyle was over in the corner on a stepladder, chipping
away at his marble while Oriana used the rest of the space to
dance. A special flooring had been laid over the original—but
damaged—wood so that she could use her pointe shoes without problems.

"Good," Novikov said, coming to stand by Coop. "You're
here." He handed a printed sheet of paper to him. "This is the
schedule. Learn it. Know it. Live it."

Coop didn't even glance at it. Instead he stared up at the
more than seven foot tall hybrid and said, "You made my piano
go away. Did it insult you?"

Novikov stared at him. "You're weird. Your sister's less annoying."

"Which one?"

"All of them." He handed Coop another sheet of paper. "I
moved your piano to the basement."

"When?"

"An hour ago."

"I didn't hear a moving crew come in."

"Moving crew?"

Coop leaned back a bit. "You moved my *grand* Steinway to
the basement by yourself?"

"I needed to get things done. Your brother and sister needed
to use this room by six thirty."

Good God! Where was Toni when he needed her? Because
this shit was the highest level of comedy, and the only one who
could truly appreciate it was Toni!

"Is the piano in one piece?"

"Of course it is. There's not a scratch on it. Oh, and your
nervous little sister . . ."

"Cherise."

"Yeah. She says acoustics are great down there. She'll be
practicing in another room in the basement. So you're both set."

"Great. Excellent planning."

"I know. Not done yet, but we're almost there."

"We're not done yet?"

"No."

As abruptly as he'd appeared, Novikov turned and walked away.

Shaking his head, Coop studied the pages he'd gotten. One was the schedule, as Novikov had said, and the other was a breakdown of who got what room and for how long per day. It was unbelievably organized.

A small hand tugged on Coop's jeans. Freddy looked up at him with eyes just like his own.

"What's wrong?" God, he hoped it wasn't Delilah again. Toni would blow an artery.

"It's handwritten," Freddy whispered.

"What is?"

He pointed at the sheets of paper Coop held.

Glancing down, Coop shook his head. "No, buddy. This is from a printer. It's been typed."

"No. It hasn't. Me, Denny, and the twins watched him do it for like an hour. He wrote out each one. By hand. We had to leave when Zoe began to cry. She was completely freaked out." Freddy leaned in a little bit more and again whispered, "I think if she'd stayed any longer, she would have stabbed him to death. And I don't think the rest of us would have tried to stop her."

Coop crouched in front of his brother and put a hand on his shoulder. "That's because you know OCD when you see it. You're seeing Troy's future. Fear that."

"Oh," Freddy said, eyes wide, "I do, Coop. I really do."

They parked a bit away so they could walk to the lake.

Believed to be the oldest and deepest freshwater lake in the world, Lake Baikal was one of the most amazing places Toni had ever seen. The water was clean and clear, the land lush and green. Not remotely what she'd think of when someone mentioned Siberia.

Ricky Lee stood next to her, both of them silent for several long minutes. Both of them taking in the scenery and the lovely land they were lucky enough to have visited.

"This is beautiful," Ricky finally said.

"Yes. It is."

"But I can't really enjoy it because all I can think about is getting you back to the hotel and naked."

"Thank God!" Toni exploded. "I thought it was just me. I've been asking myself, 'How can you not enjoy all this beautiful nature?' " She looked directly at him and admitted, "But, you look so damn good naked."

He took her hand in his, stared deeply in her eyes, and said, "We *both* do. And how are we supposed to focus on anything else when we both look so dang good naked?"

Toni laughed. "You're ridiculous."

"No. My baby brother is ridiculous. I'm just a little goofy. A fine mix between Reece's ridiculous behavior and Rory's uptight lifestyle." He tugged her hand and had the audacity—audacity!—to tip his head down and look up at her through his rather long eyelashes.

"Come on, darlin'," he coaxed. "Let's go back to the hotel, get naked, and be all awed about how good we look."

"But we're in Siberia," Toni whined. "It's not like we get out here every day. We should be exploring or something. Something touristy."

Ricky didn't say anything, but he tugged her closer and closer . . . until he could slip his arm around her waist. Then he slowly brought her up against his body and Toni's skin went hot. She might be sweating.

He stared down at her mouth. Just stared at it. Without saying a word.

"But it's not like Siberia is *going* anywhere." Still feeling guilty about not taking full advantage of a rare opportunity, Toni briefly chewed her lip and Ricky growled in response. "Lake Baikal has been here for, like, a bazillion years or something. I'm sure it'll be here next year . . . or the year after that."

The hand holding her around the waist slipped lower, his fingers gripping her ass and pushing her pelvis closer to him until she felt nothing but his amazing erection pressing against her.

Toni let out a shaky breath, her eyes briefly closing. "Oh-

kay, yeah. This lake is giant. It'll be here forever. And don't forget jet lag. I'm sure we're still having jet lag. And that can only
be dealt with in a . . . a bed."

Grinning, Ricky Lee stepped back, took hold of her hand
again, and began to walk back to the car.

Blayne sat at the kitchen table in the Jackal House—as
she liked to call it—and watched as one of the Horde of
Offspring—as Bo liked to call them—carefully cut an apple into
equally sized slices.

Because he was making sure that all the sizes were exactly the
same size, he was taking a rather long time.

"Would you like me to make you something to eat, Troy?"

"No." He blew out a breath and sat back in his chair, shook
his head, and offered, "Do you want these?"

"Your apple slices?"

"Yes." He handed the paper plate to her, took another paper
plate from the pile in the middle of the table and another apple
from the bowl beside it. Then he began again.

Honestly, when Bo Novikov says, "That kid is *seriously* ob-
sessive," you really have a problem.

Concerned, Blayne leaned in and began, "Honey—"

"I'm already in therapy for this sort of thing, so just let it go."

"All right then."

Blayne ate the apple slices and watched the kid go through
two more apples before he was happy with what he did. That
was around the time when Oriana came into the room, sweating and smiling in a black leotard and pink stockings, her toe
shoes still on her feet, white leg warmers on her legs, and a
towel around her neck. She grabbed a glass from the cabinet
and went into the refrigerator. When the girl pulled out the
bottle of pulp-free juice, Blayne squealed and jumped up.

"Not that one!" she yelped, leaping across the room to pull
the offending bottle out of Oriana's hand.

"Is there something wrong, Blayne?"

Blayne's eyes narrowed when she saw the girl smirk. "Have
you been talking to Livy?"

"Don't know what you mean."

Blayne put the bottle back in the refrigerator and took out an unopened one. It had pulp but Oriana would just have to deal with that. Once she handed it off, she turned in time to see one of the older siblings walking past her.

"Hi, Cherise!"

Cherise froze. It was like she thought she could blend into the backsplash behind the sink.

Not looking at her, Cherise nodded. "Hi, uh, Blayne."

"Are you ever leaving?" Oriana asked Blayne. "Or are you and the Incredible Hulk moving in for the summer?"

"Stop calling him that, and we're just here until Bo is convinced this whole schedule thing is running perfectly. He doesn't want to disappoint your sister."

"Why not? We disappoint her all the time."

"That's . . . adorable." She turned back to Cherise but she'd almost sneaked out the back kitchen door. Blayne rushed up to her. "Hey, Cherise?"

Cherise jumped and spun around. "Yes?"

"I was wondering if you'd like to come out with me tonight."

"Why?"

"It'll be fun!"

"You don't know me."

"No. But that's how one learns about someone, by hanging out with them. You'll get to meet my best friend, Gwen. You'll like her. Maybe. She is feline and you're canine. But I'm canine and she's still feline and we get along great."

Oriana put her arm around Blayne's shoulders and looked at her sister. "Oh, Cherise, you *have* to go. Because that sounds like so much fun for *you*."

Blayne nodded. She couldn't agree with Oriana more! And how nice of her to say it!

"Come on! It'll be a blast!"

Cherise shrugged and finally admitted, "I don't really like to go outside."

"Then you have to go outside! And you'll start liking it."

"It's that easy!" Oriana cheered. "You just have to go!"

Cherise smiled—although it looked a little pained—and nodded. "Okay then."

"Great!"

And, excited for her sister, Oriana lifted her arms in the air and cheered, *"Great!"*

Blayne started back to her apple slices when she heard Oriana yelp, "Ow!"

Blayne turned and found the girl holding her foot and hopping up and down.

"Are you okay?"

"It's my fault," Cherise confessed. "I stumbled and stepped right on her instep. Too bad I didn't hit the tip of her shoes instead. That wouldn't have hurt at all, huh, Oriana?" She kissed her sister's cheek and again headed toward the back door. "So sorry, sweetie."

Shrugging, Blayne picked up an apple slice and popped it into her mouth. *Such a lovely family!* she happily thought to herself.

CHAPTER TWENTY-TWO

There really was something about a naked woman sitting behind you, her long legs wrapped around your waist, one arm around your neck, and her other hand sliding down your abs to your groin until she could grasp your cock and hold it tight.

Ricky let out a contented sigh as Toni kissed his neck, his shoulder. He relaxed into her, her breasts pressing against his back. Nothing had ever felt so damn comfortable before. He used to think "comfortable" meant boring, but Ricky Lee realized he was very wrong. There was nothing boring about Antonella Jean-Louis Parker.

Her leg stretched out a bit, her foot curving around until she could tuck it under his knee. She nibbled on the tendons of his neck, but he didn't feel the instinctual need to protect them like he usually did when a She-predator got too close to that part of his body.

"You really are beautiful," Ricky sighed out.

Toni chuckled. "I bet you say that to all the She-dogs who have hold of your dick."

"No. I don't." He glanced back at her. "In fact I don't say much."

His motto had always been "Get in, get out, enjoy yourself while you're there." But with Toni, Ricky realized he enjoyed himself whether in or out.

Toni suddenly pulled away and Ricky worried he'd gone too far. She-predators didn't like it when males got too clingy, too sentimental. It made them feel trapped. But Toni didn't run away from him, instead she maneuvered in front of him and pushed him onto his back. Grinning, she straddled his chest and then stretched out on top of him, her knees on either side of his hips.

"I am so glad you're with me on this trip," she said, nuzzling under his neck, nibbling his ear. "I think it would have been so dull otherwise."

"Nothing seems to be dull when you're around, darlin'."

Ricky gripped Toni around the waist and rolled her until she was beneath him. "Strange and random, maybe. Dull?" He chuckled. "Never."

Leaning down a bit, Ricky sucked Toni's nipple into his mouth, his tongue flicking it. She groaned, her hands digging into his hair. He loved when she did that.

When he had her writhing nicely, he asked, "What do you want me to do, Toni?"

She didn't hesitate. "Eat me."

Ricky began working his way down Toni's body. "Did I mention," he asked, grinning up at her, "that I love a woman who knows what she wants . . . and ain't afraid to demand it?"

"That's good," she gasped out when he nipped the inside of her thigh. "Because I can be really demanding when I want to be."

"Just what I love to hear, darlin'. Just what I love to hear."

Toni stretched her arms over her head, laughing as Ricky Lee flipped her over onto her stomach.

"You're wolf-handling me!" she accused, groaning as his tongue licked up her spine.

Ricky Lee did nothing but growl at her and that's when she felt a fang graze across her back.

"No fangs!" she ordered. "No fangs!" Toni had been around enough wolves in her life to know what fangs during sex could turn into and she had no idea if either one of them was ready enough for that level of commitment. At least not yet.

Strong, large hands gripped Toni's hips and pulled her to her knees. Ricky entered her roughly, his fingers digging into her skin. She wished she could say she hated it, but she'd never been so turned on before in her life.

He held her like that for a long moment, buried deep inside her. He leaned into her, his breath hot against her neck.

"You're making me crazy, darlin'."

"I didn't do anything."

"Liar," he whispered.

Toni stretched her entire body this time and Ricky groaned again.

"See what I mean?" he accused.

"No." Then she tightened her pussy around his cock and that groan turned into a vicious growl.

"Damn evil female!" He sat up straight, his fingers now claws, digging deep into her hips.

Ricky pulled his cock out and pushed it back in.

"I don't know what you're talking about," Toni panted as she tried to push herself up with her arms. But a swift slap to her ass had her yipping, snarling, and coming, all at the same time. She'd never felt anything like it. And once she began coming, Ricky began fucking her harder, pounding into her, extending her orgasm as he sought his own.

It was so powerful, she couldn't breathe, she couldn't think, she couldn't even scream. She just kept panting and hoping she didn't pass out. She wasn't sure she could tolerate the ego boost the wolf would get if she blacked out on him during sex when liquor wasn't involved. So it was with some relief when she heard him roar like a lion male before dropping onto her back like a sack of really heavy laundry.

When he hadn't move after several minutes and the tremors racking her body had stopped, Toni rammed her elbow into Ricky's stomach until he rolled away. Took a few times, too, before he seemed to get the message.

Once Ricky Lee was flat on his back, Toni turned over and rested her head against his shoulder.

"You called me evil," she reminded him.

"Well, you are Satan's pet."

Raising herself up, Toni grinned down at him. "And aren't you glad about that?"

Ricky grinned back. "Actually . . . I really am."

Cherise really didn't understand how she'd let this happen. At what point had she lost control?

Okay, okay. She rarely had control. She knew that, but this . . . this was outrageous!

How did she let one wolfdog talk her into this?

"Blayne . . . I really don't know about this."

"You'll be great! Won't she, Gwen?"

The gold-eyed feline hybrid finished tying up her skates before looking over at Cherise. "She looks completely freaked out, Blayne."

"She's not. Are you, Cherise?"

"Well—"

"See? Besides. This is just tryouts."

"You see, Blayne," Cherise tried again, "I can't really do this. I shouldn't. Because of my hands."

Gwen stood up, studied Cherise's hands. "What's wrong with them?"

"Nothing. That's the point. I need to ensure nothing's wrong with them. They're my livelihood."

"Are you a surgeon?"

"No. Cellist."

The feline stared at her as only a feline could. "Oh. Is that really a job someone has . . . in the world?"

"Gwen!" Blayne snapped.

"What? It was just a question."

"Rude!" Blayne took hold of Gwen's arm and lifted it. "See Gwen's hands, Cherise? Her nails, specifically."

How could Cherise miss them? They were unreasonably long, painted red and black with sparkling rhinestones on the tips. Like something out of one of Cherise's nightmares.

"If she can keep her nails this long," Blayne reasoned, "you can keep your hands safe!"

That didn't seem like very thought-out reasoning, but before

Cherise could debate the point, a hand tugged her hair. Startled, she yipped and spun, ready to make a run for it if necessary.

"What are you doing?" her sister's best friend blandly asked.

"What are *you* doing here?" Cherise shot back at Livy Kowalski.

"Coop sent me. He would have come himself to get you but some very large Neanderthal pointed at a giant Post-it note and said it was his practice time."

Blayne stomped her skate-covered foot. "He's not a Neanderthal! He's misunderstood!"

Livy, never comfortable with the overly emotional, eyed Blayne once before focusing back on Cherise.

"Why did you bring Freddy?" Cherise asked Livy. The boy should be at home, getting ready for dinner. Not hanging out on the streets of New York. Toni wouldn't like that at all.

"I told Toni I'd keep an eye on him. This is me keeping an eye."

Cherise's brother held Livy's hand, his eyes wide as he stared up at all the females of many breeds and species, even hybrids. As soon as they saw little Freddy, the women surrounded him, oohing and aaawwwing over him. He didn't seem to mind. Thankfully, he appeared to take more after Cooper than Cherise, loving the attention but not needing to drown in it like Delilah, nor simply expecting it like Oriana and Kyle.

"Can I hold him?" a She-lion asked.

Livy frowned at the feline. "He's not a puppy, dude."

The cat sneered and Cherise quickly asked her brother, "Do you mind, Freddy?"

His answer was to raise his arms and the She-lion happily lifted him up, turning around to show him off to the other females. "Isn't he flippin' adorable!"

Livy yawned and motioned to Cherise. "So . . . what are you doing here?"

"It was me," Blayne explained, and Livy's cold, black eyes locked on the hybrid.

"You?"

"Yeah. I thought it would be great for Cherise to get out of the house. The whole time Bo and I have been at the house, she never seems to go out."

"Do you want to get out?" Livy asked Cherise.

"Not really."

"But you haven't tried yet!"

Livy folded her arms over her chest and looked over at Gwen. "Do you guys have a quota? A certain number of people you have to bring to tryouts?"

"Of course not!" Blayne exclaimed.

"Yep," Gwen replied. "It's not required by the team or anything but Blayne insists on having her own quota."

Blayne glared at her friend. "Snitch."

"That's what I thought." Livy motioned to Cherise. "Do you want to stay or go?"

"I thought you were coming to get me."

"What am I?" Livy asked. "Your mother?" She thought a moment, then changed it to, "Toni?"

"It's just us," Blayne told them. "Just the team and our coach. This isn't a bout. Just a chance for you to get out on skates and see if you like it or not. No pressure."

"Once you do what she says anyway."

"Shut up, Gwen," Blayne snapped before she smiled again at Cherise. "It'll be fun! I promise!"

"Well . . ." Cherise looked around, and all the females stared at her. "I am already in skates."

"Yes!" Blayne cheered. "You won't regret it!" She hugged Cherise, which Cherise didn't like because she didn't really like to be touched.

Gwen rolled around Livy, sniffing her.

"If I feel that nose on me again, feline," Livy dryly warned, "I'll start removing pieces of you."

"What are you?"

"Death."

"Olivia!" Cherise chastised.

"She asked."

"Are you a hybrid?" a very large She-liger asked, standing behind Livy.

"No."

Gwen stood in front of Livy, looked her over. "What about you?"

"What about me?"

"You trying out tonight?"

"To be on your derby team?" Livy smirked. "You don't want that."

"Is it because you're a hybrid?" one of the other girls asked. "Because we have lots of those on this team."

"I'm not a hybrid. And you don't want me on your team."

Gwen shrugged. "We're always looking for potential jammers."

"She's not a jammer, O'Neill." The She-liger shook her head. "She's a blocker."

"Her?" Gwen sized Livy up again. "She's smaller than me."

"But she's mighty." The liger handed Livy a helmet and gestured to a row of quad skates. "Let's just find out how mighty she is."

They had food delivered to their room and ate it while lying in bed wearing nothing more than a sheet.

It was wonderfully decadent.

"You seem much better," Ricky observed before licking the cream sauce from his chicken off his thumb.

Toni shrugged and speared another roasted potato onto her fork. "I finally have a handle on what's going on, my siblings have been texting me considerably less, and Bo texted that he's about to finalize a schedule."

Ricky blinked. "The man hasn't finalized a schedule yet?"

"The man has moved into our house. With Blayne. My father is completely freaked out. But Bo's getting the job done. And he's getting it done without me."

"Is that the only reason you're feeling better?"

"Yes."

Ricky leaned in closer. "You sure?"

"I don't know what you want me to say."

That's when the wolf moved, knocking their plates off the bed and tackling Toni back.

"The maids are going to hate us!" Toni complained through giggles as she weakly struggled against him.

"We'll tip them."

"That's not the point! Ricky!"

"Would you stop squealing and let me work on this delicious neck."

"No! I will not stop squealing. And I wasn't done eating, either."

"There's more food on the table. I got us enough to last the whole night."

"Not if you keep tossing it on the floor!"

Ricky, pinning her to the bed with his body, gazed into her face. "Are you going to keep complaining or are you going to kiss me?"

"Actually, what I'm going to do is thank you."

"Well, yes, I *am* good in bed."

"Not for that, you cretin." She laughed. "For taking such good care of me while we've been here and for getting me to relax. I know I can be kind of uptight sometimes."

"When did you have time to be uptight? Every time I saw you, you were busy taking care of a bunch of cranky prodigies. So I would not label you as uptight."

"Everyone else does."

"That's 'cause they don't understand you."

"But you do."

"I find you fascinating." He raked his gaze down her body, his hand pulling the sheet away from her. "And beautiful." He tossed the sheet down by her feet and kissed her cheek. "And sexy." Kissed her jaw. "And smart." Kissed her throat.

"Please don't say sassy." She hated that term to describe women. It was like they were talking about a housecat that brought dead birds home for the family.

"I'd only say that to you if I wanted you *not* to have sex with me."

Toni put her arms around Ricky's neck, grinning widely into his handsome face. "Okay. You do know me well."

"Told ya."

Gwen O'Neill reached over and grabbed Blayne, yanking her close so that she didn't get hit with their leopard teammate who'd just been tossed off the track like so much trash.

"Cherry was right," Gwen admitted.

"She's always right."

"I thought the little bitch was just full of bullshit. You know, all talk. But she is as mean as a snake."

"I know."

"She'll be great."

Blayne frowned.

"What, Blayne?"

"Don't you think she's a little cruel?"

"Cruel? Babe, the Marquis de Sade was cruel. This chick is a class-A cunt. I think she'd cut her own mother if the woman got in her way."

"Then why—"

"Because I like to win."

Blayne sighed. "God, you and Bo."

"I still don't know what you see in that man, but I do admire his focus."

A big arm slipped around Gwen's waist and a nose nuzzled the back of her neck.

Smiling, she turned and leaped into the arms of her mate and fiancé.

Lock MacRyrie hugged Gwen and kissed her. She knew he'd come right from his workshop because she could smell the different types of wood he'd worked with that day. Lock had been able to work full-time on his woodworking business for about a year. It had been a scary transition for him. He liked the security of his software business, but he hated the work. Now he did what he loved and he was like a different bear. Gwen loved seeing him happy, although his desire to up the budget on their wedding was setting her teeth on edge. She knew what was motivating him, too. Not only the extra money he was bringing in from his business, but his uncles, who were goading him into making "the biggest MacRyrie wedding *ever*!" Something she'd been trying to avoid. Desperately.

Luckily, it was going to be a double wedding with Blayne and Bo, and the one thing Gwen was starting to use to her advantage was that Lock's uncles didn't want to go near Bo Novikov. Very few people with sense did.

And Blayne was known to be rather sense-free.

"How did it go today?" Gwen asked once Lock put her back on the ground.

"Pretty good. Sold that marble and wood dining table." Her eyes narrowed and he quickly added, "For the amount you suggested. I promise. I didn't give any discounts."

"They either made you mad or they were full-human."

"They were snobby . . . and full-human."

"Whatever."

"I think I was wrong about Cherise," Blayne said, rolling over so that she could give Lock a welcoming hug.

"The mouse?" Gwen asked. "I'm surprised she's not under the bleachers."

Lock chuckled. "Jess Ward style!"

Gwen glanced at Blayne and then at Lock. "We have no idea what you're talking about."

Not bothering to explain, Lock pulled out one of those plastic bottles of honey. The ones shaped like a teddy bear.

"So how much longer?" he asked, motioning to the tryouts.

"Another forty minutes. That okay?"

"Sure." He opened his mouth, tilted his head back, and squeezed an ungodly amount of honey into his throat.

By the time he was done, Kowalski had skated over to them.

"So," Gwen said to the freaky little unnamed shifter. "You in or out?" She didn't bother with niceties with this woman. She didn't know why, but she didn't see the point.

"I don't know. Maybe. I am feeling less aggressive at the moment, which is usually a good thing." She suddenly faced Lock, and Gwen watched the bitch stare up at her fiancé. Gwen cracked her knuckles and Blayne skated in front of her, briefly stopping Gwen from house-catting the boyfriend-stealing whore's face.

"Can I have some of that?" Kowalski asked Lock. She sounded almost polite.

"This?" Lock held up the bottle of honey.

When the female nodded, he handed the bottle over and she did what he'd done. Leaned her head back, opened her mouth, and poured an ungodly amount of honey into her throat. When she was done, she handed the now-nearly empty bottle of honey back to Lock.

"Thanks."

"Yep."

With that, Kowalski skated back to the track.

Gwen and Blayne moved closer to Lock, each of them on either side of the grizzly.

"Hey," Blayne whispered, "is she a bear, too?"

"She doesn't smell like a bear," Gwen said. "But she doesn't smell like a hybrid, either. But the honey thing . . ."

Lock looked back and forth between the women. "She's not a bear."

"She's not?"

"You guys really don't know what she is?"

"It's been driving me nuts!" Blayne continued to whisper loudly. "I've been around her for days and I can't figure it out." She began to bounce up and down on her quads. "Please tell me, Lock! Please!"

Lock shrugged. "She's a honey badger."

Gwen rolled her eyes. "So now you're just making shit up? Just admit she did that whole honey thing to flirt with you."

"That woman doesn't flirt. She wasn't flirting. She wanted the honey. She starts off nice because I have something she wants. But trust me . . . if I'd said no, she'd have ripped it out of my hands, possibly taking a few fingers with her. Her claws are longer than yours."

"These are not claws." Gwen held up her expertly done nails. "These are a fashion statement."

"Claws."

"But, Lock," Blayne reasoned, "I've never heard of a shifter honey badger."

"They're unbelievably private. I mean, you think we're private with the government, but they're private with *everybody*. Of course, that could have a lot to do with them being thieves."

"Like foxes?"

He chuckled. "Foxes are like kids going into a bodega and stealing candy bars. Honey badgers steal real shit."

Gwen watched Kowalski smash her fist into the face of a six-nine grizzly female. There was no fear in her expression. Just some hidden rage that Gwen didn't even want to think about. "She does seem mean enough."

"The meanest animals and shifters in the world," Lock said. "I realized that when I joined the Marines."

"What do you mean?"

"You know those military guys who say very little but they're always standing right off to the side of what's about to explode into a problem? They're usually short, powerful look-ing . . . and smirking. Then when shit does explode, usually in a bar right outside the base, they're the first ones in the middle of it all, kicking ass and ending up in the brig for doing the worst damage although they always look the least harmed? Yeah . . . *those* are honey badgers. And the females are defi-nitely worse."

Blayne happily clapped her hands together. "That's so—"

"Shut up, Blayne," Gwen snapped before the word "cool" could come out of her mouth.

Blayne immediately calmed down and they continued to watch the tryouts. Cherise had disappeared for a while, but she came back out at some point and got on the track. Appearing typically terrified.

"We should get her out of there," Gwen suggested.

"I was thinking the same thing." Blayne started to skate out when Kowalski cut in front of her. Blayne squealed at the sight of the dangerous female and quickly skated back to Gwen's side.

"You want me to handle Cherise?" the female asked, appearing unfazed by Blayne's hysterical response.

"You don't have to kill her," Blayne said, panic in her voice.

Kowalski rolled her eyes and headed out to the track. She stopped by Cherise's side and whispered something. When she was done, Kowalski returned to them.

"Okay," she said.

The first whistle blew and Cherise, and another girl trying out for the jammer position shot off. A second whistle sounded and the rest of the pack went after the two females. Whichever jammer got out in front first would earn points by passing the girls on the other team. It sounded easy, but trying to bypass a seven-two She-bear with mommy issues was easy for no one.

What blew Gwen away, though, was not that Cherise was screaming every time one of the players got close to her, but that Cherise was moving so fast. Unbelievably fast. While squealing and screaming and slapping bodies, hands, and anything else that came too close to her, out of her way.

It was entertaining in a really horrifying way.

"What did you say to her?" Gwen asked Kowalski.

The female shrugged. "She's got a thing about germs. I just pointed out that no one trying out today had bothered to wash their hands in the last two hours, not even the ones who went to the bathroom. She's a canine who runs on fear. You just have to find ways to use that fear to your benefit."

Appalled, Blayne said, "But you're like family with her."

"Yeah. That's why I know how to manipulate her. That's what family does to each other."

And that made Gwen laugh—because the honey badger was right.

"Don't encourage her, Gwenie!"

"I can't help it!"

"I think there's something we need to talk about."

Toni sat up and stared at him. They'd somehow ended up on Ricky's hotel room floor. Toni continued to surprise him, not remotely concerned about little things like having sex with him on the floor.

"I told you I was sorry," Toni said. "I didn't even break the skin this time."

"I'm not talking about that." Although the pain he was feeling all across his back suggested she *had* broken the skin, but he wasn't going to argue the point. It had just been her claws. It would be a different discussion if she'd used her fangs. "I just want something clear before we go see the bears tomorrow."

"I know. I know," Toni said with a wave, stretching back out across the floor, her head landing in his sheet-covered lap. She was allowing him to play with her curls, but she'd insisted, "Only before I get into the shower. After that, no touching!" Well, they'd see about that.

"Don't put my feet on the table," she went on. "Russians consider it rude. And don't stand around with my hands in my pockets. They hate that. I wonder why. Does it suggest you're hiding something when you put your hands in your pockets? I just do it because I like to have something to do with my hands other than play with my fingers. Cherise plays with her fingers and she always looks like a nervous wreck."

"I'm not talking about that damn meeting tomorrow."

"Oh. Sorry."

"I just want it to be clear that when we get back, we ain't really done."

"We ain't?" She blinked. "I mean, we're not?"

"No. Don't see why this has to be a one-night stand."

"I thought that's what we agreed to."

"When did we do that? I merely suggested wolves are great for the occasional one-night stand. I didn't say that's what we had here."

Toni sat up again.

"I ain't done with your hair," Ricky complained.

"Forget the hair."

"I can't. I love it."

"What if it falls out tomorrow?"

"Why would it fall out tomorrow?"

"It might!"

Ricky could see the panic in her pretty eyes. Knew she was just scared. Didn't blame her. He wasn't exactly sure what the hell was going on, either, but he knew he didn't want to go back to the States and pretend the last two nights had never happened.

"Is this because I'm a poor country boy from Tenne—"

"Oh, shut up."

Ricky laughed, unable to keep the pathetic look on his face. Didn't matter. She always saw through that in seconds.

"This has nothing to do with any of that and you know it. But we are from different worlds."

"You're Romeo and I'm Juliet? Wait." Ricky thought a moment. "Switch those."

"That's a stupid comparison, but it's not far off. I'm a jackal. You're a wolf. I mean," she went on, "can you imagine *me* being part of a pack? Living only for the needs and wants of others—and my God! Why didn't you tell me I sounded so idiotic?"

Chuckling, Ricky admitted, "I figured you were smart enough to figure that out on your own." Because her whole life had been about living for others.

"Look, darlin', all I'm saying is that when we get back, I don't want to pretend that we don't even know each other."

"We can't do that. Then *everyone* will know what we've been up to."

"That's a good point, but you know what I mean."

"I do, but—"

"But . . . when we get back you'll need to spend time with your family, making sure they're all taken care of and that Kyle hasn't finally gone to prison."

"That is a worry of mine."

"I know. So of course you'll go see your family when you get back. Just like I'll have to check in with my idiot brothers."

"Make sure Reece isn't getting more artery surgery?"

"You'd be amazed how many of those surgeries the boy has had."

"I've met Reece . . . not that amazed."

"So do we agree?"

"What are we agreeing to?"

"When we get back, we keep things going. At least until we figure out if whatever this is . . . is actually what we want."

"It won't be easy. We're both pretty busy."

"I'm as busy as I wanna be. And I like your kin. Don't mind being around them."

She rolled her eyes at that. "Sure you do."

"They bring the entertainment to me. And we both know that's all I ever ask."

"I really can't argue that point with you, can I?"

"Not really."

Ricky reached over and pulled Toni sideways onto his lap. He stroked her back and kissed her shoulder.

"You think we're really going to head back home tomorrow?" she asked softly.

Ricky glanced at his watch. "More like today . . . and yes, I do." He pulled Toni closer, his arms around her, her chin resting against his collarbone. "I think when we're done . . . those bears won't know what the holy hell hit 'em."

Chapter Twenty-three

With Freddy attached to her like a backpack and Cherise and Blayne by her side, Livy headed back to the rental house. It had been a long night but a good one. She'd had fun.

Of course, the entire derby team hated her, but whatever. She had her family and friends and that was all that mattered to Livy. She didn't need more friends. A small group of loyal friends was more important to her than a bunch of drinking buddies. So not going out with the team after the tryouts had been no big deal for her. Instead she'd been Responsible Olivia as Coop liked to call her when she said she needed to get Freddy home.

Cherise had gratefully tagged along and Blayne pretended that she wasn't happy about it, but even Livy knew she just wanted to get home to that walking landmass she called a fiancé.

Standing on a city street, Livy waited for the light to change. As she did, she glanced around, taking in her location, surveying any nearby threats. It was a skill taught to her by her parents before she could feed herself.

And it was while she was looking around that she saw her. Across the street, coming out of some church.

"Hey. Cherise." She nudged her best friend's sister. "Do you see what I see?" There wasn't much in this universe that stunned Livy, but seeing Delilah Jean-Louis Parker coming out of a god-damn church was definitely one of them.

"Holy crap!" Cherise burst out. "Is she robbing churches now?"

"Even *my* mother wouldn't sink that low."

Except that Delilah was talking to people from the church. Talking and hugging.

Livy shuddered at the thought of hugging Delilah.

Blayne stepped up beside Livy. "That's not a church. Well . . . actually, it depends on what you think about religion and what you consider a religion and what you consider a—"

"Blayne," Livy cut in. "Get to your point before I start hurting you."

"It's a cult. They took over the church a year or so back, but the people in the neighborhood have been trying to shut them down. Something about young people joining the church and then disappearing to some farm upstate."

Livy sighed. "Lovely."

Deciding she'd talk to Toni about it when she got back and was settled from her trip, Livy hiked Freddy up on her hip and continued on to the rental house.

When they arrived, Livy trotted up the stairs, Freddy giggling as he bounced around on her back. She reached the door and pulled out her key, unlocking it. But as soon as she stepped in, she froze in the doorway. She lifted her head, sniffed the air. By the time Cherise reached her, Livy was shoving Freddy into her arms.

"Take him across the street. Blayne, go with them."

Cherise moved without question, just as she'd been taught. But Blayne . . .

"Are you—"

"Protect Freddy."

That seemed to work and Blayne followed behind Cherise.

Livy silently stepped deeper into the house, sniffing the air, listening for any sounds. Glancing back and seeing that the others were now safely on the other side of the street as the wild dogs' front door opened and they were welcomed in, Livy unleashed her long, steel-hard claws. She scented humans. Full-humans in her family's home. At least her unofficially adopted family and if something—anything—happened to them while Toni was away because Livy didn't protect them, she'd never forgive herself.

She locked on the strongest remaining scent and headed up the stairs. She could smell that the full-humans had been in each of the bedrooms although everything appeared untouched. Honestly, if she wasn't a shifter, she'd never have known anyone had been here.

Livy went floor by floor, clearing each one, quickly realizing that no one was home. Although most parents had their kids in bed at this hour, the Jean-Louis Parkers were known to do things their own way when it wasn't a school night. So chances were they'd gone out for ice cream or something. But when Livy reached the stairway that would lead to the fifth and final floor, she stopped and sniffed the air again.

"Jackie," she whispered, and then charged up the stairs and into Jackie's practice room. She pushed the door open and went inside, stopping immediately when she saw Jackie's body on the couch, facing the back of the seat.

Heart breaking, Livy slowly approached Toni's mother and, when she was close enough, she gently touched Jackie's shoulder.

Which was when Jackie Jean-Louis screamed and flipped over.

Livy stumbled back as Jackie laughed hysterically.

"Goddammit, Livy! Don't sneak up on me like that! You scared the life out of me!"

Livy had scared *her*?

After several seconds, Jackie's laughter faded away. "Hon, what's wrong? You look upset."

Livy took a breath and said, "Someone broke into the house. I thought they'd killed you."

Jackie blinked. "What? I didn't hear a thing? Oh." She held up her earbuds. "I was listening to Johnny's playing before I fell asleep. It's possible they came in then." She studied Livy for a moment. "You look like you're about to cry. Is that because of me? Oh, sweetie!"

"Jacqueline!"

"Sorry. Sorry."

"Where's everybody?"

"Paul took them out to get ice cream."

"Good."

Suddenly Jackie got to her feet. "Oh, my God . . . Irene!" She ran out of the room, and Livy followed right behind her to the only other room on the floor.

Jackie threw the door open and Irene spun around in her office chair; computer equipment, papers, and books covered the two desks. A small bed was on one side of the room and looked very unused.

"What is wrong with you guys?" Irene demanded.

"We've been robbed!" Jackie shot back.

"No, no," Livy quickly corrected. "We had a break-in. But I can't see that they took anything. In fact, if I hadn't scented them, I don't think any of us would have known they'd been here. They're good."

"Government good?" Jackie asked.

Livy shrugged. "I guess."

That's when Jackie locked on her friend. "Again, Irene?"

"How do you know it has anything to do with me?"

Jackie's eyebrow went up and Irene sighed.

"I'll go home."

"No." Jackie shook her head. "We can't assume this is about you. And if it's about Freddy or Troy, I'll need you here."

"We'll get security," Livy said.

"And contact Dee-Ann," Irene said.

Both Livy and Jackie took a step back.

"What the hell for?" Livy demanded.

"If there's one person I know who has connections you and I can only dream of and, more important, can terrify those connections into giving her answers about why strangers are searching this home . . . it's Dee-Ann Smith."

As always, Irene was right.

"You take care of that," Livy told her. "I'll deal with security. But do me a favor, go over and wait at the wild dog house until I get back. Call Paul so that he knows to bring the kids back there rather than here."

"Where are you going?" Jackie asked when Livy headed to the door.

"I'll be back. And Jackie . . . make sure no one texts or calls Toni." She narrowed her eyes on the woman she'd briefly mourned. "And that means you, lady."

"But she should know—"

"Jackie!"

"Oh, all right! I promise! And you can just put those vile-looking claws back, little miss. There's no need to threaten me!"

Reece Lee had just turned over, his dream about skating naked in front of an audience of beautiful She-predators making him smile, when a scent he'd just learned to recognize woke him up. He thought maybe he'd left the *Infamous Book of Smells* lying on the bed with him, but when he opened his eyes he saw the vicious honey badger standing at the edge of the bed, staring at him.

"Aaaah!" Reece screamed, scrambling back until his shoulders hit the headboard.

"You scream like a girl," she observed.

"Why are you here? Have you come to kill me?"

"It's crossed my mind, but no. I need a security team and I heard the company you work for is really good."

"Can't this wait until tomorrow?"

"No."

Realizing that he wouldn't be able to just get this feral little woman out of his hotel suite without a fight, Reece admitted, "Look, if you want the full team on this, it's gonna cost you, darlin'."

Livy lifted a dark green duffel bag from the floor, unzipped it, and turned it over, dropping a veritable shit-load of money onto Reece's bed.

"That enough?" she asked. And when he only stared, she added, kind of defensively, "It's clean."

"You know, darlin', I wasn't actually going to ask you that. But now that you offer it up, it makes me think this money wasn't always so clean."

"Do you want it or not?"

"Don't get tense. I was simply making an observation."

"Can your people start tonight?"

"Yeah." The company had a plan in place for last-minute protection teams. "I'll take care of it."

"Okay."

"Is it just you?"

"No. The Jean-Louis Parker family."

Reece sat up. "Toni's kin?"

"They're all okay and Toni's still in Russia."

"Yeah. I got a text from Ricky. They're so far ahead, he's afraid of calling when I might be sleeping."

"We need to keep the family safe," she said after a time. "I can't have Toni coming home and—"

"Don't you worry about it. If you think Toni will have your ass if something happens while she's away, it'll be ten times worse where my brother's concerned." He grinned. "He's got a little thing for your friend."

"I don't think it's little, but you're male—I wouldn't expect you to understand that."

Reece's grin widened. "Want me to toss this sheet aside and show you how male I am?"

And with no expression at all, Livy replied, "Do you want me to cut your dick off?"

Reece swallowed. "Not really."

"Then I'd suggest keeping that sheet on until I'm in the next room. Okay?"

"Yes'm."

"Good." She walked out and Reece let out a relieved breath.

"Either that girl is gonna end up killing me," he muttered, "or end up one of my best friends."

"More like I'll end up killing you," she called out from the living room.

Reece shrank down into the bed, pulling the sheet up to his chin. "Honey badgers are just mean," he whispered, praying she didn't hear him. *"Mean."*

Chapter Twenty-four

Vic stopped the Range Rover and turned off the engine. "Everyone ready?" he asked.

"Yes," Toni said from the back. Ricky would say she looked "brave," but she didn't. She looked determined. He found that much scarier than brave because when the woman made up her mind . . .

"And remember the rules." Vic looked directly at Ricky. "Keep your feet off the table."

"Why do y'all keep telling me that?" he demanded.

"Because you'll put your feet on the table," Vic and Toni said together.

"Fine, but I don't see what the big problem is. Bears and all their dang rules."

They opened the doors and stepped out.

Toni cracked her neck and moved her shoulders. She looked like she was about to step into a boxing ring.

"Ready?" Ricky asked her.

She nodded. "Let's go bag some bears."

They headed down the hallway to that room where the bears had continued to stick Toni every time she'd come for a meeting. She let one of them lead her toward that room, Ricky and Vic right behind her, but she cast for a scent and when she locked on it, she immediately made a left and headed down another hallway.

"You! Dog! Where you go?" demanded the bear behind her.

Toni ignored him and kept moving until she reached a room where she heard male laughter and scented bear. Lots of bear.

Taking a breath, she pushed open the door and walked in. "Morning, gentlemen!" she said, smiling. "How is everyone doing today?"

The laughter and words died, but Toni ignored all that and moved toward the long table. She spotted an open seat and walked over to it like she knew it was just for her. She didn't ask permission, she didn't stop to look around. Instead she remembered what Ricky had said about always looking like you know where you're going, even when you don't. She sat down, placing her messenger bag on the floor beside the chair.

"Okay," she said, making sure her grin was large and confident. "Let's get started."

The bears looked at each other and then one with horrible facial lacerations—she assumed he was Yuri Asanov since he was the only one in a wheelchair—nodded his head.

"Good," Toni said, reaching into her messenger bag and beginning to dig out papers.

While she pulled folders out, she saw from the corner of her eye one of the bears pushing away from the table and standing.

Toni looked up and said, "Where are you going, Ivan Zubachev?"

Walking toward the door, Zubachev didn't bother to look at her when he replied, "I have business that cannot wait."

"Then we'll just sit here and wait until you get back."

The grizzly stopped. "What?"

"No deal gets made in this town without you, Ivan Zubachev. I'll be wasting my time talking to all these handsome but relatively useless bears if you're not here. So we'll wait for you. All day if necessary. All century."

He slowly faced her, but said nothing.

"Let's be honest here, Ivan. This isn't about what Bo did to your boy." Toni looked over at the team's coach and said, "By the way, the wheelchair's a bit much." And when Yuri Asanov's cheeks grew slightly red, she knew she'd been right. "But I do apologize, Yuri Asanov, for what he did to your face." Because that was bad.

She looked back at Zubachev. "This is about what Novikov did to *you*. And what he did to you, Ivan Zubachev, is turn down your job offer."

Zubachev folded his massive arms over his enormous chest but still said nothing.

"What you failed to understand was that it was not personal. The bottom line is that playing *with* your team would not have been a challenge for him. A team filled with bears, Siberian tigers, and *Novikov*—will do nothing but win. He knows that. *You* know that. That's why you wanted him. But Novikov needs a challenge. He needs to know that he can't just waltz off with a trophy. He wants to *earn* that win. So let's forget the past. Let's forget about cages. Let's forget the insults. And let's talk about *money*. Because a game between our teams in a neutral, shifter-only location, will have money coming down on us like snow in Siberia."

That made Zubachev smirk and, after a moment, he walked over to the chair he'd just left, pulled it out, and plopped down into it.

He briefly lifted his hands, then dropped them. "Let's negotiate . . . little doggie."

Toni grinned. "Yes. Let's. You big, adorable bear, you."

Twelve hours. Twelve hours to negotiate one goddamn hockey game. During that time, Ricky and Vic had stood behind or beside Toni—Vic sometimes briefly stepping out to answer phone calls—while Toni handled it all like a pro. She never looked tired, even though Ricky was sure that she was exhausted down to her toes. Nor did she snap when the bears made things difficult. And like most bears, these Russian bears certainly enjoyed making things difficult.

Like now, when the bears had agreed to almost all the terms except one. Although they wouldn't insist on putting Novikov in a cage, they were insisting that the man was to be shackled before and after game time. Toni kept reminding them that the damage done to their coach had happened *during* a game, so what would be the point of chaining her player before and after? But the bears wouldn't be moved on this point and Ricky was thinking Toni was about to give up and decide to head on home. Especially when her cell phone went off.

Toni glanced at the screen, while one of the bears muttered, "Rude," as she did.

"Everything all right?" Ricky asked her.

"Just Cooper." She sighed, glancing up at Ricky. "He's wondering when I'm heading home."

"I can't believe Cooper Jean-Louis Parker is your brother," Vic suddenly announced . . . rather loudly. So loudly that both Ricky and Toni looked at the man. He shrugged. "Just an observation."

"Cooper Jean-Louis Parker?" Zubachev repeated, and all the bears' eyes locked on Toni. Ricky stepped even closer and placed his hand on her shoulder. Standing there for the last twelve hours had allowed him to come up with all sorts of exit strategies should things turn nasty. "You know Cooper Jean-Louis Parker?"

"He's her brother," Vic said, moving closer to the table and Toni.

Zubachev snorted. "Lie. The freak cat lies."

"I find that very hurtful, Ivan."

"Shut up." Zubachev glared across the table at Toni. "Prove he is your brother or I believe nothing."

Toni shrugged and again looked at her phone. She began scanning a ton of pictures—*how much memory does her camera have anyway?*—but instead of choosing, Toni kept muttering things like, "Nah. Not that one, I look too fat. No. Coop has that ridiculous smile. No. If I show that one, Cherise will be mad."

Fed up and exhausted himself, Ricky took the phone from her, flipped through a couple more pictures until he found one that showed brother and sister hugging each other and grinning into the camera. He sent the camera skidding across the table right at Zubachev.

The bear stared at the tiny screen, the other bears soon getting out of their chairs and surrounding him, all staring at the small phone in his giant hand.

After nearly a minute, they all looked up at Toni.

"You truly know him," Zubachev said. "You know The Coop."

"I better," Toni muttered. "He used to throw his dirty diapers at me. I better not have gone through that for no reason."

"The Coop," another bear said, grinning. "The man."

Then Ricky watched twelve bears of varying sizes and colors pretend to play air-piano.

It was . . . weird. Yeah. That was the best word for it. Weird.

"You talked all sorts of crap about canines," Toni reminded Zubachev, "but you love my brother?"

"He plays music like god," Zubachev cheered. "Species does not matter when man play like that."

"He's still a canine."

"He is The Coop," Zubachev insisted, as if that explained everything. "You should be proud to be his sister!"

"I am!" Toni snapped back, her exhaustion finally catching up with her. She leaned back in her chair, huffing and puffing a bit, when Vic kneed the back of her seat. Glaring, Toni looked at the man. Vic raised his brows and motioned to Zubachev.

After a moment, Toni focused back on Zubachev. She studied him and, finally, said, "You know . . . He's doing a tour in Russia in September. I'm sure I could get him to add this territory to his itinerary."

Zubachev smirked. "What price?"

"His usual rate, because that's the least he deserves. The concert would be open to all species and breeds and, of course, dinner with his host. But *no* chains for Novikov. Instead, we will rely on Novikov's commitment to me not to harm anyone. This, of course, is only in effect if none of you"—and she looked hard at all the players at the table—"challenge him while off the ice. Commit to that, and my brother will happily do this favor for me."

Zubachev tried for a casual shrug. "I don't know."

"I'll make sure he plays 'Flight of the Bumblebee.' "

A few of the players gasped and then they were all whispering to Zubachev in Russian.

Ricky crouched down next to her. " 'Flight of the Bumblebee?' Heard that one was hard."

"Yeah, it is. Written by a Russian composer." She glanced at Ricky and said out of the corner of her mouth, "Coop mastered it when he was three."

Ricky snorted just as Zubachev looked over at them.

"It is deal, little doggie." The grizzly grinned. "You negotiate like Russian sow."

"Awww," Toni said, her returning smile warm. "Thank you! That is so sweet."

Only to other shifters, maybe, but that worked for now.

"Now we toast!" Zubachev announced. "Aleksai! Get the vodka!"

Vic tapped Ricky's shoulder and motioned him over to a corner with a tilt of his head. His gaze still on Toni while she winced and cringed her way through a shot of homemade Russian bear vodka, Ricky stepped next to Vic.

"What is it?"

"I'm coming back with you."

"Why?"

"Orders from Dee-Ann. Plus she wants us to keep an even tighter watch on Antonella."

"But she knows The Coop," he said dryly.

Vic chuckled. "Yeah, I don't think that's the problem. She said we'll find out everything when we get back. I've already notified the airline we're coming. Okay?"

Ricky eyed the hybrid closely. "You sure you don't know any more than that?"

"If I'd spoken to someone else, I might be lying. But you know Dee-Ann. Do you really think we had a long, meaningful conversation about issues?"

"Well, we all know what a chatty little love bug she is."

Shaking his head, Vic walked away and Ricky faced Toni, who was currently being bear-hugged off her feet by Ivan Zubachev. She didn't seem too happy about that, but for her job . . . she was putting up with it.

He let out a breath and forced a smile. The last thing he wanted to do was freak her out before they got her home. Not because she'd be worried about herself. She wouldn't be. He knew that now. But if her family was in trouble . . . ? Well, to quote Ricky's fellow New Yorkers, *Oy.*

CHAPTER TWENTY-FIVE

Dee-Ann unlocked the front door and walked into the rental house the jackals were living in. She made it halfway down the hall before any adult jackal came out. It was Jackie Jean-Louis. She nodded at Dee as she rushed by and headed up the stairs.

"Morning, Dee," she called down from the top stairs. "There's Danish in the kitchen and dining room if you're hungry."

"Thank you kindly," Dee called back, disturbed that no one seemed to notice a near-stranger in their home. No wonder shady government types were wandering around the house, undetected.

Dee walked a few more feet, and that's when Cooper came out of the dining room. Like his mother, he appeared completely distracted as he walked, ate a raspberry-filled Danish, and stared down at the floor.

"Mornin' to you, Cooper."

The jackal stopped, blinked several times as if trying to bring her into focus. "Oh. Morning, Dee-Ann."

"Everything all right here?"

"Define all right?"

"Pardon?"

The swinging kitchen door at the end of the hallway flew open and Dee and Cooper came face to face with Jeff Stewart, a security specialist who worked at Bobby Ray's company, and a lion male currently covered in flour. Seemed kind of pissed off, too.

"We have a problem," the feline announced.

"What problem?"

"We thought we were protecting older kids, Smith. No one said anything about toddlers."

"What? You can't handle a few toddlers?"

"I'm a lion male."

"You feelin' the need to kill the toddlers so that their mother will go back in heat?"

Gold eyes narrowed. "No. But I'm a professional. I don't handle toddlers."

"How bad can they be?"

Stewart turned, a shower of flour hitting Dee and Cooper in the face.

Coughing and brushing the flour aside, they followed Stewart back to the kitchen.

Flour, ground coffee, coffee beans, sugar, cocoa, and gobs of peanut butter were everywhere. Absolutely everywhere.

Dee shook her head, disgusted. "You couldn't get control of two little girls before they did all this?"

"They're not little girls," Stewart snapped back. "They're demon spawn!" He pointed at the two girls. They calmly sat on the counter, both clean except for their hands, which had lots of peanut butter . . . oh, and jelly. Their little feet swung back and forth, kicking the wood doors of the counter with their heels.

"*Bonne journée,*" said one.

"*Guten tag,*" said the other.

Then they both smiled.

"I'm out of here," the lion told them.

Cooper raised his hand. "Wait. I'm sure we can figure out something so you don't have to worry about them." When the lion's eyes narrowed . . . "I promise."

The lion pushed the swinging kitchen door open. "Whatever."

"I love cats." Dee smiled at the shocked expression on Cooper's face. "They're all so dang moody."

Facing the twins, Cooper demanded, "What did I tell you two?"

"Du hast gesagt—"

"In *English,* Zia."

The two girls took each other's peanut butter–covered hands and began simultaneously in English, "Stay with us—"

"And do not quote *The Shining.* You know people freak out when you two do that."

Their smiles suggested that yes, they *did* know that freaked people out.

"Have y'all thought about getting these two a nanny?"

"Nanny?" Coop repeated, as if he'd never heard the word before.

"Yeah. A nanny. Rich people have 'em all the time."

"But we're jackals."

"Your family is also damn weird. If you're freakin' out the king of the jungle, you might need special care. Or, at the very least, someone with a high tolerance for weird."

They both looked at the twins, and in response the girls pursed their lips and made smacking sounds. Air kisses. It was cute and terrifying all at the same time because they did it in unison.

"A *very* high tolerance for weird."

Cooper shook his head. "Toni's going to freak out about this. Shit." He pulled out his cell phone. "When does she get home again?"

"Shit," one of the twins repeated, smiling.

"Shit," her sister parroted.

"Merde."

"Hovno."

"Stront."

"Merda."

"Mierda."

Dee stared at the three-year-old twins. "Lord . . . how many languages do y'all know?" Then she frowned and focused on their brother when she realized something else. "And how the heck do they know about *The Shining*?"

"Why are you looking at me? It was probably Kyle who let them watch it."

"Kyle's eleven."

"Physically, maybe." He held up his phone. "Found the text. She should be back tonight."

"Good thing. Y'all run wild when she ain't here."

A kiss on her forehead woke Toni up, her cheek resting against his chest while Ricky held her.

"We're almost home, darlin'," he whispered. "Time to put your seat belt on."

Yawning, Toni sat up and pushed off the blanket covering her. She put on her seat belt and glanced over at the seats on the other side of the aisle.

"Why is he here?" she asked again. She'd asked when Barinov had checked in with them at the airport in Russia, but Ricky had given her some vague bullshit answer she didn't buy. Yet she hadn't bothered to push for an answer then. She was too far away to do anything if something had gone wrong at home, and she didn't want to start freaking out on the flight. So she'd waited. But with their plane descending, she wanted answers.

Ricky seemed to understand that when he replied, "There was a break-in at your rental house. Everyone's fine. The kids weren't home."

Toni nodded. "Okay."

"I talked to Dee-Ann before we got on the plane. Your honey badger friend apparently went into action as soon as this happened. She pulled in my company and your aunt Irene called in Dee-Ann."

"Whatever for?"

"Irene seems to think the government was involved. Whoever it was tried to make it look like no one had been there, and if we weren't shifters, we wouldn't have known they had been."

"But everyone's safe?"

"Very safe. Darlin', you can't get safer than when Dee-Ann's involved. Unless you're on the wrong side of her."

"Good."

"I'm sorry I didn't tell you earlier, but—"

"No, no. I understand. I would have just spent the whole flight freaking out, and that's how jackals end up on shifter no-fly lists. I can't afford that." She studied him. "But any other time . . . don't hide anything from me about my family."

"I know." She could tell from his expression he took her warning seriously. "Trust me."

And she did. At least about this.

"You're exhausted," he murmured, brushing her hair off her face.

"I am. But so are you."

"I'll get you home and then we'll figure it out from there. Okay? No decisions when we're this tired."

"Fair enough."

He kissed her then, and Toni began to wonder what would happen when they were fully awake and over their jet lag. Because this simple kiss had her toes curling inside her boots.

"I'm sorry," one of the flight attendants said, a smile on her feline face. "You need to put your seats up. We're cleared to land."

Nodding, Toni brought her seat up. Once the flight attendant walked away to check on the rest of the passengers, Ricky leaned over and whispered, "You keep kissing me like that, darlin', and we won't be figuring out anything except which side of the bed you like to sleep on."

It wasn't even seven a.m. when Oriana sat down at the kitchen table with a bowl of hot oatmeal and a bottle of cold water. She'd been up since five thirty so she could get warmed up for the day's classes. Plus there was a competition coming up that she was excited about because it could lead to huge possibilities for her career.

Her career. That's all Oriana really ever thought about. Dancing and her career as a dancer. She knew that most girls her age were spending their summers hanging out with friends, going to movies, listening to music, and trying to get the cutest guys to notice them. But Oriana knew she wasn't "most girls."

She'd been given a gift and she wasn't going to waste it on shitty music, annoying frenemies, and some guy who would end up sleeping with her best friend or something. Besides, Oriana had her family and with them she didn't have to make excuses for why she couldn't go out or why she didn't care about the latest blockbuster movie.

Honestly, all she cared about was getting her turns perfect, her extensions long, and her position as a world-famous prima ballerina secure.

Anything else didn't mean much to her.

As Oriana worked her way through her oatmeal, her siblings came to the table. Five-year-old Dennis and the twins would be staying with their father for the day while the rest of them had classes all over the city. Well . . . all except Delilah, but she never really figured in their family plans. If Oriana was to be honest, Delilah never seemed part of the family at all. As horrible as Oriana, Kyle, and Troy could be to anyone who got in their way, Delilah was definitely worse. Like a dangerously unstable visiting relative rather than an immediate member of the family they were all forced to tolerate.

And while the rest of the kids tore into the breakfast their mother had made, Delilah silently slipped out the back door, probably not to be seen again until much later tonight.

Involuntarily shuddering, still seeing that blade perilously close to her eyes, Oriana went back to focusing on eating her breakfast when she saw Freddy's head snap up. He sniffed the air again, his little face twisting as he tried to make sense of what he was smelling. But then his eyes grew wide, his face flushing with excitement, and he jumped off his chair and took off running.

When their mother and father grinned at each other and pushed away from the table, Oriana knew that Toni was home. The rest of the kids followed their parents except for Oriana, Kyle, and Troy.

"I guess she's back then," Kyle muttered into his plate of eggs and bacon.

Troy pushed his food away. "Finally. Thought she was planning to *stay* in Russia, she took so long."

"Maybe she should have." Oriana scratched the back of her neck.

"Yeah," Troy agreed. "Because we don't *need* her."

"Right." Kyle nodded. "We don't need her." He briefly toyed with his bacon before adding, "And we should tell her that to her *face.*"

Agreeing, the three of them jumped up from the table and headed for the front door. To tell their sister how they didn't need her. At all.

Toni had just put Freddy back on the floor after hugging the little bugger off his little feet and she was reaching for Dennis when she was tackled by three insolent bastards. She would have hit the floor, too, if Ricky hadn't been standing behind her. He kept her standing as Oriana, Kyle, and Troy all hugged her tight.

Shocked, Toni immediately looked at Coop. He was no help, though, laughing and turning away from her.

"How dare you!" Oriana snarled. "How dare you leave us alone with that . . . that . . ."

"Neanderthal!" Troy filled in.

"He got you guys a workable schedule, didn't he?" Toni asked, awkwardly patting the backs of Oriana and Troy while Kyle hugged her waist.

"That's not the point!" Troy argued.

But Toni knew what the point was. While Bo could organize anything, he wouldn't be nice about it. He wouldn't take sensitivities into account the way Toni would. Of course, she'd known that when Ricky had suggested him . . . and that was the main reason she'd eventually agreed. Because someone nice would only get run over by the Jean-Louis Parker Family Train.

As Toni's dad always said, "When dealing with ancient Romans, you really need a Hannibal the Great to kick their ass."

Her father was a bit of a Roman history buff.

"You all seemed to survive," she reminded her siblings.

"Barely," Troy muttered.

Toni watched her own Hannibal the Great stomp down the

stairs of her family's rental house with his duffel bag. Behind him was . . . somebody.

"You're back," Bo said when he stood in front of her.

"I am. Do you want an update on what hap—"

"Later. I need ice time."

"Well, thank you for—"

"Whatever. I need ice time."

"Okay."

The hybrid stared down at her and Toni stared back, not sure what he wanted.

"I need ice time," he repeated.

"Yes. I know."

"But you're in my way."

"Oh. Right." Toni quickly stepped out of the way of the door, pulling her siblings with her. But while she wrangled her sisters and brothers, she'd abandoned Ricky and Vic Barinov, whom she couldn't seem to shake since they'd landed in the States.

"Hi, Toni!" said the somebody with Bo.

"Oh. Hi. Um . . ."

The somebody's face fell. "Blayne."

"Right! Right." Toni nodded. "Hi."

"Are you gonna move?" Bo asked Ricky.

"Sure. What do you want to see? The Cabbage Patch?" And then the crazed wolf began to do the goddamn Cabbage Patch. Right there. In her hallway, with her family watching, and *at* Bo Novikov.

Pushing Oriana and Kyle behind her, Toni reached over and grabbed Ricky Lee's forearm, using all her strength to yank him to her side.

Which left Bo Novikov staring down Vic Barinov.

And it was intense. Like something out of *Mutual of Omaha's Wild Kingdom* intense. Two bear males squaring off over a deer carcass intense.

Lips pulled back over fangs that extended out of gums, saliva pouring onto the floor as forehead rammed against forehead, and then there was the roaring. Good God! The roaring! It was so instantaneous and rage-filled that Toni was sure they knew each other.

Toni immediately looked to her parents, but they were already moving, the twins in her father's arms—both girls fighting their father because they wanted to see the bloodshed—her mother holding the hands of Freddy and Dennis. They disappeared down the hallway, knowing Toni would take care of the older kids. Yet even though Toni was willing to put herself between danger and the others, she knew she wouldn't have to. Kyle and Oriana would never risk any harm that could stop them from doing what they loved. Cherise was already easing away. Coop was pretty fast when he wanted to be and he'd take care of Troy. Delilah wasn't even there and Toni never worried about her anyway.

Contingency plans, however, were unnecessary once Dee-Ann Smith ambled down the hallway. To Toni's eternal surprise, Livy was right behind her. Surprise because Toni really thought Livy would have ditched her family by now. Not permanently or anything, Livy just wasn't for staying in one place for very long.

Of course the fact that she had stayed said the break-in was probably more serious than Ricky had let on. So, without letting anyone know what she was doing, Toni opened up her senses to everything around her while still managing to focus on the male idiocy going on right in front of her face.

Dee-Ann stopped about ten feet from the two unbelievably large hybrid males and, after studying them for a long moment, went for that bowie knife of hers that she always had tacked to the back of her jeans or strapped to her thigh. She'd just pulled it free from its sheath when, uh—Blank? Was that her name?— jumped in front of Dee-Ann.

"You can't!" Blank yelled. "You just can't!"

That's when Livy's eyes crossed and she walked past all of them and right between the two males. Compared to seven-four Bo Novikov and seven-foot-one Vic Barinov, Livy was like a mite on some wolf's fur. Yet, as always, she never let size stop her from doing whatever she needed to do.

She pushed her way between the two males and rammed her hands against their chests. Then she shoved, forcing both males back a step. Maybe even two steps.

"Cut it the fuck out," she ordered, not even angry. "Novikov. You were leaving."

"Yeah. I'm leaving." He stormed around Livy and Barinov and walked out. Blank stopped long enough to wave at everyone, then pointed at Cherise and Livy. "See you gals tonight!" she cheered.

Toni, unsure what that meant, waved at Bo's fiancée. "Bye, Blank!"

She stopped, spun around, and snapped, "It's *Blayne.*"

"Right. Blayne. Sorry."

Shrugging, Toni closed the front door and faced Barinov. "Tell me you at least knew Novikov."

"That was Novikov?" When everyone merely stared at him, he added, "I'm not really a hockey fan. I like football."

Sighing, realizing how exhausted she was, Toni asked, "You're not going to continue to hang around, are you?"

"That's up to her," he said, pointing at Dee-Ann. "She hired me."

Knowing there was no point in discussing this any further with Dee-Ann, Toni pushed past Barinov and caught the back of Cherise's T-shirt before she could escape into another room.

Once she had her sister facing her, she asked, "Why did Bland say 'see you tonight'? Why are you involving yourself with Bland?"

Cherise tried the evasive maneuver, which never worked on Toni. "I think her name is Blayne."

"I don't care."

"Are you sure you're not just saying her name wrong because you don't like perky people?"

"I like my assistant. She's perky. And don't try to distract me. What did she mean?"

"Cherise and I," Livy said from behind Toni, "were asked to join the local derby team and we have a practice tonight. With Bland."

Toni rubbed her temples and finally asked the universe, *"Really?"*

They sat in the backyard at a long marble picnic table with matching benches. Cherise brought out coffee and freshly purchased muffins from the bakery down the street. Coop brought out a big pitcher of orange juice.

Once he'd placed the pitcher in the middle of the table, Coop went to sit down by Toni, but before he could, the wolf sat down first. He straddled the bench so that he was facing Toni, his knees touching some part of her.

Unable to help himself, Coop glanced at Cherise and Livy.

To stop from giggling, Cherise desperately shoved a muffin into her mouth. An entire, giant muffin. But Livy, not well acquainted with the wolf and naturally distrusting, merely locked narrowed black eyes on the interloper.

Cherise began to choke on her muffin and Toni quickly poured her a glass of OJ while Coop patted his sister's back until she waved him off.

"All right," Toni said to them once they'd gotten settled. "Talk to me."

Cherise wiped her mouth and began. "I'm just going to play one bout. Just to see if I like it."

Coop saw his eldest sister gaze at Cherise. Toni was clearly exhausted. He saw it in her face, in her body. This wasn't just jet lag, either. Then again, she hadn't been on vacation. She'd been negotiating with bears in a foreign country.

"Cherise, I don't care," Toni told their sister.

Cherise's bottom lip jutted out a bit into a sad little pout. "You don't care at all?"

The wolf squinted at Coop, but he just shook his head. It was the way of his family, wasn't it?

"Of course I care, Cherise, but you have to make that decision for yourself. I will suggest," Toni went on, unable to help herself, "that you don't play a week to two weeks before your concerts. That way if you hurt your arms, wrists, or fingers during a game, you'll have time to heal. Okay?"

Cherise smiled. "Okay."

"Where are we at?" Toni asked Livy.

"I went to Ricky Lee's brother Reece. Had him pull in your company's team, Ricky."

"I would have done the same thing," Ricky said.

"He's been great. Jackie loves him."

"He does have a way with the older ladies."

"What else?" Toni pushed her friend.

"They've secured the house."

"No, Liv. I mean what aren't you guys telling me?"

Livy peered at Coop, raised her brows at him.

"Tell her," he urged, knowing his sister wouldn't stop until they did.

"Irene called in Dee-Ann."

Toni leaned back. "And why was that again?"

"Honestly? I think Irene feels guilty."

"Did she do something?"

"I don't think so. But your mother won't let her leave and I think Irene's worried that if something happens to one of the kids, it'll be because of her."

Toni sighed. "I guess that's why I have that behemoth following me around."

"Who is he anyway?"

"His name's Vic Barinov. He was part of my protection detail in Russia along with Ricky." She looked pointedly at Livy. "What do you think?"

Livy shrugged. "Bringing in Dee-Ann is not my favorite idea." She glanced at Ricky. "I don't have anything personal against your friend, but—"

"But you don't usually call in Dee-Ann Smith unless you want someone to die," Ricky finished for Livy. "Same thing with her daddy. But we also use Dee-Ann and her daddy when we want to prevent problems. If there's one person who can get to the bottom of this, quickly and quietly, it's Dee-Ann Smith."

Toni nodded. "Then leave it alone. If involving Dee-Ann makes Irene feel better, then let her do it. Besides, I want this done."

Livy agreed. "Then it's done."

"Anything else?"

"Nothing urgent," Cooper said, worried about how tired his sister looked. He really hoped this job of hers was worth all she was going through.

"Okay." She stood up. "Tell Mom I'll be back for breakfast in a few. Livy . . . come with."

She walked off and Livy followed her, the women walking into the house.

Ricky moved around on the bench until he could face both Coop and Cherise.

After a long minute of silence, Ricky said, "Your sister was amazing in Russia."

Coop was about to answer, "I know," but Cherise spoke first.

"My sister's amazing all the time." Cherise grabbed a muffin and squeezed it until it began to crumble in her hands. "And if you ever forget that and make her cry the way that worthless full-human did, I'm going to make you sorry you ever left Tennessee." She got to her feet, started to turn away, but then stopped and added, "Which is a lovely state but that's not the point!"

Coop watched his younger sister march off, leaving a trail of muffin crumbs behind her.

"I sure do like your family," the wolf said. And Coop looked over at Ricky Lee, saw the smile that told him the man was being completely serious.

"They are great, aren't they?" Coop agreed.

Toni sat on her bed, pulled off her boots. "Okay." She looked right at her friend. "What haven't you told me?"

"I saw Delilah coming out of a church."

"Great. She's stealing crosses now?"

"Blayne said it was a cult. They took over the church when the original congregation had to move."

Toni suddenly laughed, surprising herself. "I wish I could say I was shocked, but . . ."

"I know. I know." Livy laughed, too. "But when you think

about it, she'd fit right in there with the pantheon, wouldn't she? Charles Manson. David Koresh. Jim Jones. She blends."

"Not quite. They were monsters, but they were all kind of mentally ill. According to Kyle there's a difference between personality disorders and mental illness. Del isn't crazy. She just doesn't have a soul."

Livy braced her legs apart, crossed her arms over her chest. "I put security on each of the kids."

Toni studied her best friend. "Why?"

"I don't know. It just felt . . ." She searched for the right word. "Necessary."

"Then it's necessary." Livy didn't do important things on a whim, so Toni didn't question her decisions.

Yawning, Toni said, "Tell me how much I owe you for all this security because Mom and Dad said they didn't pay for any . . ." But Livy had already walked out of the room.

"I will pay you back, honey lover!"

"Shut up!"

Toni chuckled as Ricky walked into the room.

"Your mother said breakfast will be ready for us in a bit."

"Okay."

He came across the room and dived onto her bed, rolling around until he was on his back. He stopped, gazed at her, then started again.

Toni laughed loud. "What is *wrong* with you?"

"I'm glad to be home." He turned onto his side, wrapped his arms around her waist, pulling her close. "Aren't you?"

"Yeah. But I should go check on the kids."

"The kids are fine. Their *parents* have managed to take very good care of them."

"Not appreciating the Southern sarcasm."

"Come on, darlin'. Let's cuddle like proper canines."

"I don't know if that's a good idea."

"That's a great idea. It's called relaxing. Taking a break. They'll call us when breakfast is ready anyway."

"Well . . ."

But Ricky Lee had already eased her down on the bed until she was cuddled up next to him and at that point she didn't really feel like saying anything else. Besides, what could a five-minute break hurt anyway?

Chapter Twenty-six

"**B**reakfast, Toni."

Toni turned over at the sound of her baby brother's voice; Freddy's small hand was patting her shoulder.

"It's okay," she told him. "I had breakfast on the plane."

The patting stopped and there was a long pause before Freddy said, "That was yesterday."

Toni shot up into a sitting position, her eyes trying to focus as she blinked. She searched for the alarm clock in her room. After a few seconds, she got her eyes to read the numbers.

"It's six thirty? *A.M.?*"

Freddy nodded. "Uh-huh. Mommy made you waffles and bacon." Freddy smiled. "I'm so glad you're home."

Toni smiled at her brother. "Me, too."

He walked to the door, stopped, and said over his shoulder, "You're invited, too, Mr. Reed."

"Just call me Ricky Lee."

"Okay, Ricky Lee."

Her brother walked out and Toni spun around, landing on her knees. "You were here the whole night?"

Yawning and scratching his head, the big wolf rolled onto his back. "I guess so."

"What the hell were you thinking?"

"That I was tired . . . that you were tired . . . that we were tired."

"But you were here all night. And in my bed. And Freddy saw us!"

Resting on his elbows, Ricky raised himself up. "It's not like we were naked."

"That's not the point. Once Freddy knows, the *world* will know."

Ricky shrugged. "Don't make me no never mind."

"Well it does to me."

"That 'cause you're ashamed to be seen with me?"

Surprised by the question, Toni immediately replied, "Of course not!"

"You sure? I know most of your friends are important artists and musicians. I ain't nothin' but a good ol' wolf from Tennessee."

"Your accent certainly does get thick when you're trying to make me feel guilty."

"Is it working?" He reached over and wrapped his arm around her waist, pulling her close. Laughing a little when she fell into him.

Toni braced her hands against his chest but didn't try too hard to pull away.

"I swear," he said, gazing at her mouth, "I didn't mean for this to happen. I just thought we'd sleep for an hour or two. Not all day and night."

"I was more worried about us being up all night. You know, from the change in time."

"I think dealing with those bears just wore us out. It was the first time you could sleep without worrying."

Toni smiled. "But that doesn't explain why you slept so long."

"That's your fault."

"My fault?"

"Snuggling up to you just makes me so dang comfortable. Why would I bother moving?" He suddenly kissed her neck before easing away from her. "Dang, those waffles smell good. Hope your momma made enough."

"How many do you need?"

"A lot." He got off the bed, headed toward the attached bathroom. "I'm gonna use your toothbrush."

"Sure. Why not?"

"No need for that tone," he teased. "You can use my tooth-brush anytime you have a need."

"Oh, well." Toni flopped back on the bed. "When you put it like that . . ."

They walked into the kitchen together and Ricky expected the treatment he'd get from his own kin and Pack, a lot of dramatic stopping and staring, making the pair feel uncomfortable. But the jackals seemed less than interested.

"Good morning, you two," Jackie greeted them. "Waffles and bacon for breakfast. How many do you want, Ricky? One or two?"

"Try six," Toni stated as she reached for one of the plastic cups on the table and the pitcher of orange juice.

"No big deal." Jackie laughed. "I had to feed that lion security guard. My God, could he eat."

"You do know, Miss Jackie, you don't have to feed the team."

"I don't mind. At least for breakfast. I don't do lunch or dinner. That's what takeout and delivery services are for."

Ricky sat down at the table, nodding at the Jean-Louis Parker siblings. They continued to eat, lost in their own thoughts, it seemed. Until Kyle bit into a piece of bacon and then asked, "So Freddy tells us he caught you defiling our sister."

Toni choked on her orange juice, quickly slapping her hand over her mouth and turning away from the table so she didn't spray everyone sitting there.

"Well—" Ricky began, but Cooper cut him off with a raised hand.

"Kyle," Coop said, "do you actually know what defiling means?"

"Of course I do."

"No, you don't," Oriana told him.

"Shut up. I do, too."

"You don't know anything. You're an idiot."

"And you're getting fat!"

"Kyle!" Toni, Cooper, and Cherise all yelled in unison.

"She started it!"

Jackie put a plate piled high with waffles and another plate piled with bacon in front of Ricky. Smirking, she winked at him and whispered, "Just stay away from my mate while he recovers."

"Recovers?"

She glanced at her now arguing offspring and leaned down to whisper in Ricky's ear, "Recovers from finding out his daughter has fallen for a wolf. Something I'm sure he'll blame Irene for. She's a bad influence, don't you know? At least that's what my mother always said."

When she pulled back a bit, Ricky softly asked, "You sure about that? The falling, I mean. Because I can't really tell."

"Because you're male and all of you are hopelessly stupid." She smiled at him and went back to the stove.

By the time Ricky dug into his waffles, Toni and her siblings had stopped arguing but were now staring at him.

"What?" he asked around a mouthful of his food.

"Are you really going to eat all that?" Coop asked.

He shrugged. "I'm hungry."

In the backyard, while the rest of her family was still in the kitchen, watching Ricky Lee dig into his *third* helping of waffles and bacon, Toni faced her best friend.

"What did you say to me?" Toni demanded.

"The wolf . . . he's in love with you."

"Shut up."

"You shut up."

"He's not in love with me."

"You're stupid. You're a stupid head."

Toni pinched her lips together. It made her frown and look fierce when what she was really doing was trying not to laugh.

"You might as well just face it. The wolf's locked on target. And I think that target's your big ass."

"My ass isn't as big as yours."

"I'm compact and powerful. You, however, are a jackal and should look more like Oriana. But if she had that ass, she wouldn't be anyone's prima anything."

"*Such* a bitch."

"And very good at it."

"I'm about to do something, Livy, that you're going to hate me for."

Livy studied her a moment, black eyes narrowing. Then, the honey badger begged, "Please don't."

"I have to."

"No. You don't have to. We can just let this go."

"We're not letting anything go. *I'm* not letting anything go. Not now. Not ever."

Disgusted, Livy snarled, "Then just get it over with."

So Toni did—by hugging her best friend.

"Thank you so much for taking care of those little bastards that I love."

"You know I didn't mind."

"I know." She hugged Livy tighter. "But it means the world to me."

"Whatever."

"You know . . . you don't have to feel ashamed if you're into me. Apparently a lot of people are right now."

Hissing, Livy shoved a laughing Toni away.

"You're such a freak," she accused. "And I told you I'd protect them."

"I know."

"I mean, I may be a cold, heartless bitch, but once I make a promise, I keep it."

"Awww. Can I hug you again?"

"No."

Toni laughed until she saw her father walking toward her, the dog her mother had brought in for her own selfish reasons right by his side. She kind of liked that her father had his own companion while he was in New York. Although he had lots of friends in their home state, he didn't have any out here and didn't feel the need to make any. So the dog, and probably Coop, gave him some relief from keeping the kids from killing each other.

"Hi, Dad." Toni smiled at her father but he didn't respond, simply wrapped his arms around her and hugged her close.

"Uh . . . Dad?"

"My poor, poor baby. I blame Irene for this!"

Toni looked over at Livy, but her friend was about to get into a fight with a rude squirrel who kept mocking her from a high branch.

"You blame Irene for what?"

"For this . . . this . . . this nightmare."

Oh, boy. "Dad—"

"You know he's not like the Van Holtzes, don't you?" Her father pushed her away so he could look directly into her face, but he continued to grip her shoulders. "He's not a chef or cultured in anything that doesn't involve a banjo."

"Dad!"

"I'm just letting you know what you're in for. Because I think you're under the misconception that wolves are better than they are. But they're not."

"Dad, you're taking this too seriously."

"It's all my fault," he went on. "I should have stopped this from the beginning. But I thought he'd be able to distract you from that ridiculous full-human you were still mourning. I didn't know you'd get serious about him!"

"Dad, I wasn't still mourning anyone."

"But you've been so down the last few months."

She shrugged and admitted, "I was starting to think that my entire life was going to be taking care of my siblings. I love them all, but spending every day ensuring there's enough money for facial reconstruction for Kyle after he pisses someone off is not my idea of a satisfactory life goal."

"I'd never allow that. Don't get me wrong. I can't imagine running this family without your help, but I had no intention of letting you become anyone's permanent nanny. You deserve, more than anyone, to have your own life and your own family." He paused a moment, then added, "A family made up of un-spoilt jackal children."

"Dad."

"I'm just saying that you take a risk when you start mixing breeds."

"This from the man who used to spend entire nights outside bars so he could get tickets to Dead Kennedy concerts? Where did my soulful, liberal dad go? Besides," she added, "we both know that being a purebred doesn't ensure anything, either."

And to illustrate, she looked over at the best friend she'd entrusted her siblings to the last few days.

Livy had shifted and was now high up in the tree, fist-fighting with a squirrel. Livy's shifted form was huge compared to a full-blood honey badger, but a hundred-pound ratal shifter was still tiny compared to the lion, tigers, and bear shifters. Of course that difference never stopped Livy from taking all of them on at one time or another.

Honestly, Livy would fight the Queen of England if she thought the woman stared at her too long.

"That's not a fair comparison," her father argued, but he winced when Livy lost interest in the squirrel and discovered a beehive a few branches higher.

"Uh-oh," her father sighed out. "I'll get the Benadryl cream from the first aid kit."

He headed toward the back door, but stopped, faced her, and smiled. "I love you, baby."

Toni grinned at her father's warm words, ignoring the sound of a breaking tree limb as Livy slammed into the ground, the hive caught between her claws.

"I love you, too, Dad."

He started off again, giving a wave. "Good luck at work today."

As her father walked into the house, Ricky Lee was walking out.

"Mornin', Mr. Parker."

"Whatever," her father growled, before moving around the wolf and going into the house.

Ricky Lee looked at her and grimaced. She felt for the guy.

No one wants to face down a canine father after he knows you've been fooling around with his daughter.

"Guess he's mad, huh?" Ricky asked once he stood in front of her.

"Just worried about me. I tried to tell him it's not serious, but he doesn't believe me."

"Of course he doesn't. *I* don't believe you."

She rolled her eyes. "I'm not hung up on you, if that's what you're worried about."

"I wasn't. But what if I'm hung up on you?"

Toni took a step back. "But you're not."

"I told you he was." They both looked over at now-human Livy, her hands still claws, her naked body covered in marauding bees while she gorged herself full of larvae-filled honeycombs. "You canines never listen to me, even though I'm always right." She held her claw out, opened it. "Larvae?"

Toni shuddered. "No. But thank you."

Chapter Twenty-seven

Ricky led Toni and Vic Barinov down the hallway to his hotel room. "A quick shower and change of clothes and we can head over to the Sports Center."

"Or I can just go by myself and meet you two there lat—"

"No," both men said.

Ricky opened his door and walked in, holding it open for Toni and Barinov.

"Until we find out why someone broke into your house," he told her, "you might as well get used to both of us tailing you around."

"I don't need protection. My siblings do."

"And they have it."

Toni faced him. She'd been a little short with him since he'd told her he might, possibly, just be getting kind of serious. Whew. It was a real good thing he hadn't told her he was definitely serious about her. She would have really been pissed then.

"Look, I don't know these people watching my brothers and sisters. I don't know what kind of job they do, if they're the right fit for the particular sibling they've been placed with—"

"The right fit? They're bodyguards."

"I found that lion male crying."

Ricky cringed, but Vic said, "It's not his fault." He shook his head. "It was those weird little twin girls."

Toni glared. "Those weird little twin girls are my sisters."

"Well, their Russian is excellent, but using it to convince that lion they are speaking in tongues and the End of Days are upon us does seem cruel."

Toni rubbed her forehead. "I'll talk to them and tell Kyle *not* to keep showing them *The Omen*!"

Ricky threw his bag aside before asking, "The original or the remake?"

"The original," she replied, walking around his couch and dropping back onto it. "The remake just didn't work for me. Although my favorite Gregory Peck movie will always be *Boys from Brazil*."

"I never saw that movie," Ricky said as he wondered why Vic kept silently motioning to the other bedroom in Ricky's two-bedroom suite.

Toni gasped. "Seriously?"

Vic made an hourglass motion with his hands, and Ricky realized that the hybrid was telling him there was a woman in his other bedroom. He immediately thought of Laura Jane and began quickly moving toward the room so he could get her out. Now.

"It's such a great movie," Toni went on. "You've gotta see it."

Ricky was only a few feet from the bedroom when a voice from inside said, "It *is* a good movie."

Ricky stopped, froze really, and stepped back. "Momma?"

Toni stood as the She-wolf walked out of the bedroom. She was tall, powerfully built just like her son with a face that would be pretty if she smiled more. Something told Toni this woman didn't bother to smile. The question was why. Was she miserable for a reason? Or did she just like being miserable? Toni wasn't quite sure . . . yet.

"Momma, what are you doing here?" Ricky asked her.

"Can't a mother come to see her son?" She looked Ricky Lee over. "Especially when he's busy having tiny hybrids beat up his ex-girlfriend."

"What?"

"Don't pretend you didn't hear me, boy. I saw that girl's face. Now, I don't like Laura Jane and never did, but having some other girl slap her around—"

"Momma, I did no such thing. I haven't even been here."

She grunted and that's when her gaze locked on Toni. "And who's this?" she asked, motioning to Toni with a sweep of her hand. "Is this that tiny hybrid?"

"I'm not a hybrid," Toni replied. "I'm a jackal."

"The devil's pet."

"Momma," Ricky glanced at Toni. "This is Antonella Jean-Louis Parker."

"Toni for short." Toni came forward and held out her hand. "Nice to meet you, Mrs. Reed."

"It's *Miss* Evans, Miss Tala Evans. I'm a wolf, why the holy heck would I bother gettin' married?" She walked past Toni without shaking her hand. "And why is Laura Jane's momma calling me and telling me that my son is lashing out at her idiot child?"

"Because Laura Jane is a crazy liar."

"I thought we agreed on narcissist," Toni reminded him, but when Ricky's mother stared at Toni, she added, "You know, it's all about her?"

"So were you the one who beat up Laura Jane?"

"Me? Fighting She-wolves?" Toni shook her head. "No, ma'am. I like my face just as it is. Attached to my skull."

"Momma, I've been in Russia. I've seen Laura Jane once since she's been in town. I've been busy with other things."

The She-wolf eyed Toni. "Have you now?" She abruptly faced her son. "You know, I'm not really surprised that Laura Jane is playing these games. That's what the little bitch does. Just like her momma, that one. But what really surprised me, Ricky Lee Reed, was how defensive your brother got when I mentioned it to him."

"Rory?" Ricky Lee shrugged. "You know how he is."

"Not Rory. Rory doesn't even know I'm here yet." She glanced at Toni. "I think sometimes I make my oldest boy a little tense."

"*Reece* defended me?"

"He called that little gal all sorts of things that I thought I taught him better about. But he was adamant. Not only that you had nothing to do with it, but he said it was some dark-haired little photographer that just didn't like the look of Laura Jane's face. Not that I blame her."

Ricky briefly closed his eyes, but Toni outright laughed.

"Something I'm missing?" Miss Tala asked.

"It's nothing, Momma."

"And what were you doing in Russia?"

"Protecting me." Toni sat on the couch. "From bears. And now, since I apparently can't take care of myself at all, he's going to follow me to my day job, too."

The She-wolf looked right at Toni. Locked on her. "Is that right?"

"Uh-huh. I'm just waiting for him to shower and change clothes so we can go." Toni tapped the watch on her wrist. "Which . . . if you don't mind."

"Well . . ." Ricky glanced back and forth between Toni and his mother. He clearly didn't want to leave them alone.

Which was probably why the She-wolf smiled and motioned her son away. "You go on, Ricky Lee. I can keep your pretty little jackal company until you get back."

"Yeah, but—"

"I said," his mother low-growled, "go on."

"I'll be *right* back." Ricky, with an apologetic look at Toni, rushed into his bedroom.

The She-wolf sat at the other end of the couch. She grinned and they both looked over at Barinov. The hybrid looked from one woman to the other, pointed at the door, and said, "Why don't I . . . protect the hallway."

Once he bolted for freedom, Toni turned back to Ricky Lee's mother. She studied the older woman and finished sizing her up.

"You know, Miss Tala, I'm so sorry you had to come out here for this."

"Are you?"

"Of course! To have to travel all the way here because you're hearing bad things about your son? Things that aren't true. He was definitely in Russia with me. We just got back yesterday morning and he was at my parents' rental home until today. I'm so sorry someone is involving you in some ridiculous vendetta." Toni leaned in, made sure her face looked appropriately concerned. "Would you like some tea? Or, even better, let's get room service. I bet an iced tea and some scones would be perfect for such a hot summer day."

"You sure are friendly."

"I have to be," Toni admitted. "It's my job to protect all my siblings. And do you think they appreciate it? No. They treat me like a nanny. Like they hired me for the job."

"Well, how many siblings do you have?"

"Ten."

"Good Lord."

"Exactly. And . . . they're *all* prodigies."

"Prodigies? Do you mean—"

"Geniuses. A scientist, a mathematician, several artists, a future prima ballerina. All of them prodigies. All except me."

"I'm sure you have some talent you can be proud of."

"I did just get back from negotiating with honey-loving Russian bears."

"That's impressive. I hear Russians are tough negotiators."

"It was over a hockey game."

"Oh." They stayed silent for a moment until the She-wolf patted Toni's knee. "Why don't we order that room service, darlin'? Seems like you could use some sweet tea and scones more than I could."

Ricky knew he hadn't been in his room that long. He'd showered, shaved, and changed clothes as quickly as possible. But when he came out, he found his mother and Toni . . . eating scones?

And no Vic! Damn feline-bear hybrids were not to be trusted!

"Everything all right out here?" he asked, easing up to the pair.

"Yes." Toni held up the plate of scones. "Would you like one?"

"Sure." Ricky took a blueberry pastry while he kept his eyes on both women. "Guess we better get you to work, Toni."

"Yeah." Toni blew out a breath.

"What's wrong, darlin'?" his mother asked, shocking Ricky with the concern he heard in her voice.

"I haven't talked to anybody. I mean I e-mailed all the details about the deal to the team's coach but . . . she's hard to read. I think I annoy her."

"What is she?"

"Tiger."

Tala Lee Evans clicked her tongue against her teeth. Her typical sound of disgust.

"Momma," Ricky warned.

"You know how I feel about those felines, Ricky Lee. Not to be trusted," she told Toni. "But you don't let some cat get you down. You walk in there with your head held high and tell her exactly how well you did for them. Understand?"

"Yes, ma'am."

"Good." She stood and motioned them both toward the door. "Now y'all go on. And I'll see you tonight at your parents' place, Antonella."

Ricky froze. "What?"

"Yes. I already texted my mom." Toni grinned. "I'm dying to know what she'll order in for dinner."

Then the two females laughed while Tala Lee led them to the door. "Have a good day, you two. And Ricky Lee . . . ?"

Now in the hallway, Ricky faced his mother, his mouth slightly open because he was so confused. "Don't you worry about Laura Jane anymore. I'll handle her."

"Wait, Momma—"

"Go on now. I'll see you tonight." She blew a kiss and closed the door in Ricky's face.

Slowly, he faced Toni. She looked up at him, smiled.

That's when he picked her up and dropped her onto his

shoulder and carried her down the hallway to the elevator. The treacherous feline-bear followed behind them.

Once on the elevator, Ricky put Toni back on her feet and demanded, "What did you do to her?"

"Nothing."

"That was not my mother. My mother is an untrusting, fairly miserable She-wolf whose only friend is the scary Alpha Female of the Tennessee Smith Pack. The woman who just shooed us away is not that."

"Well—"

"And what did she mean about coming over to your parents' house tonight? Why is my momma coming over to your parents' house?"

"Don't yell at me."

"This is not yelling. This is panicked loud talking!"

"Yeah." Vic decided to chime in. "His yelling's not usually this high-pitched."

"Shut up, unhelpful!" Ricky shot back.

"Why would you be panicking? I like your mother."

Ricky couldn't help asking, "Why?"

Toni rolled her eyes and stepped out of the elevator now that the doors had opened on the main floor. "That is a ridiculous question."

"No, it's not."

"It is. Your mother is perfectly fine and considering she successfully raised four children says a lot about her."

"She had my daddy and an entire Pack behind that."

"You don't give her enough credit."

"Look, I love my momma, but I have no delusions about her. And I like your parents. They are wonderful, good-natured people, and I really don't think we should force them to spend time with my mother."

Toni stopped and spun around to face Ricky. "Why don't you admit, you just don't want your mother spending time with my jackal parents?"

"Because that's not true. I don't want your jackal parents spending time with my mother."

"What's the difference?"

"Huge difference. It's just like I don't want your parents hanging around Reece."

Toni shrugged. "Well, that I completely understand."

Toni stepped off the elevator in the Sports Center and headed toward the team offices. Behind her were Ricky and Barinov. It seemed they really were going to follow her around all day.

As Toni walked, she caught sight of Cella heading toward the practice rink. She picked up her step, wanting to catch up with the feline but not look like she was running.

"Hi, Cella."

Busy reading a newspaper and drinking a cup of coffee, Cella glanced back at her. "Oh. Toni. Hey. How's it going, hon?"

"Good. Did you get all the deal particulars I e-mailed you?"

"Yeah. Yeah," she said, still reading that paper. "The deal looks pretty good."

"*Pretty* good?" Ricky asked, but Toni waved her hand at him to put a lid on it. So maybe she hadn't impressed Cella Malone. Felines were notoriously hard to impress, but that didn't mean Toni needed Ricky Lee to push the issue for her.

"Yeah. Like I said. Pretty good. Uh . . . nice job."

Well, even Toni would have to admit that Cella didn't sound like she meant that last part.

"I have something else for you to do," Cella went on.

"Oh, yeah?"

"Yeah. A few things I need you to organize in my office."

"Organize?"

"Yeah." Cella stopped outside the practice rink doors. "You said you'd help out with my workload, right?"

"Yeah. Sure."

"Great." She motioned to the rink. "Come on. I'll give you the list while I'm setting up for morning practice."

"Okay." Toni worked hard to not audibly sigh. It was a big drop to go from negotiating with Russian bears to cleaning up the coach's office, but it made Toni even more determined to impress Cella Malone. She *would* impress her.

Toni followed Cella into the rink, swinging her backpack around so that she could pull out a notepad and pen to take notes. But as she stumbled to a stop, digging into her bag trying to find her stupid notepad, she heard banging. A weird banging.

Toni looked up and blinked, her mouth dropping open a little in surprise.

Because the entire Carnivore team was on the ice in their hockey gear, including their home jerseys, banging their sticks against the ice while the office staff, including her assistant Kerri, and the team's current staff photographer, Livy, stood outside the ice clapping and cheering.

Reece Lee skated across the ice, his arms behind his back. When he reached the very edge of the ice, which was right next to where Toni stood on the carpeted floor, he stopped and brought his arms around. He held two dozen roses wrapped in cellophane in one hand and a box of expensive chocolates in the other. He grinned at her and winked.

With shaking hands, Toni took the gifts and Reece skated backward. That's when he howled and the rest of the team joined in. Except each player did their own thing. So the room filled with roars, growls, howling, and violent hissing. She didn't even realize she was crying until the tears hit her bare forearm.

Cella slung her arm over Toni's shoulders and hugged her in close. "After the way you fucking rocked in Russia, little girl, you better start getting your family ready. Because the Carnivores are not letting you go anytime soon." Cella shook her head and added with a laugh, "And Ivan Zubachev called and, after praising you to heaven and back, he wanted to know if you were single."

That made Toni laugh until Ricky, standing next to her, said, "Nope. She's not."

Both Toni and Cella looked at him, and the wolf shrugged. "What? You're not."

Chapter Twenty-eight

Toni couldn't believe how busy her day turned out to be. She had meeting after meeting, and a bunch of phone calls to handle. Yeah. Sure. Everyone was really impressed with what she'd done in Russia, but now they expected her to keep impressing them.

She didn't know if she could manage that. Maybe the Russian negotiations were just a fluke. And she had had Vic Barinov's help, hadn't she? So she'd need to tread carefully to make sure she really deserved all the attention she'd gotten today.

Well, if nothing else, being so busy meant her workday had flown by. It was already four o'clock and she was ready to head home, check on the kids, and order dinner before Ricky's mother showed up.

Toni peeked over at Ricky Lee. He'd sat in that chair all day, taking phone calls and remotely working on other jobs for his security company. Surprisingly, he didn't seem to mind being stuck here with her. That was good. She didn't know if she could keep him entertained when she kept having to answer e-mails from Bo Novikov every couple of hours asking about team travel.

"You ready to go?" she asked.

"Yep." He and Vic Barinov, who occasionally left the office to do a "sweep of the area" as he called it and get coffee and more food than seemed natural from the food court, stood.

That's when Livy walked into the office, a tablet computer in her hand.

"Hey, hey."

"Hey." Toni smiled at her friend. "Where did you go? I haven't seen you since this morning."

"I wanted to finish this up."

Livy put the tablet in front of Toni and touched the screen. Toni's face lit up. "Oh!" Then her smile began to fade. "Oh." The smile faded completely, replaced by a frown. "Oh . . . my God! *Why are they naked?*"

Ricky and Vic practically sprinted across the room to see what Toni was looking at.

"Good Lord!" Ricky stepped back from her desk. "Why am I looking at my brother's penis?"

"What's wrong?" Livy asked. "This is some of my best work that didn't involve getting shot at."

"So to speak," Vic mumbled under his breath.

Toni flicked through the other photos. They were mostly in black and white, but some were in color but just gave the illusion of being black and white. Each player was beautifully lit, showing off every muscle and vein. Yes. This was some of Livy's best work.

And completely useless for Toni's needs!

"What am I supposed to do with this, Livy?"

"What are you talking about?"

"I needed team pictures for the fans. For the kids. Not boudoir pictures for their wives."

"Come on, these are—"

"Useless to me!" Toni leaned in closer. "I don't even know who this is. He's headless!"

"He has kind of a 'butta' face."

Barinov snorted a laugh at Livy and walked back to his chair.

"What's so funny?" Livy snarled at him.

"Do I really have to tell you?"

Toni stood up and she did something she'd never done before. She made demands.

"Fix this," she ordered her friend.

"What do you mean?"

"I mean"—Toni faced Livy—"fix. This. I don't want your bullshit art. I don't want moody lighting. I want amazing, *use-ful* pictures of the team. That's what I'm paying you for. Remember? Check out *Sports Illustrated* for ideas or something."

"*Sports*—"

"*Sports Illustrated,* Livy. *Not* Mapplethorpe. Mapplethorpe is not and should not be your inspiration for what I want for this job. Do you understand me?"

Livy looked off and Toni snapped her fingers in her friend's face. "Do you?"

"Yes. I understand you."

Toni grabbed her backpack, swung it onto her shoulder. "I'm heading home. Talk to Kerri about setting up new appointments with the team."

"Fine."

Toni stopped. "If you can get releases from the guys, I'd suggest using these for an art show."

"I don't care what my brother signs," Ricky said, pulling the office door open and holding it for Toni. "I better not see his naked ass or penis on anyone's damn wall."

Livy's eyes crossed and she swiped her tablet off the desk. She stormed out, pushing past Ricky.

Shaking her head, Toni followed. As she walked past Ricky, she complained, "Artists."

While sitting on the couch in the Jean-Louis Parker living room, Cooper stared at his sister. "You need me to do *what*?"

"I need you to play in Siberia."

"Why?"

She cleared her throat, clearly uncomfortable with asking her brother for this favor. "Because I promised the bears you'd go out there and play for them."

"They're real big fans," Ricky told him. "Once they realized Toni was your sister, they couldn't help her enough."

"Can't they just come to Moscow or Saint Petersburg to see me . . . like everyone else in Russia?"

"I promised."

"You promised without asking me. You used my name to get what you want." He wiped a non-existent tear. "I'm so proud."

"Oh, shut up!"

"Maybe Kyle's right. You'd make a great business manager for him."

"Is that a yes or a no?"

"It's a 'my agent will handle it.' "

"They'll want dinner with you."

Coop snorted, elbowed Ricky. "Great. Dinner with bears. I know that's something I love to do."

"You do it in Italy all the time."

"Do you know how the Italian bears eat? Like gods, big sister. Like gods."

Toni and her brother laughed. Ricky didn't even think they noticed when Dee-Ann silently entered the room and stood behind the couch. But they did. Both immediately stopped in mid-laugh and slowly looked over their shoulder.

"Hi, Dee-Ann," Toni said, trying to smile.

"Hey."

"Is there a problem?"

"Nah. That badger around?"

Toni quickly looked at Ricky, her eyes wide.

"Why?" she asked Dee.

"Yeah," Ricky chimed in, "why?"

"Ain't your never mind, Ricky Lee."

"I will not never mind if this is about Laura Jane."

"Laura Jane's on her way home. Your momma handled that right quick."

"She did?"

"Yep."

Ricky was surprised. His mother had arrived at the Jean-Louis Parker house less than an hour after Ricky and Toni. She hadn't said another word about Laura Jane. But she had come with groceries, planning to make her famous fried chicken. Jackie had told her it wasn't necessary, but his momma wouldn't hear it. She'd been busy in that gourmet kitchen ever since.

"Besides," Dee added, looking around the room, "some of those lacerations that badger gave her had gotten infected."

Ricky cringed at that. He didn't want Laura Jane to suffer or anything, he just wanted her to forget he'd ever existed since he was sure she didn't really care about him.

"Anyway," Dee went on, "y'all see her, tell her I need to talk to her. Ya hear?"

"Okay."

With that, Dee-Ann ambled out of the room and Ricky's momma walked in. She had a paper grocery bag in her hands and it smelled delicious.

"Here," she said, handing the bag to Ricky.

"What's this?"

"Your dinner and dessert. Y'all get now."

"Get now?" Ricky looked at Toni and she shrugged. "What are you talking about?"

"It seems Miss Antonella has her own apartment. I think it's high time she learns to enjoy it. And her momma and daddy agreed with me."

"But I thought we were all having dinner together," Toni said, getting to her feet.

"We'll do that. For now, I think y'all need some time away from these kids."

Toni blinked, her head tilting. "Why don't I hear them?" she asked.

"I've been keeping them busy making cookies."

"You kept *my* brothers and sisters busy making cookies? Really?"

"It wasn't that hard. I just had Dennis and Kyle design the look of the cookies—told them to try and outdo each other—while Oriana analyzed the fat content and tried to come up with a less fattening cookie, and I got Troy to help her with that by dealing with the actual percentages. Cherise monitored them all and the twins watched and tried to sneak licks of the batter. See? Easy."

But before Ricky could congratulate his momma on her skills managing the kids, Toni beat him to it, suddenly racing over to Tala and hugging her.

"Oh, Miss Tala! Thank you!"

Tala chuckled and patted the She-jackal's back. "Good Lord, you're just like your momma."

Reece walked into the room. "Hey. When are we gettin' to eat?" he began, but Toni turned on him like a snake.

"You be nice to your mother!" she roared at him, one finger pointing.

Reece stumbled back. "I was just asking a question, woman!"

"Ask it nicer!" She hugged Tala again. "This woman is a saint. A saint! And you boys don't forget it or I'll come down on you like the wrath of God!"

Reece shrugged and whined, *"But I'm hungry!"*

They walked into Toni's apartment. Sitting on the side table by the door was a small stack of mail.

"I'm already getting mail here?" she asked him.

"Seems so. And someone to bring it in."

She looked around, sniffed the air. "I smell Lysol. I think I have a maid."

"I'm sure you do."

Ricky headed into the dining room and set the food out. By the time he went into the kitchen and retrieved plates, glasses, and silverware, Toni was sitting at the table pulling things out of envelopes.

"What's all that?" he asked as he put down place settings.

"The lease for this place. Ric wants me to sign it. It's apparently a rent-to-own."

Ricky flinched. "I'm afraid to ask how much that'll cost ya."

Toni didn't answer, just stared.

"You're kidding?" he asked. "That cheap?"

"I could put it on a credit card." When Ricky's mouth dropped open, Toni giggled and said, "I'm kidding. It's not that bad. But . . . Ric is definitely charging a hell of a lot less than he probably should."

"You're family, darlin'. What did you expect him to do? Charge you a bazillion dollars?"

"Yes. I did."

She took in a deep breath, eyes closing. "Man, that chicken smells *amazing*."

"My momma's award-winning fried chicken. And you'll hear that award-winning part more than you want to."

"It smells like she has a reason to be proud."

"I hope she gave us enough to have cold chicken tomorrow. Nothing is better than her next-day fried chicken with a couple of cold beers."

Grinning, Toni stepped closer to Ricky. "How about her couple-hours-later fried chicken?"

Ricky returned her grin and wrapped his arm around her waist, tugging her closer. "That might be the *best* way to eat it."

He leaned in and Toni could already taste him on her lips, feel his hands on her body. Until . . .

"Dinner ready?"

Snarling, Toni spun on her best friend. "Livy!"

"What? I'm hungry."

"You're not staying here."

"You were serious about that?"

Toni started to head over to her friend, but Ricky kept his grip on her, pulled her back to his side.

"Dee-Ann's looking for you," he told Livy.

"Dee-Ann who?"

He scratched his head. "Smith."

"Oh. Why?"

"No idea."

"And did you attack Laura Jane Smith?" Toni asked.

Livy gazed at Toni. "Who?"

"The She-wolf you attacked a few days ago?"

"You'll have to be more specific than that."

"I think my brother was involved," Ricky said.

Livy thought a moment. Nodded. "Oh. Yeah. Okay. I think I know who you mean."

"Why?"

"Why what?"

Toni growled a little, then asked, "Why did you attack her?"

Livy had to think on that for a second, as if she attacked so many people during the day, she couldn't just recall them easily. "It was time for his appointment with me and she was in my way. Plus," she added, "I didn't like her face. So I slapped it around."

Ricky studied the woman closely. "So, Livy . . . what are you?"

He expected her usual, "None of your business response," but this time she was as direct with her answer as she was direct with her beat downs.

"Honey badger."

"Ahhhh." He nodded. "Explains everything."

Then Ricky had to laugh.

"What's so funny?" Toni asked.

"Laura Jane pissed off a honey badger," he said, unable to hide his smile. "It really doesn't get any better than that."

Toni put her arm around his shoulder. "It really doesn't."

Dee-Ann disconnected the call and walked into her house.

Irene had been right about one thing. This break-in to the Jean-Louis Parker house hadn't been . . . minor, but that was all she knew. That there was activity among her full-human brethren. Stone-cold killers like herself who did specialized work for the government. These were not people to fuck with. But if they wanted someone dead, they would have moved by now. So death wasn't what they wanted. It was something else.

And she was going to find out what it was and end it. Because Dee-Ann got a little cranky when pups and cubs were involved. That had always been the line she never crossed when she was in the Marines and definitely not now. Even if it was hyena pups, deadly from birth, she waited until they were at least in their early twenties before she considered taking them on.

Dee walked into her living room.

"I—" was the only word Dee heard before she'd pulled her

.45, spun, dropped down to one knee, and locked on her target.

"—heard you were looking for me," the honey badger finished without missing a beat.

With fearless black eyes, Olivia Kowalski stared at Dee. She wasn't challenging her. She wasn't backing away.

Fearless. Yeah. That was exactly it. And just what Dee-Ann needed.

Dee-Ann stood up, put her gun back in the holster. "I need to hire you."

"I don't kill on order."

"I don't need you to kill, darlin'. I need you to follow the family business."

"I don't do that anymore."

"Don't bullshit a bullshitter. You'll get paid. Well."

"Why don't you do it?"

Dee-Ann shrugged. "Not my area of expertise," she admitted. "When I get into someone's house it's for one reason and one reason only."

"Is this about what's going on at Toni's house?"

"No. This is another case. I'm dealing with Toni's first. But once I'm done with that, I'll need your help. And you won't just be helping me out. This is important work, darlin'. Something you can be proud of . . . for once."

Kowalski walked toward the exit. "I'll think about it."

Dee waited until the front door closed and she knew the badger was gone. She pulled out her cell phone and speed-dialed Malone.

"What up?"

"Kowalski's in."

"She is?"

Dee shrugged again. "She will be."

Chapter Twenty-nine

Toni rolled over in her bed and stretched.

"Morning," she heard Vic Barinov say.

Yanking the sheet up to her chin, Toni sat up in bed and yelled out, "Ricky!"

Ricky walked out of the bathroom, fresh from a shower, a towel around his waist, shaving cream on one side of his face, and a razor in his hand. Honestly, if Toni hadn't been so freaked out to find Barinov skulking around her bedroom, she would have enjoyed the delicious view. The man looked damn good.

"What the holy hell, Vic?"

"Sorry. Didn't mean to startle you. We have a problem, though."

"A problem?"

Barinov looked at Toni. "It's the twins."

Livy watched her best friend pace back and forth in the ballroom while the EMT guys did what they had to do. She knew that Toni wouldn't handle this well. Nope. Not well at all.

"What were you thinking?" Toni bellowed. "I just don't understand!" She leaned down so that she could shake her finger right in the faces of Zoe and Zia. "You were bad. Bad, bad, bad, bad, *bad!*"

The EMTs were shifters from a shifter hospital, and when one of them said, "Brace yourselves," Livy instinctively cringed even before she heard them snap that lion male's bone back into place.

Paul rushed into the ballroom with his pet dog by his side. "Why is there an ambulance out . . . oh." He briefly watched the EMTs secure Jeff Stewart to a gurney built with bears in mind.

As they wheeled him out, he screamed at Ricky Reed, "I expect disability for this, Reed! You understand me? Tell Llewellyn I want disability!"

Paul walked up to Livy. "What the hell happened?"

"I'm not sure," Livy admitted. "I heard him scream and came running in to find him on the floor with a broken leg and the girls sitting there eating Danish."

"Tell me that's raspberry on their face."

"It's not blood."

"That's something." Paul let out a breath. "Did you ask Stewart?"

"I did. He wouldn't tell me anything, just kept saying 'This goddamn job isn't worth it.' Over and over again."

Toni walked away from her sisters, past Ricky Lee, and over to Livy and Paul.

"I seriously can't leave for a night!" she complained.

"The girls didn't do anything physical to him. I think they just messed with his head. He did the rest to himself."

Paul walked toward his twin daughters. "Toni, I'll handle this. You go to work."

"But, Dad—"

"No buts. I can handle my own children."

"Fine." She kissed her father on the cheek, crouched down, kissed her sisters, then shook her finger at them again. "Bad, bad, *bad!*"

Livy followed Ricky and Toni out into the hall. As they walked, Ricky said, "I'll get on the phone with Rory and find someone to replace Stewart."

"Someone better," Toni snarled. "No more lion males if they can't handle a couple of bratty three-year-olds."

Bratty three-year-olds the twins might be, but that didn't mean they were any less dangerous. But Livy wasn't about to say that to her best friend. Not when she was this angry.

They reached the front door and Toni faced Ricky. "I know your brother handled this job, but I want you to evaluate all the personnel involved directly with *my* siblings. You understand them, Reece doesn't."

"Done."

Smart wolf. He knew better than to argue with Toni when it was about her siblings. Because there would be no winning that fight. Only lonely nights.

"Good." Toni grabbed the doorknob and yanked the door open. Her limo driver reared back.

"Oh," he said. "I was just coming to—"

"Just go already!" she yelled at him.

"What are you screaming at me for?" the feline demanded. "I didn't do anything!"

"Shut up and drive, you idiot!"

Bickering, the pair stormed out of the house. Ricky looked at Livy, sighed, shook his head, and followed.

Livy did not follow. She knew better.

It took Ricky nearly half a day to get his brother on the phone. Rory had been in client meetings and other than texting him to "stop bothering me," he'd been pretty quiet. But now that Ricky had him on the phone, he was forcing Rory to go through each team member he'd brought onto the Jean-Louis Parker job and which kid that team member was attached to. His brother wasn't happy about this—he never liked it when anyone questioned him but especially when it was Reece or Ricky. But with Stewart stuck in the hospital in the throes of an ugly fever while his leg healed, Rory knew he had no choice.

So far, though, Ricky was fine with the team Rory had assembled to watch the kids—he wasn't about to blame any male, even a feline, for being freaked out by the Jean-Louis Parker twins. Then Rory told him who he'd put with Freddy.

Sitting in Toni's office, which was filled with flowers from individual players—especially the ones of Russian and Mongo-

lian descent who would now have a chance to visit distant relatives at team cost—and other Eastern Europe shifter hockey
teams who'd clearly heard about Toni through Zubachev,
Ricky told his brother flatly, "No."

"What do you mean 'no'?"

"I mean no. I don't want Roy with Freddy."

"Why not?"

"He's lazy."

"Dude, come on. How much effort is needed to watch a
seven-year-old?"

"I don't want Roy on this."

"Who then?"

Ricky thought a moment. "What about Miranda?"

"Miranda? Is she remotely good with kids?"

"I don't care. And I can promise you Freddy's sister won't
care. It's about whether he'll be safe, and Freddy has a lot of
outside classes. So put her on it."

"Okay. Okay. Lord, you are gettin' snarly. Startin' to sound
like Daddy."

"Only because you're irritating the shit out of me."

"I said okay! I'll take care of it. But Miranda's in Queens today on another job. I can pull her, but it'll take a bit to get her
back to the city, so Roy will have to stick with the kid while
he's at school."

Ricky looked at his watch. "Yeah. All right." He'd replace
Roy himself but the coyote would wait until Ricky could get
there.

"Have her meet us at the Parker house."

"Yeah. Okay." Then his brother chuckled. "Parker house.
Aren't those rolls?"

Yep. The Reed family secret—Rory was kind of goofy.

"Does your hot, new girlfriend smell like rolls, too?"

Ricky looked over at his "hot, new girlfriend."

"Rory?" Ricky said to his big brother.

"Uh-huh?"

"Momma's in town."

"Wait. *What?*"

"Bye!" Ricky disconnected the call and then turned his phone off.

"What's going on?" Toni asked. She was focused on her computer monitor, her hands flying across the keyboard, and he didn't think she'd been paying attention.

"Just freaking my brother out."

"You mentioned Freddy. What's going on with Freddy?"

Damn, the woman was good.

"I'm going to go pick up Freddy from school today."

"I'll come with you."

"You don't trust me with your brother?"

"I don't trust that he won't talk you into letting him drown himself in a chocolate sundae as big as your head." She smirked. "He's quite persuasive, my baby brother."

"And I wonder where he learned that from?"

"Quiet, you."

Freddy Jean-Louis Parker hated school. He hated professors. They always got so mean when he corrected them. How was it his fault when they got it wrong? How was it *his* fault that they didn't know as much as they thought they did?

It wasn't! It wasn't his fault! And it wasn't fair to yell at him! He didn't do anything wrong. And even when he did do wrong things, his parents didn't yell at him. Even Toni didn't yell at him and Toni yelled at pretty much everybody. She did slap those matches out of his hand that time, but he didn't blame her for that. But then she calmed him down. Toni always calmed him down. She was real good at that.

Freddy walked out of the class, the man named "Roy" behind him. Freddy wasn't so sure about Roy. He kept sighing and seemed really bored. How could anyone be bored by nuclear and particle physics? True, the professor wasn't as knowledgeable as he thought he was, and that made him a little boring, but the field itself was fascinating! Whenever things got bad for Freddy, whenever he got real tense about something, he focused on the world of science and things got better. Toni and his therapist, Dr. Mathews, had taught him that. Because when things were better, Freddy was less inclined to . . . do things he shouldn't.

Walking down the hall, Freddy felt really small. Everyone around him was so big . . . and old. But what Toni always told Freddy was that these people might be physically big, but Freddy had something none of these people had besides being smart—he had his family. Even when they were physically apart, even when they were arguing, even when they threatened each other with copyright and trademark lawsuits, they were still family. They would always be family.

Because of that, Freddy kept his head high and walked through that crowd of people with Roy right behind him. They got outside and Roy's phone rang.

"Yeah? Yeah. Okay. Hold up, kid."

Freddy stopped on the third step and looked back at Roy.

"We need to wait here. Ricky Lee's coming to pick you up."

Freddy smiled. "Okay!" He liked Ricky Lee. A lot. He was funny and nice and made Toni laugh. Their dad had started calling him "that bastard wolf" lately, but Freddy wasn't fooled. He knew his dad liked Ricky Lee, too. He just didn't want to admit it.

Roy glanced down at Freddy. "Do you need me to hold that backpack for ya, kid?"

Freddy shook his head and gripped the straps. "No, thank you."

"Okay. But let me know if it gets too heavy."

Roy looked around; saw a pack of girls nearby. Grinning, he stepped over, introduced himself, and started talking. Bored, Freddy started to move away.

"Hey," Roy said, catching Freddy mid-step. "Do not wander off."

"Okay."

But Roy was still talking to those girls and Freddy was still bored. He got tired of just standing there, so he moved over to the building wall and leaned back against it.

As he waited, he saw students from the class he'd just been

in, as well as the professor. Not wanting to deal with them again right now, he eased around the wall until he could peek at them from the other side.

Those students had laughed when Freddy had corrected the teacher. Then they'd stared at him when they found out he was right. Stared at him like he was a freak.

He wasn't a freak! Toni said he was smart and amazing! And Toni was never wrong. Not ever!

He hated school.

"Hi," a female voice said from behind him. Freddy looked over his shoulder. She was old. Like Toni's age old. But real pretty with dark hair and bright eyes. She was dressed real nice, too. And she had a pretty smile.

"Hi," Freddy said back.

"Could you help me?"

Freddy faced her. "Help you?"

"I lost my puppy and I was hoping that—"

"Stranger danger!" Freddy screamed, just like Toni had always taught him. Well, he didn't remember the exact words she'd taught him to say, but the screaming should be enough. *"Stranger danger!"*

The woman's pretty face changed. First she looked shocked, then she was angry and she reached for him. So, still screaming, Freddy started swinging his arms and kicking his feet.

The woman squealed when he got her right in the knee, and that's when he took off running around the building. And the entire time he screamed, *"Stranger danger! Stranger danger!"*

He was looking for Roy, but Freddy saw Toni running right for him. He knew he'd be safe with her, and he dived into her arms. She lifted him up, and Freddy wrapped his arms around her neck and his legs around her waist, holding on tight.

"What happened?" Toni demanded, shaking him just a bit. "What happened?"

Freddy pointed at the corner of the building. "A woman. She tried to grab me."

Toni held him tighter while Ricky Lee and Roy took off running. Another man, he said his name was Vic and he was there to protect Freddy's sister, stood by them. He looked mean and ready to hurt people. The big students started moving away from them, giving them space.

"Are you all right?" Vic asked. Freddy realized the man wasn't mean. Not like that lady had been mean. He was concerned. Freddy's dad got that way sometimes. Like when Cherise panicked when a possum jumped out at her from behind a tree at their house and knocked herself out cold by running into another tree. The rest of them were laughing, but Daddy had looked upset and yelled at her and everyone else. Freddy finally figured out it was because he was worried about her. Worried Cherise had hurt herself bad. That was how Vic looked right now.

And although Freddy knew Vic would protect them, and that he was big enough and strong enough to do it, that didn't matter. Not to Freddy. Not when he was holding on to his sister and knew without a doubt that he was safe.

Because with Toni, Freddy knew he'd always be safe.

Ricky charged around that corner, catching sight of a long leg seconds before it disappeared inside the passenger side of a car, the door closing behind it.

"Stay with Toni!" he ordered Roy.

"Wait—"

"Just do it!"

Ricky Lee took off after that car, dodging through the vehicles of pissed-off New York drivers as he sped across the street when the car turned a corner.

The car turned again, and Ricky continued to follow, pushing people out of his way and ignoring the rude things they were screaming at him. The car made several more turns until it ended up in an alley.

The engine still running, the vehicle sat there. Moving slow, Ricky eased up to the car until he could look into the windows. It was a late-model Mercedes. Really nice with darkened windows. Leaning in close, Ricky was about to press his nose to the space between the window and the door to see if he could scent anyone inside. But he stopped before his nose could touch anything when the cold barrel of a gun pressed against the back of his neck.

"You sure are fast, kid," a male voice said from behind him.

And to prove the man right on that point, Ricky turned fast, caught the man's wrist with one hand, and rammed his free hand into the man's elbow.

The bone snapped and ripped the skin apart as it jutted forward.

The man started to scream, so Ricky slapped his hand over the man's mouth and slammed him against the wall.

"Let him go." A woman. Another gun.

Then another, as a male voice said, "Now."

Ricky knew he had one chance at this. If he blew it, he was not leaving this alley alive. Since he had plans for the weekend, he decided that wasn't an idea he liked much.

So, still moving fast, he ripped the rest of the man's arm off and used it to slap the woman in the face. She shrieked and ducked as blood blinded her. Then Ricky tossed the screaming man into the other and scrambled up onto a Dumpster, caught the bottom of fire stairs, and headed up.

By the time he was standing on the roof, the woman was trying to wipe all that blood off her face while the man was trying to find Ricky. He didn't look up, because it never occurred to him that anyone could get up the stairs to the roof that quickly. So these people were definitely not aware they'd become involved with shifters. But, they were definitely government. Which government, Ricky had no idea. Not yet.

Ricky waited until the remaining couple placed the now-one-armed man into the backseat. The woman got in with him, screaming that they had to get to a hospital. But Ricky got the feeling that the other man had no intention of bothering with that as he tossed his partner's arm into the front seat like he was tossing in an old bag of laundry.

The car pulled out of the alley and sped off, and Ricky took his phone out of the back pocket of his jeans. His eldest brother answered immediately.

"What's up?" Rory greeted him.

"Track down Dee-Ann for me."

There was a long pause and then Rory sighed out, "Well, that's never a good way to start a conversation."

Nope. It sure wasn't.

When Ricky arrived back at his truck, he found Toni still holding her brother, flanked by Vic and Roy, who were warning off the full-human students and professors just by being themselves. Ricky could tell that the full-humans wanted to help. But they didn't, and he knew why. They were terrified of the predator holding the child more than they were of the much larger and scarier-looking predators surrounding her. Because at the moment, Antonella Jean-Louis Parker saw *everyone* as a threat—and there was nothing more deadly than a predator female who felt one of her own was in danger.

Ricky stepped in front of her to block her glower from the full-humans nearby. "Why don't you put him in the truck, darlin'?"

"You don't have a child seat."

Something told him it wouldn't matter if he did; she didn't want to let her brother go.

She held her phone in one hand and raised it. "I didn't call nine-one-one. I should, though, right? I should do something."

"We don't need the cops." He reached for Freddy but Toni's grip tightened.

"It's all right. Give him to me."

After a moment, she released the boy and Ricky took Freddy from her.

"I want Mommy."

"I know. And we're going to get you home right now." Ricky pulled open the back passenger door and placed him in the seat. While he buckled him up, Ricky told him, "You were so smart, Freddy. The way you handled that. You should be real proud of yourself."

The little boy gave a brave smile. "Toni taught me what to do."

"And you listened. Good boy. Now Vic here's going to sit in the back with you." He leaned in and whispered, "Ask him to show you his claws. They're *huge*."

"Really?"

"Yep. Isn't that right, Vic?"

"Enormous." Vic got into the SUV beside Freddy. "You wanna see?"

"Yeah!"

Ricky closed the door and stepped closer to Toni. She leaned up against the SUV. Her entire body was tense, ready to strike like a cobra.

"We're gonna take care of this," Ricky promised her.

"It was them, wasn't it? The ones who were in our house."

Ricky nodded. "The scents matched, yeah."

"Government?"

"Probably. Don't think they were after Freddy because of what he is, though. They didn't know what that was."

"If we hadn't been watching out for him, Ricky—"

"We were. He's safe. And we're gonna keep him safe. Let's get him home."

"And then what?"

He took her hand, held it tight. "Then there'll be hell to pay."

CHAPTER THIRTY

By the time they reached the house, Dee-Ann was sitting on the stone banister, her long legs stretched out in front of her. To someone passing by, Toni would guess she looked innocuous enough in her ancient jeans, worn Led Zeppelin T-shirt, and black baseball cap with absolutely no logo on it.

But Toni knew better. She knew that Dee-Ann simply sitting and waiting was one of the most dangerous things in the world.

With Freddy in her arms, Toni walked up the stairs. She stopped by Dee-Ann, and the She-wolf tugged on Freddy's T-shirt. "Hey, little man."

"Hi, Dee-Ann."

"Heard you were brave today."

"Brave?"

"Yeah." Dee leaned in and whispered, "And Ricky Lee Reed don't say that about just anybody, ya know? So you must have been amazing."

A little embarrassed and overwhelmed, Freddy smiled and buried his head against Toni's neck.

"Go on and take him inside," Dee-Ann coaxed. "Me and the boys will be right in."

Toni nodded and continued on up the stairs. As she reached the top step, the front door opened and her mother stood there. She'd been crying, but she was trying to hide it. She opened her arms and Toni handed Freddy off. Jackie held on to her son with one arm and reached for Toni with the other, hugging her daughter tight.

"It's going to be okay, Mom," she assured her. "It's going to be okay."

The front door closed and Dee focused on Ricky Lee.

"You've got blood on ya."

He looked down. "Oh. Yeah."

"Any cleanup necessary?"

"They took him away. He was alive last I saw him but doubt it'll last unless they get him to a hospital. Something tells me they won't."

"Why would they want the boy?" she asked.

"I don't know. I thought for sure it was Irene they wanted."

"Use him for leverage?"

"Maybe."

"But that don't sound right, does it?"

"No. The kid is brilliant on his own, Dee. We picked him up from a university class. He's seven. When we were driving back, he said the teacher hated him because he corrected his equations or somethin'."

Dee looked around Ricky and nodded her head at the big buck standing behind him. "Barinov."

"Dee-Ann."

"You got any thoughts?" The feline-bear shrugged, which meant he did. She hated when he was evasive. She didn't like chatty men, but she wasn't much for shy ones, either. And that was his problem, though he hid it well. "Say it now before my patience wanes."

"If they just wanted to take the kid," Vic finally said, "why didn't they just take him from the beginning? Why bother breaking into the house first?" He folded his arms over his chest. "I don't think it's the kid they really want."

Dee thought on that a brief moment, then slipped off the banister.

"Where are you going?" Ricky asked.

"To find out what they could possibly want."

★ ★ ★

Jackie waited until Toni had sent Freddy upstairs to get his homework done before she talked to the rest of the kids. She knew that what she was about to tell them would not make them happy, but that was too bad.

She walked into the living room. They were all waiting for her except the twins and Dennis. Those three were still at the age where they'd go anywhere they were told. But the rest of this group . . .

There was, of course, one missing. Delilah. But she was rarely home these days. She'd turned eighteen and realized her parents had no legal way to get her to come home, so she didn't bother. Then again, Jackie didn't worry about her daughter like she did the others. She simply didn't have to.

"What's going on, Mom?" Oriana demanded. She had several pairs of toe shoes spread out in front of her, sewing on the ribbons that wrapped around her ankles. "You're crying. Aunt Irene is trying to get in touch with Uncle Van. And there seems to be a growth of hillbilly wolves in our house."

"Hey," Toni warned, standing next to Jackie. "Be nice."

"What? You're dating a hillbilly, so now we all have to tolerate them?"

"Yes," Toni shot back at her sister. "You do!"

"Both of you stop it." Taking in a breath, Jackie announced, "We're returning to Washington. Tonight."

Troy turned to Kyle. "Now what did you do?"

"Shut up."

"Kyle didn't do anything," Jackie cut in before there could be an argument. "This is about Freddy."

Oriana sighed. "Oh, God. What did he burn down now?"

"Or steal," Troy tossed in.

"He didn't do any of that. My God, what is wrong with you people?"

Kyle snorted. "Perhaps one should look to the upbringing of troubled children."

"You're not troubled, Kyle. You're troubl*ing*."

"Stop it," Toni ordered. "All of you. For once, this isn't all about you. It's about family."

"How is Freddy burning someone's house down *our* problem?"

"He didn't burn anything down!" Jackie roared.

Thankfully, Toni just came out with it. "Someone tried to kidnap Freddy today."

"What do you mean 'kidnap'?" Kyle asked.

"I mean they tried to grab your younger brother off the street."

"Whatever for?" Troy asked. "For slave labor in a foreign country?"

Toni looked at Jackie and then back at her brother. *"Really?"*

"Why do you sound shocked? That sort of thing happens all the time. And he's a strong little boy and quite tidy. He'd make a good little worker in a sweatshop."

"Okay, stop." Toni took a breath. Tried again. "We're going back to Washington . . . for safety."

"No."

Jackie wished that had come from one of the kids sitting in front of her. Because she'd expected it. But sadly . . . it didn't.

"Freddy—" she began, but it was too late. Her little boy had heard everything.

Freddy, standing under the archway, shook his head. "We're not leaving. Not because of me."

"Freddy." Toni tried to soothe, walking toward her brother. "I know this is hard to understand—"

"I'm not stupid!"

Oriana stood and Jackie cringed until her fifteen-year-old said, "We're trying to protect you. This is about family, Fred. All of us. We protect you, you protect us. Even when we think you're an untalented little bastard," she added, her gaze moving to Kyle.

Who came back with, "Or a chubby, overbearing witch with *huge* psychological issues."

Confused, Freddy asked, "You guys won't be mad? If we go back? I mean . . . you guys have all your classes and stuff set up."

He pointed at the wall covered in giant Post-it notes with Novikov's careful handwriting on it. "Our schedules."

"Our talent goes where we go," Oriana said, managing to be loving and smug all at the same time. It was a gift she did possess. "Those of us who have talent. In all honesty, I'm not shocked someone's trying to take you. You are a Jean-Louis Parker, after all. We'll always be in demand. Right, Mom?"

"Uh . . . yes. Very true."

"Besides," Oriana added, "going back is better than if you were actually taken. Because then we'd have to mourn or whatever, and spend our time searching for you."

"Wow." Troy sighed. "I hadn't thought of that. What a nightmare!"

"Exactly."

Toni put her hands on her hips. "Oriana . . . *really*?"

"What? I plan to be in the Royal Ballet by the time I'm seventeen. Can't do that if I'm busy handing out milk cartons with Freddy's face on them."

"Oh, my God!"

"Antonella," Jackie cut in, giving a quick shake of her head, "let's just go with what we have?"

"Narcissistic children?"

"Yes!" she told her eldest daughter. "That's what we have. So deal with it."

"Toni," Troy asked, "are you going to be coming with us?"

"No," Oriana answered.

"How the hell do you know?" Toni demanded.

"Because you've finally found something you're good at. And, even more important, you enjoy something you're good at. You can't walk away from that."

"And you know this because . . . ?"

"Because you've been getting flowers and gift baskets all day from people. The flowers we put on tables all around the house, but the lion security people ate the meat from the baskets and the bear security people ate all the fruit. I have to admit, I'm not sure that security company pays their people enough, because they seem awfully hungry."

"The idiot's right," Kyle told Toni. "Although I've always planned for you to be my personal assistant and business manager . . . it'll be a few years before I need you full-time. It's best you get some outside training before I add you to my team."

"Gee," Toni said dryly. "Thanks, Kyle."

He smiled. "You're welcome."

"Look," Toni said. "We'll worry about all that later. For now I still plan to head home with you guys. Now, everybody upstairs. Get packed."

"You'll need to get movers to transport my marble," Kyle said.

"Can't we buy you new marble when we get home?"

"I've already started!"

"Kyle!"

Jackie took Kyle by his shoulders and turned him toward the door. "We'll discuss this with your father later. For now . . . get packing."

While the kids walked out, Jackie and Toni crouched in front of Freddy.

"You all right?" Toni asked him.

"I thought they'd all be mad at me."

"Nah. Not for something like this." Toni kissed her brother on the cheek. "Now go upstairs and get packed. I'll try to get us out tonight, but if not, definitely tomorrow morning, so be ready. Okay?"

"Okay!" He hugged Toni, then Jackie, before sprinting out of the room and up the stairs.

Toni waited until she heard his little feet hit the second floor before she said, "I'll make sure I set up an appointment with his therapist for the day after tomorrow and get rid of any matches in the house."

"Great. Thanks, baby."

Toni smiled, as always comfortable in her role as sibling protector. "You're welcome, Mom."

Freddy was packing up his suitcase, carefully folding his Batman T-shirt, when Delilah suddenly sat on his bed.

"Hi ya, Del," he said, smiling at his sister.

"Hi, Freddy."

"Where have you been?"

"Out with some friends."

"Did you hear?"

"I did." Delilah leaned in and whispered, "Actually, Toni sent me."

Freddy didn't understand. "Sent you?"

"Yeah. She wants me to take you out of here."

"No. I'm going with the family."

"Oh, hon. She doesn't want you putting them in danger, too."

"But they said—"

"They were just being nice. For Mom. But you want to do what's right for the family, don't you?"

"Of course I do."

She smiled. "Then come with me. I'm going to take you someplace safe."

"Just the two of us?"

"For now. Don't worry. We'll have you back with the rest of the family in no time. But you wouldn't want to risk them, would you? If something happened to them, wouldn't you feel awful?"

It was the first time Freddy had ever felt this way. It came over him, falling on him like a blanket. He knew the word Toni would use, too . . . instinctual. He *instinctually* knew Delilah was lying to him. Had been lying to him. Was still lying to him right now.

"Freddy?"

"What do you really want, Del?" he asked her.

"Where's that notebook, Freddy? The blue composition one you had stashed in your backpack."

"I got rid of it," he said.

"You're lying, Freddy."

He shook his head. He was, but he knew giving it to Del would be wrong. It would be . . . dangerous. "I'm not going to tell you."

"But you know what's in the book by heart, don't you? You can write down exactly what's in there, right?"

Toni had always told him to trust his instincts, and Freddy knew what his instincts were telling him to do now. They were telling him to run.

Freddy turned and ran toward the door. Had his hand on the knob when Delilah caught him from behind and put something over his face that smelled funny.

He tried to fight but . . .

Oriana was in the backyard, putting off packing until she could finish this letter to her favorite teacher. She knew how important it was to make a good impression. Maybe one day she could afford to be a demanding diva with others besides her family, but until then, she'd have to do what she could to make sure those who would be helping her career only had good memories of her. So they would not only remember what an amazing dancer she was but how easy she was to work with.

As she struggled over her second paragraph, she heard the back door open, but didn't bother to raise her head from what she was doing until she heard that Roy guy greeting someone with, "Hey, sweetheart."

Worried he was hitting on Cherise—who God knew, couldn't handle the pressure—Oriana looked up to see the big idiot walk into the kitchen and close the door behind him. Then she heard the side gate open and glanced over. It wasn't Cherise, though—it was Delilah, which Oriana couldn't care less about. But then Oriana saw that her sister held an unconscious Freddy in her arms . . .

Oriana knew he was passed out because poor little Freddy rarely slept. He especially didn't sleep at nine o'clock at night. She shot off the bench and went after her sister, using her hands to flip her body up and over the gate since she didn't want to bother opening it. When she landed on her feet, she charged flat out for Del's back, ramming into her with her full weight.

But Delilah was surprisingly strong. Other than a small stumble, she didn't fall. Instead she turned and shoved Oriana off, then continued walking, heading toward a running car on the street.

Oriana charged again. "Give him to me!" she ordered her sister.

With one arm holding on tight to Freddy, Del grabbed Oriana by the back of the head, turned, and using the energy of that, rammed her face-first into the side of the house.

And that was pretty much the last thing Oriana remembered.

Kyle saw Oriana running and disappearing over the side gate in the backyard. He knew his sister. Oriana didn't run. She didn't jog. She definitely didn't flip herself over six-foot-tall fences—unless she really had to. Glancing at Troy—they'd come out here to fight in peace about . . . something, he couldn't even remember now—Kyle ran after his sister. Unlike Oriana, he had to stop to open the gate, but by the time he made it through, he saw Delilah shove Oriana into the house. Hard. Heard something crack. Saw blood splatter even in the darkness.

"No!"

Kyle ran over to his sister's side, sliding to a stop on his knees. Troy ran past them to follow Delilah as she got into the waiting car and drove off with Freddy.

Troy yelled after the car, just screamed Freddy's name.

When Kyle couldn't wake up Oriana, he leaned his head back and let out a wailing howl until every adult on the street was there.

CHAPTER THIRTY-ONE

Chuck Roberts left his office in the church and walked to the back door. Someone had been knocking for a bit and he'd chosen to ignore it as long as he could. The rest of the church members had gone to the farm, but Chuck had stayed behind because he refused to buy into this con. He knew better.

He and Chris had been friends for a long time and they'd always enjoyed money. But Chuck had no illusions about what they were or where they'd come from. Chris, however, had begun to buy into all this bullshit. Believing the worship. Crazy.

And yet beneficial. Because Chris was so focused on the worshippers—especially the young female ones—he didn't notice that Chuck had been pulling money out of the Cayman accounts and moving them to his own in Geneva. Another couple of days and Chuck was out of here. He'd be leaving the crazy far behind.

Opening the door just a bit to see who was standing there—a lot of homeless people came to the church asking for food or a place to sleep for the night and Chuck was definitely not in the mood to deal with any of that bullshit—he saw a gorgeous, dark-haired woman standing there in tight jeans and a V-neck T-shirt. She smiled at him.

"Hi," she practically purred.

"Hi." Unable to help himself, Chuck eased the door open. "Can I help you?"

Her head tilted and her eyes reflected the streetlight back at him. Like a cat's.

Without thought, only abject fear, Chuck went to close the door in the woman's face, but a hand from behind dug into his hair and a knife pressed to his throat.

"Hello, darlin'," another female voice growled in his ear. "You don't mind, do ya? But me and Malone here have just a couple of questions for ya."

The one he assumed was Malone walked inside the church, closing the door with her foot. She smiled again, and that's when Chuck would swear he saw fangs.

"Come on. Let's go someplace comfortable to talk."

Then the woman who held him, who was so damn strong, dragged him down the hallway and Chuck knew this couldn't possibly end well.

"A notebook?" Toni shook her head at Dee-Ann's words. "What notebook?"

"No idea."

"If all Delilah wanted was a notebook, why didn't she just take it?" Cooper asked. "She had to know that taking Freddy would set us off."

"I can only think Freddy didn't have it for some reason."

"He probably hid it," Oriana said softly while holding a bag of frozen peas against her swollen forehead. "He does that sometimes. Like a Labrador, he'll dig a hole and put something that means a lot to him in it."

"Well, it can't be one of his notebooks," Toni reasoned. "He doesn't care about his own shit. So it had to be something he stole and . . ." She looked across the kitchen table to Irene, but her mother's best friend immediately shook her head.

"I haven't had anything missing and you know I'd notice unless it was food." But then Irene looked off, her hand briefly covering her mouth. "Oh, no."

"What's wrong?"

"I think I know where this started." She rested her elbows on the table, dug her hands into her hair. "Miki."

"Kendrick?" Irene's mentee and friend who they'd just visited at the hotel only a couple of weeks ago. "What about—" Toni nearly slapped her forehead. "The box of tissues."

"The box of tissues."

"He stole a box of tissues?" Cella asked.

"No. But he was alone in Miki's room for a bit. He adores her. He'd take one of her notebooks. His way of keeping her close. He wouldn't give that to Delilah."

"So she took him?" Ricky asked.

"He has a photographic memory. If she couldn't get the notebook, taking him would be just as good."

Standing tall by Cella, Dee-Ann folded her arms across her chest, and stared hard at Toni. "What do you want us to do?"

Toni didn't hesitate. "I want you to find out who she's going to sell this information to. I think they wanted to bypass her and that's why they broke into the house and then just tried to take him." She pushed her hair out of her eyes. "Dee-Ann, I want you to find out where this is coming from and deal with it."

"And you?"

"What do you think? My mother's upstairs sobbing. My father's trying to keep the younger kids calm." She gestured to her fifteen-year-old sister. "She split Oriana's head open." Toni barely managed to bite back a growl when she saw how swollen poor Oriana's face currently was. "I'm going to go get my brother back."

Ricky didn't bother arguing with Toni. There was no point. Instead, he turned to Vic. "What do you have?"

"We traced the license plate number Troy got off that car to a farm upstate. Dug a little, it's owned by the church."

"Good." Ricky focused on his brothers. "Reece, I want you to stay here. I want this place locked down until you hear from me."

"It's done," Reece said, then he got up and walked out of the room.

"Rory, I want you with me."

"Yep."

"Y'all take care of this," Dee-Ann said. "Take Barinov and Malone with you."

"Don't you need backup, too, Dee?" Oriana asked, sounding remarkably kind since that hit on the head.

"Aren't you just the sweetest little thing?"

"No," Oriana answered honestly. "Not really."

Dee snorted and headed out. "Y'all be careful," she ordered before she left.

Toni got to her feet. "Irene—"

"I'll take care of your mother. You just . . . fix this, Antonella. Fix it."

"I will."

Yeah. Ricky didn't doubt that for one second.

Chapter Thirty-two

Dee-Ann stopped the rental car in the driveway, a healthy distance from the mansion. She looked through the windshield and gave a little whistle. For a bunch of classless, lowlife bikers—her daddy's words—the Magnus Pack must have some serious cash lying around in order to live so well in Northern California.

Opening the driver's side door, Dee-Ann stepped out onto the gravel and went to stand in front of the vehicle. She just stood there, waiting. She didn't go to ring the doorbell. She didn't howl to get anyone's attention. It was how one shifter wolf handled entering another shifter wolf's territory.

Dee had been standing there for a good twenty minutes when she heard the roar of engines behind her. She glanced over and saw several tricked out motorcycles ride up the curved driveway. They passed the car and kept going a bit farther before pulling to a stop. The wolves got off the bikes, took off their helmets, and headed into the house. Only one, a female, stopped to look at Dee. She looked but said nothing, and eventually walked into the house, closing the door behind her.

It was another five minutes before that front door was flung open and a female in nothing more than a Dallas Cowboys T-shirt and holding a shotgun came marching out. Yep, this could only be Sara Morrighan, Alpha Female of the Magnus Pack and all-around crazy bitch, according to any other Pack, Pride, or Clan leader who'd had the misfortune of meeting her.

As the She-wolf stormed over to Dee, she cocked the shotgun she had in her hands and Dee really wondered if the insane heifer was just going to shoot a strange wolf on sight or if this was all for show.

A familiar-looking Latina dressed in a very tiny nightie came charging after the angry She-wolf and grabbed hold of the shotgun. The two females struggled over the weapon until the Latina rammed her foot into Morrighan's knee.

"Ow! You whore!"

Yanking the shotgun away from her friend, the Latina backed up and snarled, "I thought we discussed this! No shooting without actual signs of aggression!"

"Just her presence on my territory is aggression!"

"That was *not* on Miki's list!"

That's when Miki stumbled out of the front door, her hand immediately shielding her eyes from the early morning sunlight.

"What the fuck is going on?" the small full-human asked her friends.

"Sara tried to shoot strangers again."

"Sign of aggression!"

Studying Dee through narrow slits, Miki asked, "Hey . . . don't I know you?"

"Dee-Ann Smith." Miki frowned at that reply. "Mate to Ric Van Holtz?" The confused frown worsened. "We met through Irene Conridge?"

"Well . . . I know Irene."

"How," Morrighan asked, "do you have a photographic memory but not remember people?"

"Is that a trick question?"

The Latina sized Dee up. "Didn't I help you get a dress once?"

Eyes wide, the other two females now gazed at Dee.

Annoyed, Dee snapped, "I've been known to wear a dress or two over the years."

Morrighan cringed. "With *those* shoulders?"

Miki had ripped her bag apart but the notebook was gone. Gone. And she hadn't even realized it.

"Well?" Angelina pushed.

Letting out a breath, Miki faced her friends and the She-wolf she should remember but didn't. "I . . . uh . . ."

"Miki."

"Okay. Lady Fullback's right—"

"Hey," the She-wolf immediately complained at the nickname.

"—one of my notebooks is gone."

"What's so special about this notebook?" Sara wanted to know. And when Miki glanced out the window, trying to figure out how to answer, her friends threw up their hands and began saying, "Oh, Miki! No! Not again!"

"You know, bitches, I don't need that accusatory tone."

"Why would you take one of your world-ending notebooks out of this house?"

"It's not world-ending, Angie. I mean . . . whole countries can be destroyed but not the world or anything. You know, plant life would survive. And cars."

That's when Angie came at Miki and they'd barely gotten in a few slaps before Sara got between them and pushed them apart.

"Cut it out! Both of you!"

"What are you blaming me for?" Angie demanded. "She's the one running around with dangerous weapons in her raggedy-ass bag!"

"Not everyone is willing to spend more than fifty bucks on a goddamn bag, you vapid bitch!"

"Stop it!" Sara ordered. "I mean it."

"Besides," Miki went on, pretending that she didn't feel guilty about all of this. "How was I supposed to know that Freddy would go into my bag and steal one of my notebooks?"

"Oh, I don't know," Angie suggested, "maybe because from what you've told us the kid's just like *you.*"

"But why would he steal from *me?*" Miki desperately tried to rationalize. "He loves me."

"Which according to his sister," Lady Fullback of Big Woman Land interjected, "is why he *would* steal from you. Because he wanted something that belonged to one of his favorite people."

"Oh."

"Yeah. Oh."

"The bigger question is who would want that notebook?" Sara asked.

"Anyone who wants to destroy a few countries?" Angie kindly suggested. The bitch. And when Miki glared at her, "Tell me I'm wrong?"

"I just don't like your tone."

"I just don't like your face!"

"For the love of God!" Sara exploded. "Would you cut it!"

They all fell silent, Angie rubbing her forehead. As they did, the bedroom door opened and Conall walked in. Miki's big wolf mate stopped, looked at the women in the room.

"What's going on?" he asked, but before Miki could answer him, he shook his head and said, "You know what? I don't want to know. Instead I'm going to ask, where's my daughter?"

"*Our* daughter," Miki again felt forced to remind him since he continually seemed to forget that fact, " is on my computer in my office."

Conall stared at her. "Really? You let her go on the computer even after that little visit we got last week from the FBI about strange computer use during odd hours when you were out of town? That computer use involving the Pentagon?"

"Well—"

"You know what I'm going to do?" he said calmly but, again, Miki could hear the *tone*. "I'm going to take *our* beautiful daughter to Ihop for breakfast, and while we're gone, you're going to go onto *your* computer and undo whatever the hell she did that could get us all arrested. Okay? Great. Love you." He nodded at the other women. "Ladies."

The door closed behind him and Angie looked at Sara and then they looked at Miki.

"Yeah," she said to her friends' unasked question. "I could do it."

"Do what?" Lady Fullback asked. She took a step back. "What are y'all plannin'?"

"To find out who wants my notebook. That is what you need, isn't it?"

"That's awful risky, darlin'."

Miki looked at Sara again. It was risky but for Freddy she was willing to take the risk. The question, however, was Sara willing to take that risk, too? This was her house and her Pack.

After a moment, Sara nodded. "Do it."

"What are you going to do exactly?" Fullback asked.

Miki got to her feet. "The same thing I almost went to prison for when I was sixteen."

When the She-wolf just gazed at her, Miki shook her head. "Don't worry. As long as I don't hack into the banks again and spread my money to my Dungeons & Dragons friends . . . federal prison time should be minimal."

The She-wolf sighed. "You genius types . . . so much damn work. I don't know how Toni does it."

CHAPTER THIRTY-THREE

It was a farm somewhere in Upstate New York where they all headed. A cheap parcel of land the church had purchased and where they sent their converts when they were ready to move to the next level of mind control.

Funny thing was, they didn't lock the small gate or secure the fence around the acres of property. So Ricky Lee just ambled on in. Just parked the SUV, and walked down the lane. As he walked, the cult members nodded at him, smiled, but didn't stop him. He made sure to smile in return, but he kept moving. He kept his pace brisk, making sure to look like he knew where he was going. Most of the housing was cabins. One-floor deals made of unfinished wood with porta-potties sporadically placed. It wasn't as bad looking as what the Manson gang had back in the day, but it wasn't much better, either.

But he did finally see a large, finished building and he immediately knew that this was where they'd put their "Prophet" as he was called.

That's where Ricky headed. He walked right up the stairs and into the building.

"Hey," he said as he passed several members working on notebook computers.

"Uh . . . sir?"

Ricky kept walking, not stopping until he reached a large set of double doors. He pushed those open and walked inside, closing the doors behind him.

"Well hi there," he said to the three men standing by the long mahogany table.

The one in the middle, looking just like a false prophet would with his worn jeans and sandals, shaggy hair, scraggly beard, and gold watch that probably cost somewhere in the twenty-grand range, smiled a little.

"How y'all doin' today?" Ricky asked.

"You've come for the boy," the prophet said.

Ricky nodded. "I've come for the boy."

"Unfortunately I can't help you."

"And you're gonna regret that decision."

The cheap, wood fence surrounding the cult's property was not exactly a challenge for Livy. She'd been trained at an early age to get around all sorts of fences, walls, armed guards . . . whatever might be between her and what she wanted. Yet Livy was under no illusion that this would be easy. Although she hadn't discussed anything with Toni, Livy knew that Delilah just wanted money. Now that she was eighteen, she wasn't about to spend her life playing second fiddle to the rest of her siblings. Nor would she allow herself to be ruled by Toni's brilliant scheduling skills. She wanted her freedom, but unlike the rest of the world, she wasn't about to do something like *work* to maintain her expensive lifestyle. So she'd come up with this ridiculous plan. Ridiculous because Delilah had to know that Toni wasn't going to just let her run off with Freddy. Of all her siblings, he was the one that Toni would destroy the entire universe to get back. Not because Toni loved him any more than the others but because he was the one that needed her protection more than the others. He was the one whose soul was so pure and loving that they all knew just about anyone with a smile and a lollypop could get the boy involved in all sorts of crap.

Even the twins, at only three years old, had that predatory edge that would keep them generally safe. But Freddy was the puppy who would gleefully romp too far from his mother, and

end up alone with a pride of lions or trampled by a herd of buffalo.

So they all felt an inherent need to protect the boy. Even
Livy, who didn't feel the need to protect anyone but herself.
But there was something about the kid that warmed even Livy's
cold heart.

As Livy moved forward, sniffing the air every few minutes,
trying to locate Freddy while avoiding any of the loser cult
members—joining a cult? Really? Were people really that
pathetic?—that might be nearby, it took her a surprisingly long
time to realize that she wasn't alone.

She stopped, spun around. Vic Barinov was behind her.

"What are you doing?" she asked.

"Following you."

"Why?"

"Because we're all pretty sure you'll be the one to find
Freddy."

"Just stay out of my way."

"How can I be in your way when I've been staying behind
you?"

She was about to answer that when she realized it wasn't
worth the effort.

Turning, Livy headed deeper onto the farm, briefly stopping
when she finally caught Freddy's scent. That's when she began
running . . .

The group had split up, knowing they could cover more
ground that way. Toni was trying to find Freddy's scent but,
deep down, she knew she was really looking for Delilah's. This
had been a long time coming. She knew it. Del knew it.

So when Toni did lock on her sister's scent, she didn't try to
ignore it. Instead she followed it right to one of the few finished
cabins. There were guards outside, but when Toni walked past
them, they didn't try to stop her.

She stepped into the cabin and took it all in. There were cur-
tains over the windows, a large bed, a bathroom, fresh fruit on

the table . . . everything a spoiled sociopath could need while everyone around her was probably starving.

"I knew you'd come yourself," Delilah said as she stepped out of the bathroom. "You could have sent Dee-Ann or that big wolf you've been fucking. But I knew you'd come."

She walked across the room until she stood in front of Toni. "But Freddy's not here."

"I know," Toni said. Then she pulled her arm back and slapped her sister full in the face, knocking her to the floor. Once she had her there, she kicked her in the gut, sending her flipping over.

By the time Del landed, she'd begun to shift. Toni joined her, her limbs, torso, and head changing, her hands turning into claws, her fangs bursting from her gums. Just as she shook off her clothes, Delilah rammed into her with such force, they went flying across the room and out the open front door.

Vic watched the bungalow where he and Livy were sure little Freddy Jean-Louis Parker was being held. On the outside, he counted four guards. All male. All armed with knives. No guns that he could see, but the way they moved suggested they'd had some training. He doubted, though, any of them had been in the military, or were cops.

He did think, however, that they were fervent believers.

Believers worried Vic more than well-trained military personnel. Because there were no limits to what true believers would do to protect their belief system.

So he'd want to move carefully on this. He wouldn't risk the safety of the boy.

With all that in mind, Vic turned to the female next to him but quickly discovered that he was standing alone.

Biting back an annoyed growl, he looked around until he finally found her—on the bungalow roof.

How she got up there, he didn't want to know.

Livy looked at him, then pointed at the four guards outside the building. Vic briefly debated killing them but couldn't. At least not yet. They hadn't done anything to prove they were anything more than desperate full-humans in need of a messiah. So he decided to go with the tried-and-true misdirection.

"I know you think you're doing the right thing," the prophet told Ricky Lee. "By coming here for the child. But you don't understand."

"What don't I understand? Explain it to me."

"It's true. Delilah did take him for financial gain. To help my church, because she loves me."

Ricky Lee chuckled. "Son . . . that girl don't love nobody."

The prophet's eyes turned steely. "She loves *me*. She loves the god I represent. And she knows I've seen the future. The boy has to be here . . . because he is the ultimate darkness. He will bring the beginning of the end."

Ricky Lee sighed. "Oh, Lord . . . I was hoping you were just a good ol' fashioned con man. Trying to make money off the boy like Delilah. But you're a true believer of your own bullshit, ain't ya? And trust me when I say that'll cost you. In tears. Because if you think that girl is going to give up cash so you can start the end of days . . . you've lost your damn mind."

"I'm sorry you don't understand."

"I'm sorry you think I came alone."

Panic raced across the man's face. "Keep him here!" he ordered his men before running out of the building.

The two already in the room moved closer to Ricky Lee, and more full-human males walked in through the now-open doorway, surrounding him, all of them watching Ricky close. They were willing to follow their Prophet's orders no matter what. Which, of course, was real unfortunate for them.

What with his big brother coming through that open window and unleashing his claws . . .

Livy waited until the hybrid had lured the guards away from the building. He was smart about it, too, luring them away with noises and possible sightings of something moving in the trees.

Once they were far enough away, Livy climbed her way up the brick of the bungalow's chimney and inside. She worked quickly, easing her way down the flue until she was right over the fireplace. Thankfully it was summer and nothing was lit, because that would be damn uncomfortable.

Livy listened carefully and she heard nothing but humming. She smiled when she realized that the song being hummed was from the Dead Kennedys. A little trick Toni had taught Freddy. "Anytime you get nervous, hum 'Man with the Dogs,' instead of picking up a lighter."

"Man with the Dogs" was one of Paul's favorite Dead Kennedy songs from back in the day, so Livy now knew she was right where she needed to be.

Livy put her hands out and, shimmying down a little farther, rested them on the empty wood grate. She lifted her head and looked around the one-room bungalow. Although she scented the few people who'd been in and out of this room, she didn't see or hear anything else, so she brought the rest of her body out of the chimney and slowly used her hands to crawl out of the fireplace and onto the hardwood floor.

Once she was completely out, she stood up and began to walk toward Freddy. He was busy with a coloring book. Although he wasn't really coloring as much as blacking out, the black crayon he held no more than a stump as he blacked out each page of the book and continued to hum his father's favorite song.

The poor kid was completely freaked out, completely panicked, and very close to losing it. In fact, the cult was lucky they didn't have a fire going in the fireplace or the kid would have brought the entire farm down to the ground by now.

Livy, not wanting to say anything and possibly alert anyone outside the building, softly clicked her tongue against her teeth.

Freddy looked up at Livy and began to smile. But when it faded and his eyes suddenly looked past her, Livy knew someone was behind her.

A strong arm went around her shoulder, and before Livy could fight, a needle was jammed into the side of her throat and poison was forced into her veins. The effect was immediate, her body convulsing, her lungs stopping, her heart seizing. She only had a second to think, *"Shit,"* before whatever they'd given her, killed her.

The sisters rolled into the middle of the road, Toni stopping to shift back to human so she could punch Delilah in the face. It was so satisfying punching the little bitch.

By now, most of the cult members had run out to see what was going on, then stopped to watch, shocked and horrified. Unable to move.

Del shifted back, too. She punched Toni in the face, the stomach. Then they shifted to jackal once more and dug into each other's throats with their fangs.

Freddy was still humming when that man named John walked away from Livy. She was lying on the floor, no longer moving, her body frozen. It looked like one of those shows Freddy saw his parents watch at night that had lots of cops staring at people on the ground and saying important things before tracking down the one who "did it."

John stopped a bit away from Freddy and stared down at him.

"He says you're the one to bring the ultimate darkness," John said, although Freddy didn't know what he meant. From what Freddy knew, Delilah jut wanted him to write out the contents of Miki's very cool notebook. Something Freddy would not do. "He says you're to be protected. So we'll protect you. You'll be safe here."

Freddy would only be safe with his mom and dad and with Toni. He didn't want to be here. He wanted to go home.

But the way John was staring at him, Freddy was just starting to think that he might never go home. That he might be stuck here with these too-nice people that terrified him.

Then, behind John, he saw Livy twitch. First her hands, then her feet. Then she sat up straight, her eyes blinking open. Freddy's heart began to race, but he tried not to show it.

Livy looked around a moment until her gaze locked on the back of John's head. She abruptly hopped up, completely silent, until she was crouching on the balls of her feet. She looked at

Freddy and with her forefinger, made a circling motion. Livy had done that before when she'd snuck into the window of his parents' home back in Washington. Between them, it had always meant, "I don't want you to see this so you have nothing to testify to in a court of law." It was their little joke, but Freddy knew it was serious now.

So, without getting up, he turned his body around until he faced the wall and, when the screaming started, he began humming his daddy's favorite song . . . "Man with the Dogs."

Because that would keep him calm. Calm was important for him; otherwise he did things, like set fires and steal.

And, let's be honest, it was stealing that had gotten him into all this.

Del, fed up with all this bullshit, shifted back to human and shoved her sister off her. By the time Toni landed a few feet away, she'd also turned back to her human form.

Bloody and bruised, the sisters got to their feet.

"You'll regret what you did," Del told her. "No one—"

"Shut up." Toni looked at something over her shoulder. "Your Messiah's here," she whispered.

Barely able to not roll her eyes, Delilah slowly turned until she was face to face with Chris.

He gawked at her as if she sported horns and a tail. Then again, of course he would. Not because of what she was, but because he now understood she was what he wasn't. Special. Different.

Powerful.

"What are you?"

"Chris—" she began.

"Kill her!" he ordered his followers. "Kill the insolent whore!"

But no one moved. No one followed his orders. So, panicking that it was all slipping away, Chris grabbed a knife from one of his bodyguards and, screaming, charged Delilah.

Del couldn't even *pretend* to be interested by this new drama.

★ ★ ★

Ricky and his brother changed back to human, threw on their jeans, and charged outside, following the sounds of screaming. They weren't Toni's screams, though, so he wasn't too concerned.

As they neared the crowd, the group parted and Ricky and Rory cut through. But the brothers had to quickly step apart as skin that—Ricky was guessing—had once been attached to the church's great prophet, Chris, landed wetly on the ground near their feet.

Rory gaped down at the mess on the ground before telling his brother, "That's just wrong."

Yeah. Ricky already knew that.

Delilah stepped back so that she could keep her eye on both the brothers and Toni. She motioned to the cult followers and, like the tragic lemmings they were, they all stood behind the blood-soaked female who'd killed their messiah. And, it seemed, had taken his place.

Staring at them with those eyes that were so like Toni's and yet so different because there was no life behind them, Delilah asked, "What am I going to do with you now, big sister?"

Toni chuckled at that and pointed at Delilah's chest. The young woman looked down and saw the telltale red dot locked on her heart.

"I've heard," Toni explained, "that Cella Malone can hit a target from more than a mile away."

"Shit," Delilah growled out.

A roar went out from somewhere in the distance and the cult members all trembled in fear as if hearing the word of God. But Ricky knew it was just the roar of a tiger-grizzly hybrid.

"Let's move," Ricky said to Toni.

She nodded and naked, she walked forward toward her sister. When they were only a few inches apart, Delilah asked, "Is this where you give me dire warnings, Toni? Tell me what you'll do if I come near Freddy or the family again?"

"No," Toni said. "This is where I say good-bye." She leaned in and kissed her sister on the cheek.

"I love you," Toni said simply and, for the first time, Ricky saw what Toni had been trying to tell him. Delilah had no idea what her sister was talking about. She didn't understand why her sister wasn't killing her, ordering the rest of them to shift and tear the cult apart. The threat of what Toni would do if Delilah came near the family again was there, unspoken. Not *needing* to be spoken. But the fact that Toni still loved her, even if she would never like her or trust her or want to see her again was beyond Delilah's simple ability to reason.

Delilah would never understand love or affection or what it meant to be part of anything that meant more than one's own life. She would never be part of a family or a good group of friends or a pack or pride.

And, Ricky had to admit, he kind of felt sorry for her. He couldn't think of a more miserable way to live.

Toni had almost reached the spot where they'd left the SUVs when she saw Livy standing by one of the vehicles with Freddy in her arms.

Letting out a sob, Toni charged over to them and pulled her brother into her own arms, holding him tight against her. Neither cared that she was naked with a good amount of blood on her.

"Freddy, are you okay? Tell me you're okay," she begged.

"I'm fine." His little arms were tight around her neck, his legs around her waist. "But you may want to check on Livy," he whispered.

With her brother safe, Toni felt confident enough to now notice her best friend.

Livy did look a little under the weather. Pale, sweaty, shaking, and also covered in blood.

"God, Livy, what happened?"

She shrugged, coughed, and spit on the ground. "Nothing I couldn't handle."

"Poison?" Toni asked. It was one of the coolest things about honey badgers—they were really fucking hard to kill.

"From the taste of it," Livy replied, "snake-based." She held up both her thumbs. "My favorite."

Toni, still crying a little, grinned at her friend. *Thank you,* she mouthed.

"What else are people who don't hate you for?"

"People who don't hate you, Livy, are called friends."

"Whatever."

Ricky came up behind Toni, smiled at Freddy. "Hey, little man."

"Hi, Ricky."

"You ready to go home?"

"I really am. I'm relatively certain . . . this is too much excitement for a seven-year-old."

Toni, now laughing *and* crying, hugged her brother even tighter. "You're absolutely right, little brother. It is."

"How's your face?" the wolf asked Oriana while they sat at the kitchen table . . . waiting.

"It's been better," she admitted, her nose hurting as it worked to heal. All she knew was that the swelling had better be down before her next class or she would be absolutely livid!

"You know," the wolf went on, "you're kind of tough."

It was a weird statement, but she couldn't help feeling it was kind of a compliment.

"Thanks, uh . . ."

"Reece. Ricky Lee's brother."

"Right. Well, thanks, Reece."

"Sure. You see, not everyone can take a hit like that to the head."

"That's because she has an exceptionally hard head."

"Shut up, Kyle."

"You shut up!"

"Both of you shut up," Cooper warned.

"Have you thought about trying ice hockey?"

Surprised, Oriana, and everyone else at the table, looked at the wolf.

"No," Oriana finally admitted when he kept staring at her as if expecting a serious answer to that ridiculous question.

"You should. I bet you'd make a mean little forward."

"I will . . . strange, burly man."

He grinned. "Darlin', are you sweet on me?"

Oriana gawked. *"No."*

"Don't get your hopes up, though; you're a little too young for me."

Before Oriana could process any of that, Dennis ran into the kitchen. "Freddy's home!" he cheered. "Freddy's home!"

The siblings all stared at each other for a long moment. Then, as one, they bolted away from the table and ran out to greet their brother and welcome him home.

Chapter Thirty-four

Toni reached into the refrigerator and pulled out one of the bottles of orange juice. Now that she was home, and Freddy was safe, she was exhausted. But she still had some things to take care of before she could get any rest so she was hoping a couple of glasses of orange juice would perk her up a bit.

With bottle in hand, she closed the refrigerator door and turned. That's when she came face to face with Novikov's fiancée.

"Oh. Hi, Bland."

The fiancée's brown eyes narrowed. "It's *Blayne*. And you can't drink that."

Toni glanced down at the orange juice. "I can't?" Because she was pretty sure she could.

"It's been opened."

"Yes. It has. That's bound to happen when you have two thousand people in your house." Because it seemed everyone and their mother had come to Toni's house, including all the Carnivores, most of Ricky Lee's Pack, and almost all of Llewellyn Security's advanced protection team. Plus the wild dogs from across the street kept wandering in and out of their temporary home like they owned the . . . oh, wait. The wild dogs *did* own the place.

"No worries!" Blayne chirped. "When Bo and I came over here I made him stop so I could pick up *several* bottles of orange juice for the entire family." She opened the refrigerator. "This way there's no problem with—"

Blayne gasped and jumped back, making Toni's hackles rise.

"What's wrong?" Toni asked, quite aware she sounded snappy.

"They've all been opened. Someone opened each bottle and drank a little bit out of each one."

Spinning around, Blayne glared at Livy.

Still recovering from her poisoning, Livy sat at the kitchen table, her elbow on the hard wood, the right cheek of her still pale and sweaty face resting on her raised fist.

"What are you looking at me for?" Livy asked blandly, her voice weaker than usual.

"I know you did this," Blayne accused. "This was you!"

"I don't know what you're talking about," Livy said. But when Blayne turned back to the refrigerator to stare at those bottles of juice, Livy looked up at Toni and mouthed, *It was totally me.*

Toni silently laughed but they both stopped what they were doing when Blayne spun back around, her accusing gaze bouncing back and forth between them.

Thankfully, before the wolfdog could snap her leash, Ricky Lee walked into the kitchen.

"Hey," he said, smiling at Toni. "My momma's here and Ronnie Lee's with her. Thought you could come out to the living room and meet her."

Toni felt a bolt of panic shoot through her system that did manage to wake her up but also brought out her anxiety. "What? Why?" she demanded. "Why do I need to meet your sister? No. No. That's okay. I'll just stay in here and hide. Or maybe I'll chew on the table leg. It looks like it needs a good chewing."

"In case you're not sure," Livy calmly told Ricky, "she *is* about to blow."

"Yeah," Ricky sighed. "I can see that."

Ricky didn't know what the problem was. Toni had gone toe-to-toe with Novikov, Russian bears, Cella Malone. Hell, she'd faced his *mother* and won her over. So why meeting Ronnie Lee would freak Toni out like this, he didn't know.

"Come here, darlin'," he coaxed.

She started to walk over to him but Blayne caught hold of the bottle of juice in Toni's hands and there was a brief—and rather ridiculous—skirmish between the pair. Blayne eventually won and she held that bottle of juice to her chest like it was the last bit of moisture on the planet.

Shaking her head, Toni walked over to Ricky. When she stood in front of him, he slipped both arms around her waist and pulled her in close.

"All right, tell me what's wrong."

"What if she doesn't like me?"

"How can she not like you? You're so dang cute. Besides, you already won over my momma."

"This is your *sister*, Ricky Lee."

"So if Kyle didn't like me, you'd kick me to the curb?"

"Of course not," she quickly told him. "But if Coop didn't like you, you'd be out on your ass."

Coop came through the kitchen door at that moment and said to Ricky, "And don't forget the power I wield, Wolf Boy of the Lost People."

Ricky frowned. "I don't even know what that means."

Coop opened the refrigerator and pulled out a bottle of orange juice—that Blayne quickly yanked from his hand.

The jackal gazed at his now-empty hand before looking at the wolfdog and asking, "Uh . . . Blayne?"

Blayne snarled, forcing Coop to step back, and carried the bottle to the sink.

Coop leaned back against the refrigerator. "I have no idea what's going on . . . but I'm *fascinated*."

The back kitchen door opened and Novikov walked in with Freddy. Both were covered in what seemed to be an inordinate amount of dirt and carrying a battered, dirt-covered notebook.

Toni pulled out of Ricky's arms and faced the pair. "What have you two been doing?"

"Getting the notebook like you told us to."

"I said get the notebook. I didn't say roll around in the dirt like two untrained Labradors."

"How do you know that's what happened?" Novikov asked.

"Yeah!" Freddy added with some forcefulness, but when his sister raised an eyebrow at him, he quickly stepped behind Novikov.

Toni shook her finger at Novikov. "Do not be a bad influence on my brother."

"Who says I am?"

"Did you let him swing from your tusks like a monkey?"

"They're not tusks," Blayne snarled as she carried more bottles of orange juice to the sink. "They're fangs. Like the mighty saber-toothed cat of yore."

Coop looked at his sister. "Yore?"

"Shut it!" Blayne snapped.

"Are you throwing out all that orange juice?"

Blayne pointed a damning finger at Livy. "It's *her* fault!"

Livy raised a finger and they all silently waited for her to shoot back a retort. But after nearly a full minute, she suddenly jumped up from the table and tore out the back door.

Smirking, Blayne nodded. "That, my friends, is karma."

"That, Blayne," Toni corrected, "is snake poison."

With a shrug, Blayne went back to pouring the perfectly good juice into the sink. "You say tomato . . ." she muttered.

Toni found her mother sitting on the couch with Ricky's mother. The rest of the kids were either on the couch with them or on the floor in front of them. They were all watching TV and eating popcorn. Thankfully, it seemed that Ricky's sister had wandered off—much to Toni's relief. She was more than happy to face that particular hurdle another time.

"Where's Irene?" Toni asked her mother.

"Bathroom, I think."

"Well, I have the notebook."

"Good," her mother said around a mouthful of popcorn. "Irene will get it back to Miki."

"Where is little Freddy?" Miss Tala asked.

"He and Novikov are bonding."

Jackie's eyebrows went up. "Which entails . . . what? Exactly?"

Before Toni could answer, a shifted Novikov charged by the living room entrance in all of his fifteen feet of bear-lion glory with Freddy hanging onto his back, giggling hysterically. Her feet frozen to the spot she stood on, Toni reached her arm out, somehow believing she could pluck her insane baby brother from Novikov's back.

As Novikov romped up the stairs, Blank came charging after him.

"I'll get 'em!" she screamingly promised. *"I'll get 'em."*

As the three of them disappeared up the stairs, Ricky Lee ambled into the room, hands dug into the back pockets of his jeans.

Toni gestured to the stairs. "It didn't occur to you to not let *that* happen?"

He shook his head. "Nope."

Disgusted, Toni sighed, and looked back at her mother, which was when Ricky felt the need to add, "Don't worry. I wouldn't let that happen with our kids."

That's when *everyone* in the room focused on them, the eyebrows of *both* mothers now raised.

"What?" Ricky asked. "Why y'all lookin' at us like that?"

"Do you really think," Kyle asked, "that a Jean-Louis Parker would ever lower him or herself to be permanently involved with a *Reed*?"

Miss Tala looked at Toni's brother. "I don't think I heard you correctly, Kyle Jean-Louis Parker. Especially if some young jackal I know ever wants to taste my award-winning chocolate chip cookies again."

Kyle forced a smile at Ricky. "Please, take my sister and permanently enslave her to your backwoods way of life. I'm so excited for her."

"Kyle!" Toni snapped.

"What?"

Toni held up the notebook. "Where is Aunt Irene so I can just give her this?"

"There's an earthworm on that thing," Troy pointed out.

And, in response, Toni squealed and tossed the notebook at

her mother, but her aim was bad and she ended up hitting Cherise in the forehead.

Cringing, Toni quickly apologized. "Cherise, I am so sorry."

"No, no. It's all right. I do so love to randomly get hit in the face with nature."

"You're frightened of earthworms?" Ricky asked her, his voice low and right by her ear. She could tell he was grinning just from the sound of his voice.

"They're *gross*."

"Princess."

"Shut up."

"You," came an accusatory voice from the archway, and Jess the wild dog marched in, dragging a clearly mortified Johnny DeSerio with her.

"Oh, hello, Jess," Jackie said with a smile. "How are you doing?"

"Don't 'hello, Jess' me."

Realizing this was bad, Toni immediately stepped in. "What's wrong?"

"Show them," Jess ordered Johnny.

"Ma—"

"Show them."

"Show us what?" Toni gently urged.

"I got this email from a . . ." He studied the piece of paper he held in his hand. "Uh, Donato Mantovani?"

Immediately recognizing the name, Toni's mother sat up straight, the bowl of popcorn barely saved from falling to the floor by a quick-handed Miss Tala. "What did he say?" Jackie demanded. "What did he say?"

"I . . . I don't think it's what you're hoping for, Jackie."

"Just tell me what he said."

"He said, 'I received the MP3s of your music sent by Signora Jean-Louis for my evaluation, and I can only say that your music did not offend me.' "

There was nearly a minute of silence before Jackie clapped her hands together and cheered, "I knew it! *I knew it!*"

Confused, Jess Ward snapped, "What is wrong with you, woman? How can you think this is positive?"

Undaunted, Jackie explained, "It's incredibly positive."

"It is?" Johnny asked.

"Do you know what he said to me about *my* music when I had a private audience with him? 'What *was* that?' "

"He told me," Cherise interjected, "that there was no shame in being a good wife and mother."

Coop, who'd walked into the room a few minutes before, offered, "He told me that I was nearly tolerable. Sort of."

"Wait," Jess cut in. "Who is this guy?"

"The long-time conductor of the Milan Philharmonic," Toni told her.

Grinning, Jackie added, "I played with the Milan Philharmonic when I was eight years old. By the time I was ten, I was playing for kings."

"I played with the Philharmonic when I was sixteen," Cherise added. "And with the London Philharmonic for Her Majesty, about two years after that."

"I was nine," Coop said. "I had my first record deal the following year."

"Wait, wait." Johnny gripped the piece of paper in his hand, his gaze on the floor. "So what you're saying is . . ." He shook his head. "What are you saying?"

Jackie stood up. "That we need to get you ready. Based on that email, I think we've got . . . three months?"

"Maybe," Coop hedged.

"Right. Maybe three months before you're playing on stage for an audience in Milan."

Johnny shook his head. "Yes, but . . ."

Jess faced her adopted son, her smile wide and bright like the sun. "*Now* can I get you that Stradivarius?"

"God, Ma, *no!*"

Livy was resting against a tree, her eyes closed, her body slowly recovering from the recent poisoning. She loved how tough she was to kill but sometimes the recovery could be a bitch. Especially when vomiting was involved. She hated vomiting.

A cool towel was pressed to her forehead and she opened her eyes expecting to see Toni, but it was that big Russian bear-tiger hybrid crouching in front of her. If she remembered correctly, Toni said his name was Barinov. Vic Barinov . . . maybe.

"You all right?" he asked.

"I'm not dead so, ya know . . . win."

He chuckled a little. "Very true."

"Where is everyone?"

"The living room I think. Do you want me to get Toni for you?"

"Please don't. She's got enough to worry about and by tomorrow, I'll be fine. And I don't need her fussing. I hate fussing."

"Yeah. I could tell that about you." He took her hand and pressed her fingers to the wet cloth, silently telling her to hold it in place. While she did, he opened up a can of ginger ale and handed it to her. "Dee-Ann was here, but she had to go. She said she'd be back later. She wants to talk to you."

Livy sipped the ginger ale. It was wonderfully cold and just what she needed—minus the fussing from Toni and her clan. That was the best part. "Do you know what she wants?"

"I'm not sure."

"Best guess?"

"There's someone our organization has been searching for. A full-human hunter. Those in charge want him. Dead or alive. And they probably need you for some breaking and entering."

"Oh."

"You don't seem surprised."

"It's what shifter Kowalskis do." She thought a moment before adding. "And Yangs." Her mother's people. "We break. We enter. We steal expensive shit."

"And mine used to tear houses off their foundations and eat the contents. The human contents. So we all have our pasts. You don't have to be trapped by it."

"No. I don't. But I also don't like full-human assholes that use us as prey. That really pisses me off."

Grinning—and he had a very nice grin—the hybrid sat down across from her and remarked, "I'm sensing lots of things piss you off, Livy Kowalski."

"And you'd be absolutely right."

"Are you sure you don't want us to go with you?"

"No." Delilah stroked the arm of her driver, John. He was one of her guards now. He'd die for her and she knew it. She used it against him whenever she could, but not if it meant putting herself in danger.

That was something she'd never do.

"I'll be right back. All of you stay out here," she said to the acolytes. They thought she was a being from the great beyond, a power sent to them directly from God.

She wasn't, but why bother them with the little details?

Delilah got out of the car and walked into the warehouse. She knew this location well, had played Texas hold 'em with the mob guys here on more than one occasion.

But, as the door closed behind Delilah, her nostrils filled with the powerful scent of blood and death. So thick she began to immediately salivate.

She turned to go, instinctively knowing the American agents from some shady division of the CIA she'd arranged to meet with were dead. She'd had it all set up. Remembering enough of that stupid notebook to fake a copy, she'd planned to hand off the book, get her money, and be gone before they realized it was completely useless. It was such a perfect plan, she'd been mad at herself that she hadn't thought of it earlier. But before she could get the door open a big She-wolf hand slammed against it, holding it shut.

"Hey, Delilah," a voice said against her ear.

"Dee-Ann. You come here to kill me?"

"No."

"Then what do you want?"

"Heard your sister took the high road. I ain't got no high road. So listen up, little girl. I already killed your friends. And the only reason you're still alive is because you're one of us. But I can end that right quick. And I will if you make me. You can play with these idiots who worship you all you want—but step outside the cult even a little bit, and you'll never be able to hide from me. Understand?"

"Yeah." Delilah sighed, unable to keep the boredom and frustration out of her voice.

She wasn't frightened by this She-wolf, but she knew her well enough to know that Dee-Ann Smith would have no problem killing her, and Delilah wasn't in the mood to die anytime soon.

One really had to know when to push and when to back off. She prided herself on understanding those things.

And Dee-Ann Smith was not someone anyone with intelligence wanted to push.

So when Smith moved her hand away from that door, Delilah went back out to those who waited for her and let them take her back to the compound, knowing that the only dangerous thing there was herself.

The car door opened and Dee-Ann got inside.

Irene started the car before asking, "All done?"

"Yup."

"Good. Give her a few years. Let her fade away." Irene started the car. "Then when the family's pushed her out of their collective minds . . . wipe her from this planet."

Dee-Ann nodded at the order from her boss's wife. "Okey-dokey."

It had been a really long day and an even longer night. Not bad, but long. Toni carried a sleeping Freddy into his bedroom and carefully placed him on his bed. She untied his little Converse sneakers and pulled them off, placing them on the floor very neatly, the way he liked. Not like Kyle who sent his shoes flying across the room, when he remembered to take them off at all before going to bed.

"Toni?"

She sat on the bed and smiled down at her baby brother. "Mhmm?"

"Are you mad at me? About Delilah?"

"No. Not at all."

"Are you mad about me taking Miki's book?"

"No. I'm not mad."

"Disappointed?"

"Not that either." Especially with that damn notebook out of their lives and back on its way to Miki Kendrick by way of someone from Uncle Van's organization. She'd thought Dee-Ann would take care of returning the notebook herself but she'd said she had something else to do. Toni knew better than to ask for further info on that.

"But in future," she went on to her brother, "let's avoid taking things from anyone but especially from those we know for a fact can destroy the universe if so inclined."

Freddy giggled even as his eyes began to close again. "Okay. Will we still have to go back home?"

"To Washington? No. I think we'll stay the summer now that everything is resolved."

"Good. I want to see Auntie Irene make my professor at the college cry. She promised she would."

"And we both know she always keeps her promises."

"Yes." He turned over onto his side. "When the summer's over, Toni, you'll have to stay here."

"I will?" she asked, amused. "Why?"

"Because Ricky loves you."

Toni barely managed to stop making that panicked choking sound that always freaked her mother out and, instead, asked, "And you know that how?"

"He looks at you the way that Daddy looks at Mommy. And if you leave him now, his heart will break. And Mommy said heartbreak is the worst."

"Oh, is it?"

"It is. And I like Ricky Lee. So you can't break his heart."

"Is that an order?"

"Yes."

"Then I'll keep that in mind."

"I love you, Toni."

"I love you, too, Freddy." She leaned in and kissed her brother's cheek. "Now get some sleep. Tomorrow we're all going to FAO Schwartz."

"The toy store?"

"Yes."

He turned his head, looking at her over his little shoulder, his eyes glinting like the wild animal he truly was from the light streaming in from the hallway. "Why would we want to do that?"

Toni could only sigh. "Only a Jean-Louis Parker child would ask that particular question about a toy store."

After another kiss on her brother's forehead, Toni headed to her own room. She passed her other siblings' rooms, hearing Kyle and Troy bickering behind one door, Zoe and Zia chatting to each other in some language they'd made up in the last couple of days in another. Little Dennis snored like a rutting rhino in his room while Oriana was gossiping on her damn phone with another dancer about which dance teacher was sleeping with which student. Toni paused at that but then decided it was too late to handle that potential situation well when she was this tired, so she kept moving. Her parents were still downstairs in the living room with Ricky's mother. She could hear laughter and was relieved that they were all getting along so well.

Cherise and Cooper were watching *Excalibur* in Coop's room. A film the three of them had watched two million times, she was sure. She briefly thought about joining them but, again, exhaustion won out.

She continued on to her room but stopped in the doorway. Ricky, fully dressed, was asleep on top of the covers, his Tennessee Titans ball cap still on his head, his back resting against the headboard. And she had to admit, nothing had really ever looked so perfect before.

Kicking off her running shoes, Toni crawled onto the bed. By the time she reached Ricky, he'd opened his arms to her. She snuggled up to his chest, resting her cheek against his shoulder and wrapped her arms around his waist. Ricky's legs were on either side of her, his chin resting on top of her head.

"Ricky Lee?"

"Mhmm?"

"I'm glad you waited for me tonight."

"Wait for you?" His arms encircled her, held her tight. "Darlin' . . . where else would I be?"

EPILOGUE

Toni looked over all the food on the kitchen table. "Mom, do we really need all this food?"

Her mother stood beside her. "I just don't know. I was told the most important thing was for the wild dogs to have ample chocolate, so I took care of that. I have a whole picnic table set up outside for that. But when I heard your entire hockey team would be attending, and those lions that are part of the Smith Pack, then I figured we'd need more food. Thankfully, Blayne—"

"Who?"

Her mother bumped Toni with her hip. "Be nice to her! She suggested the caterer," she said, pointing out the window at the team getting the food tables organized. "They apparently handle shifter weddings and all-lion events, which seems to be some sort of code meaning they could feed anyone." Her mother clutched her hands together. "I just want everything to be perfect."

"Are you still sucking up to the dogs, Mom? I mean, they seem to be entrusting you with Johnny now that Donato is interested in him."

"I've always felt you can never suck up enough in some instances. This is one of those instances."

Jackie reached out, and moved a few of the side dishes around. Then, suddenly, she asked something that she hadn't before, her gaze still focused on the table in front of her, "Delilah won't be coming home . . . will she?"

She made it sound like she meant, "Would Delilah be coming home for the party?" But Toni knew what her mother was really asking her. Knew it was hard for her to ask such a thing about her own child. A child she'd given birth to and had loved like she'd loved all her other children. But even so, something had gone wrong. And nothing they did now would change that. They both knew it.

So Toni wasn't surprised at her mother's relieved expression when she replied, "No, Mom. She won't be. But don't worry, she's in a good place now." As good a place as they could hope for anyway. Hey, it wasn't a prison cell or a shallow grave.

Her mother suddenly hugged her. "I love you, Antonella. I love you more than you will ever understand."

Toni hugged her mother back. "I love you, too, Mom."

The doorbell rang and Jackie pulled away. "They're here," she announced. "I'll go let them in."

"Okay."

Jackie walked out and that's when Toni heard, "Pssst. Toni?"

"Dad?"

Her father eased into the room from another doorway. "Where's your mother?"

"She went to answer the door."

"We have a problem."

Toni sighed. "Uh-oh. What now?"

He leaned down and whispered to her, "The Royal Ballet wants your sister."

"What? She's only fifteen."

"Let me rephrase . . ." And that's when Toni rolled her eyes. She loved her father but . . . oy.

"The Royal Ballet *School* has offered her a spot in order to train her for the Royal Ballet."

"That makes sense."

"And then there was the call I got before that—"

"You got another call?"

"From this art school for gifted children in Milan. They want Kyle."

"Well—"

"And then—"

"There's more?"

"Well, this one I've been kind of keeping to myself."

"Because that's a good idea."

"There's been so much going on."

"What is it, Dad?"

"Troy was accepted to Harvard undergrad in their math department."

"Of course he was."

"That one I'm not sure what to do about."

Toni could hear her mother and some of the guests heading this way, so she turned to her father and said, "You're going to have to let Oriana and Kyle go. Coop can keep an eye on them when he's doing his European and Russian tour in the fall. Plus, we have lots of contacts in both Milan and London, so no worries there. As for Troy, he's too young. I think you should look at Aunt Irene's University for his undergrad. By the time he's ready to go for his master's or PhD, he can go to Harvard without a problem. And trust me, they'll still want him."

"Okay." He hugged her, and Toni wondered what the hell was going on.

"I'm so proud of you, baby."

"Me?" Toni had to laugh at that. "The Royal Ballet didn't call about me, Dad."

"But none of that would have been possible for any of the kids without you. Never forget that, Toni. I know I won't." He kissed her forehead just as Jackie and a pack of wild dog children walked into the kitchen, heading to the backyard.

"Toni!" the pups cheered.

"Hey, guys! Where's Johnny?"

"He's coming," one of the kids said.

Then another screamed, "There's chocolate out here!"

They took off running, quickly followed by the adults of the wild dog Pack.

The three Jean-Louis Parkers huddled together until the

danger had passed, then they all let out relieved breaths. "Good Lord," Jackie said. "It's just chocolate."

"Yeah, Mom. I probably wouldn't say that around *them*."

Ricky moved up behind Toni and put his arm around her waist.

"Where have you been?" she demanded, sounding adorably cranky. He knew why, too . . . it took a lot for a body to manage wild dog pups.

"I had a job with Reece."

"Everything go all right?"

"Yep. Just fine." He leaned down and kissed her neck.

"You better stop . . . my Dad is totally watching you."

"He loves me. He's just not ready to admit it yet."

"Yeah. You go on believing that."

Ricky stepped away from Toni and took her hand. "Come on."

"Where?"

He didn't answer, just pulled her inside the house and up the stairs to her bedroom. He closed the door and got right to it.

"I might as well cut to the point here and tell you that I'm in love with you and I want you to be my mate."

"Are you sure about that? Because you sound awfully pissy about it."

"I am positive, and I sound pissy because I have no idea how you're going to respond and that makes me tense."

"I guess my only concern is that you don't understand what you're getting yourself into."

"You mean having Novikov hanging around? Because as long as he's picking on Reece, I really don't care."

"No. But there's not just me. There's my entire family. Even if I stay here—"

"*If?*"

"Although it's highly likely that I will stay . . . my family will never be far away. In other words, I don't come unattached. The Jean-Louis Parkers never do."

"I'll put up with yours if you put up with mine."

"What's wrong with yours?"

Ricky walked over to the window and motioned Toni over. He pushed the window open and she leaned out. Together they watched Dee-Ann, Sissy Mae, and Ronnie Lee loudly sing "Rocky Top" to Brendon and Mitch Shaw.

"What's wrong with that . . . other than they are supremely out of tune."

"The Shaw brothers hate that song. A hate so strong, mind, that it's almost become a living, breathing thing. Which is why the females are singing it to them."

"Because the brothers hate it?"

"Yep."

"That seems cruel."

"Yep."

"Yet highly amusing." She pointed over to Kyle. "See how swollen his head is?"

"You mean that lump?"

"Uh-huh."

"Yeah. I see it."

"He got that from Oriana when she physically attacked him with one of her toe shoes."

"Again?"

"Do you know why?"

Ricky cringed a little. "He called her fat?"

"No. This time he told her she had a man-jaw."

Ricky laughed. Hard.

"Yeah," Toni went on, also laughing. "And Oriana didn't appreciate that, so she hit him with her toe shoe. Actually . . . she *beat* him with her toe shoe, which is vastly different."

"I don't know." Ricky looked back and forth between the two families. " 'Rocky Top' . . . toe shoes? 'Rocky Top' . . . toe shoes?" He shrugged and looked at her. "I really can't decide."

They leaned back in, Toni smiling up at him. "Look, if you think you can handle this level of crazy—"

"Handle it? You've met my mother. I've been living this all my life."

"Then I'm in."

"Better be. Because I am *really* liking that apartment of yours."

"I've noticed you've made yourself quite at home."

"Why should you get all the closet space?"

"Yes. I know you need room for your many Tennessee Titan hats."

"You don't have to be jealous of my hats; you know I'll get you one."

Chuckling, Toni went up on her toes, looked him in the eye. "I love you, too, Ricky Lee Reed."

"Good."

She kissed him and Ricky hugged her tight, pulling her close into his body, returning that kiss.

"Thank you," she finally said when she pulled back a bit, their arms still around each other.

"For what?"

"For everything. But mostly for your amazing patience."

"Well"—Ricky shrugged—"it's like I told ya from the beginning, Antonella . . . if you wait long enough, the entertainment comes to *you.*"